Love Knows No Boundaries III
Pandora's Box

Lock Down Publications
Presents
Love Knows No Boundaries III
Pandora's Box
A Novel by *Coffee*

Love Knows No Boundaries III
Pandora's Box

~Acknowledgments~

My readers who have been extremely patient with the final coming of LKNB, I have a special place in my heart for each of you, known and unknown.

To each of my **readers on Facebook**, you have embraced and lifted me even when I didn't know I needed it. So, when I call you *fam* and not *fans*, know that it's official. My extended family rocks!

My peoples who chill hard with me in *Coffee's Lounge*, you know what it is. What happens in *Tha Lounge stays in Tha Lounge.*

T. Michelle, not every woman is able to get a two for one special in a relative, but I do. You're my big sister and my BFF, *forever or never.*

Nola B., my round, a little sister's very own super hero. Life is so much sweeter with you in it. May we remain closer than close.

Ca$h, every time I pick up a pen I am reminded that this platform in which I present my art had been made possible through you. It was your constant encouraging that I am now the author of three books and a contributor to our anthology, *Cum For Me.* How can I not give abundant thanks?

Last but definitely not least, the entire **Lock Down Publications'** squad. The **LDP** arsenal is locked and loaded with hollow point writers. Don't sleep on us. *The Game Is Ours.*

Coffee

Special Thanks

I often find myself asking: *What would I do without my brother, Nola B and sister, T. Michelle?* That's how much y'all add to my life. A triple thanks to the both of you and all that y'all have done to help the *cutest* amongst us, me, throughout this creative process.

Thank you, **Nikki Tee**, my fellow New Orleanian author, for allowing your characters, Shaunie and Keyz of *These N****s Ain't Loyal,* to make an appearance in this install and congrats on your banging series. Part 3 is coming soon. **#LDP #TNAL**

Thank you, **Reds Johnson**, for your appearance in my book and congratulations on your recent release of *Silver Platter Hoe 2* and Closed Legs Don't Get Fed this month. Keep doing great things. **#SPH #IAmRedsJohnson**

To my fam bams: **Shenae "Butter Beans", Tanika "Cleo", Zanete "My Reader Boo", Tondie "Tondilicious", Paulette "Pee", Devin "Diggity", Diana "Big Fine", Sonja "My Sunshine", Ronnie "The Homie", Alverda "Teedy", Kanari "Diamond Girl"** and my lil' cuz, **Tasia Lee Akem**, thank you all for the individual roles you all played in this install. I love you each to tiny, microscopic pieces.

Last but not least, **Kim LeBlanc**. We be epped out on the daily, so you already know how I feel about you. You're my peoples, my round, my boogie down. Sisters for life!

Coffee

Chapter 1

"...Is there any among you that object to the marrying of these two standing before me today?" Reverend Willis questioned the few people in attendance. "Speak now or forever hold your peace."

The gentle brush of November breeze swept across Minnie's face as she slightly looked up beyond the umbrella of trees and out at the clear blue skies.

The day was textbook flawless. Her idea of an outdoor ceremony in the heart of City Park was a perfect plan and she was marrying the perfect man to go along with it.

Minnie gushed with overflowing love as she stared back at Yuriah, who facially emoted her exact happiness.

"Can't wait to be your wife," Minnie mouthed during the ceremony, easing a smile onto her best friend of almost twenty years face.

"You will be soon," Yuriah mouthed back.

The Reverend was seconds away from continuing with the nuptials when a disturbing voice boomed with animosity.

"I object, muthafuckas!" G'Corey came from behind an oak tree, approaching them slowly and with caution.

He threw the balled up Lagniappe section of the newspaper displaying the elated soon-to-be on the ground as he took calculated steps toward them. His eyes were blood red and his lips curled tightly into a ball, barely able to contain his fury.

Several months had passed since the last time he saw his beloved Minnie. There wasn't a day that came to its dawning that he didn't long for her, wondering where she was and how his bud was doing. So to finally see her for the first time wearing a ceremonial gown standing alongside another man, preparing to dedicate her life to another, a life that belonged to him *only*, was unbearable.

He click clacked one into the chamber. *Shit ain't even happening like that,* G'Corey grimaced. With his gun at his side, he continued his creep.

Yuriah whipped his head toward the sound of the disgruntled man, instinctively maneuvering his bride-to-be behind him.

"Oh, God!" Minnie grabbed ahold of Yuriah as she stumbled on the length of her dress, finding her place behind his broad frame. She then tilted her head off to the side so she could see what drama she was being shielded from. She gasped when she saw the eeriness that permeated off of her ex-husband's face.

When Yuri saw it was G'Corey, his expression turned stone in the face of his enemy. His groom's men, Munch and Kamal, masked scowls as they immediately went on red alert, preparing to stop shit before it started.

"Who the fuck this thuggah is, Drop?" Munch asked of his cousin while he removed his jacket, throwing it to the ground, taking a few steps forward to find out for himself.

Kamal was on Munch's heels, preparing to do the same. "I'm 'bout to get in son ass." He cracked his knuckles.

Yuriah swiftly stretched out his arm to stall them out, "Chill, fam. He bitch made and I got this." Yuri spoke clearly and audibly to be understood by both his mans and G'Corey, who was steadily approaching.

Munch temporarily paused, but how long he'd keep the leash on was another topic because he had no manners when it came to addressing pussies in the streets.

"Handle dat, 'fo I do," Kamal spat at the ground as if it disrespected him.

G'Corey never forgot their last encounter. He saw flashes of it damn near every day and with each step he took, he became angrier.

Yuriah should have known he was going to strike back.

Initially, G'Corey came to only lay Yuriah down but his boys, who were standing there flexing, were about to get it, too. He had more than enough ammo to distribute to anyone who wanted to feel it.

G'Corey raised his gun and took aim.

The wedding guests of ten stooped lowly behind their seats, seeking partial cover when they saw the gat in the gunman's hand.

When G'Corey was close enough, he finally spoke. "Die slow, bitch!" He smiled sinisterly before setting it off.

Boc!

By the time Yuriah saw the gun, he only had enough time to spin around and push Minnie down and out of the way. When Kamal spotted the hammer, he dove and tackled Yuriah, knocking him to the ground to take cover, but the hollow point whizzed through the air quicker than Kamal's ability to move his boy out of the way and it bull's eyed the intended target.

The searing metal jacket tore through Yuriah's flesh on his right side, cracking a rib which punctured his lung, forcing him to gasp for air almost immediately.

The small crowd erupted in full-fledged screams and scattered confusingly to dodge harm's way.

"Yuriiiiii!" Minnie scrambled over to him, hovering over his body in a protective manner, oblivious to the looming danger around her.

Minnie's hands trembled as her eyes searched his entire body. The noises grew louder from the frenzied cries of people, but she was unable to concern herself with the chaos around her because she was too much in shock at what lay before her.

Just as G'Corey was squeezing off another shot, Munch pulled out his Glock from the small of his back and began to let it rip.

Boc! Boc!

Munch's steel piece delivered its deadly bullets G'Corey's way. One shot missed him, but the other one penetrated his shoulder, jerking his left side backwards and offsetting his second shot, hitting nothing.

G'Corey recklessly starting firing shots as quickly as his finger would squeeze the trigger before he took off zig zagging through the park with Munch kicking up dust behind him in hot pursuit.

Kamal kneeled down beside Yuriah and pressed his hands against his wound. "Minnie. Minnie!" He finally got her attention. "Reach inside my jacket pocket and call 9-1-1."

She bobbed her head quickly and nervously as she patted his lapel, feeling for the device. Minnie fished out his phone and proceeded with the call.

"9-1-1, what's your emergency?"

"My fiancé been shot! We're the wedding party in-in-in-in umm umm City Park by the museum. Hurry up, please, hurry up!"

The dispatcher informed her that a unit was less than two minutes away. She also asked that Minnie remain on the line but she dropped the phone and focused back on Yuriah.

"Help is on the way, baby. Hold on. You gon' make it. Just hold on. Okay," she bobbed her head rapidly. "Just hold on."

"Minnie, take my place. Hol' ya hands right here." Minnie shuffled to the other side of Yuriah's body while Kamal took off his jacket and ripped his vest off. He then removed his shirt, leaving his wife beater on and tied the long sleeve shirt around Yuri's body to bridge back the bleeding. But it took no time soaking through the shirt.

Shit! Kamal had to think on his feet. He needed something that would do a better job of suppressing the crimson flow oozing out of him. "Stay with 'em."

Yuriah took strained breaths. His eyes reflected his struggle to retain air, but he was still alert.

Minnie ran her red stained hand over his forehead, swooping it downward to cup his cheek. Her eyeliner drained down her face as the downpour of tears drenched his.

"It's gon' be okay. It's gon' be okay. It's gon'—" She mechanically repeated over and over as she rocked back and forth. She was doing her best to convince them both.

Less than thirty seconds later, Kamal returned with a plastic covering he found draping the gift table. In a rush, he bumped Minnie out of the way as he created space to undo the knot in the drenched shirt and replace it with the plastic, instead.

Yuriah stared up at Minnie, barely able to lift his arm, he feebly pointed to The Reverend who was perched not too far from them, praying aloud. "Fini—" His lips hardly moved as his weakened voice quaked.

Reverend Willis only prayed louder as he was too fearful to stop.

Kamal looked to the man who was too shaken and caught up in his prayer babble to hear Yuriah call out for him. "Yo, Rev! Get over here."

Reverend Willis jumped at the boom of Kamal's voice, snapping out of his zone. He quickly drew a cross over his chest, then hesitantly crawled over to where Yuri lay and looked upon his body, chillingly so.

In a raspy tone, Yuriah mumbled. "Sayyyy it!" He forced his words out as best as he could.

Meanwhile...

G'Corey was getting further away from meeting his fate. The Ferragamo dress shoes Munch was wearing didn't provide enough traction and he wasn't able to keep up, but that didn't stop him, though. Come hell or high water, he was going to stand over the man that stood against them.

G'Corey pressed his right hand against his left shoulder where he'd been shot, trying to slack the blood that was profusely discharging. He was growing faint and his labored breathing intensified the harder he ran. He needed to catch a second wind, but when he looked over his shoulder, Munch wasn't far enough behind for that to happen. So his feet propelled him through the throng of people, pushing past them with urgency.

Some of those same individuals were unaware of his injury while others noticed the fresh crimson tint on his white t-shirt, shoo-shooing to whoever stood nearby.

"You see that?" One woman shockingly questioned her friend as she pointed to G'Corey as he jetted by them. Twenty seconds later, she gasped and grabbed her friend's hand to pull her out of harm's way when she saw a man with a gun in hand.

When Munch was finally able to clear a shot, he paused long enough to take it. He didn't care about potential witnesses because if they were able to identify him, they would know not to.

Coffee

In the streets of New Orleans, he was a known head buster. On 6th and Clara St. out of the Magnolia projects in the uptown area, the hood coined him Munch for the way he ate a thuggah up with the fair ones or the gun. So, it was safe to say his reputation preceded him no matter where his feet were planted in the city. If any person in the crowd didn't know about him, someone amongst them was sure to let it be known.

Right as he was about to pull the trigger, an elderly couple holding a little one walked in his line of fire, making it impossible for him to shoot.

"Shit!" Munch hustled to regain ground, pushing and knocking over people in his pursuit.

The natural low gaze in his eyes from all of the Kush he smoked daily were made even tighter as he grew more impatient. The cat and mouse chase only infuriated him and made him more determined to have G'Corey's soul kiss the sky.

In the meantime...

Yuriah continued to fidget with excruciating pain the more his fight to breathe increased. His flushed face was evidence of his battle.

The Reverend was confused. "Say what?"

"Finish the ceremony. What the fuck else?" Kamal snapped.

Yuriah's eyes blinked rapidly, pushing tears out of their corners.

"Baby!" Minnie fearfully called out for him. Then she looked off into the distance. "Somebody help ussssss!"

Reverend Willis looked around but nervously abided. "Ah, ummm, by the power vested in me, me, me, me by the state of Louisiana, I do pronounce you hus—husband and wife."

Minnie burst out crying even harder. That was all she could continue to do.

Kamal had seen many men get ate up with choppas and heavier hammers than what G'Corey came spitting with and survived, so he held steadfast that his dude would pull through just the same.

With as much composure as Minnie could muster, she leaned down to kiss her husband and feel his warm lips when he suddenly sprayed blood into the air. His airways were becoming progressively restricted.

His eyes grew big and his body began to shake. He was going into shock.

"Oh, my God! Nooooo!" Minnie jumped back and freaked out as she saw her husband's life disintegrating right before her eyes.

"Shit! Fuck! Fuck! Fuck!" Kamal started pacing a tight walk as he tried to think straight. He didn't know what else to do, but he knew he couldn't just let him die. "Fuck dat!" He was seconds away from throwing Yuriah on his back and getting him to the hospital himself when he heard sirens blaring in the distance. He dropped down to his knees. "Hol' on, bruh. Just hol' on."

"Kamal, he can't breathe! Oh, my God! He's dying. Do something, Kamal. He can't die!"

Minnie's father finally rushed over to his daughter after ensuring his wife, who'd passed out from the commotion, came to. He tugged on her arm. "Baby girl, let me get you out of here."

"Don't touch me! Move!" Minnie became irate, crying non-stop as she resisted her father pulling her away from her husband.

"You don't need to see this." He wrapped his arms around her waistline, attempting to lift her up and away from the devastation.

"Stopppppp! Stopppp!" She screamed at the top of her lungs. She swung wildly as if she was trying to escape the arms of a kidnapper.

The medic team of two rushed over with a spine board and gurney as the lead technician squatted by Yuriah, barking out his directives. After a quick assessment, he said, "He has blood in his pleural cavity. I need a chest tube placement for decompression."

"What's happening?" Minnie panicked her question to the gentleman kneeling over her husband as she tried to wiggle from her father's bear hug.

He didn't answer as he concentrated on locating the section between the second and third intercostal space at the mid clavicular line to make his incision and then insertion.

In that moment, life or death depended on how quickly the air and blood was aspirated.

The female medic started two large bore IVs, then checked his pressure. "He's unconsciousness. We need to intubate him now!"

She grabbed an endotracheal tube, placing it in his mouth and down his throat. She then attached an airway apparatus over his nose and mouth and began ventilating his lungs mechanically by squeezing a reservoir of oxygen through his orifices.

The paramedics were on red alert to save a life they were in imminent danger of losing.

Moments later…

After losing G'Corey in a sea of people gathered about for some sort of celebration in the park, Munch threw his hands up and dolefully turned back around. "Muthafucka!"

He couldn't aimlessly pursue him any longer although he wanted to. He had to get back and check on his cousin. He'd get up with G'Corey at another time, he had no other choice. He was now marked for death.

Several minutes passed and midway through his run, he spotted an ambulance and a couple of NOPD cruisers. Instinctually, he hauled ass even harder to get over to them.

The closer he drew to Yuriah were the heavier his steps became. The weight of cinderblocks rested on his feet as his heart embraced the unknown. He slowed down to a crawl when he observed his family lying on the stretcher. He didn't know what to think. He only hopped they made it in time.

Off to the side of the paramedics hoisting Yuriah into the back of their medical wagon was a small crowd of uniforms.

He then saw Minnie trying to fight her way out of her father's hold, belligerently screaming and pointing at the ambulance. It was clear she wanted to go along with them but he refused.

"Let me goooo!" Minnie jumped up and down as she had a conniption over her restraint.

Scattered about were a couple of guests willing to speak with detectives.

Then he looked over to his peoples who was still standing where Yuriah's body once lay, trembling in anger. They made uncomfortable eye contact and Munch balled his mouth tightly. Kamal bit down on his bottom lip intensely and then shook his head *no* from side to side as he started to make his way over to Munch.

Gun still in hand, Munch brought his hands to his head in disbelief. "Not my dawg, mannnn! Fuck!"

Coffee

Chapter 2

Munch's emotional outburst drew the attention of the neighboring police. They approached him with apprehension.

"Drop your weapon!" One police officer aimed his gun at Munch, while his partner discharged his Glock from its holster and ordered the same of him. Seconds later, another armed cop inched up on the presumed suspect.

Munch looked each of the three uniforms in the eyes as he brought his piece to his side. "Ain't this a bitch?"

"I said drop it. Now!" The policeman yelled vehemently.

Kamal treaded lightly toward them and then shot his hands up when one officer turned his gun on him. "Mannnn, what the fuck is y'all doing?" He barked at them in a heavy voice.

"Stand back. Do not come any closer," he spoke.

"That man ain't do shit, ya heard me." Kamal disregarded his command.

"Take another step and I'll blow your fuckin' head off!"

Kamal dropped his hands. He was never one to be passive especially with those that were being aggressive. Police or not, Kamal didn't take his threat kindly and was a moment away from seeing who would blow whose head off first.

"You good, son," Munch told Kamal. He could read on his face that he was about to enter the zone where *no fucks were given* so he became compliant to the officers' petition.

Munch slowly placed his gun onto the ground and proceeded with standard protocol for a black man from the hood: *Get on your fucking knees. Hands behind your goddamn head. Get treated like a muthafucking dog.*

They quickly walked toward him. One cop kicked the gun off to the side before picking it up while the other pushed his foot into Munch's back forcing him to lay in the dirt. He then dropped his knee into his back while forcing his arms into the arresting position.

"Aaaahhhh! Son of a bitch!" Munch groaned.

"Say, dawg. He already surrendered, bruh. Why you gotta do him that?" One guy off to the side questioned the officer rough housing him, but no response was given.

Munch was brought to his feet and pushed in the direction he was to walk. "Mannn, y'all some pussies for real. You ain't gotta be handlin' a thuggah like that, man. Fuck wrong with y'all?" He grimaced at the tightness of the cuffs around his wrist. "You bitches automatically think a mu'fucka guilty, with no questions asked. Hate you hoes."

"You have the right to remain silent. I suggest you do so mutha-fucka! Anything you say…" The most antagonistic officer of the three manhandled him by the grab of his arm, walking him to a ve-hicle as he read him his Miranda rights.

Munch glared off to the side of him, studying his face and then his name tag.

The officer looked down at his shirt and then back to him. "San-temore, bitch! Remember it."

Munch shook his head up and down rapidly, smirked and then spit at Santemore's feet. "I will."

Santemore wore a chip on his shoulder. The way he despised young black men would have one think he too wasn't from the same ghettos he terrorized from behind his badge. Whether Munch had a record or not, he was a criminal in his mind and he treated him and all brown men who looked like him as such.

He threw Munch in the back of the unit, slamming the door be-hind him. "Get this piece of shit processed. And you," he pointed at Kamal, who had his fist clutched, when he turned around, "stay out of trouble or this could be you."

"Fuck you!" Kamal spat.

Once Munch was detained, the other cops moved about.

"Oh, Mal. They headin' out. Let's go!" A friend of the family pointed to the ambulance disappearing through the park.

"Fuck!" Kamal's head was smoking. He was between two very fucked situations.

Kamal gunned for his car, passing the unit holding Munch hostage. They caught eye contact for a brief second before Kamal ran a little faster. He already knew the play.

With that, he reached into his pants pocket and retrieved his phone as he took a seat behind the wheel of his Monte Carlo. Pressing the number two on the screen and then the send button, he speed dialed his lady. She picked up on the first ring.

"Hey, baby daddy. How was the wedding?" Shenae answered.

Without returning the pleasantries, he spoke sternly. "Muthafuckas arrested Munch. I need you to go downtown and see to it that he comes out looking the same way he walked in."

"What?" she asked shockingly, bolting upward from her lay position on the sofa. The side of her that cared for Munch like a brother freaked out, but then the attorney in her controlled her nerves. "Never mind that. Will you be meeting me there?"

He blew out hard. "I'm headin' to the hospital. Mannn, Yuriah been shot."

She grabbed at her chest. "Oh, my God! Baby? Is he…"

"Barely."

Okay—okay, she mumbled under her breath. "I'll take care of Munch, ASAP. And you? Which hospital are you going to?"

"I'on know. I guess Mercy. Mannn, fuck!" A flash of G'Corey entered his mind and in a rush of anger, Kamal hit the steering wheel repeatedly. "Fuckkk!"

Tears welled in her eyes at the sound of her love's pain. Her heart broke into tiny pieces. He was the strongest man she knew and to hear him vulnerable made her feel weak. She wiped each eye one at a time with the base of her palm, then toughened up. "Consider it done. I'ma see you afterwards, okay, baby?"

Taking a few deep breaths, he responded. "A'ight."

Kamal tossed his phone into the passenger seat and floored his way to Mercy Hospital, since it was the closest ER facility.

Shenae immediately rushed over to the window in their front room, peering through the blinds to see if her best friend's truck was outside. *Good. She's home.* Shenae reached into the playpen, grabbed Double, Kamal's junior, and then called out for her daughter. "De'Asia, baby, put on some shoes. You're going by Auntie Tondie."

"Yayyyy!" De'Asia sang as she put on a pair of tennis shoes. Grabbing a tiara and two of her dolls from off of her bed, she left out of her room minutes later. She ran to the opposite end of the hall and stood at the doorsill of her mother's bedroom. "Ready, mommy."

"That's my big girl. Now go stand by the front door and wait on me, okay?"

"Okay," she shrilled, doing as she was told.

Shenae multi-tasked between quickly dressing herself and her son all the while making a call. After the second ring, her bubbly assistant answered.

"Tanika Council speaking."

"Where are you?" Shenae spoke directly.

"Wherever you need me to be," she responded upon hearing the urgency in her boss' voice.

"Go down to Central Lockup. Client's name? Kareem McMillan."

Tanika had been working at Crimley & Associates as her right hand for over a year, so she didn't need any additional details. "I'm on it."

Shenae ended the call, stuffing her phone into her pants pocket.

"Come on, big boy." She picked her son up off of her bed as she reached for both his diaper bag and her purse.

Entering the hallway, she paused long enough to enter the alarm code on the keypad. With a minute to exit, she opened the front door and left out with her daughter in tow.

She locked up then hurried next door, jogging up the steps that led to her friend's porch. As Shenae was about to knock on the door, Tondie opened it, jumping back.

"Oh, shit! You startled me," Tondie replied, instantly short of breath.

Shenae could plainly see she was heading off somewhere and passing her kids off to her would be an imposition, but she needed her help.

"Sorry, sis. Look, I don't want to talk around my children but something really urgent has happened. I need you to watch them." Shenae hurried her words as she pushed Double further up on her hip.

Tondie shook her head *yes* while she opened her door wider, escorting De'Asia inside as she reached for the baby. "Handle your business. They'll be straight."

Shenae kissed her on the cheek, then backed away from her with her hands pressed together in prayer manner. "Thank you, bestie. Thank you. Thank you." She turned around and ran off to her car parked in her driveway.

"Call me!" Tondie called out behind her, stretching her thumb and pinky finger against her ear.

"I will," Shenae yelled back without looking, disarming the alarm to her car. Once inside, she quickly started the engine and pulled off.

She needed to make it to the precinct either before the police arrived with Munch or at the same time as them because it was no secret that *The Boys in Blue* were dirty.

Coffee

Chapter 3

Elias bounced his knee as he reminded himself to be on his best behavior. He didn't want to embarrass Blu with his known sarcasm or blunt responses. After all, he was sitting amongst The Huxtables.

He looked around the table and everyone was smiling with the exception of her dad, but he was the typical *tight in the ass* father, so he didn't expect much sunshine from him anyway.

Mr. Cormier was an ornery man who wore a straight face at all times. Whether he was happy, angry, or sad, his expression never changed.

He stared at Elias with a judgmental eye for a time before he let the questions rip. "Mr. Dupree, where do you work?"

Elias glanced at Blu, giving her the *is this thuggah serious* look before he directed his attention to her father. He answered bluntly. "I don't, sir."

"You don't work? Humph. This generation is lazy. So, you looking to leach off my baby girl?"

"Daddy!" Blu bucked her eyes in an effort to silently tell him to *stop*. She turned to Elias, placing a consoling hand on top of his. "He doesn't mean it." She projected an uncomfortable grin. She had asked her father ahead of time not to turn family dinner into Judge Brown's courtroom, but it was clear court was in session.

"Like the hell I don't mean it, little girl." He looked at her firmly.

Don't do it, E. Hold your tongue. You knew her ole punk ass daddy was gonna be extra, Elias cleared his throat and looked him in the eyes. He felt insulted, but he brushed the dirt of his shoulders and responded with the pride of a man. "Not at all, sir. I have my own money."

"How? You selling dope? You some kind of hustler?" He shifted in his seat and sat at attention as he faced Blu while he pointed his condemning finger at Elias. "You brought some drug dealing, kingpin lord into my home?"

"Daddy! He's none of that and he gets his money honestly, so please stop."

"Honey, this young man is a guest in our home. How 'bout you treat him with a little kindness, dear." Lauren gracefully smiled, but he could read the duplicity in his wife's request. The upward curl of her lips said *please*, but her eyes said *you better!*

He looked over at Elias, then he digressed. "Umm hmmm." He'd have a man to man conversation with him when the protection of his two Mother Hens weren't around because he was far from done.

Lauren walked over to her husband, placing a tender kiss on his forehead. He came off abrasive, but the family knew all in all he meant well. "Thank you," she whispered. Changing the temperature in the room, she spoke more vibrantly standing at his side. "Well, I hope everyone brought their appetites because Mama has cooked enough to feed the block. We have seafood gumbo, stuffed bell peppers, potato salad, homemade mac n cheese, two types of vegetables. You name it, I made it," she chuckled as she retreated over to her seat at the other end of the table, grabbing her chair.

Langston looked at the time on his wristwatch. It was 5:57 p.m. Dinner always started promptly at six in his home and his daughter who had been M.I.A. since she arrived knew that. "Blue Diamond, go call your sister from up there. Don't make no goddamn sense how she comes over here just to alienate herself," he grumbled.

"Yes, Daddy." Just as Blu was excusing herself from the table, she heard the click of her sister's heels descending the hardwood stairs. She sat back down. "Here she comes now."

Although uncomfortable from the cheap shots fired at his character, Elias made small talk by complimenting the chef. "All of this smells good."

Elias took another deep inhale, but what he registered this time wasn't the hot, steamy buttered rolls sitting before him.

He tilted his head slightly in curious wonder as he purposely did a triple sniff to identify the foreign yet familiar scent invading his nostrils.

It had been nine months, but the soft lingering scent of J'adore jolted his recall.

Awww, hell no. If I turn around and it be that bitch, he thought.

"Eli," Blu tapped his shoulder. "I'd like for you to meet my sister."

Before Elias could turn around fully, he venomously spoke her name right as Blu introduced her.

"La'Tasha," they said.

Blu turned to face her beau. "You know my sister?"

Elias zoned out for a second and went inside of his head. He had to think carefully before he answered. "Yea, but I don't know her, *know her*."

"Oh, really?" She rolled her neck in a sista gurl kind of way. "He's being modest, lil' sis, but he knows me, *knows me* both inside and out. Tell her, Elias." La'Tasha casually walked around the table observing the spread in front of her before taking a seat directly across from him as if she didn't just drop a hint of their sexual past. "Ummm, everything looks great, Mom."

Elias narrowed his eyes and glared at La'Tasha as if he could hypnotize her into holding her breath and killing over.

Blu leaned into him. "What is she talking about?"

"She ain't talkin' 'bout nothing." He barely moved his lips as he answered, looking straightway.

"Her snide comments says otherwise." She tried to whisper, but La'Tasha heard it clearly.

"You can ask me, La'Toria. I'm sure to be more forthcoming than lover boy over there." She twirled her finger in his direction all the while projecting a smile that hinted sneaky suspicion.

"La'Tasha!" Her mother's face was twisted with astonishment as she looked over at her middle child.

La'Tasha smacked her lips. "What? She wanted to introduce him to me and all I was saying was none needed to be made."

Blu rolled her eyes upward and shook her head. She bit her tongue because she didn't want to have their infamous sibling rivalry fiasco unfold as it tended to do regularly, but she definitely had questions for the both of them.

"Don't sass your mother," her father made clear.

La'Tasha threw her hands up. "Didn't know I was, but okay."

It was quiet around the table for what felt like an eternity to Eli.

He had to check his face on a few occasions because he found himself mirroring the look of a growling pit each time his eyes caught hers.

Blu looked long and hard to her left at Eli, but he didn't return the favor. He was focused on controlling the anger brewing at the pit of his stomach. Seeing her again was like pouring salt into an open wound.

It took several months for him to shake back after she cracked his face, his ego, his heart. But as long as she was out of sight, she was out of mind. However, every unsettled pissed off feeling he hadn't dealt with, bubbled to the surface just seeing her stanking ass again.

He could feel her pretty browns taunting him and he didn't like how lopsided the scales of justice were. He didn't give her the proper payback because if he had, he wouldn't feel the impulse to lay hands on her to wipe the stupid smirk off of her face.

Blu then looked across the table to La'Tasha and unlike her boyfriend, La'Tasha looked her squarely in the eyes, daringly.

"What are you looking at?" Blu finally spoke up, interrupting the conversation her parents were having. She was tired of La'Tasha eyeing her.

La'Tasha choked on her swallow at the disgruntled look on her sister's face and then she laughed out loud. "You getting a lil' sporty in front ya boy, huh?"

"Girls, stop it before it starts!" Lauren looked between them.

"Nah, Mama, forgive me but I'm going to answer her question." She looked from her mama and then back to Blu. "You wanna know what I'm looking at? Well, I'm looking at my sucka for love having sister and *my* leftovers sweating under his collar as he tries to get through dinner without having to explain the uncomfortable vibes you're picking up."

"Leftovers? What do you mean—leftovers? Eli, what is she talking about?" Blu turned toward him.

Langston pinched the bridge of his nose, resting the weight of his head on them. He hated the cattiness between his girls. It was never-ending. "Enough."

Blu snapped her head toward her father before Eli had the chance to answer her question. "Daddy, I'm tired of her. She can't stand to see me happy because she's too jealous hearted. Can't stomach me having what she doesn't."

"Correction, baby girl. I did have him. Ova and ova." She allowed the words to roll off of her lips slowly and sensually.

"What did you say?" Blu scrunched her face.

Lauren over-talked Blu and questioned La'Tasha as well. "Why are you doing this? This is family dinner, not a family feud."

"Ma, why am I always the one charged up? Your child the one huffing and puffing over there. Check her!" La'Tasha despised how her little sister was protected by her parents under any and all circumstances. She was always the sinner and her goodie two shoes of a sister was always the saint.

While La'Tasha was stating her case, she didn't notice Blu getting out of her seat and rushing up on her. She pushed the back of her head with her pointing finger. "No. You check me."

With her head still facing her mom, La'Tasha chuckled. "Trust me. You don't want that."

Elias and Langston immediately stood up from their seats but Eli walked up on Blu, tugging at her arm. "She tryna get a rise up outcha but don't let her. Let's just be out."

Ignoring Eli, Blu openly admitted her true feelings. "I can't stand you! You're selfish and mean spirited and if mama and daddy weren't sitting right here, I'd spit in your face."

La'Tasha rose to her feet and Eli switched positions with Blu so that he stood in the middle of them.

La'Tasha looked past Eli and over to Blu. "The day you do that is the day you'll know what an ass whippin' feel like."

Blu tried to push past Eli's but was met with resistance. "Step outside and try me."

Langston slammed his hand on the table. "I said enough, goddammit!"

Coffee

"But, Daddy, she started—" La'Tasha pointed at Blu.

"*But Daddy* my ass. This here is gon' stop—*today!*"

"Why you gotta look at me when you say that as if little Miss Princess don't deserve—" Her words faded to nothing as she listened to Eli coach Blu to a calm.

"Sister or not, she ain't worth getting all worked up over, ya heard me." Elias looked down at Blu as he rubbed the sides of her arms up and down in a consoling manner.

Disregarding her father's order to put an end to their arguing, she started back up again. "Oh, I may not be worth it to her but I damn sure was worth it to you, remember? I was *your* Dark N Lovely, the woman you once fiend for. Remember you were so in love with me that you bought me diamonds and other expensive toys to prove it? I don't know but either I was worth it then, or juicy had you crazy." She doubled patted her lower abdomen to represent her sex.

Blu's face turned from *I'ma get in her ass* to *How could you, Eli?*

Elias read her disappointment. In all of the months he'd been knowing her, he never seen her hurt—until now.

He found La'Tasha's outburst unnecessary and he knew she only did it to be spiteful. He didn't know what to tell her. All he could do was shake his head as her tears began to fall.

She didn't need to find out this way, he thought.

Blu's shoulders sunk at the sound of La'Tasha's confession and her body deflated in his arms. Her eyes marbled all over the place as she searched for a comeback she didn't have. Then she looked at Eli's hands on her. "Let me go!" She pulled away from his hold and stepped back.

Lauren looked over at her husband who was unmistakably annoyed and then to a laughing La'Tasha.

Ha! Ha! Ha! "Wittle baby mad?" *Ha! Ha! Ha!*

"Oh, you bitch!" Elias had enough of her taunting and he snapped. He turned around to face La'Tasha and unconsciously found his hands wrapped around her throat, shaking her furiously as he tightened his squeeze.

30

Aarrgghh! La'Tasha's tongue projected out of her mouth as she gagged.

"Eli!" Blu instinctually shouted for him to let up off of her sister. Her and La'Tasha would never be bffs but she was still family and she didn't want to see her harmed.

Langston pushed Blu out of the way to clear his path to Eli and placed him in a choker in an effort to make him, in turn, release his child but Eli maintained his hold. "Let her go!" His voice resounded in the room.

"Oh, my God! Stop it!" Lauren cried. She became overly excited at the commotion going on in front of her.

Grandma LuLu lifted her eyes from her plate but carried on eating her meal. She was too old to care about the ruckus taking place at the opposite end of the table.

"Daddy! He can't breathe." Blu went from trying to pry Eli's hands away from La'Tasha to pulling at her father's sturdy clamp around Eli's neck. "Everyone stopppppp!"

No one listened. La'Tasha was gasping and clawing at Eli's weakening hands while Eli was losing consciousness from his own lack of air. She looked over to her father who was calling for Eli to put a stop his assault as he tried jerking Eli backwards and away from La'Tasha, holding his neck hostage in the cross of his arm.

"Mama, do something!" Blu frantically ran up to her as she pointed over to the melee before running back to the fighting trio. "Eli," she tried reasoning with her eyes. "Elias! Eli—" Her words trailed off.

Several uncomfortable seconds passed and Elias still hadn't responded.

Suddenly, Elias jolted back to reality as he finally registered that his name was being called. He was stunned to silence the moment he saw it was La'Tasha standing behind him. He was thrown for a loop and an instant visualization popped in his mind of how the evening could turn out for everybody if she played the game raw.

He then looked to Blu and saw her lips move in slow motion but he still couldn't make out what she was saying.

"You know my sister?" Blu wore a surprised look on her face.

Blu snapped her fingers in front of his face to fully grab his attention and pull him from whatever trance he was in. "Eli?"

Of all the women I could have settled down with, he thought. He blinked hard and shook his head as if it would straighten out his feelings. "My bad, Blu. Nah, what was you asking me?"

"I asked if you knew my sister." Her eyebrows crumpled as she repeated herself. She couldn't help but notice the sudden artic change in his demeanor. It made her look at him crossly. "Are you okay?"

"Yea, I'm straight." He forged a smile and then replied, "Yea to your question."

"Okay. How?"

"I know her from the salon. Yah goes there and I've been with her a time or two."

"Oh." The answer seemed to appease her. "Well, Labelle, this is my charming boyfriend. Boyfriend, this is one of my sisters."

Elias swiftly nodded his head upward. He didn't want to do *that*, but it was better than flipping her the bird and setting it off. He then leaned over to her and spoke into her ear. "Why you call her Labelle?"

Blu giggled and whispered, "Because she acts like a diva."

Fitting, Eli thought.

Breaking up the *shoo shoo'n* between them, La'Tasha interjected. "Yea? So, how long have y'all two been hooking up?"

Blu twisted her lips. "I said nothing about hooking up. This is a relationship. Thank you very much."

"Have it your way. How long have you been in a *re-la-tion-ship*?" La'Tasha said the words retardedly slow.

"I said I wanted to introduce you to my guy not sit through one of your interrogations. So save it." Blu knew where her snootiness was going so she nipped it in the bud.

"Calm down. It ain't that serious." La'Tasha rolled her eyes.

"Girls, stop it before it starts." Lauren looked between them.

Elias looked over to their mother as if he'd seen a ghost when she said the exact words he heard her say in his vision.

Love Knows No Boundaries III
Pandora's Box

Déjà fuckin' vu.

Coffee

Chapter 4

Samiyah agitatedly looked at the time on her cell phone's screen. It read: 6:00 p.m. They'd been there all day and the *run around* feeling the staff appeared to be giving them was wearing her thin. She blew out her frustration and glanced over at her husband who was sitting beside her, looking equally bothered.

"Damn! How much longer?" She was becoming extremely anxious, as was Gerran.

She understood worse things could have been wrong with her angel but even a mild fever would have been cause to ring the alarm in her mind. Lil' Acacia was the miracle child that made it unlike the other pregnancies, so there was no way she was willing to take anything concerning her daughter lightly.

"This is messing with my nerves, yea." Gerran cracked his knuckles every few minutes that passed as they sat in waiting.

Samiyah placed her hand over his to stop his anxious jitter. Anytime he was antsy, he fidgeted. So in an effort to give them a more positive vibe, she changed the topic.

"How did you feel when the doctor told us about the baby surprise I'm carrying?"

Gerran's shoulders instantly relaxed and a smile crept up on his face. "It blew my mind in a good way, ya heard me. I'm kinda hoping for a boy this time. Name him after me. He'll be my Lil' Gee." He placed his hand on the small pooch of a stomach their child left behind.

For a tender moment, they relished in the bliss of the new bundle until the door creaked open and snapped them back to the reason they were there. Both Gerran and Samiyah shot up from their seated position.

The nurse stepped into the room. "Thank you all for being so patient with me. I have the results here in my folder." She took a seat behind her desk. "Please, sit down," she offered.

"We're good. Just tell us what do we do now?" Gerran was anxious to set things in motion.

Coffee

Fifteen years of being a nurse still wasn't enough preparation to deliver bad news to her patients or their care takers. She sighed and then clasped her hands together. "After reviewing everything twice, I'm afraid you won't be a candidate to donate blood for Baby Babineaux, sir."

"Why not? What's wrong?" He felt a pang in his heart.

Samiyah was in a state of shock. She needed to know what was really going on with the treatment of their baby. "What are you talking about?"

Confusion rested firmly on both her and Gerran's faces.

The nurse looked very uncomfortable but then she spoke, "Tests came back and the results show you're not a match."

"What are you saying, lady?" Gerran's initial woeful look turned menacing.

"Sorry to say this, but sir, you're not the father."

"I'm not the *what*?" Gerran's response came almost immediately after the words left her mouth. He looked off to the side with creased brows, attempting to process the lie his heart felt she told.

Samiyah's mouth flung open. She was one hundred percent stunned.

The nurse's face saddened as she observed the couple handle the news differently but she had to continue with her next recourse for plan of treatment.

"Mr. and Mrs. Babineaux, I understand you all need time to process this and I don't want to seem insensitive but if we can discuss—"

Gerran walked up on the nurse and snatched the manila folder out of her hand, startling her. "Show me where it says I'm not the father because I don't believe you."

"Sir, I'm going to ask you to step back and calm down, please."

Gerran didn't budge. He wanted proof that the little girl he sung to in broken pitch while she was baking in his wife's womb wasn't *his* child. He needed to know he wasn't a fool by embracing another man's family under false claims. It had to be an inaccurate reading. It had to be.

The nurse became alarmed when she saw a mixture of devastation, confusion and brooding anger etch across his face. One side of her felt heartbroken while the other half feared what the now emotionally unstable man would do.

Samiyah fell weak and staggered backwards into her seat. One hand covered her mouth and the other her stomach when she thought what this could mean to her growing family. She then probed her mind for the answer she was certain her husband was going to demand from her. She felt sick and the unavoidable urge to vomit came gushing forward.

Bluh! Aaarrgh! Bluh!

While Samiyah spilled her guts, the nurse took the opportunity to slip out of her office while Gerran changed his focus and looked at the repulsive fluids pouring from her mouth and onto the floor.

She wiped the remnants off of her lips and started crying before she looked up. She knew he was staring at her and she was right.

Suddenly the initial shock of Lil' Acacia not being his settled in his mind. "You knew I wasn't the father, didn't you?" She didn't answer quickly enough, so he jabbed at the wall next to him, causing her to jump. "Didn't you?"

Samiyah shook her head *no*, but she knew he wasn't going to believe her. His eyes told her so. "I—I thought she hee—hee was yours." She hyperventilated through her response.

He stooped down close enough to her face to kiss her. "Bullshit!"

Samiyah's head jerked backwards at the boom of his voice as her hand wiped away the spittle that flew from his mouth.

He then stepped back and began pacing the floor anxiously. "So who the daddy? Is she Cedric's?"

Samiyah opened and closed her mouth as she took feeble attempts to release her words. She shook her head *no* as her response. "Gerran, I'm sorry."

"Damn, Yah. Well, who the fuck is, then?" Gerran shouted loud enough for others outside of the office to hear him clearly.

Just then the nurse returned with security. "Mr. Babineaux, you're being disruptive and this is a hospital!" She needlessly reminded as she pointed outside into the hallway at inquisitive employees and visitors. "I'm going to ask for you to leave."

He ignored the nurse and continued drilling Samiyah. "Who is he?"

"That's enough, sir. Ronnie?" She looked over to the guard so he could intervene and escort Gerran off of the premises.

"Let's go." The young man motioned for Gerran to walk out on his own.

When Gerran didn't budge, Ronnie touched his elbow to help him along. He jecked his arm back. "Don't touch me, dawg."

"Well, let's go," Ronnie reiterated.

Gerran walked up on him, staring him in his eyes, but Ronnie stood his ground not flinching at the intimidating glare glowing from Gerran's orbs.

Gerran curled his lips tightly in the same manner his broken heart twisted. Then suddenly he looked back at a crying Samiyah, became disgusted and stormed out of the room, bumping shoulders with Ronnie as he did.

"Make certain he leaves the hospital grounds." The nurse instructed.

"Okay." Ronnie followed behind him to ensure he'd leave.

The nurse then reached for three sheets of Kleenex from her desk and handed them to Samiyah. "Let's step into a different office. We must discuss another viable plan for the baby's treatment."

***

Elias couldn't shake off the premonition he was feeling. He didn't know if he should or even how to tell Blu that the dog bitch he referred to as Cujo, the woman he openly admitted loving, was her sister.

"Whoever this Cujo person is really did a number on you because you really got it bad. The way you hate her wouldn't surprise

me if you still loved her." Blu sat Indian style on the floor in front of Eli as he laid stretched out on the carpet, humming to the song playing on FM 98.

He turned his head to face her before looking back up toward the ceiling. "Get yo mind right, lil' one. I don't have two fucks to give that broad. If she was on fire, I'd drink my own piss before whippin' it in her direction to put it out. She'd be well the fuck done waiting on me to give a damn."

She pushed her finger into his side. "See what I mean? Who you tryna convince? Me or you? I say if she called you right now and apologized for being a jerk face, you'd take her back, ASAP."

Still looking up and into nothingness, he impulsively responded. "How can I want fuck face when I want you?" His eyes curiously drew inward as soon as the words left his mouth. 'Where da fuck that shit came from?' he thought.

She laughed at his comedic ways, then questioned him disbelievingly. "You're shittin' me, right?"

There was no way that Elias "I Got All the Hoes" Dupree was being serious in her mind. He had to know wanting her required monogamy.

Elias got up on his elbows and faced her. "Why? Is that a bad thing? Me wanting yo lil' skinny ass to myself."

She blushed and buried her chin into her chest. "No. It's not a bad thing. After all, I am wantable, feel me?"

He muffed her forehead and she went backwards.

"Hey!" She yelled out as she balanced herself from falling all the way back. She then got on top of him, covering Eli like a spider monkey. "You wanna play games, huh? Huh? You wanna play with me?" She laughed.

He chuckled at her play punches before he pulled her body flatly on his. "Nah, I'm being for real. I want chu unless, that is, you don't want me."

Her giggles went mute as she searched his eyes. It had only been a few months since they'd been kicking it virtually every day but something inside of her told her that there was no bluff in him. "I been wanted you."

"So, it's official?"

She shook her head up and down, giddily. "It's official," she confirmed.

It was then that they shared their first kiss. A kiss that would seal the deal of a union Elias wasn't sure he was ready for but none-theless a chance he was willing to take. She was too amazing to stand by and watch another man have. He'd been there already with Samiyah.

What started off as her pressing her lips upon his in repeat mo-tion turned into a sensual lustful dance between their tongues.

It felt incredible to him. He'd never been kissed so passionately before. Humming noises escaped her mouth as he began to pummel her ass, grinding it against his already hardened dick. The pressing need to take it there grew the deeper, the longer they were orally intertwined.

After a few minutes of tantalizing tension, they broke their oral connection.

He stared into the smile parading around in her eyes and asked in the sweetest way he knew. "Now you gon' give me some of that cutty?"

She burst out laughing. He knew how to go from Romeo the prince to Kermit the frog in the span of a second.

Still on top but now sitting up, she sweetly said, "Wait for it. I'm worth it."

If his past with La'Tasha was going to come to light, he thought he should be the one to tell her. But how?

It was obvious the sisters beefed over the smallest things and there was no telling how big this cat would be once released from the bag given La'Tasha's need for theatrics and Blu inability to ig-nore them.

He shook his head. He knew it was an omen to get into a rela-tionship especially since his uncle tried to convince him to leave it alone.

"You're in a relationship?" His uncle squinted his eyes and uglied his face like he smelled something putrid. "Son, why you gon' go and do something silly like that? You tryna protect the pussy or something? Make sure no other cat can lay pipe in it but you? You do know you don't have to wife no bitch to make her pussy answer to you only, right?"

"Nah, Unc, it ain't like that." Elias grinned because he could relate to his line of questioning and why his face held a look of shock. Choosing to make Blu his girl fucked him up in the beginning, too. "Don't trip. She cool peoples."

"Cool peoples?" He mimicked, shaking his head disappointingly as he walked up on his nephew, sniffing around his collar.

Elias leaned his head back and looked at him oddly. "What you doing?"

Flint stood in front of him and grabbed his shoulders while looking him in the eye. "You smell pussy whipped, boy. Is ya?"

"Never dat!" He answered quickly.

Elias definitely wasn't P-whipped because he had yet to break her off. However, he was caught up. She gave him the same schoolboy feelings he had when he and Samiyah first started kicking it.

He brushed those foreign spirits off of him back in the day and denied them heavily the longer he and Yah remained friends. And as a result of not keeping it all the way real with himself and her, she was now married to another man.

He reasoned it was probably in her best interest although it bothered him to officially see her chained to another by God's law, but he also knew he wasn't the jump the broom type of brother and she was the kind of chick that wanted a ring on it.

Learning from his past, he didn't want to make the same mistake with Blu, so he chose to make her his. Besides, it was too late to make noise over Samiyah now if he wanted to.

When Eli came out of his own thoughts, he caught the tail end of his uncle's sermon on women and why they were only good for a night or two.

"Relationships are cancer, son. It starts in your heart but then it travels up to your head and makes you stupid as fuck if you don't cut that thumping lil' piece of shit out of you before it spreads."

Since a youth, Elias took every word his uncle said as gospel and he listened to music that further perpetuated a 'love them and leave them' lifestyle. So, choosing to settle down was undoubtedly going against every code he grew up respecting and clearly violating every verse The Geto Boys told him about bitches, but he had to go with his gut.

Besides, Willie D, Bushwick Bill and Scarface were speaking of hoes and La'Tasha, not Samiyah—and not Blu.

"I hear you, Uncle Fly, but ya boy got this." Elias laughed as he extended his hand to G-dap the old pimp, pulling him into his square.

Flint knew Eli better than Eli knew himself, so he felt, and that meant he was in no way a one woman's man. Flint believed he could try to convince himself that he could be, but the truth was just going to have to set him free. He was a Dupree and Dupree's were intended to fly the coop not be pigeon trapped in one.

He shook his head one last time and then wrapped his free arm around his shoulder, hand still interlocked with his. "Relationships are the devil, son."

"Eli?" Blu tapped his arm. "Your phone has been going off nonstop. Aren't you gonna see who it is?"

He snapped out of his thoughts and looked at her blankly because he didn't hear her question. "Huh?"

She pointed down toward his side. "Your phone? Are you gonna answer it?"

He then noticed the vibration on his hip and heard the faint buzz alerting him of a call. "Excuse me for a moment," he said when he noticed the caller was Samiyah. He stood up from his seat and stepped off to the adjacent room for privacy.

Blu watched him as he excused himself from the table, shaking her head at how weird he was acting. She wasn't sure if it was his nerves getting the better of him or if it was something else. She'd ask him about it later but for now, she continued to carry on conversation with the family.

"What's up? My G-baby doing better?" Eli referenced Lil' Acacia, his god-child. He knew Samiyah had been at Children's Hospital all day and she would be calling to give him updates on her status.

"Nooooo," Samiyah broke down crying. "Shit just went south. Way down south."

Elias' brows wrinkled and he stared off intently as he probed her for clarification. "Stop crying and tell me what's up with my baby, man."

Samiyah's body trembled so vibrantly her voice quaked as a result. "What's up is neither Gerran nor I was able to give blood for her transfusion."

"Why the hell not? What's going on?" He unknowingly raised his voice as he became worried for the baby he affectionately called Peaches.

She took a deep breath and went full speed ahead. "I'm pregnant so I can't do it and Gerran's not," she hesitated and then grabbed at her shirt, clutching it as if it would reduce the speed of her racing heart, "he's not the father."

Eli's eyes widened with surprise but before he could respond, Blu walked into the room and cautiously asked, "Boo, is everything alright?"

"Hold on," he addressed Samiyah and lowered his phone. "I'ma step outside," was all he said to Blu as he hustled through the house and out of the front door. He walked down the porch steps and stood out on the sidewalk. He put the phone back to his ear. "What you mean he's not the father?"

"It means exactly what I said. He's not the father because—" she stalled. That made him antsy.

"Spit it out, Yah!"

She took a deep breath in and on her exhale she blurted, "Because you are!"

Elias was flabbergasted. He didn't want to hear her repeat herself so in full shock, he quickly removed the phone from his ear and sent it crashing to the pavement, shattering it into two separate pieces.

Chapter 5

"**H**ow the hell?" Elias spoke out loud to himself. He was dumbfounded and totally caught off guard by Samiyah's shocking reveal. There was no doubt he loved her baby. He adored her as if she was his own but never in a million lifetimes did he expect to have a child.

He stared off to the side of him, at nothing. "*I'm* a baby daddy? That shit don't even sound right."

"What don't sound right?" Blu walked up on him, noticing his broken phone. "What happened to your phone? What's going on?"

Now wasn't the time to break everything down, and he wasn't going to attempt to do so. Instead, Elias told her what he needed. "Look, run me to my house to pick up my truck."

That didn't answer her question and based on how short he was being in his reply coupled with the distraught look on his face, Blu knew something was definitely wrong. "What's the matter, boo?"

Eli ran his hands down his face and the weight of his stress appeared suddenly. "I need to get to Children's, ya heard me."

The baby! Something's wrong with Peaches. She immediately understood his bothered disposition. "Why don't we just go together? We can leave straight from here." She stretched out her hand to rub his bicep in an effort to let him know he wasn't alone.

He moved away slightly as if her touched burned. "Why don't you just do as I asked? Damn, bruh!"

Blu looked at him strangely. He was harsh toward her and without good reason to be. She thought to respond to him snapping on her but opted not to. She didn't want to make a bad situation worse by pressing him for answers. "Let me get my keys, then."

The tone Elias took with Blu brought tears to her eyes but she refused to let them fall, especially not in front of her already leery father and most definitely not in front of her hating ass sister.

The moment she entered the dining room, she concealed her hurt. She headed toward her father, hugging him from behind, she kissed his temple.

He twisted his neck to face her. "Blue Diamond, I know you're not leaving already, are you? It's just 6:41."

"I know, but something urgent came up and we took my car so I have to bring him where he needs to go."

"Well, do you at least have time for mama to fix you two a plate, baby?" Her mother stood from her chair and attempted to dash into the kitchen to make *to go* plates.

Blu blocked her way, opened her arms and gave her a hug while she kissed her cheek. "That's alright, Ma. We really have to go."

"Well, alright. I'll just freeze you some and you can get it tomorrow or something."

Blu smiled and then said her parting words. "Love you, Mama. Love you, Daddy. See you later, sis."

La'Tasha pursed her lips. "Bye, La'Toria." Then in a stuck up manner, she wiggled her fingers to wave bye.

Blu put a pep to her step as she grabbed her purse from off of the sofa in the living room. "I'm locking the bottom lock," she called out before she left out, closing the front door behind her.

Elias was leaning against the passenger door with his arms folded, thinking.

Yah trippin' on this one. How could she be mine when I stay strapped? That's right. We used condoms. Damn straight.

A smile suddenly creased his lips but then it deflated just as quickly as it appeared when he remembered he did hit it raw to start.

In an angry manner, he quickly slapped his hands together upon the realization that this wasn't some sick November's Fool's joke. "Fuck!" he groaned out. "I am the—"

The sound of Blu disarming the alarm on her car cut Elias' talk to himself short. Without acknowledging her, he opened up the door and got inside.

Blu rolled her eyes as she shook her head. The part of her that was anxious to know what his malfunction was wanted to drill him but she knew cooler heads prevailed, so she remained quiet as she started the engine and pulled off.

The ride from her parent's home in the eastern part of New Orleans to the seventh ward in the downtown part of the N.O. was a very silent one.

Elias' mood was melancholy. It was bad enough to discover Blu's sister was the same broad on his shit list but to find out he was being forced into fatherhood was really blowing his top.

So many thoughts were swirling in his head, zooming through his mental in the same manner the cars Blu surpassed on the I-10 as she pushed eighty miles to speedily get him home.

"When it rains, it fuckin' pours, bruh!" He complained out of the thin air.

"What does that mean?" She glanced over in his direction but then realized he was looking out of the window and not at her. "Oh, never mind."

It was clear his statement was an outburst and not a pathway for conversation, so she officially left well enough alone. Blu pressed on the accelerator, hiking the speedometer to eighty-five to get him home and give him the space he wordlessly and rudely demanded.

Less than ten minutes later, she pulled up in front of his house. She wasn't even able to place her gear into park before Elias opened the door.

"Well, damn!" she blurted. What started off as concern, turned into anger. She couldn't believe how tightly he was holding his lips. "What happened that pissed you off that's making you take it out on me?"

Eli paused for a moment and looked at her, really looked at the confusion displayed on her face. For the first time since hearing the news, he registered the shoulder he was giving Blu was cold. He wanted to apologize right then and there when he saw her eyes glisten with a layer of tears but he knew there was more to be sorry for, so he'd wait until later to say everything all at once.

He leaned over and kissed her lips. "I'ma holla atcha, ya heard me."

Appalled by his reply, she stuttered. "Wha—what?" She then threw her hands up in a *that's it?* kind of way.

With his keys in hand, he got out and closed her door.

Coffee

Chirp. Chirp.

The alarm to his truck sounded off before the shut of the door slammed behind him and the roar of his engine came to life. Blu watched him back out of his driveway and onto his street as he sped off with no apparent regard of the clueless state he left her in.

She wiped away the one tear that slid down her cheek with the back of her finger as she shook her head slowly. Blu sat a minute longer as she made a call. Two rings and her best friend picked up.

"House of Beauty. This is Cutie. What's up, lil' ugly?" Kanari joked as she blew a cloud of blueberry into the evening's air.

"Where you at, best friend?"

Kanari detected the trouble in her voice. She placed her bong on the table and stood to her feet. "Somebody fuckin' with us?"

"No—no." That brought a smile to her face. "I want to come by if you're at home, is all."

She sat back down on her patio furniture, grabbing her Heineken as she folded her legs and sat on them. She took a swig. "Oh, I was 'bout to say. But, yea, I'm home. I'm in the backyard so just come straight to the back."

"Alright. I'm on my way." She pressed the end button and then slid her phone between her thighs.

Blu looked over at Eli's house for a moment, shaking her head as disappointment filled her chest before pulling off. She couldn't believe how he danced around her questions but she'd be damn if he two stepped the very next time they talked.

Chapter 6

G'Corey barely made it out of the park and down the block where the crack head rental he scooped from a clucker was stationed. Had Munch continued his chase, he would have been a dead man because he was fatiguing and growing dizzier by the minute.

G'Corey tossed the empty gun into the bushes before he reached the car. He had no concerns of a ballistics' team finding his prints because he wore gloves and the gun was hot, so no heat would come Black's way for supplying him with the steel.

Finally reaching the beat up four door, he slid into the Toyota Tercel and grabbed the keys he left in the ashtray.

"Ahhhh! Fuck!" he groaned as he crossed over his body with his right hand to close the door. It felt like a bomb detonated inside of his shoulder.

He started the engine then bit down on his bottom lip as his adrenaline decreased, his pain became blatant.

He needed to get to a hospital but he couldn't risk going to the closest one, so he swerved out onto the street to set out for a further one.

Driving in the city was stop and go, considering the red lights and casual drivers on the road. Becoming very impatient with typical delays in traffic made G'Corey cross.

"Come on, man. Fuck!" He yelled at the driver in front of him. His nerves were on short supply.

"What the fuck was you thinkin', bruh?" G'Corey asked himself out loud when he glanced at himself in the rearview mirror. Looking at his disheveled reflection, it was then he knew he hadn't thought at all.

He had no plan, only an impulse which led him to do irrational things he now had to make right if he was to win her back. And regardless to how slim his chances were, he still had hope.

Killing Yuriah ruled out the possibilities of her moving on for now. And with much convincing, she would have no choice but to return to him. G'Corey wasn't oblivious to Minnie being petrified, initially, but he decided he'd make her see that in a twisted way he did it for love.

And as for Yuriah's henchmen, he'd serve them the same fate as their friend because nothing was going to stop what was in motion.

He wasn't fooled into thinking this would be an easy feat. G'Corey even suspected it would be a long shot but he was a gambling man.

Finally making it onto the freeway, he thought back to the day he knew he'd come face to face with this moment.

A week ago...

"Wake up! I said wake up!" Mama Dee stood over her son as he lay sleep on her living room sofa.

G'Corey groaned as he came into a state of consciousness, still laying with his back toward her. "What, Mama? What you want?"

She was irritated and if he would have rolled over and opened his eyes, he would have been able to see the frustration on her face.

"What I want is the damn truth. Now wake your ass up."

G'Corey blew out hard before jerking the covers from off of him, swinging his feet to the floor and sitting up to face her. "Damn! What you waking me up for?"

She raised the back of her hand, stopping it at her neck line. "Boy, I outta slap you for taking that tone with me."

Rubbing the sleep from his eyes, he readjusted his attitude. "What's up, Ma?"

"Are you ready to tell me the truth about you and Minnie?" she asked, holding the morning paper in her hands as she stared down at him.

"Ma, what are you talking about? I've told you the truth. Me and Min—"

"Bullshit! No you haven't."

"Ma, I didn't come over here for this. I told you that me and Minnie are having some problems that we're working out and once she says I can come back home, I will happily leave yours."

50

"When was the last time y'all talked about making things right for the baby's sake, if nothing else?"

"I'm giving her space but we talked a couple of days ago. Why you with all these questions?"

Her mouth curled into a tight knot, giving the appearance she had no lips. "When did you begin feeling like you had to lie to me? Your mother!" She raised her voice.

G'Corey stood to his feet and blared, "I'm not lying about jack!"

Her eyes bucked with surprise, seeing her son chest up to her. She dropped the paper and began slapping him. "Who is you talkin' to? I will take you the fuck out!"

"A'ight. A'ight. A'ight. Damn!" He carefully blocked her hits while trying to pin her arms to her side. "Stop hitting me and tell me where all this coming from?"

She pulled away angrily, bending down to the floor and picking up the Lagniappe section she pulled from the Sunday's newspaper. She shoved it in his face. "Y'all reconciling things, huh? If that be so, tell me how is she getting married next week? When did y'all get a divorce? What's going on with my grandbaby? When were you going to tell—"

Mama Dee was hollering and carrying on but G'Corey couldn't register a word of it when he saw in black and white that Yuriah LeBlanc and Minyoka Mitchell were planning to marry.

G'Corey fell back down onto the sofa with his head hanging low, looking down at the paper. A ball of emotions rushed over him but the one most evident was shock.

'What the fuck? When did she divorce me? I never got no papers? This shit is a fake. Gotta be because she's a Daniels, my wife, with my baby. My baby? What did we have and when did she have it? What the fuck is really going on?' G'Corey thought to himself.

After he read the sordid details of how they planned to wed, his eyes gravitated back up top to their picture. Yuriah caught an elated Minnie inside of his arms with their lips glued together.

That told him much although he wrestled not to believe it.

51

He wasn't oblivious to the hurt he caused her, but there was no pain on the planet that should have prevented her from telling him about the birth of their baby and her desires for a divorce.

She moved on and that reality seared his heart like the scorch of a branding iron.

He was suspended in a state of stupor until Mama Dee slapped him on the back of the head, forcing him to the here and now. "Answer me."

He threw his hand up to brick wall her as he rose to his feet. "Not now."

G'Corey folded the paper, placing it under his arm as he slid on his tennis.

"Where are you going?" she questioned.

He didn't answer. He just grabbed his keys, phone and wallet before heading out of the door.

Mama Dee shook her head as she followed him out of the house with her hands on her hips. Judging the look in his eyes, she could tell he was up to something.

G'Corey tossed the paper onto the seat, pulled out and headed to Black's. He wasn't certain what he was going to do but he was sure he needed a burner for whatever plan he'd come up with.

G'Corey was finding it harder to focus on the road. He was nodding off, going in and out of consciousness.

Virtually slumping over the steering wheel and barely lucid, he still managed to push sixty mph while weaving through traffic. That was until his head completely fell slack and his foot rested heavier on the acceleration, propelling his speed even more until sudden impact brought him to an eerie stop.

Chapter 7

The EMT's hurried Yuriah through the doors of Mercy Hospital, briefing the attending physicians on his status as they jogged alongside the gurney.

"We have a GSW victim, appears to be in his late twenties early thirties. The insertion of the chest tube on the right side revealed massive hemothorax..."

The medical team took him to the back and began fulfilling the reasons they became doctors, to save a life.

Minnie and her parents arrived minutes after the ambulance had. Mrs. Mitchell let them out at the ER's entrance as she looked for parking.

Minnie hiked her dress up and kicked off her shoes, leaving them where she took them off.

Once inside of the facility, an air of uncertainty hovered around Minnie, suffocating her.

The sight and sound of the hospital overwhelmed her, bringing her grim reality to the forefront. She slowed down to a crawl.

"Baby girl, you alright?" Her father detected change in her stride as he held her by the arm.

"My *husband's been shot*," she mumbled before her eyes rolled to the back of her head, collapsing afterwards.

"Help!" He called for assistance as he laid her flat on her back. "Someone?" Mr. Mitchell caught the attention of a passing medical staff member.

She kneeled down beside her, taking her pulse. "What happened?"

"One minute, she was walking and then the next, she blacked out."

"What's her name?"

"Minnie."

In a calm voice, she began speaking to her. "Minnie, do you hear me?" She tapped her on the shoulder lightly a few times. "Minnie, can you hear me?"

A few seconds elapsed before she opened her eyes. When she came to, she tried sitting up but the nurse removed her jacket and folded it under Minnie's head, encouraging her to lay back down.

Minnie tried resisting but between the nurse and her father's pinning her by the shoulders, she couldn't budge an inch.

"I have to check on my husband." She cried in a pleading manner.

"You just fainted. I need you to lay her for a little while but I'll check on him. What's your husband's name?"

"Yuriah. Yuriah Leblanc."

"Don't move. I'll get a follow-up, okay?" She looked to her father. "Make sure she doesn't get up."

He bobbed his head and coaxed his daughter into calming herself.

Ten minutes later, she returned and assisted Minnie to her feet and walked her into the waiting room area where Kamal and a few other members from the wedding party waited.

"I checked on your husband. There isn't anything to report other than he is alive. Our doctors are doing everything to stabilize him here, but he will need to be transported by helicopter to Charity for his major surgery."

Minnie panicked. "Wh—why can't he be treated here?"

She reassuringly grabbed her arm. "We're not a trauma facility, but God willing, we will do everything in our power to sustain life and get him over to one that is."

Minnie began to shake as her anxieties kicked into high gear. She heard but then again she didn't hear what was being explained. All she knew was she was in a predicament that could turn the white dress she was wearing into a black one.

***

Twenty minutes later, Elias arrived at Children's. He didn't get the chance to tell Samiyah he was coming but given the situation, he assumed she would know he would.

His thoughts were so jumbled with the unfolds of his day he couldn't get his mind right. All he knew for sure was that he'd do whatever it took to get his peachy baby straight and he'd deal with her actually being *his* when it was all said and done.

He parked his truck in one of the vacant spots in front of the hospital and got out of his vehicle in a hurry. He was about to walk into the entrance when he saw one of two guards drop their keys seconds before bending over to retrieve them. It then occurred to him that he didn't lock his doors.

Elias patted his pockets for his keys but they weren't on him. He made a gruff sound and turned back around to retrieve them from out of the ignition where he absentmindedly left them.

Fifteen steps into the brisk jog back to his Escalade, Eli stumbled forward in a tumbling manner.

"Aaaahhh!" A groan escaped Elias' lips as he barely caught himself from falling to the ground. He then grabbed the back of his pounding head as he spun around and locked eyes with Gerran, who was now charging at him.

He considered the fact that Gerran would be on one but he didn't think he'd pull a hoe move and sneak him from behind.

Eli felt ambushed and if talking man to man was ever on Gerran's to do list, he ruled out those chances because now it was time to lock horns.

Gerran got up on him and threw a clobber type punch. Had it connected across Eli's face as he intended, it would have damn near knocked his head off of his shoulders. But Eli swiftly ducked the throw as if he was going underneath a clothesline and countered with a direct jab to Gerran's throat. That stopped him in his tracks.

"Huah! Huah!" Gerran choked for air as he clutched his neck and dropped down to one knee.

Amped up and pissed off, Elias was seconds away from laying a hard right across his jaw but security ran up on him, suspending his cocked arm in the air.

Tussling to get Eli to back down while in the midst of his aggression proved to be a bad idea for the guard. In full beast mode, Elias elbowed him in the mouth to get him to unhand him.

"Let me the fuck go!" Eli barked.

Security had been at the door to clearly see he was only defending himself and there was no need to treat him like he agitated the fight to start.

The officer massaged his chin slightly before making a stronger effort to contain his wild movement.

With Gerran neutralized and unable to attack, Ronnie rushed over to his co-worker to help assist in restraining an uncooperative Elias.

"This some bullshit! What the hell you cuffing *me* for?" Elias was furious.

"Public fighting, sir." One of the men responded.

"You saw that man run up on me. So what the fuck?" Elias tried stating his case.

"I did and I'll let the police know what I saw but I'm still gonna have to hold you 'til they arrive."

"What? You gotta be shittin' me." Elias couldn't believe what was happening.

"I'm sorry, man. I really am. But this is protocol and it's my job." Ronnie leveled with him.

Once they immobilized Eli, the other guard headed over to Gerran, who was now back on his feet. He had his second wind.

"Hands behind your back, sir. Let's just do this the easy way." Security walked over cautiously toward him, showing his silver bracelets.

Gerran's hands were balled into knots. His chest heaved up and down as his nostrils inhaled air and then exhaled fire. He stared down Elias, who was equally upset with his ass, too.

Eli looked over at Gerran, pathetically, shaking his head. He wasn't the only one jacked up over Samiyah's *baby daddy* shocker. Eli still couldn't come to terms with it and had Gerran been man enough to talk to him like one, he would have known there was malice against him when the slip up happened.

A third guard came up from behind Gerran and cuffed him before he had the opportunity to follow his predator's instinct and rumble with a vulnerable Eli, who was disadvantaged by his chained limitations.

Gerran grimaced and made agitated sounds as he was surprised by the metal confinements being placed around his wrists, but he said nothing as he was escorted inside of the facility.

Once Gerran was secured in a separate room, Ronnie walked Eli into another room where he too would be detained until the strong arm of the law came. As the young guard was leaving out, Elias called out for him.

"Say, bruh, can you at least get my keys up out my shit and leave them at the desk for Samiyah Babineaux to pick up or something?"

Ronnie allowed his eyes to drop to the floor as if he had to ponder doing the decent thing. "Alright," he bobbed his head. "What's your vehicle's description and location?" Elias gave him the year, make and model and directed him to where he parked. "I'm going to need to verify the registration against your license before leaving them for the young lady." Ronnie looked at the disgusted look Elias shot him and threw his hands up as if to say, *It's protocol.*

"Whatever. Do what you gotta do, dawg." Elias wolfed his frustrations.

Ronnie walked out of the room, locking the door behind him. When Eli heard the click of the shut, he slouched down in his seat. Hands cuffed behind his back, he shook his head and complained out loud. "Can this day get any more fucked up than it already is?"

Coffee

Chapter 8

Several hours later, Yuriah was brought into Charity Hospital's trauma unit where he was rushed into surgery.

News of G'Corey's fatal attempt on his life traveled as quickly as an amber alert, so everyone within his family unit showed up in droves.

The waiting room was filled with talks of optimism from some and retaliation from others.

More of his peoples trickled in as time elapsed, one of them was on fire and in desperate need of answers.

Keyz ran into the ER and hustled his way to the nurse's desk, oblivious to the recognizable faces surrounding him. He had a one-tracked mind, which was to check on his brother.

Once he stood before the woman who greeted him plainly, he placed his hands on the partition to sturdy himself because he was moments away from losing his shit.

"Yo, I'm looking for Kamal Jones," Keyz said on short breath.

She looked up at him and then to her scene and began punching the keys on the keyboard. Only seconds went by but already she was taking too long.

"We don't have a Kamal Jones in our—"

"Look again!" He impatiently cut her off.

"Sir, I checked and we—"

She was stopped short in her tracks. This time by the interruption of another man.

"Keyz," Kamal called from behind him.

The sound of his voice brought a sense a relief to Keyz instantly. He then rushed up on his half-brother, extending his hand to him. They connected in a dap and pulled each other into a G-hug.

"You good, boy? I thought you got shot." Keyz was automatically breathing easier to see that it wasn't so.

Moments later, they broke their embrace. "Shot at but this blood on me ain't mine, it's Yuriah's."

Keyz shook his head. "Mannn, my fuckin' heart dropped to my nuts when Shaunie told me what happened. I was thinking it was you who got stretched out and that shit blew the fuck outta me. But shit, knowing it's Yuriah who caught one don't make it no fuckin' better. How is he?"

"I know as much as you. But the fact that they ain't come over here talkin' 'bout speakin' to next of kin is good news right about nah. They're silence is our hope."

"So, what's up with the pussy mu'fucka that clapped at y'all?" Keyz spoke on low tone.

"Munch got in the wind after him but he got ghost."

"That's an easy fix, ya heard me. Give me his name and whatever else you know. You can keep watch over the big homie and I'll get a team of hittas together ASAP and light that boy up, dumping his body on Almonaster Rd., somewhere." Keyz barely moved his lips as he goaled to keep his volume loud enough for Kamal's ears only.

"That won't be necessary. It don't take high numbers to get at a low level clown, so less is best."

"A'ight," his reply sounded more sarcastic than it did convincing.

Keyz knew his brother was a fool with it and he didn't need him stepping in but that didn't stop him from wanting to handle his lightweight.

Aside from his last name, Kamal was the only connection to their father and he'd be damn if he let somebody get a second chance at taking what was his from him.

Kamal saw the unsettle in his eyes and grabbed him by the nape of his neck firmly, locking eyes with him. "Say, bruh, me and Munch got this, ya heard me. Trust me."

Keyz never doubted him for a second. It's just the ink on his right fist that read: *I Am My Brother's Keeper* meant there wasn't a beef Kamal would have to face alone.

"A'ight. Fa'sho," Keyz pounded him off, sounding believable this time.

Keyz then looked around at all the concerned faces that stood and sat around in the waiting area, not seeing two in particular. "Where Munch and BG at?"

Kamal ran a hand down his face. "Shenae didn't tell ya girl what all happened?"

"I didn't give Shaunie a chance. She was all hysterical when she called letting me know to get c'here, ASAP. She told me *you* were involved in a shooting and I hung up. I didn't need to hear shit else. I was on the way."

"Well, Munch got yoked up by them fuckin' people but Shenae went down there on big dawg status, ya heard me. They got him on gun charges but they can't hold him. So, they gon' lay up there and give him his day in court. Once his bond set, his girl gon' pay that shit and he'll be out that bitch. But you know it's the fuckin' week-end so he gotta sit 'til Monday."

Kamal shook his head at the thought of how sugar could turn to shit in second before he finished answering the rest of his question.

"And BG outside, running through a pack of Kools like it ain't nothing. Youngin' nerves are through. He ain't gon' be one hunnid 'til his brother is home and his cousin pull through. Shit, I ain't either," Kamal admitted.

A moment of silence fell between them right before Keyz' cell phone vibrated against his hip. He removed it from the holster. "Let me step out and take this. It's Shaunie."

Kamal nodded his head upward and watched Keyz place his phone to his ear and step outside of the facility before he took a seat next to Minnie, who had yet to speak more than two words since arriving.

***

"He's coming to now. Call the doctor." One of the nurses instructed of the other when she observed his eyes opening.

She spoke very softly as to not alarm him. Placing a hand on his shoulder to alert him of her presence, she soothingly said, "Sir, I'm Nurse Akem and you're in the hospital."

Coffee

His eyes opened fully but he started blinking them in a disorientated manner as he looked around the room, registering his foreign scenery.

"How did I— What happened?" He groaned when he attempted to sit up.

"Don't move. Relax, please." She readjusted the incline of his bed before pulling out his chart. "You were shot and you were in a three car accident. Do you remember any of this?"

"Who are you?" G'Corey squinted his eyes at her, wearing a pained expression on his face.

"I'm your nurse. Nurse Akem." She smiled genuinely at her patient.

Then the opening of the door caught both of their attention. The attending walked in and stood at the end of G'Corey's bed.

"How are you? I'm the ER physician, Dr. Jackson." The nurse handed him his chart and he thumbed through the pages in it. "We didn't find any identification on you. Can you tell us your name?"

"My name?" G'Corey repeated.

"Yes, your name."

G'Corey's eyes roamed from left to right as his mouth opened and then closed. "I don't know."

"Do you know what happened in the shooting you were involved in?" He pointed at his left shoulder.

"I was shot?" G'Corey looked as if he wanted to shed real tears.

"Do you know the year we're in or the current president of our country?" The doctor further probed.

G'Corey was becoming flustered at the questions.

The doctor could see he was becoming vexed by his inability to answer him, so he told him to relax. "Wait right here, buddy. I'll be back." The doctor left out of the room.

"I was shot?" G'Corey feigned concern and then gently brushed over the covering on his blade where he had been shot.

"Yes and you were lucky, may I add. You see, the shoulder contains the subclavian artery, which feeds the brachial artery, the main artery of the arm, as well as the brachial plexus, the large nerve bundle that controls arm function. Had that bullet hit you just a quarter

62

of an inch toward the right, you would have needed surgery to deal with blood vessel damage, severe pain and loss of motor function. But it was a clean shot and all you needed were stitches, anti-inflammatories and pain meds."

"What about my memory, though? Why don't I remember what happened?" G'Corey asked as he rubbed his scalp in a circular motion.

"Sometimes with a concussion, which you suffered, you can sustain short term loss that can range from minutes to hours, but you will regain full memory. We've ran some CT's of the head and we'll know more shortly after reading your films."

"Ah, Miss, where are my clothes?" He looked underneath his sheet and discovered he was draped in a gown.

She pointed off to the side. "There in that bin but what you're wearing is sufficient until you're discharged."

Nurse Akem remained at his bedside and that made G'Corey made feel uneasy. He didn't like being under her watchful eye, even though her intentions were to administer care.

He grabbed at his throat. "Umm, Miss, could you get me some water, please?"

"Surely," she exited the room.

G'Corey sprung out of bed. "Aaahhh!" He moaned at the dizziness he felt once he stood to his feet. He staggered over to the spot where his clothes were located and clumsily stepped into his jeans as quickly as using one arm would allow. He then slipped his feet into his tennis shoes, walking on the backs of them as he headed to the door.

He peeked his head out, waiting impatiently for a moment to slick out. The halls were busy and no time seemed appropriate but it wouldn't be long before his nurse returned, so G'Corey decided now had to be the time.

"Fuck it!" he said below his breath, swiveling her head one last time before he walked out, hurriedly.

Clutching the back of the open gown, he walked at a moderate speed but not too fast as he didn't want to draw suspicion on himself.

G'Corey walked a few feet before he turned slightly behind him to see if any medical staff was following when he bumped into a doctor.

"Ahhhhh!" G'Corey groaned the moment they brushed into each other, gritting down on his teeth from the stinging sensation that surged down his arm.

The doctor asked, looking him over. "Are you alright? What are you doing out of your room? Come on, let me walk you back."

Shit! G'Corey thought to himself. He didn't want to stick around for them to probe him for answers on who he was or make any connections to what was done earlier that day when news of the shooting became public knowledge, if it wasn't already. So he couldn't afford to be under their scrutiny.

"Which room is yours?"

"Ahh, it's room—"

"Excuse me, Doctor, can you please sign these discharge papers." The nurse kindly interrupted.

The doctor turned away to place his John Hancock on the form she held up for his signature. And in the fifteen seconds it took for him wrap up with her, G'Corey was gone.

"Where did he go?" The doctor spun around but didn't see G'Corey anywhere.

She hunched her shoulders before stepping off to tend to her patients.

"Humph," the doctor looked about before carrying on, just the same.

A few minutes later, G'Corey was walking out of Touro Hospital and down Prytania St.

The cloak of darkness the midnight hours brought covered him as he walked to the Discount gas station on St. Charles Ave.

G'Corey had to get from off of the streets, but he had no means to do it by himself. So as he waited off to the side of the building, he asked a few people for change but was turned down before he could even get the words out.

Finally, one man walked up on him. "You alright, lil' brother?"

"Nah, I'm in need of some change, Unc. I have to make a call so I can get home."

The older cat reached into his pocket and dumped the crumpled dollars and loose coins into G'Corey's hand. "There you go, fam."

"Take yo bills, Unc. I only need these quarters, ya heard me."

The man did as G'Corey asked and then walked away after he thanked him for his help.

G'Corey walked over to the pay phone, looked down the street both ways and then dropped the coins into the slot, punching the numeric buttons.

The phone just rang, so by the fourth ring, he hung up before the operator came on and he lost his money. He dialed him again.

"Come on, bruh. Pick up yo fuckin' phone," he spoke into the receiver, impatiently. On the final ring right before he was going to hang up and dial again, Hakeem answered. "Finally! Yo, I need you to come pick me up. I'm uptown, in your area at this gas station on St. Charles."

Right there, Hakeem spoke under his breath to his baby's mom before addressing him. "Say, G, you caught me at a bad time, dawg."

"Well, it gotta be the right fuckin' time because I need you. Shit is real."

"Hang up the phone, baby," she kissed up his chest before tonguing his ear.

Damn, Hakeem moaned when he felt the warmth of her swirl. He knew she was trying to convince him to stay put.

G'Corey was already impatient and now he became irritated. "Dawg, I know you heard me say I need you!"

Fuck! Hakeem moved the phone from by his mouth. "Keep that on ice 'til I get back, ya heard me. I gotta make a run real fast."

G'Corey could hear the girl expressing her disapproval.

"He always need you to get him out of some shit. You really need to stop messing with him. He's nothing but trouble, for real."

"That's my boy, bae. I'ma scoop him and be right back, ya heard me."

"Mmmhmmm, but you heard what I said. He ain't nothing but trouble."

Hakeem brushed it off and returned back to the phone. "A'ight, where you at?"

G'Corey wanted to respond to his girl having too much unsavory shit to say about him, but instead he gave him the particulars and then they disconnected after he was told he'd get picked up in ten minutes.

Again, G'Corey eyed both directions of the street before he walked back to the side of the building and kicked over a crate to sit on as he waited in the shadows. He rubbed his hand carefully over his wound.

Shit is about to get really real!

Chapter 9

It was 2 a.m. Monday morning. Minnie was sleep deprived and stressed. She hadn't left the hospital since Yuriah was admitted. Although urged by everyone to go home and get rest, shower and eat, she refused all of their advice to take care of herself and remained steadfast. Had it not been for her mother, she would still be in her stained wedding dress with not even a morsel of food in her system.

She was mentally exhausted as well. After what she thought was a successful surgery late Sunday morning, immediately turned into another emergency, calling for a second operation when one of his lungs collapsed. Now having to undergo another procedure, there was no way she'd leave. It was simply preposterous for them to think otherwise.

Kamal refused to leave also. He always had reason to ride out any situation with or for Yuriah, but what solidified his eternal debt was what took place twelve years ago.

Yuriah could have left him hanging that night, but he didn't. And for that, Kamal could never turn his back on him.

"Ain't this a bitch?" Kamal pulled onto the shoulder of the I-10 when a state trooper flagged him over. Fuck! He mouthed as he looked out of his rearview mirror and saw two men walking toward him at a cautious pace.

Yuriah was in the trail vehicle behind Kamal, so he saw when they hit the lights and rode up on him. Yuriah bypassed the spot where Kamal parked, pulling off of the side of the highway just a few yards up ahead.

The bright flashlights the two officers held shoulder high while approaching both sides of his car were blinding. They drew near and once they were up on his car, the officer on Kamal's side tapped his window.

"Let yer winder down and stick yer hands out dat der winder slowly and don't try no funny stuff, ya hear?" The officer spoke with a thick of confederacy dripping from his tone. His left hand trained

his light directly in Kamal's face while the right rested on his gun still on his belt.

"You don't gotta shine that shit in my face, no." Kamal's voice could not hide his aggression.

The hick cop didn't bother to acknowledge him. He simply proceeded with his questions.

"You got any weapons or drug paraphernalia we should know about it there?"

With his hands still out of the window and his face forward, Kamal asked a more pressing question. "Whatchu stoppin' me fa?"

"Answer my question, boy."

Kamal whipped his neck to the left and almost retracted his hands to open his door, step out and show him who wasn't a boy but he kept his cool. He was riding dirty and he didn't need to give those back wood, redneck muthafuckas a reason to hem him up more so than they were already. His record was long enough from his run ins with the law.

"Nah, I don't got shit. So, like I said, whatchu stoppin' me fa?"

"You didn't use yer blinker back der when you were changing lanes and dat der qualifies you for a traffic stop. So, I'm gon' need yer license, ID and registration. You do have that, don't cha?"

Kamal didn't answer. Instead he went to pull his hands back so he could get the requested information. The second he did so, both officers drew their weapons and pointed them at his head.

He heard the sounds of their bullets being chambered and then the officer on the right spoke. "Don't try nothing stupid."

The corner of Kamal's lip went into a high arch as he grimaced, swiveling his head from side to side as he tried his best to see beyond the shine of their lights and at the peckerwoods who were dying for a chance to kill from behind the badge.

'Before I die tonight, I'm taking one of these crackas with me,' Kamal said to himself as he angrily collected what was asked of him.

"Thank you, boyyy. We'll be right back."

Kamal placed his hands on the steering wheel and squeezed it tightly as his lips balled into an even tighter knot. Had he had his piece under the seat as he usually did, he would have roasted him two pigs.

Yuriah was still sitting in his car with the lights off but the engine running just in case he had to ride back and let his Glock 9 put something on their minds.

After waiting idly for a few minutes, his phone lit up with a call from Kamal. He hurriedly answered, "What's goin' on?"

"Mann, I would get stopped in the worst fuckin' parish there is. Pussy, racist ass bitches stopped me on not using a turn signal. But I don't got no warrants or attachment so we should be rolling in no time."

"A'ight just keep your cool and keep your phone on you so I can hear what's goin' on until they leave," Yuriah advised.

"Here they come, nah." Kamal locked his screen and then he slipped his phone into his jacket.

The same officer stepped to him and handed his things back. "Looks like everything checked out on ya. Surprised the hell out of me." He laughed but Kamal didn't find shit funny.

The other officer cased the vehicle, shining his light through every window. He then came on the same side as his partner and began sniffing. "I smell weed. Do you smell weed, Jim?"

"I surely do. Do you have weed in the car?"

"Are you fuckin' serious? You don't smell no goddamn weed 'cause I don't smoke that shit," Kamal glared at them. It became clear to him that these two good ole boys weren't gonna sleep easy until they locked him up for something.

The second, instigating officer pointed his light into Kamal's astray. "Then what's that?"

Kamal didn't turn his head, he just answered. "That's a Black n Mild. A cigar. There's a difference. Can I leave, nah?"

"Sure. Right after we check the inside of your vehicle."

"I don't give you no fuckin' permission to check my shit and you got no fuckin' grounds anyway." Kamal's body temperature elevated, causing him to produce a light sweat all over.

"Step out of the vehicle. Now!" He readied his hand on his pistol.

"Mannn, what the fuck? I told you I don't have no mutha-fuckin'. Ooooh!" He bit down on his bottom lip and angrily stepped out.

"Against the hood."

"But this bitch hot." Kamal had been driving nonstop from Texas and his engine was still running.

"Are you resisting, boy?"

Kamal stopped talking. There was no need to exchange any more words with an identified enemy. He angrily got on the heated hood of the car and waited until they did their illegal search.

The interior of the rental was clean. Nothing was inside except for a half empty bottle of Ever Fresh juice and the half smoked cigar.

"It's clear. The one performing the search yelled out to his partner.

"Pop the trunk and check it." The officer watching Kamal told the other.

Upon opening the trunk, he saw one suitcase. He opened it and shifted through the clothes, finding a brick in the trough.

"Yee doggie. Looks like we done struck gold." He celebrated.

The other officer spit out his Copenhagen tobacco and began reading off Kamal's right.

Kamal wanted to head butt him, relieve him of his gun and try his luck on getting away but that would be taking penitentiary chances for sure. So, he let the reckless thought pass.

"Shit!" he said below his breath.

One officer took the keys from his rental and locked up the car. They'd call for impound to pick it up for evidence. Meanwhile, Kamal was placed in the back of their unit and hauled off to Lake Charles City Jail.

Thirty minutes later, they arrived at county. "Welcome home, boy." He got a good kick out of that.

They walked on either side of Kamal until a voice behind them caused them to stop and turn around.

"You got the wrong man," Yuriah yelled out to them as he walked toward them.

"Whatchu say?" One of them spoke up.

"I said you got the wrong man. Those drugs are for me, not him. He didn't know shit about it being in there. That's my charge."

Kamal shook his head no. "Nah, that—"

"That's why he couldn't tell you shit. He didn't know shit. So, go 'head arrest me." Yuriah over talked him.

The officer nodded off to his partner for him to escort Yuriah inside while he walked in Kamal. It made him no never mind as long as he met his quota of locking a brother up for the day.

After they were both booked and processed, they were placed in a holding cell. The moment the officer walked away, Kamal went in.

"Bruh, what the fuck you doing? I knew the risks. I'ma take my own lick, ya heard me."

"Don't be stupid. This will be your third fuckin' strike. I'm guaranteed to come home but you'll never touchdown. Aside from all that, your girl just told you she's pregnant. You really wanna leave Shenae to raise y'all child on her own? Shit is bigger than you. Think about that."

"Fuck! Mannn, I can't have you go down for me. I won't let you."

"How you gon' stop me? Look, it ain't up for discussion, bruh. Stick to the plan. Do what you need to do and then get the fuck out, go legit and raise your family."

"Shit ain't that simple," Kamal argued.

"Real life never is."

"Nah, I gotta think this over, round. Shit not sitting right with me."

"Go on and think. I'm resolute in my decision." Yuriah was immovable. The system already fucked them into a position where selling dope was the only avenue for them to take to escape poverty, he wasn't going to let it rob his mans of his freedom too.

The next day, Yuriah Leblanc signed an affidavit, stating the key of coke belonged to him and Kamal Jones had no knowledge he was transporting drugs for him.

Coffee

Yuriah was charged with conspiracy with the intent to distribute and sentenced to five years with parole in three. To see his boy free, he pled guilty. There were no regrets there.

The day Kamal left court, he felt guilty but Yuriah insisted he shouldn't because he believed if the outcome will be great, the sacrifice, regardless of loss, is nothing by comparison.

Over the years of Yuriah's incarceration, Kamal stuck to the plan. He hustled nonstop alongside Munch until they were able to turn illegitimate revenue into legitimate bank.

Kamal also made it a point to visit Yuri twice a month and would bring his daughter, De'Asia, to see her uncle when she was big enough to go along. He kept money on his books and held him down in every way he was supposed to.

Kamal's phone buzzed and brought him out of his reverie. He removed it from the clip and looked at the screen. It read: *Wifey.* He cleared his throat and then answered.

"What's good? Everything a'ight?" His voice carried concern when he looked at the time and saw it was a quarter past two in the morning. It was odd for Shenae to be woke at that hour.

"Everything is good over here. I'm breastfeeding this greedy son of yours right now, so I decided to call to see if anything changed and if you were okay."

"I'm straight, ya heard me." Kamal yawned into the phone as he stretched his legs and sunk into a slouch position in his chair.

"How is Minnie holding up?"

"She goin' through it. She tryna stay optimistic, ya dig, but this shit is taking a toll on her."

Shenae nodded her head up and down although he couldn't see it. "I trust everything will be all right, it has to be. Oh, not to change subjects but De'Asia wants to see you, she misses you. So, I am going to swing that way after I pick her up from school today."

"That's what up. But is she the only one missing daddy?"

"Of course not," Shenae softened her voice. "Double misses you, too." She referred to Kamal Jr, his twin.

"You got jokes, huh?" He chuckled.

Shenae was glad to hear him laugh. She giggled herself before she cleared things up. "I miss you, too. Can't wait until—"

"I gotta call you back." He rushed out his words before he hung his phone up. Kamal sprung to his feet the moment he saw the doctor approaching them.

Minnie was exhausted and in a daze but she perked up when she saw the doctor. She was both anxious and hesitant the second she heard her name called.

She wanted to stand and greet the physician but she didn't have the energy to hold herself up if she was about to receive more devastating news that would knock her back down, so remained seated.

"Mrs. Leblanc. Mr. Jones," she looked them each in the eyes. "The surgery was successful and Mr. Leblanc is stable."

The breath that Minnie held released itself with a hard exasperated sound. She then leaped out of her seat and into the doctor's arms who braced herself for the hug she saw coming at full speed.

Kamal snappily clapped his hands once and walked in a tight circle as he excitedly shouted, "Hell yea!"

Minnie pulled back from the doctor and then headed over to Kamal. They shared a hug to express their joy and relief.

The crooks in their necks, the backaches, the discomfort that took root at the base of their bellies was all made worth it, hearing that he was alive.

Tears streamed from the corners of Minnie's eyes as she threw her head back. "Thank you, God. Thank you, God..." She repeated the same line over and over until she found herself crying just as hard as she had the moment tragedy struck. Difference was, this time it was tears of rejoice.

The doctor stood there, wearing a smile. She was elated she was finally able to bring them good news. However, what was to follow was surely going to be a downer of their celebration.

***

G'Corey wasn't wearing a watch but he knew it was well beyond an hour by the time Hakeem pulled into the gas station. He walked over to where he parked, tapped on the window and then opened the door when he heard the lock pop up.

The scent of sex wafted up his nostrils upon opening the door. "You smell like pussy, you couldn't wait on getting yo dick waxed?"

"And you smell salty than a muthafucka, dawg, so bring that shit down one thousand. I had to get her right, but fuck all that I'm here, ain't I?" Hakeem slumped in his seat and looked over at G'Corey. "And what the fuck happened to you anyway?"

G'Corey was bristling from having to wait so long. Coupled with the incident from earlier and Hakeem playing him for a duck, his words were reflective of his annoyance as he spoke. "I snapped off and killed that muthafucka, Yuriah, while at his wedding to, get this, *my* fuckin' wife."

Hakeem scrunched up his face. "Run dat back. You said what?"

"You heard me right."

"Whew!" Hakeem whistled. "So, what the fuck is you gon' do, nah? You know Drop's people ain't gon' let shit go until you faced up. That's how they rockin'. So, what you knock them off, too?"

"First, I'm gon' lay low in LaPlace by Skits for a minute. The city gon' be hot over that thuggah. I'ma heal up, put together a fire plan to eliminate his peoples and literally get my house in order with Minnie."

"Wait a minute, dawg." Hakeem tapped the tips of his fingers into the center of his palm, calling for a time out. "Getcho girl back? You were supposed to sling rocks not smoke them bitches. Hate to break this shit to you but Minnie ain't gon' want you after you went all ape shit at her wedding. How you plan to shake back from that?"

G'Corey shook his head, refusing to accept that Hakeem could be telling the truth. "Nah, I'll make her understand. Did I fuck up by flatlinin' that chump? Yes. Only because she had to see it but I don't regret that shit. I don't know what the fuck he did to convince her to divorce me and marry him but my throw away made that shit null and void. And because I cleared the way, I'm gon' get her back. I'ma show her that I'm prepared to do whatever I have to just to get her and keep her. And that's on everything."

Hakeem shook his head. "You crazy as bat shit."

"Maybe I am. But come on, man, let's get the hell from 'round here. Roll me through the set. I'ma get my car and get the fuck before sunrise."

Before pulling off, Hakeem had to ask, "Dawg, you sure this what you want? To wage war with Drop's peoples?"

G'Corey momentarily forgot he was injured and jerked his body forward to aggressively check him but he coiled back into his seat when the painful sensation from moving too fast settled him back down.

"Aaahhhhh! Fuck!" he groaned out, clamping his eyes shut as he tolerated the excruciating surge pulsing through his body. "Listen, I ain't sure about shit except that I want my life back, starting with my wife. And I don't give a fuck what odds are stacked against me, we vowed to death do us part. So, as long as we breathing, we gon' be together."

"I hear ya, dawg. Hakeem finally pulled off, choosing to let it be. He has had G'Corey's back on many things but this by far was the wildest shit ever.

G'Corey twisted his wedding band around his finger, thinking: *My love knows no boundaries, baby. You gon' see.*

***

"Excuse me, Mrs. Leblanc," she tapped her on the shoulder.

Minnie turned around to face her, wiping her tears away with the inside of her shirt. "I'm so sorry. I got caught up and didn't let you finish because you just answered my prayers. But what else did you want to say? Did you want to take us to him? Are we able to see him right now?" Minnie went a mile a minute.

"Yes, you may. But there's something I need to tell you first."

Minnie became panicked when she saw the plastic smile and heard the extra calm in her voice. Her smile went flat and she looked intently at the doctor while she waited for her to speak.

Kamal stepped in closer as his antennas raised a touch higher as well. "What's the matter?"

Coffee

The doctor offered them a reassuring look but what she said next wasn't as pleasant as the warmth she extended. "He never came out of his coma."

Chapter 10

Monday morning greeted Blu but Eli still hadn't. A few more tick tocks of the clock will make it 48 hours since she had seen or heard from him. And the mere fact that she had no way to call him and he made no attempts to call didn't sit well with her.

"Ummmm," Kanari stretched her arms above her head upon waking as her internal alarm told her it was 10 a.m. and time to make moves for the day. She had stayed over by Blu's place, as she would anytime she didn't feel like driving the twenty minutes it took to get to hers after they closed the bar at 3 a.m.

Kanari turned on her side and faced Blu only to see her sitting up clutching her cell, wearing the same salty look on her face she'd been sporting all weekend.

"You keep lookin' at your phone like it's gonna make him call. Didn't yo grandma tell you *a watched pot never boils?*" Kanari snatched her phone out of her hands and put it on the nightstand beside her.

"Uggghhh! This isn't like him. And I'm starting to bug the hell out. I don't want to be upset with him if something is *reeeally* wrong but then I don't want to give him the benefit of my patience if this is all over some bullshit."

"So, you tryna be his peace meanwhile he isn't giving you any? He got'chu worried and me messed up. I just hope for his sake that something *reeeally* is wrong or he's going to find himself in a real fucked situation." Kanari pulled back the covers, got out of the bed and headed into the bathroom to relieve her bladder.

Blu followed behind her and stood in the doorway as Kanari pulled down her panties and sat on the toilet.

"If this was your situation, what would you do?"

"Hold up. It's hard for me to give you the best advice with a sober mind. Let me get that Bob Marley in me and I will be able to conjure up a plan from the gods." Kanari wiggled the last of her pee out before wiping herself.

"I should have known you had to wake and bake as you call it," Blu smiled.

Standing over the sink, Kanari examined her mountain sized pimple on her chin as she washed her hands. "Girl, I need to get laid. Waiting on the right one is gon' have me looking like a crater face gremlin. Ugghhh! How long has it been?"

"It'll be a year next month."

"See, that's why you my bitch! You keeps up with ya girl."

"We been stitched at the hip since second grade. I know everything about you except your blood type."

"O positive. Nah, you know it all." Kanari confirmed.

"It's a shame to say this but you're closer to me than the sisters I actually have. We have eighteen years of tightship and a lifetime to go."

Kanari bobbed her head slowly. "Tou fuckin' ché', mi best amiga."

Cutting off the bathroom light, they both walked back into her room. Kanari headed to the oversized chair positioned in the corner, grabbed her purse off of it and pulled out her gunja kit.

"I bet your lungs are Incredible Hulk green with as much grass as you smoke." Blu poked fun at her.

"No one calls it *grass*, Lame-O." She tossed a throw pillow her way but Blu ducked. "And quit tryna clown me. It's squares like yourself that will never know the ecstasy that bud smokin' brings, so zip it and come with me outside." Kanari smiled her way before walking out of her bedroom.

"You know what happened the last time you sat on the back porch with just your t-shirt and panties on." Blu reminded her of her lurking neighbor.

"Yea, I do. But this my comfy wear. Besides, I'll fuck lil' mama up if she cross onto your property line with those plastic dick ambition of hers. I can't fuck with a man who got hoe in him so you know a bitch don't stand a chance with me. Let her try." Kanari brazenly said as she pushed open the French doors that were off of her kitchen, leading onto the deck that overlooked Blu's backyard.

After a couple of minutes of inhaling the good, Kanari turned toward Blu, who was sitting on the ledge of the wooden porch beam.

"WWKD, huh? What Would Kanari Do? Well, Kanari would stop off at his house. If he wasn't there, then she'll roll up to the hospital where he was last known to be. And let's say he's there. She'll get up on him and be like, *'Baby, are you alright?'* Once he says he good, then she'll mush his face backwards and say, *'Bitch, then what the fuck was yo problem, then?'* Straight G-check him," she spoke of herself in third person.

"That's not my style. Too disrespectful." Blu shook her head before resting her chin back onto her bended knee.

"Then why did you ask me? You already know how I am. Maybe that's why I don't have dick nah." She laughed at herself.

"I ask because you always keep it real with me. I'm just not into all that rah rah behind a man like you 'bout."

"You right. Okay then, bring it down a couple watts. Let's just find him and then you freestyle how you want to handle it from there? Whether you be calm or go crazy, I got your back, but after I get something to eat." Kanari rubbed her stomach as she took another pull before smothering the flame at the end of the cigar.

"I know you do. Mucho thank you, chica." Blu hopped down off of the banister and walked back inside with her friend in tow.

Operation *Where the Hell Eli At?* was about to be in progress.

***

The weekend had been exhausting. What started off as one problem, Lil' Acacia needing a transfusion, evolved into ninety-nine of them.

The only silver lining she saw at that moment was that her baby received donor blood and so far she was receptive to it.

Other than that, Samiyah was bummed. She rested her head on the steering wheel of Eli's truck as she sat in the parking lot of the hospital. She had to compose herself before going inside to visit her baby in the NICU, but it was hard. Her life was coming unglued all over again.

Coffee

She was now pregnant with what was supposed to be her husband's second child but as fate had it, she wasn't.

"Who makes the same mistake twice?" Samiyah questioned herself out loud as she reflected on what she told Elias about Cedric less than a year ago.

"I knew I should have never bedded my friend. Bad shit always happens when friends cross boundaries."

"Why didn't you fuckin' listen to yourself?"

Samiyah was disgusted because she knew better than to allow a moment of weakness to write another check her ass couldn't cash.

She didn't see her and Eli's train wreck coming, but surely the consequences of a similar past with Cedric was an unfadeable lesson she felt she should have learned from, but yet she sat faced with another chicken that was coming home to roost.

Desperately needing someone to talk to, she picked up her phone to dial Acacia but then she remembered her calls couldn't reach beyond the clouds. Samiyah felt weighed with sadness as if the news of her death was just delivered to her. Three months had passed since her untimely demise and she still had to remind herself that her number was no longer in service. *Damn!*

Then she wanted to reach out to Minnie, but she was out of the country on her honeymoon for the next two weeks, no doubt having the time of her newly married life.

Eli wasn't an option because he was rocking the same boat as she, plus he was in jail as of result of the fight Gerran instigated.

Here I go again, same messy triangle but this time with Eli.

***

"Roll your window down if you wanna catch a breeze because the A/C isn't working." Kanari advised the moment they both got inside of her beloved ride.

Blu slightly lifted the door upward so it would latch when she closed it. "When are you gonna get a new car?"

"Nevaaa," Kanari spoke animatedly. She was literally going to ride until the wheels fell off.

"Tell me again why we just don't take my car?"

"Because we need to be incognito. He never seen ole Benny here." Kanari ran her hand over the dash covering of her Delta 88.

"You really think we need to be inconspicuous, like we gon' see something that calls for low-key riding?"

"Don't get me wrong, I like Eli. So, I am hoping I'm overdoing it. But you said it yourself, he was acting weird since dinner, he took a call that threw him for a loop, then shut you out afterwards and now he's M.I.A. If he's up to no good, I rather we spot him first before he spots us. You know, have the upper hand in the situation."

Blu didn't think the extra mile was necessary, it gave the impression that she was expecting something to be wrong. But then again, it didn't hurt to have an edge. "I suppose."

"Fingers crossed that we don't see anything that'll make us go postal. But either way, it's best to be in the know, so let's roll."

Blu nodded her head and blew her breath upward to move her dangling curls from in front of her eye. "Let's roll."

On that note, Kanari roared the engine of her Oldsmobile and drove off.

***

Samiyah walked into the facility and was greeted by the staff. She waved and smiled at them but there was no denying it was a fraudulent attempt to be pleasant.

She signed in at the front desk. Afterwards, she was escorted into the room where Lil' Acacia lay, resting.

Turning to the nurse she asked, "What happens now and how much longer until I can take my baby home?"

The nurse looked into her chart and began explaining. "We are going to observe her over the next couple of days. See how her body responds and monitor her complete blood count, ensuring they replicate at a normal rate. Once we are satisfied with her tests and her health is restored, she can go home and lead a regular life. And from there on out, you'll be able to follow up with your baby's pediatrician."

"That's great news. Thanks."

"No problems, Mrs. Babineaux. I'm right outside if you need me. Take your time." The nurse smiled compassionately before stepping out.

Samiyah walked over to Lil' Acacia and her eyes lit up like Christmas morning. The pink onesie she wore had Children's Hospital written across her adorable pot belly as it exposed her chunky little rolls in her thighs. She couldn't wait to love all on her.

Pulling a seat next to the incubator, she sat down and leaned close up on it. "Hey, mama's sunshine. How have you been feeling? You look to be resting peacefully, sweet angel. That makes me happy because mama has been so concerned about you. I should have known you'd be alright, though, you're so strong. But as you grow up, you'll see that I am bound to panic over the littlest thing and that's because you are my very first baby love and I'm learning as I go, so be patient with me, okay?"

Samiyah sat back in the chair and stared at her daughter. She was in awe at what she created.

Regardless to how you came about and with whom, you were the best thing I've ever done.

"Oh, mommy almost forgot." Samiyah reached into her purse and pulled out Mr. Trunks, the stuffed baby elephant. "When you wake up, you'll see what mommy brought you from home. It's your favorite fury friend."

Samiyah paraded the animal around her bed until she pulled it into her chest, inhaling Lil' Acacia's scent off of it before crying softly. Wiping the tears away, she began singing Monica's *Angel of Mine*. That was the song she sang to her every night since she was born.

When I first saw you/I already knew/There was something inside of you/Something I thought that I would never find/Angel of mine…

Her eyes were closed sweetly as she rocked side to side holding Mr. Trunks tightly against her bosom as if he was her sweet pea.

Midway through the song her phone rang, startling her. "Oh, crap!"

She didn't mean to have her ringer on but when she saw it was a jail number, she was glad she did.

"Be right back, angel."

She jumped out of the seat and sprinted for the door. Once she was out in the hallway, she answered. She waited for automation to ask if she'd accept the call. Whether it was Gerran, whom she hadn't heard from since he stormed out, or Elias, she was taking it.

"Hello. Samiyah?"

"Yes. Hello."

"How you holdin' up?"

"I'm still standing, considering the circumstance. How are you?"

"Been better but shit is what it is. Where you at? The hospital?"

"Yea, I just got here a few minutes ago."

"How is Peaches?"

"The transfusion went smoothly and she is doing great."

"That's good to hear. Well, I called because I needed you but I don't want to pull you from her, so I'll just hit Jacobi."

"Nah, what do you need?"

You have one minute remaining. The automated recorder interrupted.

"I need you to bond me out. They set my shit but I don't want you paying from your joint account with that asshole you married, so I need you to run to my house, get my debit card from off the nightstand and get me right. Can you do that?"

"Of course, I can always come right back."

"A'ight. I'll call you from a payphone when I'm released because I'm gonna need a ride and we gotta talk anyway."

"Okay, we most definitely do. But I'll take care of that for you now. What's your pin number?"

"It's 5036. 5-0-3..."

The line went dead but she heard him clearly. She went back inside the NICU, told her baby she'd be back as well as the nurses and then she headed out.

***

They were a few streets away from Elias' house when Blu made Kanari pull over.

"Why am stopping?"

"Girl, I'm getting nervous."

"What the hell for?" Kanari's brows drew inward.

"What if he's home and just doesn't want to be bothered with me? I feel like I'm intruding on my own damn relationship."

"Well, you're not. You're just concerned and there's nothing wrong about that. You're doing the right thing. It's not like you tryna charge him up. You just want to know if he's alright and what's going on."

"True, but let's just wait a minute. Give me a little time to feel less stupid about going to him after two days of nothing. "

Twenty minutes had passed by the time Kanari looked back at the time. "Do you feel less stupid now?" she asked facetiously.

"No."

"Well, suck it up, sister, because we heading to the crib. You just need to get it over with. If he's home, y'all will talk. If he's not, then we will find him, wherever he may be." Kanari pulled off without waiting for the green light.

Minutes later, they pulled up in front of Eli's house. Blu let out a disappointing breath when she didn't see his truck in his driveway. "He isn't here."

"Plan B it is. To the hospital." Kanari pulled into his driveway, reversed her Buick then headed back up the street.

As they were approaching the stop sign up ahead, Blu saw Eli's truck roll past them and her heart raced. She quickly slouched down in her seat, so he wouldn't see her and assume she was spying on him.

"What the hell is your prob?" Kanari looked at her crossly.

"There he goes!" Blu blurted out in relief.

"Word? I'ma back Benny up and drop you off, so y'all can talk. Cool?"

Blu rubbed her chest as to simmer down her nerves. "Yea, that's cool."

Kanari checked her rearview mirror and once she saw her path was clear, she placed her car in reverse and backed it up toward his house.

Blu lowered the visor so she could check her face. As she continued to spot check herself, her body was jerked forward and then back suddenly. "What the— Why'd you slam on brakes?" Blu frowned at her abrupt driving. "Good thing I had my damn seatbelt on."

Kanari didn't answer. Instead, she just back hand tapped her repeatedly on the arm while looking outside of her driver's window. Her eyes were stuck on the female that was using a key to get inside of Eli's house.

In a high pitch and stunned voice, she asked, "Harpo? Who da fuck is dis woman?"

Coffee

Chapter 11

Blu didn't answer her fast enough and that was okay with Kanari because she was on her way to find out for herself. She opened the car door. "Oh, he's cheating on us?" Her voice squealed.

Blu reached over and grabbed her by the arm, yanking her back inside. "Calm down. That's Samiyah."

"And?"

"Anddd she's nobody to worry about. She's his friend, plus she's married."

"*Tsss.* You said that like her being married is a repellant to getting fucked by your man."

"Well, damn! Say how you really feel." Blu was offended.

"Come on, sis. She's the married friend who just got out of *his* truck and who's now using a key *you* don't even have to get inside of *his* house. The bitch got privileges I don't see you with. That's all I'm saying."

Kanari pulled at both of her earlobes to ensure she didn't have earrings on. It may had been in Blu's nature to be diplomatic and exercise reasoning but Kanari was the fighter type and she was ready to question Samiyah and get her right in the event she went left.

Blu was thinking, trying to process her jumbled thoughts but it was hard to do under the scrutiny filled eye of an impatient Kanari.

"Well, you gon' go check her?" Kanari twisted her neck and bucked her eyes at Blu because she was ready to see something happen.

Blu's cool exterior was in no way an indicator for the fire burning within. She was confused as hell, for real.

Why is she driving his truck? What's inside for her? Where is he? What does she know that I don't? Why would she know what I don't?

There was only one way to handle it at this point in Blu's mind. "No, I have nothing to confront her about. But we are gonna follow her to see where *his* truck is going."

Coffee

Kanari closed her door and backed up four houses. Waving her hand in a dramatic flair, she spoke. "Ooh, I swear to God if she pulls up at a hotel, if I see them boo'd up or anything that looks remotely suspect, I'm telling you now, get my bail money together. 'Cause I'ma whip his ass with my tire iron and hers too if she tries to save him."

***

The nurse checking Yuriah's vital woke Minnie up unintentionally when she bumped into her. "I'm so sorry, ma'am."

Minnie lifted her head off of Yuriah's bed and released his hand to move out of the way. Wiping the sleep from her eyes, she spoke. "You're fine. I'm in your way."

Minnie skirted off to the side and watched her press buttons on beeping machines, check tubes, IVs and draw a fresh vile of blood. Her stomach churned to see him unresponsive but she tried imagining him as taking a much needed nap.

Minnie found the rim of her finger trimming the dampness that accumulated in her eyes. She didn't want to cry anymore. If she intended to dwell with a spirit of expectancy, then she knew she didn't have room to be sad. *Speak it into existence, Minnie. Your husband's health is well.*

"I'll be back in an hour to check his vitals again." The nurse headed for the door.

"Excuse me, Miss. Have you seen Mr. Jones, the guy who's been with me all this time?"

She softly snapped her fingers in a remindful manner. "Oh, yes. He stepped out for fresh air. He didn't want to wake you. It slipped my mind to tell you. My apologies."

"No apologies needed. You deal with a lot. Thank you for all that you do."

The nurse nodded and smiled before she left out.

Minnie turned to face Yuriah, caressing him gently. "Baby, I've been thinking. God spent entirely too much time preparing us for one another. I need you to wake up, so we can begin our new life

88

together. We have plenty babies to make and places to go. There's…"

Kamal walked in and Minnie stopped talking.

"Need me to step back out?"

"No, you're fine."

Kamal walked over to her, handing her a plate he picked up from the food truck parked on Tulane Ave, in front of the hospital.

"I'm not hungry, but thanks."

"Eat some of it, ya heard me. It doesn't do you no good not to. Plus that man don't need you stretched out in another room from malnutrition or some shit like that. So, take it."

Kamal had been a godsend. He made sure she looked out for herself especially considering how absentminded she'd been lately.

"You're right and let me say this while it's on my mind. Thank you for everything. You have a family that needs you but you're here with us."

He missed his girl and kids but he knew Shenae was going to hold things down and be alright in the process. Besides if the roles were reversed and he was the one laid up, Yuriah would do the exact same thing.

"I wouldn't have it no other way, ya heard me."

***

Kanari was on I-10W following behind Eli's truck, keeping a three car radius between them.

"Alright, so tell me the story on this chick?" Kanari wanted to get a complete rundown on her.

"There's nothing to tell. They've been really good friends for a long time. End of story."

"And you okay with that? Like for real?" Kanari never understood how Blu was alright with him having a female sidekick. A dawg was supposed to be a man's best friend, not a pussy.

"He's been very open with me about everything. And to be honest, I'm only following her because I'm curious about his well-being, not what he's doing. So, yes, I am okay with him having a female friend because I trust him. Besides, they're more like brother and sister anyway."

Kanari smacked her lips the minute she heard that. In her experience, men screamed brother/sister to cover up the truth of them being bed buddies just like women passed off their side pieces as their cousins. "Brother/sister my ass. Did they ever fuck?"

"Kanari! No! They never!" Blu was insulted again. "We were friends first and he would have told me that. Damn!"

Kanari usually played devil's advocate in many of their talks but Blu never jumped out of the bag because of it. "My bad. I just don't understand it."

"Exactly, you don't! So, please, let's just see what we see and let that be it."

Kanari frowned. She didn't like being scolded for keeping it real with her. She was only speaking her truth. However, she closed her mouth and turned on some music to fill the silence. She had nothing else to say about it.

Blu cut the radio off almost immediately. She couldn't allow bad vibes between them, not even for a second. "Look, I'm sorry. I didn't mean to come at you like that."

"Mmhmm, it's cool."

"You sure?" Blu already knew she wasn't by the way she was responding.

"Mmhmmmmm."

"Don't sound like it."

"But it is."

"Smile, then."

"I'm not doing all that? I said I'm good."

Blu wouldn't let up, so Kanari cracked the driest smile her way before turning her attention back to driving.

"Not good enough." Blu reached over and tickled at her side to get her to offer up a genuine grin.

"Stop it. You gonna make me wreck." Kanari tried to hold onto her chuckle.

"Smile, then."

Kanari wiggled and giggled, breaking out into full laughter at Blu's relentless finger attack. "You gon' kill us!" She screamed.

Blu let up but kept her hand in place to give her the business again if she had to. "Is we cool, then?"

Kanari hesitated, popping her mouth in an *around the way girl* manner. "You know you my boo." She gave her the Colgate smile she was looking for.

"Better be," Blu threatened, worming her fingers at her. They both laughed and that changed the air between them.

Ten minutes later, they followed Samiyah pulling into the parking lot of Blair's Bail Bonds on Tulane Ave.

"What the..." Blu scrunched her face. "Is he in jail?"

"There's only one way to see." Kanari parallel parked her car by one of the empty meter spaces. "Get in the driver's seat and make the block if you see one of those raggedy ticket writing heifers coming this way. I'ma go inside and see what's good."

"Don't say nothing to her." Blu warned.

"I won't." She reached in her purse and pulled out her shades, slipping them over her eyes. She then stretched her body into the back of her car, locating her camouflage fitted cap. "Be right back."

She exited the car and Blu slid into her spot, looking behind herself as she watched Kanari walk inside of the building. Blu then faced forward, checking for cops and thinking things through.

I hope he's not in jail but if he is that would explain why I haven't heard from him. God, I hope he's alright, though. But why didn't he call me?

Three minutes later, Kanari was trotting back to the car, except she was sliding into the passenger's seat. She looked at Blu who was eyeing her the moment her hand touched the handle of the door.

"Well?" Blu was curious.

"Yep, yo trade is in jail and she is there to get him out."

That brought relief to her immediately. It was obvious she'd been waiting to exhale by the expression on her face.

"What now?" Kanari asked, keeping her more flavorful questions to herself.

"Back to my house. He'll call me when he's released and we'll talk this out from there."

"Cool. Although I hate that your peoples got arrested, I'm just glad it's not the bullshit I was thinking." Kanari admitted.

Blu agreed as she pulled off and headed back to the eastside of New Orleans. While relieved he was safe, she couldn't help but wonder, *Why didn't he reach out to her at all?*

Chapter 12

Seven o'clock that night...

Elias sat at the Broad bus stop, where he waited for Samiyah to drive by and swoop him up.

Looking at the courthouse across the street, he shook his head disappointingly. It fucked him up to be in the penal system, especially over some avoidable bullshit.

Damn!

There were three things at twenty-seven years old he had bragging rights over: One, he had no children. Two, he never been to jail. And three, he never had an STD.

But as of today, he could only stand by one.

Eli stared vacantly ahead as a slew of thoughts flowed through his mind.

I gotta baby? Me? Elias Devin Dupree has a daughter. A daughter? What do I know about raising a child, more less a girl? This shit is too much. First Cujo pops her dog ass up, then Peaches is mine, making me and Samiyah parents and leaving me to sort all of this out with Blu. Too many splits to have to deal with at once. Fuck!

The wrinkles of his skin congregated at the center of his forehead, displaying sign of his deep thoughts. Dazed by the chain reactions each cause effected, Eli didn't notice his truck parked in front of him.

Bonk! Bonk! Bonk!

Samiyah pressed on the horn as she rolled down the window. "Eli!"

He snapped out of his daze and headed to his vehicle. Once he was in, he stared for a moment before speaking. "What's up, Yah?"

"Too much but that's obvious." She pulled off, continuing her course down N. Broad St. when she finally noticed, thirty seconds later, he never removed his eyes off of her. "Why are you watching me? Are you mad at me or something?"

"I don't know what I am, to be honest. Right now I'm feeling all type of ways. I'm shocked, stunned, in disbelief and most definitely I'm throwed the fuck off, but I don't think I'm mad you."

"I understand. Well, we have a lot to talk about, so where am I going? Your house or mine?"

"Mine. I'm liable to make you a widow if I see yo ole punk ass husband right nah." Elias' jaw twitched.

"I'm sorry he tripped out on you. He's just having a really hard time with this."

"You don't say," Eli said in a *no shit Sherlock* kind of way.

Samiyah frowned at his flippant response. "You don't have to be stank, no."

He didn't reply to her statement but in an aggravated tone, he said, "Make this U-turn and pull up at the store. I need some liquid chill in my system." Eli pinched the bridge of his nose and shook his head slowly.

Samiyah knew the only time Eli drank Crown was when he was in party mode or brooding and because of what she laid on him, she knew it didn't call for a Soul Train line. He was contemplating but what exactly, she didn't know.

She made the Uwie, then in a probing manner, she questioned. "When you were just her paran, it was cool. But now that you're her daddy, it's a problem, huh? Be real."

"Don't go there, Yah. I love Peaches and you know this but you also know I never wanted children of my own. Remember when I told you *I never wanted children of my own?* So my reaction shouldn't surprise you. I told you I'm fucked up 'bout it, ya heard me. This is a lot of shit to take in. And in addition to the *you are the pappy* bomb you dropped, that ain't all that's on my plate. A lot of shit happened this weekend that you don't know dick about, so quit with the damn paranoia and let me process this shit. Damn!" Eli opened up the door once she parked, closing it behind himself harder than he intended.

Samiyah smacked her lips while her eyes followed him walking past the truck and into the store.

Fifteen minutes had passed and he was still inside. The store didn't appear to be packed and buying a bottle of brown should have only kept him for three minutes, tops. Samiyah was fixing to get out of the truck and see what was taking him so long when she saw the push of the glass door birth Elias.

Placing the keys back into the ignition, she restarted the engine. The moment he opened the door, she could smell what kept him. The aroma of honey barbeque and sweet and spicy wings filled the air.

He sat the plastic shopping bag between his legs, pulled out the brown paper bag containing the pint of Crown, twisted the top and took a shot to the head.

Samiyah placed the truck in reverse to back out of the space.

"Yah, before you pull off, let me tell ya I'm sorry, ya heard me. I probably should've put a little cut on my words. It's just that pill ain't only hard to swallow but that bitch stuck in my throat."

Samiyah tilted her head as she swam in the vulnerability in his eyes. "I know how the news had me, so I should have known not to push you. I'm sorry, too."

Elias turned his head to look out of the window and up at the evening sky as he tried to grab ahold of one of the many thoughts that were running a marathon through his mind.

Samiyah pulled out of the driveway and back into traffic. Glancing over at him, she knew he was having a difficult time dealing and her heart went out to him seconds before her hand covered his. She gave it a small squeeze as if to silently say *you're not alone.*

She went to remove her hand, but he stopped her and held on to it.

At that point, she knew he needed her in the same way she knew she needed him.

***

Blu had called down to Central Lock-Up periodically to see if Eli had been released, so when they informed her that he was no longer in their custody, she was able to breathe a sigh of relief.

Slipping her phone into her pocket, she headed into her kitchen and grabbed the plate of shrimp quesadillas Kanari had fixed.

She walked outside onto her deck to join her. Taking a bite into one of slices, she instantly moaned. "Ummm, girl, this is sooooo damn good. Who taught you how to make these?"

"Girl, me. I always find myself hooking something up and loving the shit I create. Plus, when you're a stoner like moi, it will behoove that ass to know how to cook."

Blu cracked up with knee slapping laugher. She was sniggering a little too hard if Kanari's opinion was solicited.

"Trick, that shit wasn't that funny. You must have either heard from ya boy or you found out your lil' jailbird a free man, which one?" Kanari swirled her tongue around her mouth and exhaled her smoke into tiny images.

Still giggling, she responded. "Ah, yes, it was that funny and yes again because he is out, which means I should be getting a call soon."

"Toss me my party hat," Kanari joked as she whirled her finger in a circle.

Blu poked out her tongue. "You're such a turd."

Kanari plucked the roach of her blunt into the air and then got up from her seated position. She crept up on Blu and snatched the slice from out of her hand.

"Hey! I think I was about to eat that."

"Now, I'm a turd who done jacked you up outcho issue. I'm out. Wake me when it's time to get ready for work." Kanari threw the deuces over her shoulder and walked inside, smacking on her food.

She shook her head at her girl but she wasn't tripping over her greedy self. Blu would give her friend the shirt off of her back but nine out of ten, she'd just be returning the same shirt Kanari would have already given her first.

Smiling at the thought, Blu looked at the time. It was 7:24 p.m. She wasn't sure when he was released but she anticipated a call no later than 8 o'clock.

Turning the Pandora on her phone on, she scrolled through her saved stations, stopping at TLC. She bobbed her head to the first song to play as she continued eating the remainder of what her crumb snatching friend didn't steal.

Two hours later...

Blu had fell asleep on her sofa but was startled awake when she heard a knock at her door. Suddenly, a smile creased her lips. *My boo.*

She flicked on the light, rushed over to the mirror in her living room and fluffed out her curls that went flat. Wiping the sleep from her eyes and then doing a five second hyper style dance, she calmed down to a cool and opened the door.

She wore a welcome smile on her face that immediately went south.

"Good evening. You ordered a large meat lover's and an eight piece hot wing?" The Pizza Hut delivery guy asked as he pulled the box out of the sleeve.

Blu was about to tell him he had the wrong house until she heard Kanari walking up on her. "Yesss!"

Moving to the side, she made way for Kanari to complete the exchange.

Blu then swiped her phone off of the sofa, pressed the button on the side to light up the screen and saw one missed call, an employee of hers. *Really?*

"Y'all have a good night," he grinned at his hefty tip.

"Come with me in the kitchen." Kanari walked off from Blu, holding the boxes. When she didn't budge, she asked. "Are you coming?"

"Yea," Blu sighed as she followed.

Taking a seat at her kitchen island, Blu cupped her chin into her hands and supported its weight with her elbows planted on the counter top. She watched Kanari grab two plates out of the cabinet.

Blu shook her head *no.* "I'm not hungry, sis. I don't see how you are. Matter of fact, weren't you supposed to be sleeping?"

Coffee

"If you were in the Puff Puff Olympics, you'd be eating like this too and I took a cat nap. I'm good, though." She took her first bite into her chicken and her eyes almost rolled to the floor.

"You alright over there?" Blu had to ask.

"Trust, I'm straight. Ha you doin' over there?"

"Eli's home but I ain't heard from him, yet. And I'm not waiting around while he takes his sweet time to remember he has a girl-friend."

"Now you're talkin'." Kanari spoke with a full mouth.

"Do you think you could…"

"Yep." Kanari already knew she wanted her to open up the bar, so she could tend to personal business.

Blu got up from her barstool and walked over to her friend, hugging her around her neck. "Anyone ever told you that you're…"

"The motha lovin' best? Haven't heard it in two days but you're welcomed to handle that."

Blu playfully muffed her head. "Don't let it get too big for your shoulders."

"I'll try not to."

As Blu was walking off, she twirled around. "I'm gonna take a shower and head out. Lock up when you leave."

"No, I'ma leave it wide open. Bye, Felicia!" Kanari waved her off.

As Blu disappeared around the corner and off into her bedroom, she couldn't help but wonder what was really goin' on with Eli.

Oh, but I'm 'bout to find out, though.

Chapter 13

It was 10:30 when Blu pulled up in front of Eli's house, but it wasn't until 11 o'clock when she finally stepped out of her car.

Seeing his truck parked and his light on entranced her. She was stuck, thinking.

He's home, but he didn't call, he didn't come by, he did nothing. Why is he avoiding me like I'm some damn bugaboo? What's going on? And do I really want to know?

She reached for her handle to get back inside of her vehicle but then the words of her Grandma LuLu echoed in her mind.

"Chile, jumping to conclusions is the worst exercise of all. Worrying won't change a damn thing. Always get your answers from the source and not from your imagination."

Ding Dong! She was at his door to do just that.

She stood there feeling low-key stupid for reaching out to him when it should have been the other way around, but she was tired of being in the blind.

The porch light came alive and seconds later, she could hear the locks coming undone.

She was starting to feel awkward.

Do I hug him and take the polite route since I can attract bees with honey or do I give him the what up nod and wait for him to kiss up since he has some explaining to do?

But her answer was simple when she saw Samiyah and two half eaten plates of dinner on his coffee table upon him opening his door. Blu then turned around to trot down his steps and dash to her car.

She had been stressing over his well-being and he was chilling? That was crushing. Blu had to step away or else it would be a scene.

He followed her and grabbed her wrist, turning her toward him. "Blu, why you leaving?"

"Why am I leaving? I should'na came in the first place. I should have made work my priority and not you. Finish enjoying *your* dinner."

"Ouch! I earned that but I do need to talk to you, ya heard me. Come inside for a minute."

"It took for me to show up for you to realize we needed to talk? I see you're alive and well. I'm good knowing that much for now. I'm about to go."

Blu's irritation wasn't going to make what he had to tell her any easier, but he couldn't let her leave like that.

"Boo, it's serious. Let me talk to you."

"You sure there's enough room on your couch for me *and* her?" She flicked her finger in the direction of his house. Her sarcastic tone was drizzled with petty.

The situation was already giving him a headache and he hadn't even opened the lid of Pandora's Box, yet. He wanted to throw his hands up and say *fuck off!* It was a lot easier to say than *I'm sorry* but she deserved to hear it. After all, she wasn't wrong in any of it.

"Blu, for starters, I apologize for how I treated you over this weekend. That shit wasn't intentional, at all. And Samiyah being over at my crib doesn't make her more important than you, if that's what you're thinking."

That's exactly what I was thinking, Blu thought.

"Shit involves her, though, and that's why she's here. So will you come inside and let me run everything down to you?"

It didn't pay off being a hard ass when the truth of the matter was her feelings were soft. She removed her front and shook her head up and down *yes*.

Elias then pulled her into him, wrapping his arms around her neck as he kissed her. With their lips still touching, he whispered, "I missed you."

"I missed you, too." Her words rang truth. Every day in one form or another, they never skipped a beat.

For ten months strong, they'd been one at the hip, laughing and learning one another. The last two of those months were spent cultivating a relationship, loving and leaning on the other for support. It was hard to stay mad with a track record like theirs.

He walked her inside by the hand, closing the door behind them. "Have a seat. Want me to fix you a lil' something?"

"Nah, I'm good," she answered.

"Well, I'ma fix me one. I'll be back." Elias grabbed his empty glass off of the table, gave Samiyah the *oh shit* look and then headed into the kitchen to refresh his drink.

"Hey, how are you, Blu?" Samiyah greeted her as warmly as she always had.

That depends on what Eli tells me, she thought. "I'm fine. How's your baby doing?"

Samiyah tensed up a little. Blu wondered if she did the wrong thing by asking about her daughter when she saw her mouth freeze in mid answer.

"She's still at the hospital but so far so good."

"Oh, that's good to hear. I'm glad she's getting better."

Elias returned and took a seat next to Blu. He and Samiyah had discussed telling her the news together, that way she could hear both sides.

"About what I wanted to talk to you about," he opened up dialogue but stopped the moment he heard Samiyah's phone ringing.

Out of the frying pan and into the fire, Samiyah thought.

"I'm listening to you." Blu tapped his knee to get his attention.

"Oh, this is Gerran. I'm gonna take this in another room." She announced as she stood up to step off.

"Let's wait for her to come back. I want her to be in on this." Eli took a swig of his Crown and then slouched into the couch, placing his hand on her thigh.

Why? You know what? Never mind. I've been waiting all this time. "Mmhmm," Blu nodded.

In the other room, nervous butterflies fluttered in Samiyah's belly as the ringing continued.

Pressing talk on her phone, she answered sweetly. "Hey, baby. It's about time you called me. How are you doing?"

He got straight to the point. "Your car is here but you're not. Where you at?"

I hate this rock and hard place shit. Closing her eyes, she just said it. "I'm over at Eli's."

Coffee

"Word? You by your baby daddy, huh?" Gerran spoke sarcastically.

"It ain't what you think. And if you let me explain…"

"You got that right. Ain't shit what I thought."

"Gerran, I'm on my way home right now."

"Nah, you already home," he stated at a regular tone before his voice bombastically elevated, "so stay yo ass over there!"

"Gerran, don't do this. Gerran? Gerran?" *Shit!* She looked at the screen of her phone when he didn't respond, only to see that it was black. He had already hung up.

It begins, she threw her head back, exhaustingly. Taking a breath and fanning herself with her hand to cool down, she composed herself enough to step back into the living room.

She waved her phone in the air. "Duty calls and I have to get home. I'm gonna need a ride."

"Fo'sho." He addressed Samiyah then turned to his girl. "You coming or you stayin' here while I drop her off?"

Blu wanted to pull a page from Kanari's playbook and go bananas and say: *"Looka here, thuggah! I ain't 'bout to go nowhere and I dare you to dot your ass out that door too. Whatchu gon' do is tell me what the hell is goin' on or else my problem is gon' be everybody's' problem."*

Blu had a good mind to do it but her grandma's voice of reasoning rang in her mind once more. *"Praise in public. Punish in private. Don't you let nobody know your business. Keep that to yourself like you would your dirtiest pair of drawers."*

Choosing to ride with her more sensible side, she answered. "I'm coming."

With that being said, she stood up and headed for the door so they all could leave out.

Thirty minutes later…

"Good night, y'all." Samiyah waved bye as she closed the back door and headed up her driveway.

Gerran's car wasn't there, but that somehow didn't surprise her.

Elias rolled down Blu's window and leaned over the console. "Oh, Yah. Call me tomorrow."

She looked over her shoulder. "Alright."

Eli and Blu both watched her get inside of her home before he pulled out of the Cul-de-sac she lived on.

When she stepped inside, it was pitch black. Their two-story, five bedroom house was too big to enter inside with it being completely dark. It always freaked her out and he knew that. But again, she didn't expect Gerran to give her any courtesy at this point.

Her hand scaled the wall in search of the light switch. When she found it, she turned on a few more. She pulled out her phone and sat down in the den as she made a call to her husband.

Answer your phone, she coached into the receiver.

"What's up?" He answered dryly.

What's up? She shook her head. She didn't even bother to question his nonchalance. "Gerran, I'm home. Where are you?" He didn't respond. "Gerran? I'm asking a simple question."

"I ain't there and that's all you need to know."

He hung up, but she called back.

"Gerran, why did you hang..." *Lord Jesus,* she exhaled slowly and called back *again.*

He answered.

"You're making it hard to talk to you and you know we need to have this conversation."

"Well, quit calling me." He hung up.

It was one thing for him to need space and time to think things over and in her mind, he would have done better saying that in opposed to being childish.

She was annoyed with his antics but called him again. He picked up.

"Hello?" She was hesitant to speak but when she saw he didn't hang up, she began talking. "Gerran, if you're gonna answer the phone after you hang up in my face, why not just stay on the phone? I'm trying to talk to you."

"You're right." Gerran hung up.

Coffee

She blew out hard. "This is so un fuckin' necessary. She called him once more.

You've reached Gee... His recording picked up immediately.

"Aahhh! I swear to God you're an asshole!" She tossed her phone on the sofa. It was clear he turned his cell phone off. But at that point, she had already decided she wasn't calling again.

***

In no mood to wait any longer, Blu opened the floor for the serious discussion he wanted to have with her.

"I'm done with being patient and we don't need a third party to have a conversation about what's going on with you. So, I'm listening."

Elias looked over at her and saw in her face that she was really on a verge of losing her shit.

Fuck it! he thought. It made no sense to procrastinate.

"A'ight, well, Saturday when I left you, I ended up going to jail because I got into a scuffle at the hospital. I bonded out and was just released some hours ago."

"With who?" She shook her head, making an O shape with her mouth as she stuttered from mild shock. "Who—who would want to fight you?"

"Gerran," was his one word reply.

In a very inquisitive manner, she delved. "Why? Aren't y'all cool? Look, don't stop and go, just tell me everything, please." Blu felt her chest tighten. Her woman's intuition was telling her to brace herself because the full story was going to piss her off.

"Gerran found out he wasn't the father of Samiyah's baby..."

Cutting him off, she jumped right in. "So he assumed when you showed up that you're Peaches' daddy? That's ridiculous." She shook her head at what she believed was Gerran's misplaced aggression toward Eli.

"He was foul as fuck for charging me up but he assumed right." Elias put the truth out there, catching Blu off guard.

104

"He assumed *what*? Did you say he assumed right?" Blu felt that squeeze grip tighter around her chest muscle.

"Dude attacked me because it turns out Peaches is indeed my daughter."

Blu waved her hand in front of herself like she was washing a window. "Wait a minute. Hold up. Your daughter? You mean to tell me you thought enough to tell me about the girl, Yvonne, whose booty you used to roll on from second grade, a girl you couldn't finger in a line-up if she stood before you today but it didn't occur to you to tell me that you slept with a woman you can put your finger on, literally? A woman I've accepted as being your sister because that's the kind of relationship you claimed y'all have?"

"She *is* fam and it only happened once." Elias defended, thinking that would lessen the sting.

"I don't care if it happened a half of one time. The point is you told me about every girl you smashed from here to Houston but you conveniently left out the one you should have mentioned above all?"

"Why does it matter that I didn't?"

She began looking around the truck like she wanted to find something to beat him over the head with. She couldn't control her hands. They were moving wildly like her emotions. "Pull over, Eli."

"What?" He gave her the side eye. They were riding on the bridge and there was no way he would take to the shoulder.

She felt her usually calm nature go out of the window, she was about to blow. To stress her point, Blu clapped her hands with every word. "Pull. The. Hell. Over!"

"Mann, you trippin'," he said below his breath as he pulled over.

Blu got out immediately and stood at the back of the vehicle. She sat on the bumper and bent over, taking deep breaths as she tried her best to contain the belligerence on the tip of her tongue.

She heard his door open. "Not now!"

Elias shook his head but got back into his vehicle. He could hear his Uncle Fly talking mad shit about this and he wasn't looking forward to hearing his mouth either.

This some real bullshit! Eli thought as he waited for God knows what.

She was still taken aback by his question. How he didn't comprehend the significance of telling her about Samiyah was beyond her. But with a fraction of a cooler head, she got back inside of the truck and answered.

"It matters because unlike any other fling, encounter or whatever you want to call the women you sexed, Samiyah is very much your present and as of today, your future."

He pulled back onto the freeway. "Blu, you going too deep with it. I'm with you."

"And you're not going deep enough. Just don't talk to me." She almost snapped on him but she caught herself. It was time to place space between them, otherwise, she was going to regret what happened next.

"So you don't have anything to say, nah?"

Blu rolled her eyes to the roof of his truck and kept them there as she answered. "Oh, I have plenty to say but I guarantee you don't want to hear it, so just leave me alone."

The last of the five minute drive was spent in silence and as soon as he pulled into his driveway, she got out of his ride and headed straight to hers.

He stepped out of his truck and walked behind her. "Blu, don't leave angry."

"What do you suggest I do? Drive off happy?" She was extremely pissed off.

"Nah, but come inside so we can really talk this thing out."

She aggressively shook her head *no*. "Not tonight *or* the next few." She climbed inside of her car and speedily pulled off.

If he thought she would be ready to head over to Sears to take a family portrait, then he was sadly mistaken.

Eli watched as her navy blue Maxima blended into the dark of night thinking, *How the fuck did I get here?*

Chapter 14

It was after 11:30 p.m. when Munch walked out of Central Lockup. His little brother, BG, was waiting for him. They spotted each other and walked into a G-dap, ending it with a firm hug.

"You straight?" BG stepped back to check him out.

"Fuck me, what's up with Yuri? He came out of that coma?"

"Not yet, big bruh."

"Damn!" He dropped his head, sighed and then lifted it back up. "At least he breathing and I'll take that over death, any day."

BG nodded his head in agreement. He then looked at a policemen going into the same building Munch just walked out of and the right side of his lip lifted into an arch. "Let's get the fuck from 'round here. We in cop central and you know I got that thang on me."

"As you should. Let's roll."

They began walking down S. White where BG had parked his ride, talking.

"Where's Minnie and ha she holdin' up?"

"At the hospital. She ain't leavin' cuz' side. And I guess she doin' better but she ain't sayin' much of nothing, so I really can't call it." BG shrugged his shoulders.

"She by herself?"

"Never dat. Mal with her twenty-fo."

"That's what's up. I'ma go up there first thing in the morning."

"That's what's up."

Once they walked up on BG's Regal, he chirped the alarm and the locks popped up. As BG got behind the wheel of his car and closed the door, he turned to face Munch, slapping his hands together once. "You know dude gotta get his issue. You don't touch fam and not expect for a mu'fucka not to clap back."

For two days straight, Munch thought about G'Corey for breakfast, lunch and dinner. No one was hungrier to avenge Yuriah than he was. But it didn't make sense for him to show the rowdy that was inside of him since nothing was popping off at that minute. "To know me is to know I'ma handle that shit, ASAP."

BG knew his brother wasn't an empty wagon so he didn't need to make a lot of noise. "I don't doubt that shit for a second."

BG cranked the ignition and his Tupac CD immediately came through on low volume as he pulled off. He handed Munch a rolled one and a lighter before reaching under his seat and passing him his Dessert Eagle.

Placing the toolie on his lap and sparking a blaze to the blunt, Munch took a deep pull. He allowed the inhale to marinate before blowing it out. "This weekend had me bent. I needed this."

"I know yo head was smokin', dawg. Shid, mine still swervin'. It's fuckin' me up that I wasn't there with you."

"I'm glad you wasn't 'cause if you would have ate one of his bull—" Munch shook off the thought and took another toke. The idea of something happening to his little brother made him feel uneasy.

He tried his best not to show it but it was a known fact that BG was his weakness, his Achilles heel. His BG was his pulse. And just like a heartbeat, he couldn't survive without him.

BG glanced over to his side. Although Munch didn't complete his thought, the pained expression on his face told the rest.

"Don't get fucked up over me, big brudda. I only be on my Dirty Harry shit when it concerns you. If you in dem waters, I got no churse but to be in that bitch too because I'm right behind ya, ya dig. But other than that, I got life mapped out, don't trip."

BG jumped off the porch early and Munch wouldn't have had it any other way. But it was important to him that BG lived a very different life than his.

Aside from the code of *kill or be killed*, Munch taught him that life was about priorities and he was proud to know that although his lil' one would bang on an opponent if need be, he did recognize there was more to strive for than solely surviving.

"Is that right? What's yo G-plan? Run it to me, then."

BG replayed Munch's words in his head before answering.

Applied knowledge is power. You can't be no dummy out'chea. Even when it comes to crushing those who oppose you, you still gotta be smart. Always step ya game up by keeping your eyes and ears to the streets but your nose in a book.

"I'ma get my muddafuckin' high school diploma, ya dig, put the rap game in a choke hold and then history gon' make itself."

That brought a smile to Munch's face. Having dropped out of school when he was fifteen to assume the full-time responsibility of providing for a then five year old BG, placed heavier pride and emphasis on him walking across the stage.

Plus, all their Pops wanted, *God rest his soul,* were for his boys to have a better life than he and their dad felt education was that key. So a teenaged Munch stood over his father's gravesite and promised he'd see to it that the youngest of his seeds make that happen.

Munch curled his hand and BG did the same, allowing the backs of their fist to touch with a slight bump. "Say that shit." Munch blew a cloud around him.

Catching a glimpse of Anita's Restaurant on his right, BG groaned. "Aww, man, I just passed up all kindsa places to eat. I know you didn't fuck with dem stale ass bologna sandwiches they be down bad for servin'. Yo stomach probably touchin' yo back." BG slowed off of the gas just in case Munch wanted him to pull up on somebody's drive-thru before he jumped on the I-10.

"Fuckin' right, but you can run me by my girl. She got me."

"Fa'sho."

Munch extended his weed to BG but he shook his head, declining. "That's all you."

Munch brought it back to his lips and took a pull. He then rolled the window down and reclined his seat. He allowed the Kush to begin clearing his mind because too much was troubling him.

His Pops always told him, *"Find a way to let shit go because pressure busts pipes."*

Tupac's *Better Dayz* was playing at a modest level. Munch slightly began bobbing his head to the contemporary Isley Brothers' beat as he was certainly in dire need of those better days, considering shit was going to get a whole lot worse on the strength of his peoples being touched.

"Cut that up, round," Munch directed as he closed his eyes and absorbed the lyrics of the best to ever do it.

...Got me thinkin' about better dayz/Thinkin' back as adolescent/Who would've guessed that in my future years, I'd be stressin'/Some say the ghetto's sick and corrupted/Plus my P.O. won't let hang with the brothers I grew up with/ Tryin' to keep my head up and stay strong...

Twenty minutes later, BG pulled into the parking lot where Munch's lil' mama stayed on Tchoupitoulas Ave.

"We'll get up in the a.m., I fucks wit'chu." Munch slapped hands with BG before leaning over the console to bring it in.

That was his way of saying he loved him. He dared not utter the actual words because he felt it was something said right before a person took that eternal ride. He was sure it was his superstition but he refused to test it.

"Heavy," BG replied.

Munch stepped out of his ride, tucked his gun inside of his waistline, pulling his button down over it. He then doubled tapped his chest, aimed his pointing finger to the sky and then through the window at his little brother.

BG did the same and then pulled off once Munch shut the door.

That was how they peace'd each other out. A double tap for the love from a beating heart to their father above and then to one another.

Munch turned around and headed to the third floor and rapped on the door of his girl's apartment.

Reds was in her office when she heard the knock. She all but ran to unlock it. She was expecting him. Without looking through the peephole, she swung the door wide open. Then she ran into him, hugging him closely around his sculpted waist.

He smiled, hugging her just as tightly. He loved his girl's energy. Reds had a way of making a shitty day feel like sunshine.

"Gimme some," he cupped the chin of her pie face in his hands and guided her lips to his.

Standing 4'11", Reds had to pull off a ballerina's act on her tiptoes just to kiss her giant. After giving him some of her luscious, she examined him in a motherly manner, shifting his face from side to side checking him out.

"I'm so happy to see you. Are you alright? Did they hurt you? What did—"

Munch leaned down, thrusting his tongue into her mouth as he squeezed her double wide booty, pressing her into him roughly. That shut her up.

"Boo, if they would have fucked wit'cha boy, I wouldn't be here. Nah, you gon' let me in or are you buying time for that thuggah to sneak out the back doe?"

Reds laughed because she didn't have a back door. "You play too much. Come on in." She stepped back inside from out of the breezeway as he followed behind her.

Munch locked the door as she headed into the kitchen to fix his dinner.

"Bae, what do you want? I made you your choice from barbeque chicken, macaroni and cheese, potato salad and corn. I also made meatloaf with brown gravy and smashed potatoes in case you didn't want the other meal."

He couldn't decipher what his stomach craved more so he opt for them all. "Give me a lil' of everything, ya heard me."

After she prepared his dish, she called him out of the living room to have a seat in the dining room. He took his gun off of him, placing it on the table and pulled out a chair.

Reds knew the man she fell in love with was no angel. He never painted a picture as such and she never questioned his moves but tonight she was curious to know something.

"Bae, why you always keep a gun on you?"

It took no time for Munch to respond. The answer came as quickly and as easily as stating his name. "'Cause it's a *dog eat dog* world and I ain't tryna be dog food."

She pondered on his reply for a short moment. And with no further questions, she handed him his utensils. "Eat up, munchy poo." She kissed his temple and headed back into the kitchen to clean up.

Fifteen minutes later, once she squared everything away, she sat down next to him.

After licking sauce off of his tips, he asked, "What'chu was doing before I got here?"

"Work as usual. I was finalizing my edits for *Thicker than Most*. You know speaking of my manuscript, you should write street lit with the company I'm signed to. I told Ca$h, the CEO of Lock Down Publications, that you are as real as they come. You should think about that."

"Nah, you'da big time author. How 'bout you write ya man's life so that my shit is told truthfully. Write a story so our sons know dey pops wasn't a merciless killa and that every man that ever stared down the barrel of my pistol earned that position. Name it something gangsta like *The Card I Was Dealt*."

Reds frowned at that. "If you don't want to write, that's cool. But you can tell them that yourself."

She stood up and removed his plate once he was done. Before she excused herself into the bathroom, she asked, "A bath or a shower?"

Munch looked down at the dirty tux he still had on from Saturday. "A bath. And thanks, bae. You'da baddest."

Reds blushed then retreated into the bathroom.

Ten minutes later, Munch was undressed and submerged chest deep in bubbles as the jets of the Jacuzzi style tub massaged his tensed muscles.

Reds sat on the edge and gently sponged his shoulders. "This feels good?"

With his eyes closed, he responded. "Mmhmm."

"Are you full?"

He motioned his head up and down *yes*.

Reds relaxed him some more as she washed over his chest, waiting for him to tell her about the incident, but he didn't. Hoping she wasn't catching him by surprise, she bluntly asked, "The person who shot Yuriah, did you get him?"

Munch opened one eye at her to catch a glimpse of her face before closing it back. "Nah, not yet."

"I see. Well, do *we* have anything to be concerned about?"

That question almost irritated him because she knew the answer to that. They had been together for *two* years and not *one* thing ever came to her doorstep.

"Nothing I do will ever fall back on you."

"I'm only asking because I'm sure he got a pretty good look at you and Kamal's faces and now he's on the loose."

That angered Munch. He sat up abruptly, splashing water around as he did. His eyes shot open and he stared at her fixedly. "And what? I got a good fuckin' look at his too. What the fuck you tryna say, Reds?"

"Look, I know you're the man in these streets and definitely in this home. But in here," she pointed at the center of her chest, "you my baby and that means I will worry sometimes. I'm sorry but I can't help that."

Munch looked at the delicate look on her face as she explained herself. He didn't mean to snap on her but it was eating him up to know he got away. Then to make matters worse, it was going to be a challenge finding him. G'Corey was the pussy type and pussies run from hard dick.

"I put too much heat on my words. My bad fa dat." He placed his hand on the back of her neck, pulling her down to kiss her.

She understood where that came from and didn't sweat it at all. "I know better than that. Relax yourself. I'll be in the other room when you get out."

Forty minutes later...

Munch stepped out of the tub, wrapping a towel around his waist. He stood in front of the mirror. Looking at his reflection, he ran his hands over his goatee as he examined the unrest in his eyes.

He finished up in the bathroom and then stepped out into the living room, planting his eyes on something that made the edges of his lips curve upward.

Reds rose to her feet when she saw Munch. Placing one hand at the curve of her shapely hips, the other hand held a stress reliever rolled in the form of a cigarillo between her fingers.

She stood there looking seductive and *ready*.

The woman who opened the door earlier looked like his homie, but the sex kitten who was greeting him now looked like his lover.

The red, lacey baby doll negligée she changed into hugged her plus sized body beyond perfectly.

Reds was everything he physically found sexy in a woman. Her skin was the color of dark chocolate. Her soft DDD breasts were bountiful, no two hands could hold them. She was pluscious. Fat ass, thick thighs and all his.

He walked toward her, allowing the towel to unravel and slide to the floor. She stirred with anticipation, eager to feel his touch.

Munch was unbelievably sexy. His cinnamon skin was the perfect canvas for the tattoos that marked his toned chest and stomach.

Across his abdomen read: *Magnolia Munch* with NO GUTS NO GLORY underneath. Across his left pectoral, right over his heart read: *Baby Goon* with a pulse line running through it. And the tattoo that made her heart leap out of her chest was the one across his rib that read: *Reds Johnson*.

She enjoyed looking at that man.

Reds lit the blunt in her hand. Although she didn't choke with him, she puffed on it until the fire kept ablaze on its own. Tilting her head to the side, she exhaled the smoke before they engaged in a deep, passionate kiss. She then placed the blunt in his mouth and he took a pull.

Expelling a fog of Purp into the air, he studied her eyes. "You my baby, yea. You know that?"

She shook her head *yes*. "You show that."

He smacked her on her booty, leaving his hand on it to feel it jiggle. "Sit that ass right there." He pointed to the sofa and she did as she was told.

With hard dick in one hand and Purple Haze in the other, he walked over to the music station. Thumbing through his CD case, he pulled out a disc and slid it into the carousel. He wasn't the romantic type but he was about his thug passion from time to time.

Pressing play on the stereo, Jae Millz' *Tip of my Tongue* started thumping through the surround sound.

Soon as I'm done with this blunt/I'ma give ya what you want/And honestly baby you can keep on them pumps/I like to put 'em in the air when I work from the front/But I love giving back shots that make your ass jump...

He placed the blunt in the ashtray on the ottoman nearby, kneeled in front of her and then separated her legs, pulling them apart as he slid her to him in one quick motion.

"Ha!" The sweep of her body drawing close to his caused a sharp sound to escape her mouth.

He then kissed, suckled and nibbled along the walls of her inner thighs as he traveled to the paradise located at her center.

The first lick between the slit of her lotus bomb placed an arch in her back and a wail imploded from her lips. "Oooohhh!"

She trapped her fingers in his long locs and he went to work pleasing her.

Hours later...

Reds rolled over in bed and noticed Munch was sitting up in what appeared to be deep thought.

She picked up her phone and looked at the time. "Bae, it's 3 a.m. Why aren't you asleep? Something's on your mind?"

He looked over at her, then clicked the lamp on the nightstand *off* as he pulled her to lay on his bare chest. "Nah, it's all good."

He concealed his truest thoughts. There wasn't a need to say everything that crossed his mental. Besides real men didn't whine about shit.

Truth of the matter, G'Corey was still on his top. He admonished himself for letting him get away. So, if his girl detected stress, that's because he was.

Coffee

Any man who thought he could breathe easy with an enemy on the loose, may very well find himself not breathing at all.

On that note, he needed to chapter G'Corey, ASAP!

Chapter 15

A few days later...

Samiyah and Gerran

If Thursday was anything like Tuesday and Wednesday, then Samiyah was expecting not to see or hear from Gerran. She accepted the news was devastating but the truth still remained she was his wife and the baby she was carrying was one hundred percent his child.

Samiyah rolled out of bed and over to her dresser. It was 10 a.m. and she needed to head over to Children's to spend time with Lil' Acacia as she had every day since she had been hospitalized.

She reached into her drawers and pulled out a pair of gray jogger capris, a simple white V-neck T-shirt and her under garments. Heading over to her walk-in closet, she stepped up the ladder that allowed her to reach the top of her shelves and pulled out the Adidas box attached with the photo of the gray and white tennis she was looking for to complete her casual assemble.

As she was heading into the bathroom to start her shower, she had to make a slight detour to the toilet and allow her insides to turn out.

Still in the kneel position, Samiyah looked down at her stomach once she was done praying to the porcelain god. "Be good to mommy, little bud. And no more sickness for the day, okay? We have to see your big sister."

Once the nausea subsided, she stood up, headed over to the sink to brush her teeth before showering.

Forty-five minutes later, she was out of the door with a double peanut butter sandwich in hand, that was one of her favorite *pregnancy go to* foods.

Thirty minutes later, she pulled into the parking lot. She was happy she was stationary because she was starting to feel queasy from the drive, which reminded her to schedule a visit with her GYN/OB.

Let me do that now, she thought as she pulled out her phone and called her doctor's office. After she confirmed her appointment for Monday morning at eleven, she got out of her car to head inside.

Before she closed her car door, her phone rang. It was Elias, so she sat back down and took his call.

"What's up, E?" she spoke exhaustedly.

"Checking on you. Yo, you got any rest 'cause you sound tired as fuck."

"Not really. It's hard to sleep when you don't know where your husband's laying his head or where his mind at."

"I can tell you where his head at. It's in his fuckin' ass. You know you married a dick, right?"

"He can be, but I need to believe this too shall pass. I mean we've weathered other storms."

"Storms not hurricanes," Elias clarified. "But fuck talkin' 'bout him. What's up with Peaches?"

"I'm actually in the parking lot to see her now. But she's doing great from yesterday's report. Thanks for asking."

"*Thanks for asking?* Don't hit me with that courtesy line, Yah. She's my child, too."

"My bad. I just know you're not thrilled about it and…"

"And nothing, ya heard me. When we talked the other night, I made it clear that this ain't what I want. I never wanted this, but she here nah and my issues ain't got shit to do with her. So don't talk to me like I'm an associate inquiring about your business when she's my business too."

"You're right. You. Are. Her. Father." Samiyah spoke the words slowly as the realization still needed to set in with her.

"Sounds weird as hell, huh? Me? A daddy." Elias shook his head at the word *daddy* like he was declining a plate of god awful liver. He had an easier time saying *supercalifragilisticexpialido-cious.*

"It does. I swear you couldn't have paid me to believe we would be parents, more less together."

"Who you telling?"

"Anyway, what's up with Blu? Is she still mad?" Samiyah was curious to see if he was able to make up with his lady.

"Yes indeed, she on fire, but I knew this when she left my house Monday night. I told you if she would have peeled off any faster, she would have time traveled. But I'm 'bout to pull up on her right now and see if these couple of days cooled her off some."

"I hope so. Well, let me go inside and check on my," she caught herself, "our daughter. I'll talk with you later."

"A'ight. Do that."

Samiyah hung up with him, walked into the building and greeted those who passed her like usual. When she made it to the nurse's station, she reached for the clipboard to sign in but paused when she saw the last name on the sheet.

"My husband, Gerran Babineaux, came earlier?"

"Yes, ma'am, but he's still here actually."

"Oh," Samiyah's cheeks went into her eyes to cover up her shock. She signed her name, dotting the I's in two places before walking off.

She then crept up on the room but didn't enter. Instead, she watched what appeared to be a tender moment. Gerran was rubbing the backs of his knuckles over her pudgy cheeks as he smiled at her. *Awww.*

Samiyah saw his mouth moving but was unable to hear what was being said but she gathered it was touching because shortly after his lips stopped moving, he dropped his head and then used his index finger to swipe away tears.

Oh, God, my husband's hurting, she thought as her heart shattered. I swear *I didn't mean for this to happen. You have to believe me. I pray to God you'll believe me.* She caressed the door as if it were his back, tenderly, soothingly.

"Are you alright, Mrs. Babineaux?" One of the nurses asked while walking up when she saw her leaned up against the door, crying.

"I am." Samiyah smiled as she wiped her face with the base of her palms.

"Okay." The nurse rubbed her back, ending it with a double pat before walking off.

When Samiyah turned her head to look back in on them, Gerran was preparing to leave.

Oh shit!

She quickly skedaddled and veiled herself behind a corner wall. Samiyah didn't want her presence to publically trigger the floodgate of pain he was bridging back.

He turned left, nodding at the receptionist as he headed out of the hospital.

Samiyah waited for the coast to clear before she came out from hiding.

Walking back to her baby's room, she pushed the lever down, pressed her weight against the door for it open and walked inside.

She could smell the scent of Gerran's cologne lofting in the air. That made her feel his absence even more as nostalgic memories hit her like a cannon ball.

Shaking off those melancholy thoughts, she looked upon her sleeping beauty and held a chat with her of her own.

"I don't know what he told you but before you're old enough to know about this mess I made, mommy will fix our family. That's my promise, angel. I *will* fix this."

*E*lias and Blu

Whether it was the right or wrong thing to do, Elias gave Blu the few days she needed to clear her head. But now it was time to see if she was rolling with him on this or if he needed to roll without her because although he wasn't ready for fatherhood, it was upon him.

He pulled up to her house and she was home like he anticipated she would be. Shutting down The Bar at Aqua Blu and making it to the house at 4:30 each morning guaranteed she'd be too tired to makes moves before noon.

Love Knows No Boundaries III
Pandora's Box

Elias knocked a few times and then slid his hands into his pockets as he turned his back to the door and looked down the street, admiring the view of her well-to-do neighborhood.

Eli looked over his shoulder when he heard the locks disengaging before he fully turned around. When he saw Blu, he smiled but she didn't return his kindness.

She stood in her doorway, leaning against the side of it. And because she didn't roll out the welcome wagon like she usually would, he knew she was still bristling.

"Good morning, Blu sky." Eli greeted her the way he would every morning they brought in together with the hopes she'd warm up to him but she was unfazed by the name that usually made her bubble with adorable smiles, for today she was still as cold as ice.

"Why did you come?" Her voice was sweet but her words were sour.

"You said a few days and I gave you that. It's time we talk for real, for real." Blu didn't budge or open her door any wider for him to come inside when he stepped forward, so he questioned. "You not gon' let me in to talk?"

"Say what you came to say. We can talk right here."

Eli looked the other way as he shifted his eyes off to the side. He didn't want to be impatient with her but it was becoming hard not to.

"Blu, this is just as much of a surprise to me as it is to you, so exactly what's upsetting you most about this situation?"

"Correction. It isn't the same surprise to me as it is to you. The baby was your surprise but sleeping with her wasn't. So, the fact that you didn't tell me you sexed her *before* I became all buddy *buddy* with her is the reason this is blowing me. I feel like an idiot having sat between y'all and the little secret y'all kept. You played me."

"I didn't play you because I didn't lie to you."

"You might as well because your omission served the same purpose."

"I understand you're hurt…"

She waved her finger back and forth as she shook her head side to side. "*Hurt?* I'm not hurt. I'm pissed and the more I think about it I want to know the reason behind you not being as forthcoming about her as you were so many others. Is it because she wasn't just a screw? Is it because you love her?" Her lips were in danger of trembling, so Blu balled them tightly.

"I didn't tell you because I didn't want you becoming all melodramatic over something that only happened once!" He began talking with his hands as a way to exert some of the bottled frustration threatening to pour from his mouth.

Her blue tinted hair was going to burst into tiny red flames if he mentioned how it only happened once, one more time.

"Do you take me for a fool? What happened once has room to happen twice and who's to say it hadn't already, huh?"

"Me is who." He angrily pointed at his chest. "So what? My word ain't bond no mo'?"

"Maybe that's why you weren't concerned with my sex because you were busy dipping off into hers. We all know how you get down."

"What?" Eli attempted to walk off but turned back around, clutching his fists. "I'm not fucking her."

"I agree with you on that. You made love to her." Blu could see she was pressing his buttons but she didn't care. He already detonated her mind missile.

"Let me get this right. You more upset at the fact that we did the damn thang over the fact that we have a baby together?"

"To be honest, both have equally angered me."

Elias felt at a loss and could tell she was willing to go tit for tat as long as he went toe to toe. He didn't like the pendulum effect their talk was taking and he wasn't built to go back and forth. So in a very firm manner, Eli decided to nip things in the bud.

"A'ight, then. Well, check this. For keeping the fact that I slept with Samiyah away from you, ya heard me, I'm fuckin' sorry! But I can't take the shit back, it happened. And there ain't no returning Peaches back to sender, so either you gon' take me as I am, right now," he pointed his index finger to ground to emphasis his argument, "or I can leave you the hell alone because I'm not about to kiss yo ass to make you understand shit else."

Blu felt insulted by his ultimatum so she said the very first reactionary thing her mind conjured. "Go on, then. You're still fuckin' her anyway, so leave and don't come back with yo hoe ass!" She slammed her door and locked it.

Elias choked the air and then grimaced at her stunt. *I got cho hoe ass*, he thought. "Relationships are fuckin' stupid any goddamn way. Fuck I look like tryna be in one?" He spoke on a low growl as he headed over to his truck to leave.

Once inside, he started his engine. He stared at her door for a second to see if she would come out but when she didn't, he placed his vehicle in reverse and pulled off.

"It is what it fuckin' is."

B*lu and Kanari*

Blu folded her arms and leaned her back against the door. Tears streamed down her face because *now* she was hurting. She never saw the day come where something that felt so right would go so horribly wrong.

She covered her face and cried into her hands when she heard him pull out of her driveway. She was hoping he'd beat down her door and tidal wave her with apologies she wouldn't accept immediately but in time, she would. But he was gone.

Blu peeled herself off of the door and headed into her bedroom where she fell onto the bed face first.

She laid there in one spot for twenty minutes soaking until she heard her front door opening. Blu jumped up, rushing to her bathroom and locking the door behind herself.

Shit! I forgot she was coming by. She needed to rejuvenate her face before Kanari detected something and started asking questions.

"Oh, bae! Where you at?" Kanari walked through her house, looking for her.

"In the bathroom. Be done in a sec," Blu yelled out. Looking at her slightly puffy eyes in the mirror, she said, "You look a hot mess, you know that?" Splashing water against her face did nothing to refresh her look, so she just stepped out to face the music and the onslaught of questions she was sure would follow.

"What's all this?" Blu asked when she saw Kanari pulling items out of a bag and spreading them out on her bed.

"I didn't know what kind of food mood you were in so I came prepared."

"Mood?" Blu attempted to front. There was no way Kanari could have known that something was troubling her because she didn't say a peep. Plus, she covered it well, so she thought.

"Yes, mood. You thought I didn't notice? You've been in one for three days now. And of course you tried to play it off like everything was Kool and the Gang, but I know when something's wrong with your ass. I just don't know what. But don't think I came over here to pry either because I also know when you're ready, you'll tell me."

It was scary how well Kanari could read her even when she thought she wasn't readable.

"Now if you are feeling like binging, I bought your fav. A shrimp on french with an order of fries. Or if you just want to eat sweets until you get a case of *tha sugar*, then I got you on that, too. I have Twizzlers, Boston Baked Beans, Chico-Sticks, Lemon Heads, Noun Laters and then some. And if you in a real funk, I got a tub of Ben & Jerry's in the freezer with your name all over that shit."

She chuckled slightly. "Cherry flavor?"

"That's an affirmative." She beamed. Turning away from Blu, Kanari popped in their *go to* DVD of all times. There was nothing like good food, movies and conversations. That combination was a guaranteed smile creator.

But when Kanari turned around, Blu had her hand over her mouth, muffling her cries. "Boo, what's the matter? Don't cry." Her eyes watered automatically as she walked over to her with open arms.

Blu cried harder the instant her head touched Kanari's shoulder. "Calm down, Blu Belle, calm down." She consoled her. After a few minutes passed and Blu was temporarily all cried out, Kanari walked her over to her side of the bed, pulled back her duvet covers and assisted her into bed. "I'll be right back."

Kanari jogged through the house, ending up in the kitchen. She opened the utensil drawer and grabbed two tablespoons, then she headed over to the freezer.

This is a job for ice cream.

Seconds later, she reentered the room. Popping the lid off of the bucket, she handed it to her. Then she cleared everything else off of the bed and placed it on her dresser.

Kanari took off her shoes and climbed in bed next to her.

Blu's shoulders were slumped and her eyes, droopy. She was definitely her name at that moment. She sniffled. "I know you want to know what's up, huh?"

"Unh unh. That's where you're wrong. I just want to eat this entire gallon of goodness with you and regret it when I'm sick as a dog later." She smiled her way while reaching for the remote. "Hot Tub Time Machine?"

Blu wasn't ready to talk about how right Kanari was although she would have told her if she really wanted to know.

Grateful that she didn't have to pretend everything was cool when it wasn't and also relieved that Kanari wasn't forcing her to spill the tea, Blu returned her smile, faintly.

"Hot Tub Time Machine," was all she said.

Coffee

Chapter 16

Minnie and Kamal

Minnie looked at the calendar on the wall. Another Saturday, making it exactly one week since Yuriah had been in a comatose state, had arrived.

She sighed but smiled a golden smile, nonetheless, as she looked at him with sweet eyes.

Minnie then looked over at Kamal, who was just as obstinate as her when it came to not leaving her husband's side.

Everything he had to do, he did in Yuri's room or within short vicinity of it.

He had been sitting on the sofa talking on the phone all morning, ensuring that all of his business affairs were in order with his multiple laundromats and dry cleaning services.

"Keyz is gonna swing by my CPA's office and pick up payroll. He'll call you and meet up with you today to drop that off. Deliver those checks to each of my managers no later than ten o'clock Monday morning and let me know if there is anything I need to personally address."

"I have it covered and I'll give you a full report when we speak at 10:01," Trena, the VP of Jones' Enterprise clarified.

Kamal hung up the phone and noticed Minnie was looking his way. "What up?"

"Oh, nothing. Just thinking about this guy, me, you and how long we all have known each other. We were yay high." She used her hand to measure two feet from the ground.

"Yea and I was bad since you knew me as a juvie." Kamal smirked at his knucklehead ways. "But things had definitely took a one-eighty in my life, fo'sho. And I owe most of that shit to my boy. He was the one person who refused to give up on me, even when I did myself."

Minnie caressed Yuri's arm. "He's such a good man. I only wish I would have known he saw me as more than just a friend a long time ago. I would have never made the mistake of getting to know G'Corey." She frowned at the thought of them having been married. "I hate him!"

Kamal nodded his understanding but didn't speak on the *G'Co-rey* topic. He was already working on finding his location so the next breath he took would be his last. But he wasn't going to share that with her.

He noticed the detestation that swam in her eyes, giving her a hardened look when she appeared to be concentrating on her ex, so he swung the conversation back to what had her in a happy place.

"You know my dude wanted to tell you on many occasions that you should be his girl. He was always sweet on ya. Everybody knew it but you."

That changed the tide of her mood immediately. She looked soft again. "I was too shy, too nervous and insecure and he was unafraid, bold and certain. Because of that, I didn't think we matched. Besides, back then I only thought he showed me kindness because he felt sorry for me being the short, chubby kid people made fun of."

"So all throughout middle and high school when Yuri was your date for proms, winter formals and spring dances, you thought he was just being *kind*?"

He gave her the *you gotsa be kidding me* look and she gave him a clueless stare, while shaking her head *yes*.

"At that time, I one hundred percent thought he was doing it on the strength of friendship and nothing more. He should have told me." She looked back to Yuriah and shook her head at him for being so hush about his feelings.

"He wanted to, ya dig. But he was living that life. Always smart but too far out there to bring you with him. He respected you too much. But from a teenager, his plan was simple. He was going to better himself and his circumstances and then make a life with you. That was all he talked about: house, kids and you as his wife. That is until the day he found out you was serious about someone."

"G'Corey?" she said his name like it left a foul taste in her mouth to say those three syllables.

"He never mentioned dude's name, but he probably the same cat Yuri spoke of." Kamal looked down at his phone to read a text message that came through. He paused their conversation to check it.

Shenae 10:46 a.m.: I'm here. Got the kids, food, and fresh clothes for the week.

Kamal 10:47 a.m.: On my way down.

"Minnie, hate to cut our talk short, but that's my girl. She downstairs with my kids. You straight?"

"I am."

"A'ight, we'll be back up in a few."

As Kamal was exiting out of the room, the physical therapist was entering. Every day, he was one of the medical staff members who came in to care for Yuriah. His visits usually lasted thirty minutes. He would do different massage techniques to promote circulation through Yuriah's muscles so he didn't get bedsores from lying in the same position from day to day.

When Kamal got off of the elevators, he saw Shenae weighted down with Double on her hip, his baby bag and a gym bag of clothes. Alongside her was De'Asia, rolling an ice cooler.

"Daddy!" De'Asia all but screamed when she saw him approaching.

He quickened his steps and lifted his big girl into his arms, flooding her with kisses.

"Save some of that for me," Shenae said to Kamal when she was close enough to be heard. "Go back there and get that chest you left behind." She directed De'Asia with the point of her finger.

Kamal placed her on her feet. "Awww, Mama."

"Do whatcha mama said. Daddy ain't goin' nowhere."

She lit up and hurried off to get it. Kamal then removed both bags from her shoulder and kissed her like he didn't see her just the other day.

De'Asia hurried back and stood at Kamal's side. She was the definition of a daddy's girl and he was cool with it because Double stayed glued to his mama.

"We gotta kill a lil' time before going upstairs." He reached for Double but he clung to Shenae's shoulder. "Oh, that's how you wanna act? Well, I got my own baby." He picked De'Asia up again. "Nah, I ain't worried," he spoke to his twin who giggled at him, making funny faces.

If Shenae didn't know him pre-kids, no one would had ever been able to tell her he was a gangster about his.

"Where do you suggest we go?" Shenae looked about.

Kamal directed his question to De'Asia. "Wanna go to the gift shop and get Uncle Yuri something special?"

"Oh, yea! Can I get something too, Daddy?"

"Are you the one who's sick?" Shenae gave her eyes that only mothers give when they expect their children to answer correctly.

"No ma'am."

"Alright, then. Don't insert your wants into every situation. This is *be nice to Uncle Yuri* Day not *De'Asia* Day. Understand?" Shenae questioned.

"Yes, ma'am."

Kamal picked up both bags while Shenae pulled the cooler. She headed to the elevator with Kamal behind her.

"Psst. I gotchu," Kamal told his baby girl and she beamed.

Thirty minutes later, the family walked into the room to find Minnie in her usual spot, right next to her husband's bed.

"Hey, Auntie Minnie. Look what I got for Uncle Yuri." She showed her the balloons and teddy bear.

"Oh, that's so beautiful. You picked that out yourself?"

"I did. You think Uncle Yuri will wake up before we leave and see what I got for him?"

"I hope so, baby, but he's really tired. But they will be right here when he wakes up."

That made De'Asia smile before scampering back over to jump on Kamal's lap.

Shenae walked up on Minnie and gave her a hug. "How are you?"

"Hopeful. You?"

"Tired, but I can't complain."

The trio went back in forth in conversation, sharing stories of Yuriah and optimism for his full recovery. Then after thirty minutes, Double became very cranky, which ultimately cut their visit short.

"I gotta get this lil' boy home before they put us out. It was good seeing you." Shenae embraced Minnie with her son still attached at her side.

"It's always good seeing you and the kids. Take care until next time." Minnie waved at the fussy baby while speaking to his mom.

"Same here. Call me if you need anything and enjoy the meals I made. Don't let Greedy eat it all from you." She poked fun at Kamal's hearty appetite.

Kamal looked at his incoming text and then to Minnie. "Munch and BG on the way up. I'ma walk them down. I'll be back," Kamal announced as if he had to. She knew he'd never be too far away or gone for too long.

Minnie saw them out and then headed back over to Yuriah.

She took her guy's hand into hers and placed it at her cheek. Then she stared at him. "Wake up, baby. I'm ready to go home, too."

G'Corey

"Aahhhh!" G'Corey yelped. On impulse, he grabbed the plastic Fisher Price bat that hit him over the eye, waking him from out of his sleep. "Aahhh!" He cried again because he reached with the wrong arm.

His little five year old cousin ran out of the room when he saw G'Corey hustle out of the bed and charge after him. Man Man ran through the house screaming until he jumped into his mother's bed.

G'Corey came storming in there seconds later. "Come here, you lil' mutha—"

"Unh unh, don't be talkin' to my son like that. Bitch, is you crazy?" Skittles looked up at him with bugged eyes.

"You need to control ya damn son, then."

"I don't need to do shit, hoe. You in his house, in his bed." She defended her deviant of a child.

131

Man Man stood behind his mama, bouncing on her bed, making silly faces at G'Corey.

"You shouldn't be treating that boy like he untouchable. Somebody gon' lay his lil' bad ass out. Might be me." G'Corey iffed at him.

"Oh, but I'll shoot a bitch for playing with my son and don't think 'cause yous family that's yo ass is an exception to that rule. Fuck with 'em, bitch, and see."

"Ahh ha! Ahh ha! You can't hit me." Man Man antagonized.

Skittles turned around to face her child. "Get yo funky ass in that bathroom and brush your damn teeth, boy. Shit smell like you ate groceries."

He covered his mouth while giggling and hopped off of the bed. He walked up on G'Corey with caution and then skirted off when he was past him.

"All he like to do is fight and you think that shit cute. See how cute it is when he clock yo stupid ass upside yo head." G'Corey warned the young mother.

"Man Man ain't crazy, but I wish da fuck he would test me." She slapped her chest. "Anyway, I ain't raising no pussy. Maybe if Aunt Dee would have had the same concept with you, your ole puss ass wouldn't be duckin' off here." She laughed as she spit out sunflower seeds into a crumpled piece of paper.

He pointed his middle finger at her. "You'sa a real bitch. Fuck you, Skits."

"Nah, fuck with me, hoe." She laughed even harder than before. His serious face always cracked her the hell up. "Let me stop fuckin' with you, cousin. You gon' tell me why you showed up at my door like a thief in the night, though?"

He sat on the corner of her bed. "New Orleans too fuckin' hot right nah. So I need to chill for a minute."

"And where the fuck yo wife and baby at, hoe?"

G'Corey turned to face her, wearing a disgusted look. "You know you got a dirty fuckin' mouth, bruh?"

"Ass. Fucker. Cunt sucker. You don't have to kiss it, bitch, so it shouldn't matter what the fuck I got." She poked her tongue out at him. "For real, though. Answer my question."

His phone began ringing from the other room. "Hold on." He got up and headed across the hall to get it. It was his mother.

He answered. "What's up, Ma?"

"That's what I want to know. I haven't heard from you in days." Irritation reeked from her voice.

"Didn't you tell me not to come back once I left?"

"Sure did but that didn't have nothing to do with you calling me. I heard that you was involved in some shooting. Is that true?"

He shook his head *no.* "Nah, Ma. It ain't true."

"Mmhmm. Just like you told the truth about Minnie, huh?"

"Ma, is this what you called me for? To vex me?"

She smacked her teeth. "Didn't know I needed a reason. Anyway, I got a letter from Tracie. Want me to read it?"

"Not really, but go ahead." G'Corey's mind wasn't on Tracie, never was. He only placated her because he didn't need her turning state, gaining her freedom in exchange for his.

She opened it, cleared her throat and began reading.

Baby,

I would ask you how you doing but you not locked the fuck up, so you blessed. Well, I'ma get straight to the point. What's up with my bail money? I know you got set back and I'm being super patient but it's been four months now. How much longer do I have to wait?

I need to see you. I need to see my son. I need to be home with the both of y'all. Be the family you promised you wanted from our previous letters. How is he, anyways? Have you been to visit since my last letter? My auntie said whenever you call her you barely ask about him. You can't be doing no shit like that if you want me to believe in what you're writing me. Let him know he is loved by you. I'm not fuckin' playin', no.

This letter is short because I had those things on my mind and I wanted to get them off. The next one will be long and nasty, though.

Coffee

Oh, yea. Thanks for putting money on my books last week but put a fire under your ass with getting me out. I don't want to sit in this bitch 'til these white folks decide to give me a trial date.

On some real shit, I love you. And you better be loving my ass back for all the hell I'm going through.

Go see your son.
Tracie

G'Corey's eyes marbled in his head. The last thing he wanted to do was appease her, but he had to. "Text me her address and I'll call you later, a'ight?" He hung up without hearing her say bye.

As G'Corey was stepping out into the hallway, Man Man tried to run past him again. G'Corey stuck his foot out and clipped him, causing him to fall and cry.

Skittles didn't know why he was boohooing but she called for it to stop immediately. "Boy, shut the fuck up with that sissified crying you doing before I come beat the shit out you."

G'Corey smirked. "Lil' punk," he said below his breath and stepped over him.

He then walked into the kitchen where Skittles was making a late breakfast. When she saw him, she resumed her questions. "How long you tryna lay up here?"

He hunched his shoulders. "I don't know."

"Okay, well, back to my other question. Where is your wife?"

"I don't know that either."

"Well, bitch, what the fuck do you know?"

"I know why yo baby daddy beat the shit outta you. Your fuckin' mouth don't stop."

"And I know if you visit that bitch over at his place, you gon' hafta give him some time to answer the door because he doesn't walk the same." She referred to the time she shot him.

"What the fuck ever. Put a fuckin' filter on your mouth 'cause I'm not in the mood to hear yo shit."

Skittles rolled her eyes. G'Corey wasn't being himself. He was acting beyond sensitive, so she chilled a bit. "Alright, then. Tell me what you do know. What's really goin' on with you?"

As much as Skittles got under his skin, she was as down as they came. So, he didn't mind telling her the truth because as big as her mouth was, she'd never open it to gossip family business.

"I fucked up, thinking with my dick, lying and shit. Minnie found out and bounced on me. Had my lil' one and didn't even tell me about it."

"Awww, she phony fa that."

"Somewhere in the middle of havin' got ghost on me, she divorced me and was preparing to marry another thuggah. But you know I couldn't let that shit play out like that, so I rocked his ass to sleep right there on the spot. Now, I'm tryna figure out how in the fuck do I make it all the way right with Minnie because I *need* her in my life. I ain't even playin'."

"Damn! You fucked up. Real talk, the best thing you can do right now is give her time."

"How much time?"

"Bitch, I mean G'Corey, do I look like Oprah? I don't fuckin' know all that. All I know is you can't be clit riding. You gotta ease yo stupid ass back in there from a distance, though. You don't want to come on too strong because I can tell you right now she ain't feeling you."

"You think she gon' forgive me if I give her a little time?"

"Shit, all things are possible. Just start off small so she don't forget why she fell for yo ugly ass in the first place. Then after that, gradually work your way in and make your efforts to win her back bigger. Make her forget the dummy shit you've done by making her fall in love again."

"That's fuckin' genius. Will you help me?"

"*Will I help you?* What in the hell could I do?" She removed the last pancake from the skillet and removed the pan from the stove.

"Get close enough to her to find out her routine and I'll take it from there."

"Bitch, you sound crazy as a Betsy bug. How in the fuck am I supposed to do that?"

"Leave that up to me." G'Corey's eyes glimmered with impossible hope as he smiled at his newly formed plan.

Chapter 17

Monday morning…

The need to puke her guts outs kept Samiyah hovered over the toilet all throughout the night. Unable to lie down for a straight hour without having another violent urge, she ended up spending the night in her bathroom on the floor.

It was 4 a.m. when she awoke yet again to another compulsion to upchuck. After the release of what felt like pure acid reflux, she continued to linger over the ceramic bowl as she began to cry.

She bawled because she was in pain, both emotionally and physically. It had been a week since she spoke to Gerran and now her bud was sending her through changes.

Grabbing some tissue from off of the spindle, she blew her nose. She threw it away in the waste basket, then slowly got up off of the floor. Samiyah then sat on her bed and thought about her family, specifically Gerran.

There was no doubt in her mind he was taking it hard, she and the baby were his heart. Everything he did in the months leading up the *I do's* and thereafter was testament of his love. In an effort to show how deep his love went for Lil' Acacia, he did the one thing he vowed never to do.

"You're serious aren't you?" Samiyah asked for the tenth time to be sure.

"It was my idea, so I'm one hunnid about it."

"You've always been against them. Remember you said 'my body is a temple?' So I won't know it 'til I see it. After you, sir." She smiled like a silly school girl while holding the door open to the tattoo shop.

"And it is a temple. That's why I wasn't marking my body up with random shit but this is different. This is special."

After a few minutes of filling out the consent form and the artist sterilizing his station, Gerran removed his shirt and reclined into the chair.

Samiyah leaned down to kiss him. "This is special to me, too."

After hours of jaw clenching pain, the buzz of the gun stopped and Gerran heard the specialist tell him, "Have a look, my man."

Gerran stood up and walked over to the full length mirror. The artist reached him the picture he used for comparison but he didn't need the portrait of Lil' Acacia held up against his chest to see that the 3D drawing of the chubby, red-skinned, curly-haired two month old was his daughter.

"This is tight." Gerran grinned as he dapped the man for doing such a spectacular job on the coloring and the script underneath her face, which read: Daddy's Angel.

Samiyah wiped the tears that were in constant stream after reflecting on that day.

She lay on her back and stared up at the ceiling. The silence was driving her mad. She needed to talk to her husband but what had been the usual pattern of their tumultuous past was becoming her present again, him leaving her alone to figure things out by herself.

Samiyah reached for her phone. It was 4:30 but she knew he'd hear his phone ringing, no matter the time.

"Hello," Elias answered with his eyes still clamped shut.

"Eli, I need you." Her voice was frail like she'd been injured.

His eyes shot open, he sat up and cut his lamp on. "What's wrong with Peaches?"

"Oh, God, nothing's wrong with her. She's fine. Matter of fact, I get to bring her home in a couple hours. I was calling for myself."

Elias laid back against his pillow, rubbing the sleep out of his eyes. "What's up, Yah?"

"I'm sick and I'm stressed and I'm scared. I can't figure Gerran out although I know exactly what's wrong. He is still refusing my calls, so we have yet to talk." The sigh she let out sounded like the burden of one who was carrying the world on their shoulders. "I couldn't be pregnant at a worser time."

He wanted to save her. He knew he could make it alright if she wanted him to. "What do you need right now to feel better?"

"I need to talk to Gerran."

"Well, that ain't happenin'. So what else do you need? From me, just to be clear."

There was silence on her end. She knew what she wanted to say but she wasn't sure if she should say it. Samiyah looked over at the empty side of her bed and then closed her eyes. The sound of her lightly gasping could be heard second before she answered in her small voice. "I need you."

The way she said those three words made the heart he promised to keep in the freezer, after the fall out with Blu a few days ago, melt.

"Get here, then. You heard me? Get here." The second *get here* sounded like he was desperate for her to come to him.

Samiyah didn't know if she was reading him right but his pull on her was a hell of a lot stronger now that Gerran was pushing her away. "I'm on my way."

Samiyah got out of bed, headed over to her closet and pulled a pair of jeans and a blouse off of a hanger. She removed a box with a pair of hot pink Mary Jane pumps inside and placed those items into a bag.

Moving over to her drawers, she pulled out some sweat pants to slide into and a bra to put on since she never wore one to sleep. She could never get comfortable with her breast being restrained by one.

Stashing some fresh underwear in her bag, she then moved to her bathroom so she could brush her teeth.

Since she had everything she needed for herself, she then proceeded down the hall to Lil' Acacia's room and picked up her pre-packed baby bag from off of her change table.

"Bags? Keys? Phone? Purse? Check," she said out loud as she headed downstairs to leave.

Two quick snaps to the left undid both locks. And as she opened the door, she shouted and stumbled backwards when the unexpected happened.

"Gerran!" She grabbed her chest as he stood there looking just as shocked as she was. Trepidation caused her breathing to become irregular for a moment, so she had to settle herself down before speaking again. "I wasn't expecting to see you."

"And I wasn't expecting to see you, leaving. Where you on your way to at four something in the morning?"

The walls were closing in on me and I had to get out, is all."

"I didn't ask you why. I asked you where?" He stepped all the way inside.

"By my mama." She regretted lying almost immediately but it wouldn't have looked good for her to tell him actualities.

"Ya mama, huh?" Gerran didn't believe her.

"You decided to come home and talk?"

"Not at all."

She was puzzled at his reply. "So why did you come, then?"

"It's still *my* house and I have things I need to get out of my office. Look, I don't want to talk to you, so chill out talking to me. And I don't want to see you, either. That's the whole reason why I came at this hour but you were on your creep shit, so here we are. But you can still carry the hell on to *your mama's,*" he spoke distrustfully.

She placed her phone and keys on the hall table and dropped her bags on the floor next to it.

She followed him into his work room and stood by the door as he cut on the light and began looking through his things. "Gerran, there's a whole lot I want to say but I need to start with I'm sorry."

Gerran didn't acknowledge her. He just continued searching through his drawers until he found the UB drive he was looking for.

"Are you listening to me?" Samiyah almost wanted to pout but she held it in.

He turned around and jabbed at the wall, leaving a deep impression in the sheet rock.

"I'm sorry, wall." He eyeballed it for a second before facing Samiyah, who was trembling with nerves. "Look at that. It's not fixed. Hell out my way!" He walked past her and through the house to leave.

She followed behind him, pleading for an opportunity to explain herself but he wasn't fazed. However, her ringing cell phone caught his attention as he walked past it. Curiously, he picked it up, looked at it and then slapped it into her hand.

"Ya mama, huh?" He glared at her so hard she didn't want to breathe.

Gerran then walked out of the door, got into his car and whipped out of the driveway in a hurry.

She felt weak seeing his car drive off to who knows where.

Samiyah locked her door and then lifelessly walked over to her sofa and plopped down. She was tired of trying to figure out how to deal with the curve balls of life alone.

Samiyah pressed the button on her phone to light up the display. She knew who called her but she couldn't help but wish for a tiny miracle that it wasn't so.

The screen came to life. *Missed call: Elias.*

She rolled her eyes and sighed. "Damn, E! Damn!"

Samiyah debated for a few minutes on whether she was going to stay home and sulk or still go over to Eli's.

A few moments of contemplation gave her the verdict she was to carry out. *It's whatever. The damage is done and I still need him.* With that, she grabbed everything she sat down and headed out of the door.

Twenty minutes later...

She parked in Eli's driveway, only taking her purse as she stepped out.

Elias was in his living room when he heard her pull up, so he was already standing on the porch waiting for her.

She walked up on him. Her lips stretched into a frown as she stood directly in front of him, looking up at him as he was looking down at her. She then allowed her bag to slip from her hand and wrapped her arms around him and cried.

Coffee

He closed his eyes for a time and then reopened them as he shook his head slowly, resting his chin on top of her head, swallowing her within his embrace.

He remembered this exact feeling, a spark that turned into a flame.

Not long after, he pulled away. He had too. "Come on. Let's go inside."

She grabbed her purse off of the ground and walked in with him.

Samiyah took a seat on the sofa, removed her Uggs and coiled her feet under her as she lay her head on the arm of the couch. Eli sat across from her, where it was safe.

The dim shine from the lamp sitting off in the corner provided the only light the otherwise dark house had. He saw just enough of Samiyah to see she was wiping tears away with the tips of her fingers.

"Talk to me."

"From over there?" she asked.

"Nah." He stood up and took a seat at the other end from her. "Give me your feet."

She unfolded her legs and stretched out on her back, placing her legs in his lap. He removed her socks and began giving her a massage.

"Talk to me," he said again as he provided smooth strokes and firm grips around her foot.

"Gerran came by the house right before I came here."

"So y'all talked?"

"No indeed, no. He don't have no words for me and you calling after I told him I was going by my mama's only made him look at me more hatefully." She placed her hand on her stomach. "What am I gonna do if he won't let me make this right?"

"Fuck him, ya heard me. And I ain't just saying that shit because he's a bitch, either."

"Come on, Eli, he's still my husband."

"Yea, a husband who treats you like shit. Should he be pissed the fuck off? Hell yea but you carrying his baby and you still his

142

fuckin' wife. That should have at least earned you a decent conversation, at minimum. But like I said, he's a bitch!" Eli held his position on it.

"This is stressin' me out. Why couldn't he be like you in this situation?"

"We were built in different elements, Yah. He was made for the sun and I was crafted for the rain. He can't handle a storm. That's why I'm here and he's not."

His words were like a blow to the heart because each trial, whether it was her fault or Gerran's, made them weaker. And now wasn't the time for them to fold. They were grown and married with children.

"I need something unbreakable, Eli, 'cause I can't keep going through this."

"Come here." He motioned with the wave of his hand for her to come lay on his lap.

She changed positions and cradled herself against his body, resting her head on his muscular thighs.

In a consoling manner, he began rubbing the contour of her physique, down and then back up. Her body was firm in places and soft in others.

There goes those sparks again, he thought.

He bit down on his bottom lip as he shook off carnal impulses. Elias didn't want to travel that road with her but it was torturous to deny them. As long as she was with Gerran and he was with Blu, he managed to bury intimate thoughts of them sea level deep. But now, those feelings were rising just like his dick had.

It jumped once. It thumped twice. Samiyah felt its movement. It was too big not too but she didn't stir.

Elias suddenly found his hand on her back under her T-shirt. His lips parted and his heavy breathing became noticeable.

He then used the assistance of his other hand to unbuckle her bra.

"Eli, what are you doing?"

"Nothing that shouldn't be happening." He pushed one strap off of her shoulder and she sat up on command, so he could remove the other.

Sliding his hand up her stomach, he felt her muscles tense as he pulled her brazier down, tossing it on the coffee table.

His tongue rolled over his lips. He then stretched his neck to the left and then the right to loosen himself up.

Then without hesitation, he grabbed the throw blanket that draped over his sofa and used it to cover Samiyah's body. He needed her comfortable and he knew she couldn't get there with a bra on.

He leaned down toward her ear and whispered. "Get some sleep. We gotta get our daughter in a few hours."

Tears dripped from her eyes as a smile creased her lips. He always knew what to do to make things better, even if it only lasted a little while. "Okay."

She nestled closer to him and fell asleep with ease under his comforting touch.

Chapter 18

One week later...

Samiyah sat Indian style on the sofa as she breastfed Lil' Acacia while eating peanut butter toast when her phone rang next to her.

She stared at it for a second and started not to answer because she wasn't in the best mood but she decided to pick up anyway and was glad she did when she heard who it was on the other end.

"Hi Samiyah, this is Zanete. Am I reaching you at a good time?"

Hell yea! Samiyah wanted to say. "Yes, absolutely. How can I help you?" She spoke professionally.

"Well, I could have called Gee but I thought it was only right that I contacted you since you're the reason Pleasure will be producing her entire album with you all. She wants to work with Gerran." The artist's manager relayed.

Despite two weeks elapsing without him being home and having the inevitable *where do we go from here* conversation, Samiyah wanted to scream excitement for his blooming success. "I'm so happy to hear that and I know Gerran will be just as thrilled as I am."

"Correction, thrilled as us three. Well, I have other producers to disappoint." Zanete chuckled.

"Thank you so much for the opportunity. Gerran will see to it that she stays number one." Samiyah rightfully boasted. He was, after all, a beast at what he did.

"I have no doubts about that. I will email you Pleasure's schedule. Match it against yours and then let's discuss studio times. Sounds good?"

"Sounds great!" Samiyah grinned.

They disconnected the phone and Samiyah all but jumped out of her seat. She was pleased because working with Pleasure was bragging rights for any producer.

Everyone wanted an opportunity to work with the fierce R&B/Rap talent who was dominating the charts, but she wanted the fresh breath Gerran breathed into the industry. Plus, she was fond of how hard Samiyah went for Raw Musik without being aggressive in the process.

"Maybe this will stop da—Gerran from giving mommy the silent treatment," she spoke to Lil' Acacia.

Over the last year and a half, she had become instrumental to his company and had been intricately working as his right hand, side by side. So, shooting him an email to update him wasn't going to be sufficient. Her accomplishment merited a verbal sit down with hopes of also being the gateway to their much needed talk.

After Samiyah got finished burping Lil' Acacia, she held her up to her face.

"Mama has some business to take care of. Do you think I can drop you off by Daddy and you be a good girl for him, huh? No throw ups and only one poopy diaper. Can you handle that?" Samiyah made silly willy faces, making her baby coo and giggle.

She played with her daughter a little while longer and then made a call to Elias.

"What up, Yah?" he answered as he continued trimming his goatee.

"I needed to know if you'll be busy in the next couple of hours because I want to bring Lil' Acacia over for a little while as I take care of some business."

"You want *me* to watch *her*?"

"Yes."

"By myself?"

"Yes, for an hour, tops."

"Will she be asleep the whole time?"

Samiyah had to laugh. His nerves had him asking the most ridiculous questions. "Probably not. Quit acting scary, will ya?"

"I'm not acting."

"You'll do fine. I promise."

"A'ight. We'll see. Come on through. I'm at the crib."

"Cool."

Eli hung up the phone and stared at himself in the mirror for a second. He wasn't ready to care for something so tiny by himself.

146

What if I'm too strong handling her and I break her? What if I'm no good at doing this? Shit, I ain't ready.
Meanwhile, Samiyah attempted to call Gerran to let him know she would be passing over to his studio to speak with him on business but he didn't answer.

"Boy, I swear." She shook her head. It irritated her to her soul how withdrawn he was being considering they still have a family and a business between them but she wasn't going to allow that to damper the delivery of her news.

Two hours later...

Samiyah was ringing Eli's bell. He opened the door, inviting her in.

She spoke as she entered, sitting the carrier on his sofa and placing the baby bag next to it. Samiyah reached inside of the bag and pulled out three bottles of breastmilk.

"I'm going to leave one out because she will be ready to eat at any time now. I'm gonna put these two in the fridge. Keep your eyes on her while I do that."

Elias nodded his understanding as he found himself smiling at his sleeping baby. *You got this, playboy.*

Samiyah returned seconds later and gave him a rundown of the *do's* and *don'ts.*

"Alright, I'm gonna head over to Gerran's and after I finish up with him, I'll be back to get her."

"Or you can stay and kick it. Maybe we go to lunch or something." Elias offered.

"Like a family?"

"Nah, not like one. We are one."

A bitter sweet feeling came over her. In one corner, she had a husband who felt no sense of duty to her, while on the other, she had a friend who did.

Swept up in a moment, she wanted to give him a harmless kiss. The kind sweethearts gave before they departed one another but then she looked at their child and realized there was no such thing as *harmless* when it came down to them.

She smiled. "That sounds like a great plan."

Samiyah bent down, kissed her baby's hand and whispered. "Mama's gonna be right back. Remember our agreement, okay?"

She waved bye as she exited his house, closing the door. No sooner than Samiyah was getting into her car, Elias was charging after her.

"Oh, Yah. Hol' on. She wants you." He lifted the car seat waist high for Samiyah to get a good glimpse at their crying daughter.

Lil' Acacia's sneeze startled her and she began to cry as a result.

"She doesn't want me. She wants comfort, so give it to her. And get use to this, Daddy. I won't always be around to save the day, ya know?"

"But what do I do? Feed her?" Eli looked absolutely clueless.

"She could be hungry. She eats every two hours, so you can try feeding her the bottle I left on the coffee table. If she doesn't want that and her pamper is dry, touch her and hold a conversation with her. She likes that."

"All of that?"

"And then some." Samiyah smiled at him as she started the engine.

He looked at Peaches and then back to Samiyah. "Keep yo phone on. Matter of fact, hold it in your hand."

"Eli, just remember to support her head when you're holding her and burp her like I showed you after she eats, okay? Don't sweat. You'll do great. You're a natural with the ladies."

"Ladies not babies."

"Be back soon, okay?" She blew a kiss at Lil' Acacia.

"Yea, a'ight."

Samiyah headed out and Eli headed inside with a crying Peaches at his side. He placed her on the sofa and tried removing her from her carrier but was struggling to do so.

"What the—" Elias couldn't unbuckle her for nothing. "Who made this?" He looked at the embroidery stitching above her head. *Damn you, Eddie Bauer.*

After a minute more, he was finally able to undo the straps.

He hesitantly pulled her out, grabbed the bottle and took a seat. "You hungry?" He put the bottle in her mouth but she didn't want it. He tried feeding her the nipple again but she rejected it. He awkwardly tried to rock her like he had seen Samiyah do on many occasions but his touch wasn't doing the trick. "You're not being a peach right now. Come on, baby."

As her cries continued and bewilderment etched his face, he bounced her some more with the hopes she'd like that enough to stop her fussing. But she wouldn't let up and he didn't know what to do.

Yep, I ain't ready.

***

Samiyah tried calling Gerran again, so she wouldn't be popping up on him. But he didn't answer, as she expected.

Pulling into the parking lot, she saw his car along with another next to it. She hoped he wasn't too busy with an artist, making it that much easier to brush her off.

When she walked through the door, the chime of the electronic bell sounded off. A lady appearing to be in her late thirties came from out of the back and approached Samiyah.

"How can I help you?" Audra held her head high with her shoulder pushed back.

He went and hired someone? Samiyah kept the sting of his action hidden behind her smile and extended her hand. "Introduce yourself, please. I'm Samiyah."

The assistant looked at Samiyah's hand and then back to her face before she obliged. "I'm Audra. How can I help you?"

There was something about her Samiyah didn't like. Audra was giving a stank vibe for no reason at all.

"I'm here to see Gerran. I'll just step in his office." Samiyah made an attempt to walk past her but Audra stepped in her path.

"Excuse me, but you can't go back there. Do you have an appointment?" She began looking through her scheduling app on her phone.

Who in the fuck do she think she is? Samiyah was puzzled.

Pictures of her were sprinkled all throughout his office. Audra knew exactly who she was, even without having met her in person prior to today.

She raised her left hand, pointing at her bodacious diamond rock. "There's my appointment. Now move, please." She gently brushed past her and Audra spun on her heels and followed behind her.

Before Samiyah was able to open the door herself, Audra reached around her and turned the knob, stepping in his office first.

"Someone is here to see you," she spoke so politely, so professionally.

"Thank you," Gerran casually waved his hand.

Samiyah gave her the side eye. *Someone's here to see you? Bitch!*

"Would you like your door left open or closed?" Audra asked with too much sugar on top for Samiyah's taste.

Samiyah stepped all the way in and off to the side. "We want it closed." She pushed it shut, forcing Audra to move with it.

He chuckled. "What you did that for?"

"Why is she here?"

"It's obvious why *she's* here but what isn't is why you are. What you want?"

"What I want is for you to treat me like the last eight years of our lives count for something. For you to talk to me because our marriage and our family is worth fighting for."

Gerran looked at her unbothered by the plea in her eyes. "That's why you came here? I could have saved you the gas."

"Are you being serious right now? Gerran, we weren't together when Eli and I happened. It was one moment of weakness. One! We had never and I do mean never had any inappropriate dealings prior to that time. And I didn't know she wasn't yours. I wouldn't have caused you intentional pain like that, so why are you deliberately hurting me?"

He looked at his watch, then flipped through the pages of his planner. "Are you done because if you aren't, it's too bad. I have a meeting in a few."

"So, you ain't trying to hear a word I say?"

"If you that good at peepin' shit, then why are you still talkin'? And that was rhetorical just in case you thought to answer it." Gerran stood up to open the door but Samiyah blocked him.

"Gerran, do you even care that I had a doctor's visit last Monday and found out I am six weeks pregnant?"

"With whose baby?"

Samiyah's lips curled. She wanted to slap the shit out of him in his mouth for his disrespect, but she bridged back her fury. She knew she deserved most of his wrath but not all. He was now flat out being cruel.

"Believe what the hell you will but I'm still your wife and this is *your* baby!"

"Both are to be determined." Gerran's words were as icy as his stare.

Samiyah didn't know how to respond to his bitterness. Everything she said was welcomed with disregard and retaliation.

She broke down for a second. Her eyes shifted to the other side of the room so she wouldn't have to look into his remorseless orbs.

A few feet over sat their wedding picture amongst other photo memorabilia. She walked over to it and snatched it from off of the shelf. She marched back over to him and he gave her a look of disinterest.

Her voice cracked but she pushed through her astonishment. "What ever happened to *for better or for worse?* You're acting like you don't even give a fuck."

He took the photograph from her and then threw it in his waste basket. "Maybe it's because I don't."

"Fuck you!" That blew her fuse and she snapped, pushing him as hard as she could although she was barely able to move him an inch.

Samiyah stormed over to the door and slung it open only to find Audra listening at it. "Get the fuck up out my way!" Samiyah bumped shoulders with her as she walked into the hallway.

"Ahh, is everything okay?" Audra took a passive aggressive method, speaking directly to Gerran but indirectly addressing his wife.

Samiyah spun around and stood in her face so closely their noses were on the verge of touching. "And if it wasn't. What the fuck you gon' do about it?"

"Samiyah! Leave!" Gerran stood between them and pointed for her to step.

Samiyah looked at him angrily. She wanted to bruise, if not damage, his ego in the same manner he was breaking her heart and embarrassing her in front of Audra.

"I shouldn't have come because you are every bit of the *bitch* Elias said you are."

That struck a chord with him. "Get the fuck out, for real." He grabbed at her arm to escort her out personally but she jecked away from him.

"Don't touch me!" Her feelings were hurt and Audra's happy response to it was puzzling her, adding to her pisstivity.

Samiyah had no idea pain would transform him into a vindictive and uncaring S.O.B. but it had.

She stormed out of his office, jumped in her car and pulled off onto Haynes Blvd.

Samiyah couldn't go back to Eli's just yet. She had to get something off of her chest, so she parked at an empty lot, got out of her vehicle and headed across the four lanes of traffic to the other side where the levee was. She scaled the steep hill until she stood at the top of the climb.

It was there that she let out a gut wrenching scream and cried a river for what appeared to be irreversible damage.

Chapter 19

"Tell me I'm not doing the wrong thing?" Blu was second guessing her decision to see Eli on the drive over to his house.

"What's wrong is denying what you feel is the right thing to do." Kanari coached her into following her heart.

"He hasn't tried reaching out to me since that day. Do you think I'm weak for going to him?"

"Are you weak?" Kanari countered with a question of her own.

"No."

"There's your answer, so quit trippin'. Have the talk. See what happens when the both of y'all can talk this thing out without being all defensive and shit."

"You're right and thank you for not trying to talk me out of this. I probably would have listened for fear of being stupid."

"Girl, friendship don't mean do what I do for me to have your back. It means I will support you in what *you* do, period. I'ma stay in your passenger seat. I'm ya rider, you know that."

"Until the wheels fall off."

Blu and Kanari have had their share of rough patches over the years but regardless to who did what, they both vowed to work whatever it was out. True friendship was hard to find and that old adage proved true when it came to her relationship with Elias as well.

"I'm almost at his place. What are you about to do?"

"Shid, I'ma smoke, eat and sleep."

"That's all?"

"Shit no! Take out the trash, too. Thanks for reminding me."

"You are stoopid, for real."

"You already knoooowwww!" Kanari said in her Big Freedia voice.

"Girl, I'll talk to you when I see you at work tonight."

"Alright. Talk to you then."

Blu dropped her phone into her purse and drove down the 7th ward streets until she found herself parked on Eli's.

Ten minutes had elapsed and she found herself still sitting outside of his house, hesitating to knock on his door. But as usual, her grandmother's sage advice rang loudly in her mind.

"Live with no regrets. Shoulda, woulda, coulda should be three words you know nothing about."

She stepped out of her car and onto his porch. The cries of an infant could faintly be heard the moment she stood close enough to the door. Blu sighed and shook her head. A part of her wanted to leave him alone to deal with the choice he made but the other side of her couldn't do that in good conscious.

She rapped on the door. He didn't answer immediately. Her guess was his hands were full, so Blu waited a little longer before knocking again.

When he opened up, the first thing Blu saw was an upset baby with rosy colored cheeks in his arms and a father who looked to be struggling.

It wasn't Blu's nature to disregard the need of another just to accommodate her own, so she instinctually reached for Peaches as she placed her purpose for coming by on the back burner.

"May I?"

He nodded his head, beckoning her inside as he reached her his daughter.

"How long has she been crying?" Blu began a motherly bounce as she used a calming voice to settle her.

"If we basing it off of dog years, she been crying for two of 'em, feel like. But maybe the last forty-five minutes, off and on. More on, though."

Blu reached for her bag and pulled out the blanket and spread it on the cushion of the sofa. She laid her on it and began taking the bottom of her outfit off. She felt her diaper. It was soggy.

"Eli! She is soaked."

He hunched his shoulders. "I didn't know that. How you know?"

She took his hand and placed it on the front of the pamper. "Squeeze. You feel that squishiness?" He nodded his understanding. "That's how I knew."

She changed her into a fresh one after cleaning her tush. "Does that feel better? He didn't mean to leave you with a wet tookus," Blu spoke to a still fussy Peaches.

"Why she still crying?"

"I don't know but we are about to figure it out." Blu leaned forward and grabbed her bottle off of the coffee table, positioned Peaches in the cradle of her arm and began feeding her.

Peaches latched on and greedily began devouring her milk.

"Oh, now she wants to eat?" Elias questioned audaciously.

"After a game of basketball, do you eat or shower first?"

"A'ight. I feel ya." Elias didn't like feeling dirty and it was apparent to him that she got his ways on that one.

After a few minutes of suckling, Peaches began looking drowsy. Sleep was imminent. Blu turned to face Elias who was sitting beside her, watching as she naturally settled her down.

"Here, take over." Blu pulled Peaches away from her body and into his arms.

"You don't want to finish?" Elias felt Peaches would notice the switch and start back cutting up.

"She's your child. You have to get comfortable doing this yourself." *Wow! His child.* It sounded weird for her to openly say that but it was true nonetheless.

He bobbed his head, taking her and the bottle from Blu. Peaches looked so angelic although she was hell a few moments ago. He couldn't help but smile at her as he watched her stop and go suction on the nipple.

When she was finished, Elias removed the bottle from her mouth and went to lay her down, but Blu stopped him.

She shook her head. "Don't do that. You have to burp her first. Otherwise, that gas will sit on her stomach and make her cranky. It's painful for them, you know?"

Elias blew out but lifted her to his shoulder. Blu searched through the bag and pulled out a cloth diaper to place over his shoulder.

"Why you doing that?"

"So she don't throw up on you."

"Good lookin' out."

Blu showed him how to cup his hand and pat her back with a gentle firmness. Once she let it out a good one, Blu told him he was okay to lay her down.

"That was rough." He admitted.

"You'll get use it and it will become easier as time goes on."

They sat in silence for a moment. Blu not knowing exactly where to start and Eli not wanting to say the wrong thing.

"So, ummm, I came by because I've spent some time thinking about our last talk and I want to have a different one this time. One where you're willing to understand me as I understand your position. Is that cool or is now not a good time?" She looked over at his sleeping beauty.

"Now is good as long as you promise not to chomp your boy head off."

"Nah, none of that. I was angry, then."

"So you not no more?"

She shook her head *no*. "I still feel some type of way, though. I feel like you could have told me Samiyah was once your bed partner. After all, y'all spend time alone. I could have determined if that was going to be a problem for me as your girlfriend. Then, I wouldn't have been upset about Peaches being your child at all because I would have known the potential was there for her to be yours. Does that make sense to you?"

"It do, ya heard me."

"So, why didn't you tell me?"

Elias thought about the answer for a second and told her the honest truth. "I only met two women in my life that I respected. And that's you and Samiyah. I guess I found it disrespectful to put our business out there like that. But I can admit it was disrespectful to you for me not to have said something."

"Speaking of disrespect, I'm sorry for calling you a hoe ass. That was dirty of me."

"Yea, you was down bad fa that 'cause I haven't been doin' *nathaniel*. Matter of fact, I been jackin' my shit for the last two months. I ain't did that since—never! But I was doin' it for you."

Blu blushed and the one dimple in her left cheek sunk deep into her skin. "If it makes you feel any better, I haven't shared myself with anyone either."

"That's 'cause your ass selfish with your kitty kat." Elias clowned her and she slapped him upside the head.

She giggled before taking a more serious disposition. "I've missed you, us. You don't just find chemistry like we have around the corner and I still want us if that's on the table."

"I'ma be honest. I've had plenty relations but you've been my only relationship so there's a lot of shit I ain't gon' do the right way but I ain't gon' stay left forever. If you can feel that, then pull up a chair."

Blu responded with a peck. A peck that turned into kiss. A kiss that turned into a full blown make-out session.

Aroused by her feel, he began squeezing, groping and gripping her body. Their brief separation brought a level of appreciation he was happy to express with his hands.

"Don't start a fire you can't put out." She panted, wanting to give herself to him in that moment.

He looked down at his hard dick from his joggers, begging that it be released. "Oh, I got something to put it out, ya heard me."

He went in to kiss her again, but she stopped him and pointed to the other sofa. "Ahh, Peaches."

"Shit! So, if she wasn't here, you would've let me hit that?"

She shook her head at his choice of words but chalked it up to Eli being Eli. "Maybe."

If it wasn't for her denim jeans, he would have known from the drench of her panties that she was powerless to tell him no.

Elias sat back and looked at his girl, admiring her ways. If she wasn't anything else, she proved she was understanding. So, while the portal of honesty was still open, he felt now was a good time to tell her about Cujo and put everything on Front St.

"Boo, I got something I want to—" Elias was interrupted by the doorbell. "Hold on, boo. That's probably Samiyah. You good?"

Her stomach tightened when he mentioned her name. She supposed it was the uncomfortable reality that Samiyah was no longer just a friend. Now she was the friend who had her man and if fate were to ever be so cruel, a friend who could have him again.

"I'm good." She suppressed her thoughts.

Elias kissed her lips and then opened the door only to see Samiyah upset. He could tell without her saying a word because her eyes never lied.

Samiyah saw Blu sitting inside and knew crying on his shoulder wasn't going to be an option, so she faked a smile and spoke to him and then to her. "Hey, Blu. How are you?"

"I'm good. You?"

"Not so good. I have an upset tummy. This baby won't give me a break." She blamed her obvious facial upset on her pregnancy.

"You're pregnant?" The shock of her statement registered on her face and in her voice.

"I am and I need to get home to rest. So, I'll just be getting my little one and leaving." She turned to face Eli, shifted her eyes off to the side where Blu sat and gave him the *are y'all straight* look. "How was she?"

He bobbed his head to answer her unspoken question first before he responded out loud to her second one. "She something else. I can tell ya that much."

Samiyah smiled and went to collect Peaches' things. "You'll be a pro before you know."

"If you would have seen me in action, you might think differently."

Samiyah shook her head at Eli and then smiled at her sleeping baby girl. "Come on, big girl. Let's go for a ride."

"I got that." Eli reached for her car seat. "I'll be right back," he told Blu as he walked Samiyah to her car.

"Bye, Blu."

"Bye." She waved back.

They headed outside.

"Is everything a'ight with you?" Eli asked the moment they stood next to the car.

"It's Gerran we're talking about, but that's a different time. You need to get back inside. You don't want her feeling insecure."

"She ain't like that."

"That's what you think. Call me when you're alone." After securing the baby, she took her seat behind the wheel and started her engine.

"I'ma holla." He stood in his driveway and waited for her to pull off before he headed back inside.

Blu quickly moved away from the blinds and hurried back to her seat. She didn't want Elias to catch her spying but as soon as he walked in, she inquired, "Is that—"

Elias already knew she was tweaking to find out. "No. Her baby is not mines. I told you it only happened once."

"Okay. I won't ask again." She zipped her lips and threw away the imaginary key.

To ensure things remained light between them, Elias hinted kinky suggestion. "I know what you need to stop all your trippin' out on me."

Elias pulled her up on her feet, wrapping his arms around her waist while kissing her long and deep.

Her eyes fluttered and she felt woozy. His kisses were always so intoxicating. She could only imagine going all the way with him and being drunk in love afterwards. That was always the reason she kept her sexual distance, too fearful of falling too deep too soon.

Pumping the brakes, she blurted, "What did you want to tell me earlier?"

She pulled back to cool down the heat stirring between them.

But Elias wasn't having that. He waited for the right time with Blu because she wasn't the average woman. She was respectful, sexy without trying, funny and caring. Just a few of the things that made dipping off inside of her love worth waiting for, but the waiting game was about to end and there was no way he was going to mention her retarded ass sister and fuck up the mood.

They were on the verge of something that was long overdue in his mind. She wanted him and he could tell. The curious look in her eye, the exaggerated breathing and the force behind the thrust of her tongue told him that she only needed a little convincing.

He couldn't bring up La'Tasha if he wanted to.

"We can talk about that later. Right now it ain't more important than what I wanna do."

He pulled her into his body and she felt the jump of his dick against her stomach.

"And what's that?" She wanted to hear the answer although she knew she shouldn't have asked.

"Don't stop me and I'll show you."

"You wouldn't be the first woman sprung off a man's good sex. So, quit thinking so damn much because what you won't do another woman will. Don't be naïve, chile. You're a rare find but pussy isn't. Keep your man happy before he ends up someone else's."

I hear you, grandma, Blu thought to herself as she took his hand and followed his leading.

***

Samiyah made it home and felt more alone than ever. She couldn't help but see images of Gerran everywhere she looked. They christened every inch of their house and with his energy stamped everywhere it was hard not to miss him, even with his Mr. Hyde personality shining brightly.

The downs of her situation made her miss Minnie much more.

She reached for her phone and dialed her up. She was certain if she would have made it back from Italy, she would have called her but she needed to try anyway.

After a few rings, the phone went to voicemail.

I don't even blame you, sis. If I could shut out the world, I would, too.

After Minnie's spiel played, the beep sounded.

"Hey, I guess you guys are having so much fun away from it all that y'all decided to stay in paradise a little longer, huh? Well, brief update: the baby is great but Gerran and I are back on the fritz. Long story short, I need my friend. So, whenever you are back and settled, please call me. I love you. I miss you. Stay enjoying your honeymoon, though. Bye."

Thinking back on Gerran, she was still very upset but with her phone still in her hand, she decided to send him a message informing him of the news from earlier. After all, there was no need to let business falter even if their relationship was going down in flames.

5:13 p.m.: Zanete called earlier to congratulate me on finalizing their decision for you to exclusively work with Pleasure. You're welcome and it's still fuck you!

That was unnecessary fuel she added to their blazing fire but it felt right to say it, since he was abusively lashing out at her.

A few minutes later her phone rang. She assumed it was Gerran calling but it wasn't. When she saw it was Minnie, she answered excitedly.

"Minnie, I'm soooo happy you're back. Why didn't you call me?"

She didn't respond with the same vigor although she was happy to hear from her as well. "I never left, sis."

Samiyah knew something was wrong by the tone of her voice. "What's the matter?"

"Girl, a lot. Too much. I'm at Charity and had been since the day of my wedding."

"What in the hell? Why didn't you call me? I would had been there? Minnie, what happened?"

"No offense but my mind had only been focused on what was before me. I honestly didn't know the world existed unless it came to our hospital room. But what happened was Yuriah was shot by my ex and has been in a coma since coming out of his second surgery."

"Oh, my God!" Samiyah's mouth flung open. She didn't know what to say but she knew what to do. "I'm on my way."

She didn't mean to hang up on Minnie but she couldn't think straight. She gathered her daughter and their things and flew out of the house. She had to get to her friend's side.

Coffee

Chapter 20

Elias sat on the corner of his bed, pulling Blu between his thighs. His hands sensually slicked underneath her shirt and up her back. As her top crept up her skin, he began tonguing her navel and kissing a trail up her stomach and onto her B cup delights through her lacy brazier.

Blu started doing slow neck rolls as she gripped his head. "Ohh! Ummm!"

With his hands still wrapped around her body, he stood to his feet to completely undress her out of her blouse and bra, now thrusting his tongue into her mouth.

With his hand resting on her lower back, he pressed her into him firmly as he used his other hand to palm her punani through her jeans.

"Ahh haa! Ummm!" she whimpered, placing her hand on his wrist to stop him from massaging her mound. "Baby, wait."

"No." Elias kept his hand in place.

"Ummm, baby," she moaned pleasure. "There are, *ummm*, no more surprises, right?" She had to be sure before she unleashed her inner whore and the floodgates of her emotional damn.

Asking him a question while his dick was harder than cracking The Da Vinci Code wasn't the best time to get honest answers.

His one-eyed monster ventriloquized his response for him because the head on his shoulders couldn't think worth a damn. "No. No surprises." He continued necking her.

That was all she needed to hear. She pulled away from him and he stepped forward, but she blocked him with the shove of her extended palm. She unbuttoned her jeans and stepped out of them, leaving her panties on.

Elias, seeing that, stripped out of everything.

Blu looked at his inflexible muscle and her mouth watered. She had to taste him. She sealed the gap between them and kissed him strongly before she allowed her body to glide downward and onto her knees.

She placed her hands on his thighs for support, allowed the tip of his dick to jump against her lips and then she opened wide to give it a warm and wet welcome.

Blu created a rhythm between the slides of her mouth going back and forth as the suction of her tongue manipulated its way around the girth of his pole.

"Ummm, ummm, mmmm, hmmm…" her moans were continuous as she enjoyed taking as much of him as she could.

"Damn! Awww! Shit!" Elias went to grab the back of her head while he spoon fed her dick but she slapped his hands away and unlatched herself to speak.

"Don't touch me!" she spoke forcefully, lustfully and it turned him the fuck on.

Eli shot his hands up in surrender fashion so she could get back to doing her thing.

Before she resumed, she hawked spit onto his caramel rod and then went for broke. Her mouth was sensational. Elias began clutching the air, bringing his fists to the front of his face as his toes tried their hardest to grip the carpet beneath them.

There were levels to sucking good dick and it appeared Blu knew them all. And after a few minutes more of her trying to suck the life force from his body his face turned into something god awful to look at.

"Oh shit! I'm 'bout to nut."

Hearing that made Blu turn up. She grabbed the back of his legs and assisted him in driving his stiffness to that gag zone in the back of her throat. She was on the verge of extracting his juice, which caused him to wrap his hands in her curls to position her for the heavy swallow.

"Ahhhhh! Shit! Ahhhhh shit! Ahhhh shit!" His cream slipped down her esophagus.

Eli didn't have to tell her how A1 he found her head game. The mere fact that he almost lost his balance twice was all the props she needed.

Blu rose to her feet. She had her fill of appetizer. Now she was ready for the meal.

"Get on the bed and strap the fuck up!" She gave the order. He followed it.

"You ain't sayin' shit!"

Eli walked over to his nightstand and pulled out a few Magnums, tossing them onto the mattress, eagerly tearing one open and sliding it on.

Blu began pulling her underwear down but Eli stopped her. He waved his hand side to side. "Fuck that! Leave them bitches on."

Now it was her time to obey. She did as she was told and then climbed into bed, sitting on top.

Blu lifted off of him just enough to dip two off inside of her throbbing tunnel. She tasted her nectar off of one and then offered the other to Eli.

With no hesitation, he allowed his tongue to wrap around her finger slicked with her honey, only to discover he was fond of her flavor. She was sweet enough to eat.

"Damn!" Eli never dined between the legs of any woman but today he was willing to change all of that.

Eli flipped Blu over onto her back as he prepared to go downtown. But Blu had different plans. She pulled him back up toward her face and wrapped her arms around his neck. Flicking her candy licker against his earlobe, she whispered, "I been wanting to fuck you for so long. Don't make me wait to feel you."

The feeling was mutual. That's why he had every intention on tearing her ass up.

Eli stared down at her, silently. Then he slowly nodded his head as he pulled her panties to the side and maneuvered his brick at her opening.

"This is going to hurt." He centered himself at her warmth and right as he went inside, he covered her mouth to quash her screams. His thickness was sure to bust her revirginized pussy wide open and that had a tendency to bring out the falsetto in a woman.

"Ummmm. Ummmm," her cries were subdued by the force of his tongue against hers. Her short nails dug into his back and as he pushed more of his inches further inside, her eyes watered.

Elias stopped mid-way in, allowing her kitty the opportunity to accept his stretch. But once her heavy panting died down to light whimpers, he hard-pressed the rest of himself inside.

"Ooohhhh!" Blu eye's rolled and her clamp around him grew tighter but that only encouraged him to keep giving her that pressure. She tried to run toward the headboard but he shook his head no.

"Nah, take this dick." He continued snaking his python into her oooh wee.

"Ooow! Oooh! It's too big. Ummmm."

"I know it is, but you gon' take it." He grunted. "Tell me you're gon' take it."

She nodded her head as she continued moaning out his name.

"I want to hear you say it, goddamit!" He stroked a long shot of dick through her canal.

"Ohhhhhh! I'm gon' take it, baby."

"Fuckin' right you will." Elias smoothed over her body as he gave her that work.

His goal was to ensure that her pussy responded to his voice, his touch, his desire and by the time they'd be through, it would be on call for sexual duty.

The sounds of their bodies slapping against each other infused with *ummms, oohs* and *aahhs* created a melody worth listening to on repeat.

And that is exactly what happened off and on over the next five hours.

***

Later that night...

"What you got good fa me?" Kamal asked the minute he answered Fo' Eleven's call, stepping out of the hospital room and into the hallway.

His street informant earned that name because one way or another he'd get the 4-1-1 on anything.

166

"That pussy you been dying to fuck is back in town. I got an address for you to make that creep if you still with it."

"Hell yea! What's up?"

"A'ight, well, you gotta sweet talk the friend first, ya heard me, and from there you good. And to sweeten the pot, I put together a lil' list that's hard to refuse. Meet me at the duck off so I can slide you that."

Unwilling to leave Yuriah's side, Kamal elected Keyz to handle it for him. "Look, my brother gon' be coming through fa me."

"That's straight. I'll holla at that boy when I see 'em, then."

"Give him 'bout twenty, ya heard me. I gotta hit 'em up."

"Straight up."

Kamal hung up the phone and dialed Keyz. When he picked up, he asked, "You still my keeper?"

That was code to alert the other that they were needed for some ill shit without discussing details by phone.

"Yes in fuckin' deed."

"A'ight, meet up with Fo' Eleven at the spot. I'm 'bout to call Munch so he can get down."

"Fuckin' right, alright." Keyz hung up the phone and got ratchet up.

Shaunie tried asking him where he was heading off to but he was already out of the door.

Kamal hit up Munch next. "What up, bro? I got something for you."

"What's good with it?"

After Kamal gave him the run down in a roundabout way, Munch headed out already knowing what to do. It was time to take care of business that was long and overdue.

An hour and a half later…

Munch and Keyz waited outside of the pool hall Fo' Eleven told them Hakeem would be at.

Coffee

Fo' Eleven couldn't provide them information on where G'Corey was laying low these days, but he was able to put them down with someone who did.

"You think this thuggah gon' talk?" Keyz leaned against Munch's car.

"There's only one way to find out." Munch kept his eyes trained on the unsuspecting man from his view through the windows surrounding the building.

"I got short patience, so let's hope this muthafucka do."

"You handled that business?" Munch double checked.

"Already in motion, ya dig."

"So now we wait." Munch kept his focus.

Fifteen minutes later, they saw Hakeem reach for his phone. His wrinkled brow gave the appearance he was suddenly concerned.

He received a text from his baby's mother that read: *10:46 p.m.: Stop what you're doing. I'm losing the baby!!*

"Oh, shit!" Hakeem dropped the pool stick and scrammed for the door. There was no way she was supposed to go into labor, she was only five months pregnant.

Hakeem scrambled to his car but stopped cold in his tracks when he was confronted with a cocked chrome to the dome. He didn't recognize Keyz so he assumed he was about to be robbed.

Instinctually, he turned around to run but was ambushed when he saw Munch standing before him. Now he knew what time of day it was.

"Oh, shit! Magnolia, mannn, I don't got nothing to do with nothing, ya heard me." He automatically began explaining himself because he knew there were only two reasons Munch, who he identified immediately, would be in a man's presence. It was either because he fucked with them or he was there to fuck them over.

"You do now. Walk." Munch was on a short supply of words.

"Fuck!" Hakeem shook his head as he turned to follow Keyz. He knew better than to further protest, a true killer didn't negotiate shit.

Once they made it to the back of the parking lot, Keyz patted him down for weapons but didn't find anything on him.

Munch opened the back door to his car and Keyz pushed him inside of it as he climbed in with him.

Munch sat down behind the wheel and looked out of each window to see who was watching, if any.

"Where is y'all taking me?" His voice went up in pitch.

Still surveying the parking lot, Munch responded. "It's where you taking us. Word is ya mans is in town and you're gonna take us to him."

Hakeem sat up straight and looked up front by Munch and then off to his side at Keyz. "I don't know where that boy at. He hasn't holla'd at me in months. There ain't nothing I can tell ya, for real."

Munch turned around to face him. "Ain't nobody gon' fuck around wit'chu. All I want is G'Corey. You gon' make that happen or not?" He preferred if he would willingly cooperate but the choice was his.

Hakeem stuck to his guns, though. "I don't hear from that boy, you gotta believe me."

Keyz stepped in. "We don't gotta believe shit!" Keyz turned to Munch. "This muthafucka think it's a game. Hold the fuck on."

Keyz got out of the car and headed to the trunk of his vehicle parked next to it. He always made it a point to travel with insurance, a little something to help a man do what the fuck he wanted.

Keyz walked back to the car and slung his pregnant girlfriend into the backseat next to Hakeem. She was petrified. With her eyes, mouth, wrists and ankles bound together, she was unaware of what was going on and who kidnapped her.

Although the soldier rag covering his face ensured she wouldn't identify him, he played it safe so he wouldn't be sorry later, considering he let her live.

Keyz sandwiched her in the middle and closed the door. "You think your baby moms is gonna tell the same story when she got a fo-five cocked at her fuckin' stomach?"

"Mmmmm mmmmm," she begged mercy upon hearing the threat.

Hakeem started sweating bullets. His involvement in G'Corey's scheme was minimal. He begrudgingly agreed to be his eyes and ears but nothing more. He had no intentions on getting his hands dirty.

"Still think shit sweet? Tell us what the fuck we wanna know or I'll stop your bloodline right here and right fuckin' now." Keyz pointed his loaded weapon at her swollen belly.

Her screams were muffled but her appeal to live was heard loud and clear. Hakeem cursed under his breath as he looked at his girl. He was helpless to do anything but cooperate.

"A'ight! A'ight! Just don't shoot her. He's meeting me at my place for one o'clock." Hakeem told them a half-truth.

If G'Corey didn't get a text that read: *I got the hook up,* then he wasn't showing up at all.

Keyz turned the gun from the girl and onto Hakeem but Munch spoke up. "You got us walking into a trap, thuggah?"

"No, mannn, I swear on my mama grave I'm not setting you up." Hakeem pleaded.

"You'll have a plot right next to her come tomorrow if you are." Keyz promised.

Then at gunpoint, Keyz ordered Hakeem to get out of the car and head over to his vehicle so he could lead the way to his place on Felicity with Munch trailing behind. He needed G'Corey to see his vehicle parked in front of his house so he wouldn't become suspicious.

Hakeem was reluctant to be obedient but he had no other choice but to comply. He, his girl and baby's life would be terminated if he rebelled.

Ten minutes later…

"Get out!" Keyz ordered of Hakeem.

Hakeem opened his door to follow the stiff instructions but Keyz had a thought and snatched him by his shirt, pulling him back inside. "Say, bruh, if you do one thing slick, I will kill yo hoe and anything else you love before midnight."

"I ain't fuckin' around."

Keyz let him go. "Bet' not be."

Meanwhile, Munch had removed the tape from around the girl's ankles so she could walk, leaving her wrists bound together behind her back and her eyes covered. He walked her from around the corner where he had parked and met up with Keyz.

Munch passed the girl to his partner and then shoved Hakeem toward his house. Hakeem looked back at his boo, remorsefully. She'd always tell him the company he kept would get him caught up. He just now realized she was right.

Hakeem led the way Munch was to shadow while Keyz stayed behind waiting for clearance.

Once inside with a gun trained at his back, Munch had him turn every light on while checking each room and closet. After he verified the house was indeed empty, he walked him back up front and signaled Keyz to come inside.

Keyz entered into the living room and pushed his woman into his arms. "Y'all muthafucka have a seat."

Hakeem caught her as she was shoved toward him, kissing her sweaty temple as he held her tightly to stop her from shaking so much.

"What's the play? How were you to reach him and let him know it's a go?" Munch knew the paranoid type would never just come off of GP, they would make sure the coast was cleared before they'd show up.

"There is no play. He's just gonna show up." Hakeem was counting on G'Corey showing up with guns blazing, since he wasn't following the plan and would assume something went awry. Or he hoped they'd see him as a non-threat and just let him go.

"This muthafucka lyin'!" Keyz caught the slight stutter in his voice.

Munch looked at the time. It was 11:20 p.m., a long ways from 1 a.m., but his predator instinct was willing to wait on its prey. "We gon' play it how it go. You stay in here with them and I'ma be outside."

Keyz nodded his head upward once and took his seat directly across from them, with his finger on the trigger.

171

Coffee

A quarter after one…

Munch had been perched alongside Hakeem's house, waiting on G'Corey to walk through the gate, so he could blast him back onto the sidewalk with his AK-47 but there was no sign of him.

Munch angrily took flight up the porch steps, two at a time, before he stormed through the door and rushed up on Hakeem with his chopper pointed to his chest. "Where the fuck is he?"

Keyz closed the door but stood watch by the window.

Hakeem panicked and threw his hands up. "I—I don't know. He—he was been supposed to be here. Magnolia, bruh, I don't got no beef with y'all and I don't got shit to do with whatever squabble y'all got, mannn. Just let me and my girl go, please."

"If he was supposed to show up and he didn't that only tells me whatever the fuck you *didn't* do gave him a head's up. That wasn't smart." Munch detested his intelligence being insulted.

"I should blow yo muthafuckin' brains out since you ain't using that muthafucka," Keyz said from the other side of the room.

Hakeem signed the shape of a cross in front of his body. "I swear to God I don't know what happened."

"Silly sucka. You loyal to the wrong muthafucka." Munch lowered his weapon and stepped away.

"What we gon' do with him?" Keyz walked over toward him, resting his piece between his eyes.

"I aint' gon' say nothin', mannn." Hakeem's eyes went cross, looking at the gun pressed at the center of his forehead as he petitioned for his life.

"That's yo call. He ain't who I want." It wasn't Munch's method of operation to randomly kill a man to send a message to another.

But that wasn't the principal Keyz lived by. His M.O. was much different: *A friend of a foe is a foe and he gotta go.*

Munch walked out of the house and onto the porch, leaving Keyz to whichever decision he chose. He looked down the dimly lit street both ways. But nothing was moving outside of the typical night crawlers: junkies, hoodrats and hoodlums.

172

Seconds later, a single shot was heard, the thud of a body dropping and then the muffled screams of a frightened woman.

Keyz stepped over to her and knocked her out cold with the butt of his gun to shut her the fuck up, sparing her life on the strength that she wasn't involved. He'd dangle a man's bitch in his face as bait but he wouldn't kill an innocent female, not unless he had to.

He stepped out of the house, standing next to Munch with his heater at his side. "This was a bust, so now what?"

"Stay alert and keep that thang ready but for now, let's get the fuck from 'round here," Munch said as they headed out.

Coffee

Chapter 21

The next day…
Thanksgiving Day

Samiyah was sitting in the living room, changing her daughter's diaper when she heard her front door opening. She knew it was Gerran, so she didn't bother looking in his direction. *Why is he here?* she thought. All he was going to do was hurl insults her way and she wasn't up for the abuse.

Between the emotional visit with Minnie last night and her hormones being all over the place, she didn't want to deal with any of his mistreatment.

Instead of bypassing her and going about his business, Gerran surprisingly took a seat across from her. He silently stared for a time, watching her every move.

She glanced in his direction but then continued the task of getting Lil' Acacia freshened up.

She rolled her eyes because the mere sight of him was disgusting. He had said a mouthful yesterday so unless he was coming with an apology, she didn't understand what else was left to say.

Gerran noticed both Samiyah and the baby were dressed and set to go out. He could have asked her where she was going and she could have responded *her mother's*. She agreed to go to her parent's home for the holidays so she wouldn't have to spend Thanksgiving alone and if Minnie were up for a visit, she'd drop her off a plate afterwards.

Instead, he allowed his imagination to run rampant with thoughts of how she was going to spend her day disrespecting his last name, sleeping with Elias no doubt.

A minute or so passed and Gerran asked, "I'm here. You're not gonna say anything?" His face nor tone was welcoming.

"It's not like I invited you over, so you can say what you came to say." She cradled her baby in her arms.

Gerran took her statement offensively, although she didn't mean it that way. But he wanted to fight by any means, so it wouldn't have mattered what she said.

"Oh, so I need an invitation? This not my home no more?"

Samiyah smacked her lips and looked at him with one eye squinted lower than the other. "I don't know why you're doing this because you care nothing about what happening over here. You made that painfully clear over these last two weeks with your absence. And for the record, this is *not* your home so don't front like you want it to be. But it is still your house."

Gerran nodded his head, looking around the place. "Well, you just made my decision that much easier."

"And what do you mean by that?" Samiyah was sure she didn't really want to know but she asked anyway.

Gerran skipped over her question and asked one of his own. "I see you're about to tramp off somewhere. Heading over to Eli's for some family time and mid-day fuc—"

Samiyah shot up to her feet and covered her daughter's ear. "Don't you dare be disrespectful and curse around my baby."

Realizing his gloves were off, she needed to put her daughter in her room, away from Gerran's toxin. She walked Lil' Acacia upstairs and placed her in her crib. After she grabbed the baby monitor, she closed her door and headed downstairs.

As she descended down the staircase, she saw her front door was left wide open. She reached the doorway and looked out into her driveway only to see Gerran closing the door to a U-Haul truck he rented, approaching the house with a handful of garment bags.

"You mind grabbing a few of those empty boxes from over there?" Samiyah gave him an angry glare. "I didn't think so."

Gerran walked past her and headed upstairs. Samiyah followed behind him into their bedroom. With the way things had been going between them, she was glad he was giving her space. But she didn't appreciate his audacity to come over under the pretenses that he wanted to talk.

"You are a real piece of work, Gerran. I didn't make shit easy for you. You had plans to leave all along." Samiyah watched him pull his clothes from out of the closet and place them into each bag.

Gerran went mute, choosing not to respond only to purposely agitate the situation. It was only fair, in his mind, that he cause her the same agony he felt every minute of every day. After all, he forgave her once for cheating on him but there was no way he was going to excuse the proof of it. She deserved his lack of understanding.

Samiyah was in the middle of asking yet another question when his phone started ringing. He smiled at the screen before he pressed the talk button.

"No the hell you didn't!" Samiyah was awed by his asshole behavior.

"What up, A?—Aww, nothing much. Just handling that business I told you about earlier.—Oh, I'm straight, ya heard me.—I don't know yet…"

Samiyah was flabbergasted at how he ignored her but the moment his hired help called, he was casually talking like it wasn't a thing, like they weren't in the middle of something important.

Samiyah walked up on him and snatched the phone from his ear and placed it to hers. She heard Audra giggling and then say, "I'll see you lat—" She hung the phone up and hummed it at him.

Gerran dodged it, barely. "What the hell is your problem?"

"You're fucking her, aren't you?" Samiyah yelled so loud her voice cracked.

He laughed but she saw nothing funny. As messed up as their marriage was, she was still his wife.

"What if I am? You're fucking Elias." Gerran accused.

Samiyah was so inflamed by his insinuation she could have wrung his neck. "Uurgghh! No, I'm—You know what, I want you to get the fuck out. Take everything you need because whatever the hell you leave behind will get trashed."

There was nothing left to say. Gerran had no good intentions. So she stormed out of the room and flew down the steps, retreating to the guest bedroom. She was ready for him to be gone.

Two hours later...

Gerran was at her door, wiggling the knob, only to find it locked. He knocked. "Open up."

"No thank you. Just go."

"Come on, Samiyah. I really gotta holla at you and then I'll bounce."

Samiyah rolled her eyes because she could forgo hearing whatever his holla consisted of, but she opened the door anyway. "What?" Her eyes were puffy.

For one brief moment, Gerran felt a twinge of regret. Seeing Samiyah so upset and fragile made him second guess being so venomous. After all, she was there when all the chips were down. And when he didn't have two nickels to rub together, she still managed to make him feel ten feet tall.

She truly was everything *except* faithful and that slice of reality brought out his fangs.

"Before I go, you should know that you're cut off, from everything." He motioned his hand to slice at his throat.

Samiyah gasped. "Wow! Really?"

"But lucky for you, though, I'm still gon' pay the mortgage because like you said earlier, this is still *my* house. But be clear on this, I ain't paying shit else. And before you think about giving me a *woe is me I'm your wife* speech, let Eli or whatever other sap thuggah you fuckin' fund you."

It took a second for his cruelty to register. Samiyah was completely blown away by the stranger standing before her. She felt weakened by his low blow but then she toughened up.

"I won't beg your wicked ass to change your mind but let me say that I am so fuckin' disgusted with you. Acacia isn't your child? You're mad? I get that. But how in the fuck could you be so damn heartless toward me while I'm carryin' your child?"

The chance that she was pregnant with his baby was there but his belief in the paternity of Lil' Acacia being his earned him nothing but heartbreak, so he refused to accept it this time around.

He hunched his shoulders. "You know what they say: *Mama's baby, daddy's maybe.*"

No words, at least not from her, could penetrate his thick skull to get him to see beyond his resentment and if he was trying to make her despise him, he succeeded.

"I fuckin' hate you!" Tears poured from her eyes and her voice quaked.

Gerran looked as though he was unaffected. "And I don't fuckin' care that you do." With the last of his things in hand, he stepped.

Samiyah was so furious, she slammed the door behind him. He crossed a line that there was no coming back from.

***

"Knock, knock," BG said as he opened the door, stepping into Yuriah's room with Munch right behind him.

"What's happening, whoa?" Kamal stood up to dap him and then Munch.

"Nothing much, ya heard me. We just swervin' through. You know how we do." BG headed over to Minnie, handing her a vase of red roses.

"Thank you." She stood up to hug him. "Yuri's going to appreciate this."

"Nah, that's for you, ya heard me." BG corrected.

"Me?" Minnie found him charming to say he was just a kid.

"You deserve a smile, ya dig." BG smirked and his set of dimples caused his cheeks to cave in a little.

"Watch that boy wake up and put yo ass to sleep, pushin' up on his girl." Kamal clowned BG's Casanova way.

BG turned around to face Kamal. "I wish he would. He been down two and half nah. He need to get on up."

BG turned back toward Minnie. "I also brought you a plate. I don't know what all you eat but I put everything on it, ya heard me. My teedy made turkey, ham, stuffin', potato salad, it's all in there."

"You're too sweet." Minnie peeked underneath the aluminum foil.

"You're fam. Gotta look out fa ya."

"Then where my plate?" Kamal threw his hands up in the air as if to say, *What's up?*

"What I look like bringin' another man dinner? I don't rock like that!" BG clowned.

"Oh? That's what's up. I'ma remember that when yo ass pull up a seat to my table," Kamal pointed his way.

BG waved him off. "Shenae loves me. You gots no control over that."

While BG and Kamal exchanged words, Munch walked over to Minnie and hugged her. "How you holdin'?"

"I'm hopeful and that's where my strength is."

"That's what's up. You gotta stay prayed up, ya heard me." Munch then grabbed his little brother by the shoulder. "Keep Minnie company while I holla at Mal."

"A'ight," he responded.

Munch nodded for Kamal to step out with him. Kamal pretty much figured they needed to have a private talk about last night since he didn't receive the *7/11* text. No text meant they crapped out.

They chatted about nothing serious on their walk outside. However, once they found a sequestered place to talk, Munch gave him the details of last night.

A few minutes later, after he broke everything down to him, Kamal only had one question since everything else was understood.

"Is the girl still alive?"

"Yea, she is." Munch shook his head *yes*.

That eased his conscious. Kamal was a firm believer of keeping women and children out of men's business and that included extorting or using them for information.

If he had known Fo' Eleven's art of persuasion included taunting Hakeem by using his girl as inducement, he wouldn't have allowed that piece of info through.

Love Knows No Boundaries III
Pandora's Box

With Kamal being a family man, he couldn't afford the price of karma collecting off of Shenae or his children. So when Fo' Eleven called him earlier today and told him he had a couple of thug misses on the same tier as G'Corey's baby's mother, Tracie, who were guaranteed to get her to talk and an address on his mother, Dee, Kamal declined the intel and told him to bring him something else.

"A'ight, cool. Well, this shit been goin' on too fuckin' long and dude ain't that smart. So, let's plug into all our underground channels and put a heavier hunt on his ass. That means we search Saint Rose, Mandeville, Laplace, Thibodaux, Houma or any city within a fifty mile radius because he ain't that far." Kamal began mapping out a strategy.

"I'm with you on that. I'm 'bout to get on the horn with Hollywood right nah and see what he got for me."

"That's a bet."

The men shook on it and headed back upstairs.

Three a.m. in the morning…

The hospital room was dimly lit and quiet with the exception of what little noises that could be heard from the traffic in the hallway. Kamal was sleeping on the other side of the room and Minnie was asleep in her usual spot, just a few feet away from Yuriah's bed.

"Minnie?"

She stirred out of her sleep effortlessly. She'd been sleeping light these days.

Minnie was unsure if she heard her name but nonetheless looked over to Kamal to respond to his calling. She noticed he was asleep.

"Mmm," she groaned. *I need to get more rest,* she thought.

Paying it no mind, she laid back down. She closed her eyes, only to open them again. She heard her name a second time.

She was tired but not delirious, so this go around she got up and walked over to Kamal.

"Kamal?" She semi-whispered his name as she stood over him but he didn't budge.

Why in the heavens would he sleep talk her name? She didn't know but she would be sure to ask him come morning.

As she headed back to her uncomfortable spot, she glanced at her husband and then jumped back. She sucked in a small amount of air in one quick breath, forgetting to breathe afterwards.

Minnie backed up slowly and back over to Kamal. She was in a state of shock.

"Kamal!" She bluntly called his name, waking him up fully.

"Huh? What's wrong?" He shot up to his feet, looked at her curiously before following the direction of her pointed finger.

She then rushed over to his bed to confirm her eyes were not playing tricks on her.

They weren't.

"Call the doctors," she all but screamed. "Yuriah is out of his coma!"

Chapter 22

Four weeks later...
A few days before Christmas

Minnie woke up in a panic when she didn't see Yuriah lying next to her in bed.

"Yuri, baby!" She threw the covers back and went searching through the house. "Yuriah!" She called again, only to discover him in the kitchen.

He looked over his shoulder when he heard her enter. "Good morning, Nervine." He kissed her when she walked up on him.

"I got your nervous. Why didn't you wake me up to tell me you were hungry?" She tried taking the spatula from him so she could finish cooking but he wouldn't allow her.

"That's because I'm not hungry. Now, go sit down and let me do something nice for you."

"Baby, you shouldn't be doing this, though."

"Says who? Because according to my doctor he returned me to full activity and cleared me off of bed rest a couple of days ago. But you, my overprotective MD, was there to know that for yourself."

"True, but I can still take care of everything for you. Home health is what I do, you know?"

"I feel you, but making my very attentive wife breakfast is what I'm doing today. Now, go have a seat." He directed her over to the kitchen table.

His physician assured Minnie that Yuriah was as healthy as a horse. All of his outpatient physical exams and repeated X-Ray screens proved it to be so.

Despite knowing that, Minnie couldn't help but be paranoid. She spent so many weeks on edge, she became accustomed to it. She thought to rebut him anyway but placed a finger over her lips and sat down like he said.

He wore a smile of approval as he plated her breakfast. He was happy to be doing something other than laying up all day. And for him, there was no better way of celebrating life than to cater to the reason he found a will to live.

Minnie sat back and watched him work magic over the stove. He moved about like nothing traumatic happened to him, to them. She didn't want to sour the makings of such a sweet day, but she found her thoughts too troubling to contain.

On one end, she was beyond ecstatic to see him so full of life and energetic and then on the other, she was fearful that it could all be taken away from her, for good this time.

Yuriah headed toward Minnie sporting a smile that only she could elicit. He placed her spinach omelet, toast and hash before her and then kissed the top of her head. "Breakfast is served."

Minnie looked up at him smiling, but it was plastic.

He detected it and questioned it. "What's up, bae?"

She fumbled her words, unsure of how to ask them. "Baby, can I have a really hard talk with you? I have been uneasy lately."

"You don't have to set me up for a conversation. If you have something on your mind, let it off."

"I'm going to just get straight to the point, then. What's going to happen to G'Corey? Is there going to be some kind of battle between you two? I mean he tried taking your life. What if he tries again? I'm scared to lose you."

"Baby, I'm Teflon. The doctors ain't tell you?" He tried taking a light approach to a heavy subject.

"Yuri, I'm being for real. I don't know what got into him. I didn't think he was capable of being so evil but no one knows where he is and when I asked Munch and Kamal what was going on, they made it seem as if it was nothing to stress about. But I am stressed."

If I ain't trippin', neither should you." He grabbed her by her chin. "Look me in my face. I ain't got no worries."

"I know but—"

"Mouse, some things are best left unsaid because once they're spoken you won't be able to get it out of your mind. You're concerned about him coming for me again and I love you for that. But know that he can't do nothing to me that I can't do to him first."

"What does that—"

"Curiosity kills the cat, so trust me enough to know when to stop asking questions, a'ight, love? I'm not goin' nowhere and I'm gon' keep you safe."

Minnie nodded her head. The looming thought of G'Corey resurfacing didn't just disappear but she wasn't going to allow it to further contaminate their beautiful morning. Besides, she always trusted him so there was no reason to go against him now.

She leaned over to him and kissed his lips. Changing the subject, she stood up to her feet. "It needs to feel like Christmas up in here."

She headed over to the counter where the remote control was. Cutting on the TV, she found the music station on Cox that played continuous holiday music. Donny Hathaway's *This Christmas* was playing.

"Now what are the chances my favorite song would be on? It's a sign, bae. Get up." She waved her hands for him to come where she was.

"Unh unh, I don't dance." Yuriah smiled.

Come on, bae. Be merry with me." She started moving from side to side.

He shook his head *no* but ended up standing to his feet when she gently tugged for him to get up. Yuriah stood there looking at her sing along into the cooking spoon, handing him a ladle to use as his own mic.

It was only moments before he too got swept up in the joy his other half was creating. And with a two-step of his own, the couple had their first official dance as husband and wife.

***

Man Man was in the living room watching a marathon of Hey Arnold and staying clear of G'Corey. His mother wasn't there to protect him and he had enough run ins with his older cousin to know better than to play with him.

Coffee

G'Corey stepped outside onto the porch to smoke, leaving the door open but shutting the screen door so he could keep an eye on Bad Ass.

He had a lot on his mind.

As he waited on a phone call, he leaned over the banister and allowed his thoughts to settle on the last conversation he had with Black.

"Say, bruh, you heard from Hakeem? I was supposed to catch up with the boy the other day but he been dodging my calls."

"That boy ain't dodging nothing, ya heard me. He was touched a couple of days ago," Black informed him.

"Fuck no! Hell no! How he die?" G'Corey couldn't wrap his head around that.

"One to the dome."

"Mannn, that boy didn't live that life. What was the motive? Was he robbed or something?" G'Corey was trying to piece how and why his people was did in.

"Nah, word circulating that Munch knocked him off. Heard that shit was over you, too."

"What?" was all G'Corey could say while suspended in a state of stupor.

"His girl was there when it happened but he left her alive. And oh, yea, just so you know, Yuriah ain't dead, either. He's in a coma, but he's still alive."

He and Hakeem didn't grow up shooting marbles together but the five years he'd known him, he'd been solid.

He didn't deserve that shit and his baby moms don't deserve that pain, but I know how to return favors, Munch, he thought.

And as for Yuriah, if he managed to walk out of the hospital, he'd see to it that he extinguish his chances to survive their next encounter.

Then G'Corey's phone rang. It was Skittles. He took a long drag from his Black & Mild and then answered, "What up?"

186

She went in the moment she heard him. "I did what he hell you asked. I put on my *Betty Do Right* voice and that shit got me nowhere. What the fuck you had me come down here if the hoe wasn't gonna put me on payroll?"

"Was Minnie there? What all happened?"

"Shit happened. And fuck no, Minnie wasn't there. Some Alveka, Alverda or whatever the fuck her name is was the only one there talkin' 'bout they're not hiring."

"A'ight, that's cool."

When the time was right, G'Corey was going to open up a position himself.

"Hoe, no the fuck that's not cool, you ole stank mouth bitch! Why you had me dye my hair this bland ass black when you knew this bitch wasn't going to hire me?" Skittles was fuming, frowning at herself in the rearview mirror of her car.

"You must listen through your asshole. I didn't say shit about you getting a job. I said I needed you to look the part so they would want to hire you."

"So, let me get this straight. I did all this bullshit and they not gon' hire me?"

"No. You don't even want a fuckin' job, so why you trippin'? Besides, I got my reasons."

You got your reasons? "Bitch, square the fuck up when I get home. It took Charmin three months to get my rainbow effect on point and now, thanks to you, I'm lookin' hit all because you said I had to look hirable. You'sa plungee hoe. I swear to God!"

"Shut the fuck up with that stupid shit or get gulfed in your mouth on sight. If having Kool-Aid hair what you're worried about, I'll have your dumb ass lookin' like a crayon again."

"No, hoe. A mermaid, you cross-eyed ug-ga-lay bitch! And you betta." There was so much bass in her voice that had she not hung up on him, he would have definitely hung up on her.

Even though Skittles had a way of tap-dancing on his nerves, he was so happy his plan was in motion he could kiss her.

He needed to do something different and what his cousin just put in motion was that something.

Before now, G'Corey sent a bouquet of red roses, her favorite, to her office along with a note that had a love song dedicated to her every Friday for the past month.

Alverda discarded them without mentioning it to Minnie but there was no way for him to know if she was in receipt of any of it. He had a gut feeling Alverda would block but that didn't stop him. He couldn't stop showing his effort, just in case Minnie was there to intercept them.

However, he had a deadline in his mind as to how long he'd tiptoe around the situation. He wanted to hear her voice, to see her, for her to know that he wasn't going to give up on them. He couldn't. He needed her too much.

He was anxious to get his girl back and square business up on behalf of himself and now Hakeem. But he knew they were expecting him to make a move and his steps were not to be calculated.

All he had to do was keep reminding himself that *slow and steady wins the race.*

***

Elias and Blu were in the food court at The Mall at Lakeside sharing a Chinese plate. They had a long day of shopping because Eli wanted to see Peaches with it all. If it was manufactured for a girl, he was buying it.

He couldn't help the urge to spoil her. She was the sweetest baby he ever laid eyes on. And the more time that passed was the more accepting Eli was of his new role.

He developed the same magic touch both Blu and Samiyah had when it came to putting her to sleep and he just about perfected changing her diaper without her poopie escaping from the sides.

Blu was feeding him a piece of beef and broccoli when her text alert went off. She checked it. It was a message from her mom asking what time they were coming over to the house.

"Bae, this is my mom. She wants to know what time we're going to pass over on Christmas Eve."

"To do what?"

"To spend the night. It's gonna be soooo fun. We watch movies, play games and eat of course. Then come morning, we open gifts while we're sipping on something nice and cooking the rest of what will be dinner."

Elias wasn't trying to be uncomfortable in the same house as La'Tasha. But that wasn't his main reason for his lack of interest in going.

"Boo, I told you I wanted to celebrate Christmas with my daughter. It's gon' be her first." Elias grinned at the thought of seeing her adorableness in the red and white dress he picked out by himself.

"For how long?" Her smile went south.

He shrugged his shoulders. "I don't know, but we gon' kick it up until you go by your peoples and then when you leave from by them the next day, we'll get up and do our own thing." Eli felt that was a good compromise.

"You're not gonna come by my family's house at all? You're going to be busy the whole day? She's only four months. It's not like she'll remember you being there for an hour or at all." Her aggravation reared its ugly head.

Elias leaned back and uglied his face. She was talking reckless. "She don't have to remember. I will! What the hell is wrong with you? I know you not jealous?"

She was beginning to feel like the side chick when it came to Peaches and her mama because over the last few weeks the world stopped for them, but she wasn't going to put it to him like that just in the event she was overreacting.

"No, I'm not jealous. But I'm concerned with how much time you're spending over there with them."

"I'm *not* spending time with them. I'm spending time with Peaches."

"But Samiyah is always in the picture."

"Is that what this is about? Samiyah? She's her mother. Where else is Peaches supposed to be?"

"You know what I'm saying."

"No, I don't 'cause you not making sense to me. What you thought? I was gon' be a weekend dad or some shit? I thought you was on board with this."

"I am but it just seems like we never get a moment to ourselves no more."

"We have a moment to ourselves right now but look how you wanna spend it."

The more Blu tried explaining her points were the crazier she sounded, even to herself. Maybe it was her imagination, but she wasn't certain if Samiyah was using the baby to get closer to her guy. She had no proof of it but she couldn't understand why else he felt a need to put her on a backburner just to see a child who slept most of the visit.

With her whole heart, she wanted him to spend time with his baby but as selfish as her thoughts were, she wondered, *Did it have to be every single day?*

"Baby, let's go to the movies."
"We gon' hafta reschedule because I got Peaches tonight."

"Baby, I'm horny. Let's make love?"
"Damn, that's tempting, but you gon' hafta keep it hot for me. I promised I'd pick up Peaches' medicine and drop it off in twenty minutes.

"Baby, come over to my place."
"In a second, boo. Let me finish feeding—"
"Let me guess. Peaches."

Blu decided against speaking her mind because she didn't want to be made the villain. "Never mind."

Eli was no longer hungry. "Pack up your food and let's go."

"Why?"

"I'm not feelin' your attitude."

"I can't voice my feelings?"

190

"Not about no dumb shit like that. Look, boo, I have a kid now. And you chose to stay with me so that means you're gonna have to make some adjustments to your thinking."

"My feelings are valid, even if you don't understand them."

"Well, get out your feelings for a minute and let me explain something to you. I done fucked a plenty women with daddy issues. They didn't get what they needed from him so a dude like me was able to swoop in and handle my business without so much as buying her a burger. So, I ain't missin' nothing when it comes to her 'cause I need to be the first man to love her enough, so no smooth talking, slick cat can get up in her head and then her drawers. You, yourself, are a daddy's girl, so how you don't understand my position?" He stood up and collected all of their shopping bags. He was ready to drop her off at her house.

Every player felt God paid them back for their mistreatment of women by giving them precious little girls. So, there was no such thing as too much of anything when it came to his daughter. He wasn't going to let Peaches pay for the sins of her father.

Blu, on the other hand, still felt entitled to her feelings but she didn't have an argument after hearing him put it that way. And moreover, he was right. Her family came packaged under one roof so it made it normal and expected for her daddy to be present for everything. She couldn't expect less of Elias when it came to his own.

She reached for his hand to motion him to have a seat. "Sit back down. I do get it, Eli, and I don't want you thinking I'm trying to block you. I was just thinking selfishly. It's not like we won't spend both days together, so there was no need for me to go there. Do you accept my apology?"

"You good," he answered casually.

Blu knew he was heated because he always switched to his non-chalant mode when he was. And since he didn't want to sit down, she stood up and whispered in his ear. "Can I show you how good I really am? You know to make up for being so bad." He didn't bat a lash. "I'll do the disappearing trick you like so much."

That got him to look her way.

Coffee

"You dirty, yea." Eli shook his head at her. She knew how much he immensely enjoyed seeing his shit in her mouth balls deep.

"Well?"

"Well, come the hell on and show me what that mouth do." Eli nodded his head in the direction she was to walk.

Blu didn't bother wrapping up the food. She just dumped it and walked with her boo, thinking how she should be praising him for being the kind of father she would want for her own.

That put a smile on her face and she was all too anxious to put one on his the moment they got home.

Chapter 23

Two weeks later...

It was the middle of January and the city was experiencing the coldest day since winter began. However, that didn't stop G'Corey from carrying out his mission, for today was the day.

G'Corey had spent enough time becoming familiar with the routine of Angel Heart Homecare Service to know the ins and outs, the comings and goings.

And as suspected, Minnie didn't physically go into the office on any of the days he had staked out the place. With Alverda, her trusted field supervisor, coming in every morning at 5 a.m. and leaving every evening at 5 p.m., it wasn't necessary for her to do so.

The office only needed to be manned by one person to handle potential clients or the employees, who'd come in every Friday to collect their weekly paychecks.

This Friday was no different.

Bonita pulled up in front of the building for 6 a. m., parking alongside the curb as she always would.

"Right on time," G'Corey said under his breath.

The skies were robed in darkness, providing him the added cover he needed to go about his mischief undetected.

As she was reaching into her backseat, grabbing her walking stick to deter strays that were often out and about, G'Corey quickly studied both directions of the quiet, one-way street before coming out of the bushes and running up on her. He slapped his gloved hand over her mouth so she couldn't scream.

Bonita's eyes bulged out of her head when she felt the stronghold yank her from her vehicle at her waist. She began moving about wildly, trying to stomp his feet or anything that would get him to release her. Then with the thick stick she had in her hand, she swung it forcefully over her shoulder, connecting it against his face.

The whap against his eye caused his lid to balloon. Nonetheless, he released his hand from her mouth and snatched the weapon out of her hand, throwing it down.

"Hel—" She attempted to yelp but was cut short with a punch to the side of the head.

She fell to the ground woozily. She tried to call out for help again, but G'Corey kicked her so hard in the face her mouth started pouring blood like a running faucet.

Bonita clawed for his leg but he stomped her hand, rendering it useless just like her ability to fight back.

Woof! Woof! Woof!

G'Corey looked up and spotted a mangy dog barking huskily at him, putting a stop to his vicious attack.

It was time to leave before someone saw what happened. He spun around in a circle looking for the stick he threw down and the purse she had on her shoulder. He managed to find them both and jumped into her car.

Alverda opened the door and peeked her head out. Mutt, as she named him, needed to be told to stop or he'd keep woofing. She was surprised Bonita didn't do it, but she'd handle it. He was too loud to ignore.

"Quit your yapping, Mutt!" Alverda sharply told him but unlike any other morning, it didn't work. She went back to her desk and grabbed her coat from off of her chair to put it on and go out to shoo him away personally.

G'Corey hustled to search through her junky hobo-sized purse for the keys. His nerves were getting the best of him because the ruckus from his relentless barking was going to draw attention his way.

"Shut the fuck up, stupid dog!" he said with his nose buried into Bonita's purse.

Alverda reopened the door and started walking to her employee's car, not paying attention to the driver. "Shut up, Mutt. Nita, get your dog," she said the closer she got up on her car.

G'Corey looked to his right and saw the image of who he knew to be Alverda approaching his way. He pulled his gun off of his waist. If he didn't find her ignition starter and pull off soon, he would have to kill Alverda because she knew who he was, easily.

"Go on somewhere. Get!" She persuaded Mutt to trot off. Alverda stopped at her passenger side, tapping on the window and then pulling on the handle. The second the door opened, Alverda said, "Nita, what are—Aaahhhhh!" She jumped back and clutched her chest. She was taken by surprise when the car sped off abruptly.

She watched her car zoom away in wonderment. She couldn't believe Bonita would do something like that. Then she looked off to the side at what appeared to be someone laying on the ground and realized Bonita didn't drive off at all. That was her sprawled out before her.

"Nittttaaaa!" Alverda cried out as she rushed over to her.

***

Minnie was sleeping comfortably in the nook of Yuriah's arm when she heard her business phone ringing. She opened one eye and saw 6:17 a.m. flash across her digital clock. She knew it was Alverda, she'd be the only one calling at that time.

I'll call her back in an hour.

Minnie had been up with Yuri all night and she was bushed. But when Alverda called her right back, she knew something had to be wrong. She didn't call back to back, ever.

Minnie cleared the sleep from her voice. "Good morning."

Alverda's anger could be heard through her words. "It's not a good morning. Bonita was car jacked and beat up real bad."

"What?" Minnie shrieked her one word reply so loudly Yuriah immediately got up from his sleep.

"Baby, what's wrong?" He turned on the lamp to illuminate the dark room.

Minnie pulled the covers off of her, bolting out of bed. "My worker just got assaulted," she addressed Yuriah. Turning her attention back to Alverda, she asked, "Where are you and where are they taking her?"

"I'm with her in the ambulance and we're on our way to West Jefferson."

"I'll meet you up there." Minnie snapped her phone shut and tossed it on the bed.

She began stripping out of her pajamas and into regular clothes. Looking over her shoulder, she saw Yuriah doing the same.

***

Early morning traffic jams coming from Mid-City and crossing over into the Westbank of New Orleans had them arriving at the hospital thirty minutes past the usual half an hour drive it would take normally.

"You mentioned a man stole her car? What type of wheels was she riding?"

"Ummm, a Nissan Maxima. Why?" Minnie was looking for a parking space as she questioned him nervously.

"Just curious to know, baby." Yuriah scanned the lot with the eye of a hawk, looking for anyone that looked like G'Corey because his street sensibility told him he may have had something to do with it because he knew a set up when he saw one.

In the game of Chess, a pawn was easily scarified to get to the queen and ultimately the king. Yuriah quickly surmised it wasn't a random robbery. Off top, no dude, not even a crack fiend, would seek to take that type of vehicle off of anybody's hands. Then the neighborhood where Minnie's office front was located sat on an isolated road where the only people who walked or drove down that strip had purpose to do so.

They parked, exited Yuriah's truck and headed into the lobby of the emergency room.

A police officer was taking Alverda's statement when Minnie saw her. After the cop concluded his questions, she walked over to Minnie and Yuriah and told them what little she knew.

Hours later…

196

Love Knows No Boundaries III
Pandora's Box

The nurse advised that only two people were allowed to go in to see Bonita.

"Go ahead. Y'all check on her. I'll wait right here." Yuriah kissed Minnie's forehead.

When she disappeared behind the curtain, Yuriah reached into his jacket and pulled out his phone. He called Kamal and from there he'd put Munch in the know.

Kamal picked up on the fourth ring. "What up, bro?"

Yuriah spoke on low volume. "I'm not sure, bruh, but I believe G'Corey made a play."

"Straight up?"

"Yea, straight up. Look, we gon' meet up and talk about this fuck shit later but I'm at West Jeff right now with Minnie, checking on her people. Anyway, I need you to do me a solid."

"Anything."

"Get on the horn with a top notch security company. Have them set up in and outdoor surveillance cameras over at Minnie's building. I want the type of shit the CIA use and I don't care how much money it takes to make it happen. I want it done today! Can you handle that?"

"This me. Where the keys to her spot?"

"At my crib, in one of my top drawers. It'll be the only set in there."

"A'ight, dawg, I'll catch up wit'chu later."

Yuriah hung up the phone and then called his little cousin, Munch. He was going to need him for something else.

Meanwhile, Minnie was doing her best not to cry. Bonita's face was badly bruised and her lips were so swollen she couldn't open her mouth to speak.

Minnie had to turn away from her for a moment so Bonita couldn't detect how horrible of a beating she sustained from the astonishment screaming from the look in Minnie's eyes.

The nurse informed them that she had two broken ribs and a fractured hand but she didn't prep them for the visual effect of the awful assault.

197

Minnie and Alverda stood on the same side of her bed, wearing smiles to mask their concern.

"The nurse said you're under a lot of medications, so we won't stay long. We just wanted to let you know we are here for you, okay?" Minnie squeezed her leg gently.

Bonita lightly nodded and then closed her eyes.

The ladies stepped off to the side and had a conversation.

Minnie placed a hand on her hip and head. "I can't believe this. I hope they catch whoever did this."

"I wish I would have caught him." Alverda looked over at the battered girl. "You don't do no stuff like that to no woman."

Minnie blew out hard. "Not to sound callous but what are we going to do about her clients?"

"About that. I already called Jessica and she'll do a double to cover both her and Bonita's shift today but how long she can do that, I don't know." Alverda looked at the schedule for the week from her phone.

"I can always fill in to compensate for being short staffed."

"Well, you know I have two applications on file from a couple of weeks ago. Both ladies passed the preliminary phase. I can check their references and then push them through to you for an interview."

"That sounds good. You can do their background check once I give the thumbs up on the candidates. And if all pans out, we can have either one on schedule by the end of next week. Call them today and let's set something up for tomorrow afternoon. Have them meet me at La' Madeline's on St. Charles for a lunch/interview."

"Okay, I'll set up the exact time and text it to you as well as fax you their resumes. Is there anything else?"

"No, I believe we have things covered."

Minutes later, Bonita's mother came and the nurse advised that one of them had to leave.

"We'll both go," Minnie told her before turning back toward Bonita. "I'll check on you tomorrow."

The ladies stepped out and walked over to Yuriah who stood to his feet when he saw them. "How is she?"

Minnie shook her head. "She looks bad but she'll be okay in time." Minnie dropped her head, grabbing the bridge of her nose and then looked back up at him. "Baby, Alverda is going to need a ride to the office to pick up her car. I'm going to close the office today."

"You don't have to do that, Minnie. I'm going to stay my shift."

"Alverda, you don't have to do that. Are you sure?" Considering what happened, she had to ask.

"I carry mace, a hunter's knife and a .22 everywhere I go. I will blind, stab and shoot me a m'fer before I let them stop what I do. I have three children to feed. But don't you worry. I'll be careful, for sure, but mama didn't raise no punk."

Yuriah liked her guts. "Well, in that case, you'll be there when my friend, Kamal, arrives with a security team to install some cameras."

"Yes, I'll be there, Mr. Leblanc."

"Let's get going." Yuriah escorted the ladies to his truck.

Fifteen minutes later, they were dropping Alverda off.

"You're sure you're going to be okay?" Minnie asked for the second time since they got inside of the vehicle.

"I am. The office is fine, your husband checked that out for himself. I'll call you if I need you." Alverda began walking away before Minnie had the chance to question her safety another time.

After seeing her inside, Yuriah turned to Minnie. "Baby, don't get alarmed, a'ight. But I need to know has G'Corey tried making any contact with you? Letters, emails, your parents, anything?"

Minnie answered immediately. "No, why? You think he is behind this?"

"I'm not saying all of that. But what I am saying is you would tell me if he tried reaching out to you, right?"

"Of course." Minnie looked over her shoulders. "Baby, I'm getting scared. Do you think he is going to show up and harm me next?"

Yuriah pulled her face close to his. "No, baby, I won't let no harm come to you. I'll protect you with my life, beleed dat. Matter of fact, don't get riled up. It was just a question and you said he hasn't. We'll leave it at that, a'ight?"

"Okay." She looked worried still.

"Give me a kiss."

She obeyed but the kiss was weak.

"A better one." He needed to stir Minnie's emotions to a happier place.

She gave him a longer kiss but he wasn't satisfied.

"Nah, take me home so I can show you the type of kiss I'm talkin' 'bout." He gave her a phony displeased look.

"You're so bad." Minnie cracked a small smile.

That was a start for him. Protecting her went far beyond making sure she was physically okay but that she was mentally safe from harmful thoughts as well. So, he planned to get her mind right before meeting up with the fellas to have a round table discussion.

Because whether it was G'Corey or not, he much rather be safe than sorry.

***

G'Corey walked into the kitchen to get a cool compress for his eye. It was throbbing unbelievably. He went to open the freezer's door but was distracted by the sound of running water. Shutting off the faucet, he noticed a thawed out piece of meat in the sink. Figuring it would do a better job than bulky ice cubes in a towel, he tore off the plastic, removed it from its package and used it instead.

Twenty minutes later when Skittles came inside from dropping Man Man off at school, she saw G'Corey stretched out on the sofa, resting.

Is that my T-bone steak? This bitch! She walked over to him. "Excuse you, your hoeness, why do you have my…" She pulled the meat cutlet off of him and leaned back and then forward for a closer look. "Ooohh, bitch! Who clocked you?" Skittles inquired, seeing his swollen eye with a nasty gash above it.

He gave her the side eye with the good one. "I tripped."

She smacked her teeth. "You sound like one of them hoes that be tryin' to cover up for a man that's beatin' that ass. Real talk. Who tagged you and why you didn't grab a frozen fuckin' bag of peas instead of my dinner steaks?"

He reached into his pocket, crumpled up a twenty and threw it in her direction. "Buy another one and shut the fuck up."

She picked it up off of the floor and slid it into her pocket. "I'll buy another one but shutting the fuck up, I can't do. So, same question as before. Who dotted your eye?"

"Why? You gon' kick they ass if I give you a name?"

"Fuck no. I just got my nails done." She wiggled her fingers in front of her face.

"Well, don't worry about what the hell happened, then?" G'Corey booted her up.

"Don't get mad at me 'cause them N.O. dudes stomped yo ass first thing after breakfast."

"Whatever, man, I bet you I can wear yo ass out."

She swung his feet off of the sofa so she could have a seat. "I'd like to see you try it, you no hands havin' hoe."

Skittles grabbed the remote off of the table and cut the television on. One of her favorite episodes of Martin was playing. "Ooh, I didn't miss my part. It's 'bout to come up," she told an uninterested G'Corey.

She was laughing and pointing at the screen saying each person's part, line for line when her cell began ringing.

Ring! Ring!

Skittles ignored it.

"Yo, who's that?"

She ignored him, too.

"You so fuckin' ignorant." He swiped her phone out of her purse.

"Don't touch my shit." She yanked it out of his hands, lowering the television's volume while cutting her eyes at him.

"Hello!" she answered roughly.

"Hello, may I speak with Tabitha Henry?"

She raised a skeptical eyebrow. No one called her by her government name except her mother, Sallie Mae or the IRS.

"Who's calling?" Skittles was seconds away from taking a message for herself.

"This is Alverda Robertson with Angel Health Homecare…"

After Skittles wrote down the time and place she was to meet with Minnie, G'Corey snatched the piece of paper from her hand.

"Thank you very much," he grinned.

"So now what?"

"If she calls you again, don't answer. I got it from here on out."

Chapter 24

One month later...

It was 5 a.m. While most people were asleep, Eli was in the *la la* land found between Blu's thighs.

There was no hair pulling, shit talking, ass smacking or other rough housing going on. It was the purest form of sex there was. Him on top of her, going in and then out.

His strokes were slow, her clamp was tight. His mouth was open, her eyes were shut. His groans were audible, she couldn't speak. However, their heartbeats were in tandem.

He stared down at her face but the darkness enveloping the bedroom wouldn't allow him to see her biting down on her lower lip.

Her lips parted. "Oooh, bae, I'm—ohhhhhhh!" A strong tingle waved from the top of her head ending at the tip of her toes.

Her walls spasm'd around his shaft, creating a warmed waterfall that could be felt beyond the condom he wore.

She wrapped her legs around his waist and he quickened his pace as he too was about to release.

His body jerked the moment his cum came shooting out of him. It was so strong it caused his body to vibrate and his lips to tremble.

Blu grabbed him on both sides of his face, pulling him down toward her. "I love you." She kissed him without needing to hear him say it back.

He then collapsed, laying sprawled on top of her for a time before he pulled himself out of her and removed the soiled prophylactic, tossing it in the wastebasket right next to his bed.

Eli then repositioned himself back on top of Blu and found his comfortable lay between her legs. She stroked the waves against his scalp, putting him into trance that he wouldn't awake from for hours to come.

Hours later...

Coffee

It was close to nine o'clock when Elias found himself on the other side of the bed, tangled in his sheets and alone.

"Blu?" He sat up and rubbed the sleep from his eyes as he walked through the house stark naked in search of her.

She stepped out of the kitchen and into the hallway when she heard her name. "Bonjour, sir. Happy Valentine's Day." She greeted him with a peck.

"Happy Valentine's Day to you, too, boo." He smiled when he saw her dressed in an apron only.

"You're just in time. Come with me." She directed him into the dining room and placed the cup of coffee she had in her hand on the table where she wanted him to sit. "Have a seat, bae. I'll be right back."

A few minutes later, Blu returned with a platter sized plate. She sat before him a stack of heart shaped pancakes topped with sliced strawberries and whipped cream, fluffy scrambled eggs, bacon and smoke sausage.

She then disappeared again to retrieve a ramekin of butter and the dish of syrup as his condiments.

"You're not eating with me?" Eli questioned when he didn't see her bring anything in for herself.

"Of course, but I had to serve my man first." She kissed his forehead. "Be right back."

When she reentered, she had removed the apron, matching her boo's skin attire.

"Damn, boo. Anybody ever told yo lil' skinny ass you sexy as fuck?"

She blushed. "Not really. Only the dude at my cleaners, and the guy at mechanic shop, or how 'bout the—"

"No, how 'bout you can get these hands if you keep playin' with me." Eli threw his sets up.

"I don't want it." She flinched and shielded herself behind her hands.

They both laughed and soon after their banter stopped, they dived into their meals, having conversations about any and everything.

After they had gotten their fill of breakfast, Elias had something he wanted to give Blu.

He wiped his mouth with his napkin. "This was good, boo, but now it's time to show you what ya boy working with."

Blu started dancing in her seat, making her upper body wave like an ocean's ripple. "Heyyyy!"

"I'ma give you a clue. If you can solve it, then you can get it, ya heard me."

She smiled brightly, rubbing her hands together, excitedly. She was a kid at heart and ready for the games to begin. "I'ma Blue's Clues genius, bring it on."

"A'ight. You'll find what you're looking for in the same place R. Kelly was trapped in."

"Too easy!" She shrilled as she pushed her chair back and headed to his bedroom's closet.

Blu searched high and then low but didn't find anything there, so she moved to the next one in the hall.

Nothing there.

"Oh, my God. Quit playing, Eli!" She ran past him with her hands waving in the air and her titties bouncing as she headed up-stairs.

"Have fun up there." Eli shouted loud enough for her to hear him as he headed back to bed.

After she opened all the gifts he bought her, he was sure she'd reward him with a special bedroom thanks.

Two hall closets? Empty. Guest bedroom's closets? Empty.

Finally, she walked into Peaches' bedroom and her closet was also empty but when Blu looked over at her dresser, it was full.

"Awwwww!" Blu fawned over the stack of boxes exquisitely giftwrapped. The colors were bright and the bows were big.

Peaches, you have a good man for a father.

Taking a few seconds more to admire the arrangement, she noticed a small gift bag from Kay Jewelers. Blu smacked her lips, already knowing who that was for. "Really, Eli?"

She reached inside and discovered two small gift wrapped boxes within along with a sealed card.

Blu stood there with her eyes closed, trying to rationalize why he would treat another woman on her day, or period. But everything in her said there was no justifiable reason.

She snatched the bag and trotted down the steps, marching into his bedroom.

"Took you long enou…" His smile went down just like his semi-erection when he noticed the expression on her face. "What's the problem now?"

She extended the bag form her body and lifted it to her eye level. "You tell me. Why are you buying your baby mama a Valentine's gift?"

""Don't start, Blu. I always get her a friendship gift on today."

"You know it's one thing to spoil your daughter, it's another thing to pamper her mother. You said I need to adjust my thinking, well so do you. Some shit has to change between y'all now that *I'm* your girl?"

"There's a lot of shit me and Samiyah don't do because of my relationship with you but nothing is going to satisfy you until she is x'd out of the picture but that ain't happening."

"I didn't ask you to remove her from your life but what you're saying is she's more important than me?"

"No, you're saying that." Elias shook his head, lifted his covers and looked at his limpness. "You be on some real dick softener type shit, bruh."

"*Tsss.* It's nice to know you're taking me for a joke."

"A'ight, it's whatever you say 'cause I ain't even 'bout to go back and forth with you. You want to finish having a good rest of the day or what?"

She put the bag down and threw her hands up. "It will be impossible to do, considering I'm going home."

Blu opened his closet door to retrieve her luggage off to the side, containing a week or more of clothes and personal items.

When she pulled it out, she saw several boxes giftwrapped in different hues of her favorite color blue, but she was so disgusted with him that she didn't bother acknowledging them. She simply got dressed and headed for the front door.

She had him tight. In his mind, there was no need to spazz out the way she would so he had to give her some parting words. He got her attention with the call of her name.

"Blu, every time you get heated you bounce. Keep that shit up and one day you gon' walk away from me and I won't be bothered by it."

She looked at him as she contemplated his words before she dropped her head. Looking back to him, she said, "Well, I suppose we're going to see if you'll be unbothered or not." Blu opened the door and left.

At Samiyah's house…

Lil' Acacia had been crying non-stop for the last thirty minutes and Samiyah couldn't help but cry along with her. Everything had been giving her the blues over the last three months.

She found herself suffering from depression. She was on and then off at the flick of a switch.

Her mind was unstable. Her heart was broken. Her back was hurting and her ankles were swollen. Nothing was going her way and now her baby was draining what little sanity remained with her incessant whining.

She walked over to Lil' Acacia and pulled her out of her jumper. "Baby, what do you want?" Samiyah cried literal tears.

After spending five minutes trying to find the answer, her doorbell sounded. She placed her back into her jumper and left out of the living room to answer it.

When she opened the door, she saw that Elias was dressed in the amorous colors of red and white, holding bags in both hands.

Samiyah wiped her face dry. "Hey, E."

He heard the baby crying in the background. "Is Peaches being a handful again? "

"That's the short answer, but I'll be fine. So come on in."

"What's wrong with Peaches?" He walked into the living room.

"Samiyah shut the door behind him and followed him into the living room. "I wish I knew so I could give it to her."

Coffee

Elias stopped by his daughter before going into the kitchen "What's bothering my baby, huh? You wanna stop hoopin' long enough and tell daddy all about it? A'ight, let me put this up and I'll be right back."

He turned around to step off and no sooner than he did, he spun around when she went from fussing to calling his name.

"Da da da da da da da da da..." Peaches started clapping.

Elias froze in place and listened as she kept saying it over and over. Then the biggest smile graced his face. He put the bags on the floor where he stood and turned to grab Peaches.

"Samiyah, you hear this? She goin' hammer."

Da da da da da...

Samiyah cupped her hands together. She was happy to hear her call out for Eli but she was most excited that she was no longer hollering.

"She stopped crying at the sight of you. Let me find out you got her spoiled."

Elias was touched with pride. "Is this her first time saying this or has she done it before now?"

"This is the first time I heard it." She smiled then looked at the dew in his eyes. "Are you about to cry?"

"Neva dat, but this makes me feel like I want to. I love this lil' girl. You just don't know how much she changed me."

"I've seen your growth. You've come a long way from there to now."

"Nah, you don't understand, Yah. She changing my mind and how I see things. Did I tell you I'm enrolling into Delgado for the spring semester? I'ma earn a business degree and do something other than chilling my life away."

"No, you didn't. I'm so proud of you. That's big."

"Yea, I never had reason to evaluate my life until she came along. All I can keep thinking about is the type of example I'm setting and how I want her to date the kind of man I'm becoming and not the one I was, so I have to boss up, ya know?" He kissed her forehead. "Love changes shit and I'm *in* love for the first time."

208

Samiyah placed a hand over her heart. "You're gonna make me cry."

Elias faked a frown. "Don't do that. You not cute when you do."

She pinched his arm. "You make me sick."

"But you love me, though." He passed her the baby. "Hold her real quick. I gotta run out to my truck."

He left out and returned a minute later with a dozen red roses in one hand and a surprise for Peaches in the other.

When Samiyah turned around to see him, she gasped. "Oh, no you didn't."

"Happy Valentine's Day." He handed her the bouquet and took Peaches from her with his free arm.

Tears cascaded down Samiyah's face and he thumbed them away, kissing her on the forehead, gingerly.

"This is beautiful," she whispered.

"Glad you like them."

"No, not the flowers. Well, yes, the flowers, but I'm talking about this thing that you're doing for me is beautiful."

And she looked beautiful to him. It wasn't her attire. It was the tenderness she often wore. Her femininity was undeniably sucking him in, more and more.

There goes those sparks again, he thought.

Elias had to move away and focus back on his baby boo. He brought his hand from behind his back and handed Peaches a single pink rose. "And a Happy Valentine's Day to you, baby girl."

Peaches went to put the plush petals in her mouth but he stopped her. She tried to do it again but was blocked, so she ended up swapping it from side to side.

Elias chuckled at her and then looked over at an emotional Samiyah. "Go 'head on upstairs, shower and put on something nice. I got plans for us."

Samiyah looked at the time on the wall clock. It was nearing six o'clock.

"I thought you had dinner plans with Blu for seven?"

"*Had* is the operative word. I ain't foolin' with her right nah. Maybe tomorrow, maybe."

"Did you cancel your date because y'all are still bumping heads over me?"

"Yea, kinda sorta, but I'ma 7th ward hardhead, she won't win."

"Maybe she should sometimes. Today is a big day for lovers and I, after all, am only your friend."

"Well, tonight you special. I'll deal with Blu later. You just go get dolled up. And I'ma get Peaches straight. Can you do that without saying anything else about her?"

She thought about it for a second. "Yea, I can do that."

Samiyah headed upstairs while Eli held onto Peaches, grabbing the bags he left in the center of the floor and bringing them in the kitchen.

***

An hour later...

When Samiyah came downstairs, she was greeted by the smell of something savory.

Elias had his back to Samiyah, taking usies of him and Peaches twinning. He had wiped her down and changed her into a red and white polka dot dress with a matching bottom to cover her pamper.

"Maybe I should have worn red and white, too, "Samiyah said as she made her presence known.

Elias turned around and was in awe. "Give me a 360°, ya heard me."

She did a little spin for him, showing her oval belly, hips and curves through her maxi dress.

"You think I can get in on a picture?" Samiyah wanted to share a frame with them.

"Wait. Lemme ask my girl. She might get jealous 'cause you wearing that dress." He shoo shoo'd to Peaches and then invited Samiyah over. "She ain't trippin', my girl said she ain't a hater."

"She better not me be." Samiyah clowned as she stood on the side of their daughter, while he snapped two shots of them.

Elias then smelled the aroma of his dinner and remembered he had to check the oven. "Take her." He passed her to Samiyah and jetted to the kitchen.

Samiyah followed him and stopped at the doorway. "What you making this time?"

"Something I saw on Food Network. Stuffed Cornish hens, wild rice and baked asparagus. I hope it taste good."

"I'm sure it will be. Your other dishes have been on point."

"Shocking shit, huh? Turns out ya boy can cook more than El Tacos for dinner."

Elias discovered he had a passion to create over the stove when he found himself making sure Samiyah was eating more than peanut butter sandwiches. Not everything he put together was magic in a pan but he was progressively obtaining chef status.

Samiyah sucked in her breath, making a hissing sound. "Don't mean to dip out on you but I need to get off of my feet."

"A'ight. I'll be in there to get lil' one in a sec." He stirred his rice as Samiyah retreated into the living room.

An hour and a half later…

Eli had finished feeding Peaches as she sat in a high chair next to him, while Samiyah watched on unable to take another bite.

"I got something for you."

"I can't. I'll explode." She rubbed her stomach.

"Nah, it ain't food. Look under your seat."

"My seat?" She leaned over to the side and looked down, pulling a bag from underneath herself. "When did you put this here?"

"Don't worry about that. Just peek inside."

She pulled out a card and two boxes. She went to open the envelope but he asked that she do that afterwards. So she obliged and opened box number one.

It was a gold bracelet with *Peaches* engraved on the nameplate.

"Awww, this is too adorable. Look, maw maw, daddy got you your first piece of jewelry. She walked over to her and clamped it around her wrist. It fit perfectly.

Coffee

"Now open the second one."

Samiyah headed back to her seat and sat down. She opened it wondering if there were earrings for Peaches in them but then a smile stretched across her face as she stared down at a locket heart necklace that was clearly for her. "This is so pretty."

"Check out the inside." He further instructed.

She opened the heart and saw a newborn picture of both her and Peaches, one on each side.

"Oh, my God. Eli, this is so beautiful. Oh, my God." She fanned her eyes to hold back her tears. Then she sat the necklace down and opened the card. It read:

There's not a gift in the world I can buy you that will amount to the gift you've already given me in Peaches. You're loved by me.

She placed the card on the table and cupped her mouth and nose as she cried tears of happiness. His words came at a time when she couldn't be feeling more unloved by her husband. "I don't know what to say."

"Say nothing, ya heard me." He stood up and walked over to her. "Let me put your necklace on."

She grabbed her long locs and lifted them off of her neck as he snapped the latch, connecting her chain.

Samiyah stood up and hugged him, looking into his eye. "Thank you."

He hugged her back, with one hand resting on the small of her back and the other gently stroking her up and then down. They held each other's stare and then suddenly they found themselves entwined in a kiss.

It had been a long time since he felt her lips but he remembered its softness as if he'd just felt them last night. She felt too good to let go of, so he questioned why he was trying.

She held his face and steadied their tongue connection. It was in the strength of her touch that Eli knew he had to make love to her again.

Still engaged in a heated kiss, Eli began walking her over to the sofa but one little person reminded them that she was in the room.

"Da da da da da da da," Peaches began talking in different octaves nonstop, causing Samiyah to break their enchantment.

Elias looked over at Peaches and then back to Samiyah. "I'll put her to sleep."

"No, you shouldn't. We shouldn't."

"Yah, tell me that didn't feel right to you."

"Oh, I felt it. We make fire together, E, but there's a problem about that happening. You're not mine, you're hers and I'm—I'm still married."

"All of that shit can change if you just say the word. You're still my best friend and having Peaches makes us family, so why don't we just do this? Gerran don't look to be coming around and Blu, I love her but she ain't you."

Samiyah was touched. She had a very sexy man standing before her confessing his desires to be with her. She knew they would be happy too. In all the years they had been friends, they hadn't had one bad day.

But she couldn't give in.

"You're right. She's Blu. Patient, understanding and dedicated. Can you imagine how hard our relationship must be on her? You're conflicted because we have an amazing story but you have an even better one with her."

"So you're saying you never thought about us being together and *saying fuck the world*?"

"I've thought about it and I still do but I'm not who you need. I have a complicated marriage and *his* baby on the way. It's not like before, E. We can't just throw caution to wind and you shouldn't want to." She looked at the time again. "It's ten o'clock. Go to Blu and apologize for whatever made you give me this wonderful night and not her." She took a deep breath and continued. "I will always be here but she won't, not if you keep treating her like she comes second."

"Well, damn, I don't know what to say behind that."

"Say nothing. Just make it right while you still can."

Elias bobbed his head. He was disappointed but he was just going to roll with the punches. Maybe she was right or maybe she was wrong, but he wasn't going to wrestle with it tonight. He was going to allow time to dictate who he belonged with.

"I'm gonna lay Peaches down and then I'll be out, a'ight?"

"She'll like that."

Eli picked up his big girl and walked past Samiyah to head upstairs but turned around when she called out to him.

"E, one more thing. You love Blu for a reason, so stop diluting it by comparing her to me. You may find out some pretty remarkable things."

Eli wasn't sure why Samiyah was campaigning for Blu but he wasn't mad at her. His girl was a gem and he knew there was no way to give two women the same benefits. But years of repressing his feelings toward Samiyah wasn't just going to go away.

"A'ight." He nodded his head and continued up the steps.

Elias walked into Peaches' room, changed her diaper and wiped off her face and hands with a wet wipe she tried sucking when it brushed past her mouth.

He was about to lay her in her crib and tell her good night but then a thought came to him.

"You know what we didn't do? We didn't dance. And you can't have a date without a dance. Daddy trippin'."

Eli scrolled through the music in his phone and came across the perfect song. He picked her up out of her crib and held her up to his face.

"Peaches, may I have this dance?"

She drooled a long line of spittle as she responded in baby gibberish, which he translated to mean *yes*.

He wiped her slobber mouth with his fingers and then onto his jeans. Now his belle was all set for the ball. With the volume at a moderate level, Elias allowed Jamie Foxx to serenade *Heaven* to his peach as he began a gentle rock with her cradled in his arms.

Tell me have you heard the story/That took place not long ago/Bout an angel up in heaven/They say she up and ran away from home/Word is she had unfinished business/So back on earth she had to flee/Well you know I'm so elated/Because she's laying right here next to me...

Samiyah walked upstairs to head to her room but was drawn to Lil' Acacia's when she heard music. She stood at the door and saw the most precious thing unfold before her eyes. She watched Eli sway to the melody with his eyes closed, holding her snuggly against his chest. So protectively. So delicately.

Then she heard him say, "No matter who's on my arm, you'll always be the one in my heart."

Coffee

Chapter 25

The next day...

It had been weeks since the incident with Bonita occurred and although G'Corey hadn't popped up and proved his connection to it, Yuriah still couldn't shake the fact that he was behind it.

As a result of his suspicions, he amped up security around his home and had Minnie shadowed everywhere she went without him, just to be careful.

It annoyed him how G'Corey eluded his search efforts. But what Yuriah knew was in time, he was going to catch him slipping. The question wasn't if, only when.

So until he crossed that bridge, he went about his day with as much normalcy as possible to keep Minnie's mental unaffected even though he couldn't have true peace until G'Corey was resting in his.

Minnie yawned and stretched as she awoke from her sleep. She looked over to her left only to see the usual empty space on his side of the bed. Yuriah never slept past 4:30 in the morning.

She got up from her comfy lay and went to the place she knew he'd be, his office. She stood at the opened door and knocked on the frame of it. "Good morning, handsome. Can I come bother you?"

He swiveled his chair away from the desk. "I wouldn't call what you do bothering me but you can come sit on my lap and be a welcomed distraction."

Minnie blushed as she sashayed over to him, taking her seat. She felt him rise almost immediately. "Don't you ever get enough?" She spoke of his growing erection.

"I can never get enough, ya heard me." He hugged her around her waist and kissed the center of her back before he scooted them over in front of his computer's screen.

"What are you typing up?"

"I was just sending out an email to my team, letting them know that I'll be in to have a mandatory meeting with them for noon."

"Is everything okay?"

"Oh, yea. I just need to show my face so no one gets too comfortable with me being away like I have been. What about you? How you spending your day?"

"I'm going to spend time with Yah and the baby but I will run a few errand before doing that."

"How long you plan to be?"

"I'm not sure. Why? You have something you want us to do?"

"Always but there's no rush with you and yo peoples. Just be ready for me to *whine and dine* you when you get back." He squeezed her tightly and started whimpering to mock the sounds she would make anytime he went down on her.

She burst out laughing. "I do not sound like that."

"Oh, yes the hell you do. You be like, *Ha! Ha! Wait a minute, baby. Oooh, hold up, baby. Right there, baby. Yes, baby!*"

"Get off me." She tried loosening his grip around her but couldn't.

"You know you like that." He let her go but she didn't get up off of him.

She twisted her body to face him. "I do but you don't have to tease me, though. I can't help but make those sounds. You working with voodoo here *and* here." Minnie pointed to his mouth and then his pleasure tool.

Yuriah one hand typed another sentence in the email before he pressed the send button, tapping Minnie on the butt for her to stand up.

Once they were both on their feet, he spun her around and picked her up.

"Yuriiii! She giggled, wrapping her thick thighs around his trimmed waist. "What are you doing?"

His meeting wasn't for another three hours, so he had time to kill. He licked his lips. "I'm not putting it off for later when I can handle that right now."

She clamped her arms around his neck and showed her excitement through her laughter as he began walking her through the house and into their bedroom.

218

Two and a half hours later...

They were both showered, dressed and ready to go. They stood on their porch and kissed before they departed.

"I'll call you when I make it over to Yah's, okay?"

"A'ight. Enjoy yourself."

She got into her car and blew him a kiss through the windshield. He caught it and held it tightly.

Yuriah watched her slowly pull off, wearing a smile that turned flat when he looked over to his right. He then nodded his head upward to his dude to take off behind his wife, remaining low-key so she wouldn't know he was having her followed.

After Yuriah got into his truck to head off to work, off in the distance, G'Corey was lowering his binoculars.

He was so angry he wanted to wait for Yuriah to return, catch him on his doorstep and off him before he had a chance to walk inside, repainting his house with his blood. But he had to think with his head and not his trigger finger. He couldn't run the risk of Minnie fearing him more so than she probably did already. So Yuriah was safe, for now.

"Aaahhhh!" He released his frustrations at a moderate volume as to not draw attention to himself. It was already odd enough that he was perched in a tree conducting his stakeout. He didn't need to be discovered doing it.

G'Corey dropped his head. He couldn't believe the lengths he'd gone through and the ones he was preparing to weather just to get her back, but she was worth it. And he was willing to use super human levels of patience to not fuck up his happily ever afters this time. He was aware it was going to take time to body three men without looking like the bad guy and being her man once again.

***

After picking up some groceries for Samiyah's house, she realized she forgot something. So she decided to stop at Family Dollar to avoid the long lines at Winn Dixie.

Minnie was standing at the cooler section, grabbing a carton of eggs when she saw a face she swore she'd beat to a pulp if she ever had the chance to.

Now confronted with whether she'd make real of her malicious intent, she found she didn't have it in her.

"Minnie?" Kawanna was shocked to see her after having gone so many months without crossing her path. "I don't want any trouble with you."

Minnie didn't respond. She didn't know how to. She just reached for her item and closed the door, heading for the checkout line.

After paying for her grocery item, Minnie realized she did know what to say to Kawanna and she set out to find her in the store. She spotted her pushing her shopping cart, minding her business.

"Kawanna." She turned around. "I have something I want to say to you."

Kawanna felt she owed it to her to listen but she hoped whatever harsh words spilled from her lips this time didn't end up in a brawl in aisle nine.

"There were two things I told you would never happen when we last saw each other and it turns out I lied about one of them. When I said we will never be friends again that was Bible but when I said I would never forgive you, that wasn't true. Truth is I forgave you much faster than I forgave myself. I just thought you should know."

Kawanna breathed a breath of relief. She hoped for a moment like this but with the way she devastated Minnie, she wasn't sure if this day would ever come.

"There's nothing I can say to justify my actions and an apology doesn't seem sufficient but I am very sorry. I was damaged and in turn, I ruined a great friendship and your faith in your husband."

"Ex-husband but like I said it's okay. Matter of fact, I should be thanking you."

"Thanking me? Why?"

"Discovering he was cheating with random women was painful but I probably would have forgiven him and stayed, knowing me. But if it wasn't for the level of betrayal I felt from you, I wouldn't be where I am now, which is where I should have always been. So, yes, thank you."

"I wish I could have opened your eyes much differently but you're welcome."

Kawanna looked a little uneasy as they stood there so in the spirit of allowing bygone to be bygones, Minnie opened the floor for mild conversation. "So, do you live in this area now?"

"Yes. Yes, I do. I couldn't stay where I was. I didn't feel comfortable there." She thought of how G'Corey had her too frightened to be at her own apartment. "But I also work in this area as well."

"Oh? Where are you working?"

"Well, I don't actually work. I volunteer at Sweet Haven's Women's Center. See, I started seeing a counselor over a year ago and she inspired me to help others, so I help oversee the *Break Every Chain* program."

"That sounds interesting."

"It is. I'm actually here because some of those ladies are in hiding from their abusers, so I do their personal shopping for toiletries and other needs until they are free to live again without having to look over their shoulders."

In that moment, Minnie kind of wanted to open up about how she felt paranoid about G'Corey but she didn't want to welcome her back into her life on such a personal level again.

"Well, I have somewhere to be as do you. Keep up the good work and take care of yourself."

Kawanna reached into her back pocket and pulled out a business card. "Hey, you'll probably never call, but if you ever need me for anything, I'm available to you."

She wasn't sure how Minnie would feel about physical contact but she was compelled to give her a hug. Minnie was caught off guard by it, but she returned the gesture.

Tears fell from Kawanna's eyes as she embraced her. She wasn't going to fool herself into thinking this was the start of something new but she was relieved to finally begin letting go of the burden she'd been carrying around for such a long time.

They separated and Kawanna returned to her buggy. She looked over her shoulder to see Minnie still standing there. She waved her bye, unsure if she'd ever see her again, but hoping that she would.

As she turned the corner aisle, Minnie exhaled deeply and looked at the card.

It was good seeing you, Kawanna.

Minnie never thought she'd think that after their last encounter but time had a way of healing all wounds.

Thirty minutes later...

Minnie was at Samiyah's house. She brought all of the bags to her porch before ringing the doorbell.

Samiyah opened up and the first thing she attempted to do was reach for some of the groceries.

"Don't you dare. You can barely carry that beach ball in front of you. Go sit down somewhere," Minnie mothered.

"I'm not helpless, no."

"I know that, but I got this. Now go on."

Minnie made the necessary trips to bring all of the bags inside and then sat down on the sofa once she was done putting them away.

"You look tired. You want something to drink?" Samiyah was seconds from peeling herself off of the couch to grab her a cold drink.

"I'll get it myself. Where's nanny's baby?" Minnie looked around.

"Upstairs sleep. Thank God. She is busy bee. I don't know how I'm gonna do it with her *and* a newborn."

"You're going to do fine and I will take Lil' Acacia off of your hands when Eli doesn't have her. Speaking of Eli, how is he?"

"He's Eli. Excellent father and a great man—to me."

"What do you mean you? Are y'all together now?"

"No, we're not together but he's been taking care of me like we were. Just yesterday he spoiled me like I was his lady and cooked me a hellafied dinner."

"What his famous tacos." Minnie chuckled.

"No. He been surpassed that. Every week he'd been experimenting and making new dishes for me to try since I haven't been in a mood to cook for myself. He actually throws down. I'm talking about butterflied stuffed pork chops, red beans and fried chicken that taste like Popeye's, anything that comes to mind, he whips. I mean some of it needs tweaking but for the most part, that shit be so good. That's probably why I'm spreading so damn much." Samiyah looked at her round belly and even thicker thighs.

"Okay, so what about Blu and Gerran?"

"Well, I told him that he has to be fair to Blu by giving her the respect she deserves. It's clear we love each other but it's too complicated for us to be anything other than friends and co-parents. And Gerran? It's still fuck him."

"He hasn't tried coming around or anything?" Minnie was saddened by his hardened heart.

"Not at all. When I tell you he ain't concerned about me and this house, I'm talking truth. He doesn't check on Lil' Acacia, which I'm not mad about, but he doesn't even inquire about the one I'm carrying. So the best way to sum up me and Gerran is—it's a fucked up situation that ain't gon' get right no time soon."

"That's so sad to hear. I thought he was better than that."

"I thought so too, but I don't want to talk about me or him. My shit is depressing as hell. And I'm tired of going through the motions over it, so tell me something good. What's going on with you and hubs?"

"We are on a cloud. I mean my imagination couldn't fathom the type of love this man gives me. But not all is well in paradise."

"What do you mean? Yuri *is* one of the good guys, right?"

"He's too good to be true but what I'm talking about is this," she paused as she looked around her living room, "where is your laptop?"

"It's in the den." Samiyah pointed.

"Be right back." Minnie got up and headed off into the other room, so she could show her what she was talking about instead. When she reentered the living room, she placed the computer on her lap. "Log into my email account. It's minniedaniels04@gmail.com and my password is blackbutterfly0714. Read the messages from theonly14u."

Samiyah did as she asked and began reading.

Minnie,
I didn't mean for that to happen that day. I only meant to scare him off. Nothing more. I know you don't know if you can believe me because of what you witnessed but you know me better than anybody so you should know soul deep that I'm not the man you saw that day. I was just crazy in love but I can promise you if you give me another chance, I will spend my life making it right.
Don't you remember you told me that you would never leave me? That you would be my forever mine? Well, you're not here and now that you're gone nothing feels the same. I just want to get back to that loving feeling. Don't you miss that? How we would curl up in bed and make love, fall asleep and make love again. I want that. I need that. So, I'm prepared to earn you again but know that I want you and I'll stop at nothing to have you.
We made a commitment that I'm gonna see all the way through. I love you now and I always will.

Love,
Your one and only

Samiyah read a few more messages but couldn't stomach reading the other pages worth of his bullshit. "G'Corey is a fuckin' retarded joke! I hate him. He has some damn nerve. Are you going to show your husband?"

"I don't know. I haven't decided yet."

"And why the hell not? He should know?"

"I know that but I can't be responsible for something deadly happening to my husband because I sent him on a chase, looking for my ex when maybe he's just talking. I mean I haven't seen G'Corey and neither has he so I'm wondering if this is even worth mentioning."

"I say *yes*! What happens if he tries something, Minnie?"

"Like I said, I don't know what I'm gonna do. All I know is I almost lost my husband once and I am not eager to put him in harm's way looking for G'Corey if all these are just letters confessing a love that will never be returned."

"I don't think that's a good idea but if this ever escalated beyond emails, will you tell Yuriah? Will you tell me?"

"I pray to God it doesn't but I most definitely would say something then and that's if I don't say something now."

"Good because you don't know where his head is and I already lost Acacia. I can't lose you, too."

Minnie stared at Samiyah in stupefaction. She didn't consider G'Corey setting out to do her personal harm but now she had something to think about.

Coffee

Chapter 26

One month later...

Samiyah knocked on Elias' door. She needed to drop Lil' Acacia off to him while she went to her 20 week check-up with her OB/GYN.

"You're ready to see Da-da? Sure you are." She looked down at her baby.

Blu answered the door, taking Peaches off of her hands as she let them inside. "Hey, Samiyah. How are you?"

"Miserably fat and I'm only halfway through this." She shook her head.

"That just means he or she is eating good." Blu looked behind herself and pointed. "Eli's in the shower, but you can wait for him."

Samiyah looked at her watch. She had a few minutes before she had to leave for her appointment, so she sat down.

The ladies shared light conversation, something that had been hard to do since finding out Samiyah's baby was Eli's. Not certain if the timing was right, but Samiyah wanted to share something with Blu that had been weighing on her.

"I want to change the subject a little bit and address the elephant in the room. I know accepting the change my daughter brought into your relationship and even coming to terms with the line he and I crossed had been trying for you. So, I wanted you to hear from me that you have a good man who happens to be a great father as well as my friend but that's all he is to me, my friend." She sliced her hand in the air.

Blu was taken by surprise but she couldn't deny that it made her feel good to hear those words coming from her. "I appreciate you saying that but may I ask why'd you feel the need?"

"We are amicable with each other but at one point we were friends outside of Eli. So, I know you're uncomfortable when I come around and I want there to be good vibes between us for our baby's sake. After all, she'll grow up seeing you as a mother-figure and I would like for us to be more than cordial, if possible."

Blu wasn't going to divulge to her that she had been experiencing four levels of insecurities when it came to her, that's what Kanari was for. But it would help to create a better environment for Peaches if she was able to move past her trust issues that got in the way of not only their relationship but the one with Eli.

Blu looked over at Peaches who was gnawing on a chew toy and smiled. "It's possible."

Samiyah smiled and then realized she had to be going. She stood up slowly. "Look, tell Eli I will be back to pick her up after my visit, please. Ummm, I've pumped more than enough milk to last her. And—"

"And we've been doing this for a while. We got it." Blu reminded her that this wasn't there first baby rodeo with her.

"You're right. Well, it was good talking with you." Samiyah headed for the door.

Blu walked up behind her. "Give me a hug."

"Awww." Samiyah turned around to hug her.

"It was good talking with you, too." Blu expressed genuinely.

***

Twenty-five minutes later, Samiyah sat in the examination room as she waited on her doctor to come in. She had been up and down about her pregnancy but today she was riding a high because if the baby cooperated, she would know what to plan for.

Moments later, the door opened.

"Good morning, mom. How are we doing today and where is your little sunshine?" Her always jovial doctor gave her a hug.

Samiyah rubbed her belly. We're fine and she's with her daddy."

"Oh. Well, if you're up to it, bring her on your next visit. My office just adores her."

"I will." Samiyah smiled.

She then pointed to the scale. "Okay, now let me check your weight."

Samiyah stepped on and stood still as she watched the doctor's fingers slide the nodule from left to right until the beam was balanced. She looked in her chart at her previous weight and again at her current weigh in.

"Oh, my. You've gained thirteen pounds from your last visit. Has anything changed in your diet?"

"No, I try to eat three times but it's all normal portions. Is there something wrong?"

"It's abnormal but let's not be quick to worry. Get on the table for me. I am going to perform a sonogram."

"Okay." Samiyah climbed on the table and laid back lifting her shirt. She jumped at the cold application of jelly that was squirted onto her stomach before the doctor maneuvered the device on top of it.

She pulled the baby up on the screen. She made grunts as she examined the monitor. "Umm. Hmmm. Okay. Everything looks normal. So, would you like to know what you're having?"

"I'm guessing another girl. Am I right?"

"You are. It's a girl." The doctor radiated.

Samiyah smiled.

"Andddd it's a boy."

Samiyah frowned. "Excuse me. Which one? Girl or boy?"

"Both. You're having twins, Samiyah. A boy *and* a girl."

"What?" Samiyah was shocked as she tried to make sense of what was being told to her.

"You're having twins. You picked up so much weight because there's another baby in there."

"What?" Samiyah still couldn't process what she was hearing.

"I take it you're surprised. Well, it looks like baby B was hiding behind baby A when we did your very first ultrasound and there was no way to know up until now. Are you excited?"

Samiyah's lips curved downward and tears sat on her eyelashes, threatening to leap onto her face. Unable to conjure other words, all she could say was, "What?"

Coffee

In the parking lot of her OB's office...

"What? Two more babies? This is unreal. I can't believe it. Three children, Yah. You're blessed." Minnie shrilled so loudly into the phone that Samiyah had to pull the receiver away from her ear.

"Unreal is right but I don't call raising children without their father a blessing."

Minnie brought it down a notch and saw it through her eyes. "I understand. Well, are you going to tell Gerran that you all are having twins?"

"Why should I? All he does is stress me out. Every time we talk, he assassinates my character. How can we be parents to these babies—Oh, God! Babies?" Samiyah began crying so hard she couldn't finish talking.

Minnie didn't say anything because she knew she needed to let it out.

Samiyah stopped crying long enough to continue. "How can we be parents and we can't even get along? He has no respect for me and as much as I want my children to grow up with him, I can't, in good conscious, allow them to see their mama be mishandled by their father."

"You're right. He can't allow his hurt and anger to infect y'all's babies. But you can't allow your feelings to stop him from being there, either. Y'all really have to work this out and you have four more months, if that, to do it. They're coming, Yah, and they deserve you both. Plus, you shouldn't do this alone. Call him and tell him."

Samiyah agreed with her instantly. It was Gerran's choice whether he wanted to be with her but it wasn't an option not to be there for their children and she wasn't going to give him the easy way out by condoning his isolated behavior.

"I'm going to call him."

"When?"

"Now. I gonna let him know that we can have a paternity test done as soon as they're born and we don't have to fuck with each

230

other unless it's about them, if that's the game he wants to play. Matter of fact, we can get a fuckin' divorce because I can't stay married to a man who can abandon ship when the waters get rough."

"You're serious? You don't want to see if this can be salvaged? Y'all have too much history, though."

"History means nothing when you don't have a future. So I'm super serious. I mean, what am I holding on for? He been showing his hand for four straight months and now I need to put mine on the table."

"You don't love him anymore?"

"I suppose I'll always love him, but what's love got to do with it? I gotta love me and my three. I gotta put this behind me so I can learn to sleep through the night without waking up to cry or becoming frustrated with my daughter because she's acting her age. I can't control these depression swings if I'm still connected to a man that makes me feel like shit. So, you ask if I'm sure, and I answer *yes*."

"I hate divorce for you but I can't say I don't understand it in this case. But do me a favor. There's enough tension between y'all already. How about you get the paternity portion out of the way first. Reach an agreement on that and then tell him you want to legally go your separate way."

"I can do that. Well, let me call him before I end up not doing it."

"Alright, call me back and let me know how things panned out."

"Okay." Samiyah hung up the phone and did as she agreed she would.

She stared at her phone before calling to rehearse how she would tell him.

Gerran, don't be a dick right now. I only called to say we're having twins and you need to get on board with taking care of them with me. She shook her head *no* at that introduction.

Gerran, when the babies are born—yes I said babies as in two. We need to get a DNA test done so you can see these are your children. We have to raise them together even if we're not.

"That's perfect, Yah." She said out loud.

Coffee

Be nice, Gerran. Please don't give me no drama today, Samiyah thought as she placed the call.

Meanwhile...

"Knock, knock. Can I come in?" Audra entered into Gerran's office when he nodded his head for her to step inside.

"What's good?" He stopped fidgeting with her cell phone and placed it on his desk.

"I wanted to check on you. I just saw the cancelation email. I'm sorry you couldn't book the spot."

"Yea, me too." Gerran cracked his neck from side to side.

"Ooh, don't do that. My chiropractor said doing manual adjustments on yourself are the worst things you can do. Let me give you a massage to work your kinks out." Audra walked over to him and stood behind his chair.

"Nah, I'm good on it." He rejected her offer.

"If you felt these magic hands, you wouldn't so quick to decline them." She loosened the first two button on his shirt, brushing her breast against him just enough for him to feel their softness.

After she got the slack she needed around his collar, she slid her hands into his shirt and began gripping his shoulders.

"That feels pretty good." He admitted.

"Yea? But I can't get it the way I want. Let me try something." She came out of her five inch heels and then walked in front of him, parting his legs with the command of her knee. She centered herself between them and went back to massaging him. "Now doesn't that feel better?"

Gerran's eyes rolled and Audra pretended not to see it but she knew what she was doing. She was privy to enough details to know he hadn't had a woman's touch in a minute and she was seconds away from changing that, if she could.

"It does." But it wasn't just the feel of her hands that was making his dick jump. It was the sit of her breast staring him at eye level, the smell of her perfume wafting up his nostrils and his curiosity to

232

know what she looked like bent over his desk that had his nature rising.

"Good, then. Just continue to relax. Relate." She bent down toward his ear and sensually said, "Release."

She traveled her hands down his chest but he grabbed them. Audra looked at him as if to ask, *Did I do something wrong?* But she got her answer when he grabbed the back of her head and drew her mouth into his.

Nothing at that point needed to be said. She wanted him and he wanted her.

In an animalistic way, he unbuttoned her pants and began yanking them down as she undid his. As Gerran stood to his feet to drop his jeans, she came completely out of hers.

She sat partially on his desk with her legs opened as he ran two of his finger over her clit and between her lips, kissing her as he pushed those same fingers up and inside.

Her head fell back and she gasped. "Haa!"

He finger-fucked her while playing with her breast and she became super soaked. Gerran had to have her now. He turned her around and pushed her back down, pulling her ass up in doggy-style position.

Gerran was so driven by lust and her eagerness to feel him that he pushed inside of her raw.

"Oh, shit!" she said upon feeling his rough slam inside of her.

He balled his mouth and closed his eyes as the feel of her snatch latched around his pole. "Fuck! Dis pussy good."

"Ummm," Audra moaned pleasure. She had been wanting to sample his forbidden fruit. He was too fine not to have tasted.

Her eyes rolled to the back of her head the moment Gerran separated her ass cheeks and began spearing his thickness into her tight tunnel.

"Aaahhh yes! Ooooh, work it, baby!"

In between the chorus of Gerran's grunts and groans and her loud moans and pleas of satisfaction, he couldn't hear the low volume of his incoming call. She thought to silence it because there was no way she wanted him to stop the thrashing he was putting on her pussy just to talk to his wife. But then she had another idea.

She slide her finger across the screen to answer it.

"Ahh! Ahh! Oooh! Shit!" Audra held back nothing.

"Hello?" Samiyah's chest instantly tightened. She looked at the phone and saw Gerran's name. She placed the right call. "Hello?" she said a little louder.

"Ooohh, Gerran, that dick so big. Oh, don't stop fuckin' me. Just like that. Just. Like. That." Audra talked their screw session play by play.

"Aarrrgghhh!" Gerran let out a thunderous roar as Audra gripped his dick so tight with her muscles he damn near lost control of his nut and almost shot off inside of her.

It had been a long time since Samiyah heard his sexual sounds but a woman knows her man's moans and she knew it was her husband's.

"Slide that dick in and out just like that, baby. Slap my ass! Oooh! Oooh! Oooh! Aahhh!" Audra's whimpers were continuous and too painful for Samiyah to hear.

Samiyah hung up the phone and placed a hand over her racing heart. It was beating so fast she just knew it would burst out of her chest. Then her breathing became so loud it sounded like she was wheezing.

"What the fuck?" She looked at the phone with disgust.

Samiyah was confused by what was going on but not about what she was going to do. She started her car and hoped to God his ass was at the studio because she was on her way there.

She drove like she was the only one on the road, arriving at his spot fifteen minutes after she had hung up.

Samiyah saw his car so she didn't hesitate to push the front door open and head straight for his office. She marched to the back, busting through Gerran's office to see them both looking satisfied.

He attempted to ask her what business she had with him but everything played out faster than he could speak.

Samiyah saw a smile in Audra's little spiteful eyes and she lost it. She grabbed her by her hair and slung her to the floor, managing two solid blows to her face before Gerran rushed over and stood in the middle of them, trying to break them a part.

"The fuck? Let her go, Samiyah!" He tried prying the strong clutch she had around her hair, while trying not to hurt her.

"Bitch, let my hair go!" Audra tried digging her nails into Samiyah's hand to get her to release her.

"Gerran, move!" Samiyah was breathing fire.

"Samiyah, you're pregnant. Stop!"

She didn't need him reminding her of that. She was fully aware but she was also the angriest she's ever been.

Samiyah tried kicking her but caught Gerran the hits instead.

The cattiness went on a minute more and then Gerran was able to separate them and bridge back a volatile Samiyah.

Audra stood her distance behind Gerran, pointing at Samiyah. "You're a crazy bitch!"

"I got your bitch, ya bitch!" Samiyah tried to move past Gerran's restraints before she looked at him. "Let me the hell go! I don't need you holding me."

"You gon' chill the fuck out with that rowdy shit?" Gerran was fuming fire of his own. He had no idea why she would come into his business and start a fight.

"I'm calm. Let me go. I'm pregnant, remember?"

Gerran examined her eyes for truth and then turned his head to address Audra. "Don't come for her when I let her go, you understand?"

"I'm not the one with the beef," she shot.

"A'ight, Samiyah." He let her go and the moment he did, she slugged him in the face.

"Fuck you, you hypocrite! I hope you fucking her made you feel good about yourself." Samiyah's glared at him through wet eyes before she turned off to leave.

"What the fuck?" He indignantly grabbed Samiyah's arm but she threatened to mace him if he didn't let her go.

He released her reluctantly and she hurried out of his studio. She did what she came to do.

She started her engine and her mind went blank. She was so frazzled she forgot she was supposed to get her baby from Eli's. Instead she went straight home.

Gerran stared at Audra. "How the fuck she knows that?"

"How am I to know?" Audra went blonde.

"She hadn't showed up here in weeks and all of a sudden the day she does is the day we got down? Nah, something ain't right." He reached for his phone.

"Fuck it! I'm not going to lie. I answered your phone when she called you."

"Why the fuck you did that?" Gerran raised his voice.

"I did it because I'm tired of you pining over her while flirting with me. Plus, she needed to know it's over between y'all. That's what you've been saying to me, right? Now she will leave you alone and we can do us freely."

"She's still my wife! And there ain't no doin' us. That fuck shouldn't have happened."

"So, what are you trying to say?"

"That you can get the fuck on. None of your services are needed. You're fired!"

"I'm what?" Audra suspended her hand in the air and then decided against trying to figure out what just happened between them. One minute he was dissing Samiyah and now he's back claiming her? "You're confused as hell!" She walked out, gathering her things from up front and leaving him to his own chaos.

"Fuck!" was all Gerran could say.

Later that day...

Gerran wasn't sure showing up was the best idea but he couldn't leave things like they were from earlier. He owed her an apology for Audra's actions.

Samiyah knew he would stop by, so she wasn't surprised by the knock at her door.

236

When she swung it open, Gerran tried coming inside but she blocked him and forced him backwards, stepping outside with him and shutting her door closed.

Samiyah was so infuriated she went in immediately. "I just knew you were gonna come but why? So you can tell me how good you feel about the fucked up shit you've done? Well, you can save it because I've had it up to here with your insensitive shit." She measured her hand above her head. "See, I convinced myself to tell you that we're having twins, but I got more than what—"

"*Twins?*" He cut her off.

"Yes, muthafucka, twins! And when I called, you or your bitch answered so I could hear you two fuckin'. Was that your idea of payback? To damage me beyond repair? While I'm pregnant on top of it?" She screamed so loud her own eardrums ached.

"I may be pissed with you but I never had sex with her or anybody else before today and I damn sure wasn't trying to hurt you by it."

"Am I supposed to believe you when you couldn't believe me?"

"Yes, I'm telling you the truth."

"Well, you've been telling me a whole bunch of shit, so let me tell you some things. We *will* get a paternity test done. You *will* see that you're their father and you *will* take care of your children, one way or another. And we—we *will* be getting a divorce!"

Her eyes casted an evil glare his way before she backed into her house, slamming the door and locking it.

Gerran ran his hand down his face. Suddenly, it didn't feel so good being on the end of one's wrath.

Coffee

Chapter 27

A few days later...

Eli was still uptown after he left Jacobi's house when he decided to stop off at Pound Puppies. Eli had read that puppies who grew up with babies were the best protector next to daddies and their shot gun, so he headed on over to grab him one. He could never be too careful with his pretty girl.

Parking was always terrible on St. Charles Ave. and the closest spot he found to park was three blocks away but it was beautiful spring day so it was all good.

That was until he walked past *her*.

It didn't occur to him that the store and La'Tasha's shop were on the same street and it was just his luck she'd be outside to see him.

As Eli was walking up on her, she spoke as if all was well between them. "What's up's, Elias?"

She wore a smile of innocence that concealed her man-eating ways because behind her allure was a black widow spider waiting to consume and spit out the heart of an unsuspecting brother. So, he kept walking like he didn't see or hear her.

She grabbed at his arm before he stepped off too far. "We're not speaking?"

"For what, bruh. What you want?" Eli vibed his annoyance.

La'Tasha didn't pay his shitty expression any mind and she didn't bother beating around any corners. "I want you back and maybe if you would have answered any one of my calls instead of ignoring them, you would have known that."

"Look, bruh, I don't fuck wit'chu and I know hearing that shit makes your girl dick hard but we ain't shit 'cause you ain't shit."

"Ouch! That stung a little bit but I know you don't mean that. You're pissed and you have every right to be. Want to punish my punani and make us do better?"

"You scandalous as fuck!" Eli was about to step off and she stopped him again.

"My bad, Eli. I'm not good with being soft but you know I'm golden. You know I've missed you, right?"

Elias was bored with the conversation. "Don't you have another man's blood to suck?"

"Come on, Eli. You changed the game up on me. I wasn't expecting you to want a relationship from me then but I want that now. I see the way you are with La'Toria every time we run into each other by my peoples' house and it makes me want what you were trying to offer before." She walked up on him. "You know, us being together."

"Oh, really?"

"Yes, really. I can admit I made a mistake but I can rebound from that if you let me."

Elias shook his head. "Nah, I'm with Blu. She's happy and I'm good, so ain't shit happening with us. So you can kill it."

"So what you're saying is if she wasn't in the picture, you would have given me another chance to say sorry, kiss you all over and make it better?"

"Well, we'll never fuckin' know, now will we? 'Cause she is in the picture and she ain't goin' no muthafuckin' where."

If she had something more to say, she would have to tell it to someone who cared because Elias turned around and walked off from her.

La'Tasha smirked as she watched him and all of his swag glory go about his business.

Elias was right when he mentioned how much a challenged tickled her lady parts, but it was the cat and mouse game they played. And he nor his junior love with her baby sister was going to change that.

In La'Tasha's mind, Blu was kitten chow in comparison to her being the cat's meow, so there was no competition to be had. Eli was going to remember that. She only needed to lower his guards down just enough for her to get back into his chest.

That's what you think, she reentered her shop.

Two hours later...

Samiyah was sitting on her front lawn with Lil' Acacia in her outdoor playpen when Elias pulled up into the driveway. He hopped out of his truck and headed straight over to his baby. He picked her up and kissed her fat cheeks.

"Hey, maw maw. You ready to roll out with Daddy?" He kissed her a few more times before putting her down to finish playing.

"Why did you leave your truck running? You 'bout to head back out?" Samiyah inquired.

"Nah, I bought a puppy for Peaches and I didn't want it getting stuffy in there on him."

Samiyah reached out her hand for help getting up so she could take a peek at it. She walked over, opened the hatch and saw the most adorable cinnamon colored pup ever.

She picked him up. "What's his name?"

"Milo."

"I like it." She placed him back into the box and closed the hatch back.

"When he is old enough and completes obedience/guard school, he can be over here sometimes, if you cool with it."

"That's cool with me." She walked back over to her seat and sat down.

"So, how you feelin'?" Eli asked when he saw her blow out a breath of exhaustion.

"Like a baby factory."

"You still shocked from the news?" Eli squatted down beside her chair and rested his hand on her stomach.

"Yep. I really can't believe it. Lil' Acacia won't even be one years old by the time I have them. How am I gonna do the simple things like go to the store, sleep, take a shower, have a little bit of *me* time? It's gonna be so hard to do."

"Hard but not impossible, Yah. You're overwhelmed and I get that shit but you strong and you got a whole village outchea to help you, ya heard me. You got ya parents, me, Blu and Minnie. You winnin', lil' mama." He encouraged her.

She smiled, thankful for having the support she had but then her smile went flat.

Eli noticed it. "What's wrong, Yah?"

She turned her vibrating phone in his direction so he could see Gerran calling.

"He's been calling me over these last couple of days but I haven't been answering because all he do is make me cry." She rolled her eyes and shook her head. "And yea I know I've hurt him too, but I refuse to allow him to make me pay for my actions with my tears any longer."

"I been sayin' fuck him, ya heard me. Every stunt he been pullin' has been a hoe's move."

"Right." She finally agreed without feeling the need to defend him.

"Speakin' of that thuggah, you ever got around to putting my name on Peaches' birth certificate in place of his like I asked? I don't want my baby rockin' his last name. She's a Dupree."

"Yea, I inquired but you will have to take a DNA test in order to have it changed. They said my marriage to Gerran and him signing for her makes her his child legally regardless to the result from the hospital, but once we get a testing done with you two, we can change it."

"I'm cool with that. We can handle that tomorrow, right?"

"That's fine with me." Samiyah made a mental note to call the Diagnostic Center.

"A'ight, well let me bounce, ya dig. I'ma go scoop Blu and we gon' get everything we need for Milo and grab some lunch or somethin'. You gon' be good by yourself?"

"Yes indeed! I am goin' straight to sleep when you leave. So thank you for taking her but are you sure you can handle a week?"

"That's my round, my boogie down. I got this."

"Well, her bag is on the sofa. She has enough milk to last her two days in the freezer and fridge and I'll have more with me when we meet up for our appointment."

242

"Straight." Elias went inside, gathered everything and loaded it in the truck, grabbing Peaches last.

After he buckled the baby into her car seat, Samiyah gave her kisses and then turned to Eli. "You're the greatest dad any little girl can have."

Elias looked at Peaches stuff her foot into her mouth and said while gazing at her still. "I know I said in the beginning I never wanted kids, ya heard me, but I can't imagine my life without her. She make me want things I never saw myself having."

She smiled at that. "Well, don't let me keep you. Call me if you need me."

Elias hugged her and kissed her on top of her head. "Same here, but like I said, daddy got this!"

***

G'Corey had been itching to talk to Minnie, but he knew he couldn't just knock on her door to do it. So, he waited and waited some more for a crack to identify itself in her daily routine. And finally, after several weeks, it happened.

Minnie went to Planet Fitness to do her forty-five minute workout, as she would every Monday, Wednesday, Friday and Saturday except this time there was no one watching her moves.

He waited a while to see if the black Camaro that usually tailed her was going to pull up but after it didn't twenty minutes later, he headed inside of the gym.

"Welcome to Planet Fitness. What's your member ID number?" the young man greeted.

G'Corey slid the guy some cash. "One-zero-zero."

Although letting a non-member through was against company policy, the guy slapped him a dap and let him through with no hesitation.

Minnie was on the treadmill toward the back of the gym with her earbuds in her ears listening to her workout mix when a call came through interrupting her playlist. She looked at the Caller ID, it was Yuriah.

"Hey, baby," she huffed into the phone.

"What's up, love? Where you at?"

"Planet Fitness."

"Why didn't you wake me up before you left?"

"Because you barely sleep, so I figured you must have been really tired if you were napping and I didn't want to disturb you."

Damn! He never felt comfortable with her being alone but he wouldn't let her know that. "How long will you be?"

"Half an hour or so. Why? Do you need anything?"

"Nah, just you, ya heard me."

That man made her feel desired. "I need you, too. I'll call you when I'm on my way." Minnie hung up the phone and her music resumed.

Get up/Don't sit there/Get up/If you wanna get there/Clocks won't stop and time won't wait/ Get up...

Minnie was singing along with Mary Mary when she was startled from the tap on her shoulder. She removed her buds and looked to her right.

"Sorry to disturb you, ma'am, but is this your towel on the floor?" He picked it up and held it up for her to see.

She looked at it. "Yes it is. I didn't notice it fell. Thank you."

"No problem." He walked off.

Minnie went to refocus on her walk but noticed an image to her left that almost made her heart leap out of her chest. She wanted to pretend she didn't see him but the buckle in her knees and the tension coursing through her body made it obvious she'd seen something unexpected.

Even with a hoodie over his head, she knew it was *him*.

"Keep walking." G'Corey told her from the treadmill on the side of her.

Minnie slowed her speed down to a crawl as her legs were having a terrible time holding her up.

She didn't want to show her fear or her anger so she tried to be casual. "What are you doing here?"

"I'm here to workout, just like you. I been wanting to see you again so it funny to have bumped into you here." He chuckled.

She gave a painful laugh as she looked at him from the corners of her eyes. Then she counted the number of people around her that could potentially help her if he tried kidnapping her.

"You're looking good but then again you always have."

Minnie looked so uncomfortable. It could be seen through the worry in her eyes. She was petrified of the man she once felt so safe with. She had to go, she couldn't fake airs with him so she stopped her machine.

"Thanks for the compliment. It was ni—nice seeing you, but my workout is done."

She attempted to get off of the machine but G'Corey grabbed her by her wrist. "Keep walking. I'm trying to talk to you," he spoke firmly, looking around before he let it go.

Minnie did as he instructed, resuming the conveyor belt and walking. "What do you want?"

"What do I want? You sounded so formal like you don't know me no more. Are you scared, baby?" He got off of his machine and stood right up on hers, fixing her shirt and rubbing a trace along her moist arm.

"Yes," she started whimpering. "You shot at me."

"Baby, baby, I would never try to hurt you. I don't even know what got into me that day but you know I couldn't harm my black butterfly. When have I ever laid a finger on you other than to make love to your body?"

She shook her head and flinched when he clutched her hand. "Never."

"Minnie, baby. Look at me. I love you and all I want is to show you how much. Please give me a chance to introduce you to the new me and allow me to give you the same ole lovin' you used to crave. Can you give me one date?"

Minnie was too afraid to tell him *hell no* so she said, "Yes."

G'Corey was surprised at how easy the answer came but he was too excited to question the validity of it.

"Let's meet up at Houston's. You still like that place, right?"

She nodded her head *yes*.

"A'ight. Tomorrow for noon and bring our lil' one." G'Corey hadn't seen her with a child on any of the occasions he'd been watching her, so he paid attention to how she answered.

Minnie thought to just agree to the terms just to get him to leave but then she said, "There is no baby, G'Corey. I had a miscarriage early in my pregnancy."

"No! No!" G'Corey gritted anger. He knew something had to have happened but he clung to hope that maybe her mother was caring for their baby while she regrouped. He placed his hand on her stomach and mourned his loss and she cringed at his touch. He looked up at her with tears running down his face. "You lost my seed?"

She shook her head *yes* and in that moment, she oddly felt sad for him. Minnie caught a glimpse of his tenderness and a small piece of her ached but the fact remained it was only a flash of him she saw because in her mind, he was a monster.

"Look, G'Corey. I—I really need to be going. My family is expecting me in a few minutes." She let it be known that people would worry about her in the event he thought to do something.

G'Corey snapped out of his remorseful state and looked at her with a slightly hardened face. "Are you trying to get from 'round me?"

"No." She shook her head *no*. "Not at all. I just really have to be going."

He looked at her oddly for a second, which made her heart pound harder, then he softened his look. G'Corey pulled her off of the treadmill and into his arms, placing his face in the crook of neck, kissing her gently.

"I love you, yea. And all I want to do is apologize for everything I did wrong and make it right, ya heard me."

She bobbed her head. "Okay."

He bent down and kissed her lips once, twice and then the final time he eased his tongue into her mouth. G'Corey knew the rhythm of kiss wasn't the same but he didn't worry about that. Just the feel of them reenergized his purpose to have her again.

246

He pulled away and then pecked her lips, gazing at her lovingly. She wanted to literally throw up but she kept her upsetness down.

"Houston's. You and me. Twelve sharp, ya heard me."

Minnie repeated after him. "Twelve sharp."

G'Corey smiled vibrantly as he headed out. This was the happiest he'd been in over a year.

Samiyah's words came to Minnie's mind, clear as day.

"...you don't know where his head is and I already lost Acacia. I can't lose you, too, too, too, too, too..."

Tears pushed from the corners of her eyes as the words echoed loudly in her head. It became obvious what she needed to do next.

Coffee

Chapter 28

Two weeks later...

"I've been thinking. Things have been going really good between us, you agree?" Elias stood in front of Blu.

"Most definitely." She smiled.

He grabbed her left hand and rubbed it gently. "I think it's time that we take our relationship to the next level. Hold up, let me get down here for a second." Elias got on one knee.

Oh, my God! Blu began fanning herself. This was so unexpected but she was ready. She never practiced how she would accept a man's proposal but how hard was it to say *yes*?

Elias dropped his head and lifted it back up when he picked up an earring off of the floor that he had lost. "Got it."

Blu snatched her hand back. "Negro, I thought you—oh, never mind."

"You thought what?" Then he looked at himself and then her and burst out laughing.

"I swear you play too much." She was annoyed at how played she felt being wrong.

Elias laughed tears out of his eyes. He swiped them away and blew out a breath. "You tryna get locked down?" He laughed some more.

"Whatever. Well, if you weren't about to ask me to marry your ass, what the hell you think it's time for?"

"For you to have a drawer or two for your clothes."

She balled her mouth to hide her smile. "I swear I can't stand you." She play punched him but he blocked it and softly slapped her upside the head. "Ooh, that's your ass." She took off running behind him.

He ran out of his bedroom and into the dining room, circling it a few times to keep from getting hit. "Come on, nah, Blu. You play too much."

"Let me get my lick back and we'll be Even Stevens."

"Damn! It mean that much to you?"

"Yes."

"Come get you, then." He stood still so she could pop him once. But the moment she got close enough to smack him, he tripled tapped her and ran out of the front door.

She chased him but stopped at the porch. "You done messed up now because the only way you can get back inside is if I get me. So you might as well come face the music."

"A'ight. Damn, I swear you childish." He clowned as he walked back inside to a barrage of hits that turned into a make-out session once he pinned her on the sofa.

After a few minutes of messing around, Blu reminded Eli that he had to pick up Peaches so they could go to Audubon Zoo. He kissed her again and then got up.

"Good lookin' out. Make sure you put on that shirt I bought you so we can be a matching trio."

Elias had on a T-shirt that read: *I'm hers.* He bought a T-shirt for Peaches that read: *I'm his.* And one for Blu that read: *I'm the side chick.*

"I'm not wearing that shit. You can forget it, buddy boy." She laughed at how silly he was, but she loved it.

"Have it your way, then." He grabbed his keys off of the coffee table.

"Bae, which drawers should I clear out?"

"The top two on the left" He unlocked the door and opened it. "Oh and one more thing."

"Yea, baby."

"Take this." He tapped her on the face and flew out of the house, getting inside of his truck before Blu had the chance catch up to him.

She stood at his window and placed her fist from eye to the other and then pointed at him. She mouthed, *See you at three o'clock.* They both laughed as he pulled off.

He really loved that girl.

Twenty minutes later…

Samiyah opened the door when she heard Elias knocking.

"What's up, Yah?" He greeted her and reached for Peaches out of her arms. "Why isn't she dressed?"

"Because there has been a change of plans."

"What's wrong? She got the loose bowels again. Did you feed her those prunes? You know that goes straight through her."

"No, I didn't. Come in the living room and have a seat. I wanna show you something."

Eli looked at her peculiarly but followed behind her, silently.

"Da da da da da..."

"I hear you talkin', lil' girl, but let's see what mama talkin' 'bout." He gave Samiyah the *I'm waiting* look.

Samiyah contemplated how to begin but she determined it was best if she didn't say anything at all. She simply handed him the letter she received in the mail.

"What's this?" He reached out for it.

"Just read it, please."

His eyes scanned the document, then he looked over at Samiyah and then back to the paper, this time reading each word slowly.

The alleged father is excluded as the biological father of the tested child. Based on testing results obtained from analyses of the DNA, the probability of paternity is...

Elias felt his breath leave his body as he dropped his head down. Peaches grabbed him and tried sucking on the side of his face as she would anytime he got too close to her mouth.

"Elias?" Samiyah called out to him but he didn't respond. "Elias, please answer me."

He couldn't. He was choking on his words.

She walked over to him with tears streaming down her face, touching him gently on the shoulder. "I'm so sorry, E. I swear I've never been sorrier in my life. Please talk to me."

Never raising his head, he faintly asked, "Who's her daddy, then?"

She didn't hear him. "Say it again."

He lifted his head and tears soaked his entire face. His big, beautiful, brown eyes were heavy with despondency. "Who's. Her. Daddy?"

In the six years she'd been knowing Elias, she never once saw him cry. And to know she was the reason for it, broke her heart.

It was just five months ago when Gerran asked her the same question. Her head hung low and she closed her eyes. When she envisioned her daughter's face, she saw the image of her father's clearly. They had the exact same eyes.

"Cedric."

***

Blu sat on the edge of Eli's bed, stupefied. Every time she finally got comfortable in her relationship, something dealing with Samiyah would happen to make her uncomfortable all over again.

She had to call Kanari so she could vent her frustrations. As she waited for her to pick up, she scanned his personal mail line for line.

"Hello." The drag of her voice told Blu she just finished smoking.

"Kanari, why I ran across some shit that just blew the hell out of me?"

"What your *seek and find* ass found now?" Kanari chuckled at her.

"This ain't even funny, for real. I was cleaning out some drawers like he asked me to do and I saw a bunch of his bank statements. Now, I'll admit I shouldn't have looked at them but I did and I found boo-coo charges for Samiyah on them."

"How do you know they're for her?"

"Listen to this. Mom & Me—$260.93, Massage Envy—$156.50, The Infinity dealership—$654.19. Double payments to Entergy and Sewerage and Water Board every month…"

"Stop! Is this the kind of relationship you want?" Kanari heard enough.

"No. He just…"

"Let me hold the mirror to your face, sis. He has been friends with that girl longer than he knew of your existence and you're acting like that relationship is supposed to disappear because you're sleeping with him. Well, it doesn't work like that and you're smart enough to know it. So, you can't keep spazzing out on him for being true to himself when he keeps lookin' out for her. All you can do now is be true to yourself. Is it a deal or no deal?"

"You're right. I can't handle his friend doubling as his baby's moms. He's doing way too much. I will never be number one in his life since that slot is already filled. I have to let go."

Tears slid down her face as gloom enveloped her. She really loved Eli and wanted to be with him but it appeared that being with him meant being in a threesome with him and Samiyah.

"So, when are you going to do it?"

"I am gonna talk with him when he gets home and let him know there can't be an us." Blu broke out crying. It was clear she didn't want to end things with him but she was either going to break it off today or postpone the inevitable from happening on another.

As painful as it was for her to admit, she just didn't fit in his life the way it was now.

"You sure that's what you want to do?" Kanari asked her to be sure.

"No, but it has to be done."

"Well, whatever you do, do not sleep with him because then you gon' end up stayin'."

Her eyes rolled to the back of her head just thinking about the withdrawals that were sure to come. "We can't do it once and call it *goodbye* sex?"

"Hellll no! Didn't you say he got the magic stick that took yo ass to a mystic land where you discovered unicorns were real or some shit?"

Blu laughed through her tears. "Yea, I told you to call me Pegasus that day."

"This is what I know. Good dick will have you puttin' up with shit you shouldn't, so don't do it."

"Damn! No more seeing purple horseshoes, green clovers and blue diamonds for me."

"I'll buy yo ass a box of Lucky Charms. Just stick to your guns, sis."

Blu stopped chuckling and took a more serious tone. "I will. I'll just tell him that I overestimated my ability to go through this situation and—" Blu removed the phone from her ear when she heard a sound. "That's him. I'll call you back." She hung up the phone and threw all of his mail back into the drawer, meeting him upfront.

Eli sat down on the sofa, resting his elbow on the arm of the couch and rubbing his thumb over his bottom lip, thinking.

She recognized his low conscious as she sat next to him. She curiously asked, "What's the matter and where's Peaches?"

"She with her mama?"

"I figured that much but weren't you going to get her?"

Elias sat soundless for a moment but then he spoke. "I'ma say this but I don't want you asking me nothing about it until I bring it back up to you?"

She shook her head *yes* without uttering a word. "Peaches isn't mine."

Blu's mouth dropped open. She didn't know what to say but she promised she wouldn't anyway, so she didn't try.

She just consoled him silently, choosing not to bring up Samiyah and the money he shelled out on her. It appeared fate had it that she wouldn't be a problem anymore.

***

G'Corey sat in front of the TV zombiefied, looking at his wedding DVD. He'd been doing the same thing every day for the last two weeks.

"Bitch, you is sad." Skittles shook her head at him, cutting the television off. "You gotta get a grip on yourself because you startin' to weird me out, for real. You don't even look the same no more. Have you seen yourself lately?"

He didn't answer her because it wasn't relevant to him. Instead, he flowed his thoughts off the top of his head.

"Skits, the woman I married would have never played me like she did. She wouldn't have looked me in my eyes, say she'll meet me only to set me up." G'Corey shook his head in disappointment. "Had I been a duck and sat up in that restaurant, Yuriah and them would have took me out. Why the fuck would she do that?"

Skittles could tell G'Corey was out of touch with reality, so she had to level him a bit.

"You a real dickhead, bruh. That girl is scared of you. You actually thought you was just gonna pop up one day, say a couple *I love yous* and shit was gonna automatically go back to normal? Yep, I'm convinced your stupid ass get a check on both the first and the fifteenth. Be honest."

G'Corey glared at her. "Do I look like I'm in the fuckin' mood to play with you?" He cut the DVD back on. "That girl is my fuckin' world and at one point I was hers. But she got too many mutha-fuckas crowding her view and she can't see that now and I've played it cool for far too long. I'm not sitting on my hands no more. I'm 'bout to move shit up out of our way."

"And what is that supposed to mean?"

"Keep watchin' the news."

Coffee

Chapter 29

Six weeks later...

"Can you believe we gon' be graduating next week?" Ace asked before he turned the grab bag of Cheetos upside down into his mouth.

"Huh, bruh. It's been a long time coming but we made it." BG held his middle fingers up. "And fuck everybody who said we couldn't do it, too."

"Yea, ole pussy ass thuggahs can all suck our dicks." Ace grabbed his crotch.

BG looked at him sideways. "Nah, I ain't inviting no man to suck my dick, ya heard me. What type of faggot ass shit you on?"

"Fuck you, man. You know what the hell I'm talkin' 'bout."

"Word that shit differently, ya dig." BG straightened him out.

"I'm tired of you playin' with me, bitch. Come get some." Ace squared up to slap box.

"These hands ain't what you want." BG got up from the stoop and met Ace on the porch.

The boys exchanged licks and dodged others. Ace was cold with his but BG was colder. After a minute of horse-playing, BG called for a time out.

"Damn! You seen her before?" BG turned Ace's head in the direction of the cutie he spotted.

Before the young girl could walk past Ace's house, BG caught her attention. "Say, lil' mama, can walk wit'chu?"

"You don't know where I'm goin'." She stopped to address him.

"It don't matter."

She looked around for a second like she had to ponder her reply. "Yea, it's cool. Come on."

BG turned to Ace. "A'ight, bitch, I'ma fuck back wit'cha in a few, you feel me." BG slapped hands with Ace twice before doing some elaborate handshake that called for forearm touches, special grips and a snap.

"Ya betta, bitch. Remember, you gotta cut my hair for tomorrow."

"A'ight."

"Dawg, come the fuck back *today*," Ace reiterated.

"Mannn, quit whining like a lil' hoe." BG grinned.

They pounded each other off again and then BG trotted down the steps of the porch to meet up with her.

He pulled up his pants to prevent them from sagging further below his behind although they still dropped back to its original spot. "Where we goin'?"

"Up'ta Keys Corner Store."

He boldly threw his arm around her neck and she automatically wrapped her arm around his waist. BG flashed his handsome smile and dimples. "I likes that, ya heard me. Hold on to yo thuggah."

She laughed like she found him funny but she liked his confidence. "My thuggah? What if I got an ole man already?"

"You don't but if you do, he lame as fuck. 'Cause if he was handlin' business, you wouldn't be cheesin' as hard as you doing." He referred to the smile plastered across her face. "So, what's yo name, bay-bae?"

"Paulette but everybody call me Pee fa short. What's yours?"

"BG."

"What dat stand fa? Born Gangsta or something?"

He chuckled, "Nah, but I can dig dat, doe. He stopped walking, removed his arm from around her and raised the sleeve of his shirt, exposing the tattoo going across his arm.

"Baby Goon," she read it aloud.

"But you can just call me Baby, ya dig." He placed his arm back around her neck and continued walking.

"Well, Baby, why dey call you dat? And is you some kinda D-boy or something?" She fingered the rope chain around his neck.

He frowned before he broke out in a grin. "What type of question dat is? You the Narc or somebody?"

She giggled, "Yea, I'm dem people and I'm 'bout to put yo cute self on my house arrest."

"Girl, you gon' make me steal a kiss." He looked down at her plump lips.

"You ain't gon' hafta steal it." She got fresh back with him. "Let me stop being bad."

"I like bad, ya heard me. And to answer your question, I don't fuck around with no dope. That ain't my life."

"That's good. Alright, next question. Booker T. Washington or LB Landry?"

"This my last year at Booker T."

"Then what?"

"Then I'ma be a rapper."

"Oh, you nice wit' it?"

"Hell yea! Ya boy got skills."

"Oh, yea? Kick something fa me, then."

They now stood on the corner of Louisiana and S. Robertson in front of the store when BG agreed.

"A'ight then. I'ma run dis freestyle real quick, ya heard me." He started shifting his hands back in forth in the same manner a deejay using a turn table would as he found a beat in his head to flow to.

If you ain't a head busta, then you can't get crap/Should have listened to ya boy when he said carry that strap/Either on ya waistline or the small of ya back/And when swervin' through the city keep that thang on ya lap/'Cause these mu'fuckas will test you, they ain't playin'/Try to knock your brains out like Kurt Cobain.

"Ah oh! That boy fire like cayenne." Pee motioned her hands in the air in a triple pat manner and then headed for the door. She turned her head over her shoulder and noticed he wasn't behind her. "You coming in?"

BG had missed a call from Munch while he was rapping that he had to return. "Nah, I'll wait out here. But get me a Delaware Punch and pay for yours, too." He reached into his pocket and pulled out a twenty.

"Alright. Thank you," Paulette walked inside.

He dialed Munch and when he heard his voice, he responded, "Wuz'am?"

"Wuz'am is yo big brother got somebody who wanna put chu on."

"You being for real? You ain't fuckin' around?" BG started walking excitedly in circles, talking with his hands.

"Come on, man. I wouldn't pull yo leg."

"Awww, man. It's 'bout to go down!"

"Where you at right nah?"

"Uptown. Where else?" he asked rhetorically. He didn't roam outside of the third ward too much. "I'm at Keys, though. 'Bout to head back over by Ace unless you need me to be where you are."

"Yea, holla at me. I'm at Raw Musik Studios. I'ma shoot you the address and I need you to get here ASAP 'cause this man waitin', ya heard me."

"A'ight. I'ma be there in a hot minute." BG relaxed his hyper for a moment and turned serious. "Dawg, I been waitin' for dis moment my whole life. Thanks, big brudda. I fucks with... Nah, fuck that. I love you, man."

Munch laughed at him. "I know dis 'cause you show dis. See you in a minute, lil' brudda. And you know I fucks wit'chu, too."

"Heavy." BG hung up and like the true performer he was, he broke out in dance and started spitting some rehearsed lines he wrote from the other night.

Paulette came outside to see him in concert mode, commanding the sidewalk like it was his stage. He was amped up. She didn't know why but she joined in.

"Heyyyy," she sang, throwing her hands in the air and snapping her fingers before she placed her hands on her knees, arched her back and lift her rump to pop.

BG turned to face her and got more excited when he saw her just as crunk as him. "You a cool lil' mama, yea. I'm feelin' you already. So let me run down some things you need to know as my woman..."

"*As your woman*? When did that happen?" She interrupted.

"You not gon' be my girl?" BG's smile was impossible to resist.

"But you don't know me."

"Yet." He interjected. "I don't know you *yet*."

"But…"

"But this," he stepped up to her and kissed her lips and when she didn't slap the red off of his skin, he kissed her again.

"Whoa!" She pulled back and smiled at how much she liked his assertiveness.

"Now like I was saying, *as my woman*, you can't be with all that fussin' because *The Kid* gonna be spending mad time in the studio. A thuggah brother just called him to let him know we on and poppin'."

"Ah ohhh!" Pee went in to dap him up but he slapped her hand away.

"You ain't the homie."

Pee blushed and then kissed his jaw. "Is that better?"

"Much."

As she was handing him his cold drink and change, his phone rang.

"Hol' on." He answered the call. "Wuz'am?"

"Man, is you on your way or what?" Ace didn't want BG fading him at the last minute.

BG looked at his watch. "Mannnn, I been gone for what, fifteen minutes and you sweatin' me? Go change your manpon, bitch." BG laughed at him. "Look here, I'ma have to postpone yo shit 'til later because I have to get to the studio, ya dig. Munch lined a lil' something up. You wanna roll with me?"

Ace quit his minor rant immediately. That was major. "Do you even have to ask? You know I'ma be dipped off in that thang with you…"

BG made a few grunts as he listened to his homie with his head down, eyeing his fresh white G-Nike.

Then a strange feeling came over him, telling him to look up. When he did, he saw Pee's eyes grow the size of saucers as her mouth opened in the form of an O. He didn't know what called for her petrified reaction but he was ready to face it and then get the fuck from off of the corner.

Dropping his phone to the earth, he lifted his shirt to pull his banger off of his waist so when he turned around he could blast, if he had to.

Sure enough when he spun around, he understood Pee's fearful expression. In a split second, he was faced with an up-close view of the barrel from the assailant's heat.

In all but a second, BG bit his bottom lip infuriatedly as he raised his gun to pop off.

With no words, no hesitation, he pulled the trigger twice.

Bow! Bow!

The shots rang loudly. The piercing sound was deafening.

Soundlessly, Pee stood there shaken, in shock, unable to move from her spot.

Moments later, the death of one man made the streets come alive. People came cautiously walking up from different directions, curiously seeking to see if the victim laid slain on the sidewalk was any friend or kin of theirs.

***

"I know dis 'cause you show dis. I fucks wit'chu, too, lil' brudda. See you in a minute." Munch text him the address to Raw Musik.

He's on his way?" Gerran asked the moment he saw Munch slide his phone into his pocket.

"Yea. He'll be here, ya heard me."

Gerran nodded his head and then smiled as he turned on a track he recently mixed down for BG's sound. He then stood up from his seat and started rocking to the hard hit of it. "Yea, this that shit right there. I can see youngin' goin' hard on this bitch."

Munch bobbed his head in agreement. He could picture BG killin' it, too.

"Your brother got skills. How old is he again?" Gerran lowered the volume and sat back down, excited to meet the young talent.

"He seventeen but he be on some next level shit, ya dig," Munch spoke highly of BG's creative flow.

Gerran looked down at his ringing phone. "I'ma take this call. You good?"

"I'm straight. Handle you."

Gerran stepped out and Munch looked around the studio, imagining BG in the booth laying down something nice.

At that very moment, he couldn't be any prouder than he was right then. If the numbers on the contract were official, then his brother was on his way to living his dream. And as of next Saturday, Nicholas McMillan was graduating at the top of his class with honors, fulfilling their father's dream.

Munch had a silly grin on his face and he wasn't even trying to wipe it off. He wondered what his Pops would tell him if he was there.

He tapped his chest twice and then pointed it to the ceiling. With a fatherly type of pride, he boasted. "We did it, Pops!"

***

"BG?" Ace heard what appeared to be his phone dropping. He waited a few moments, surely he'd pick it up. A few uncomfortable seconds passed and right as he was about to call his name again, he vividly heard two gun shots ring out. "Yo, BG, what the fuck? BG?"

Shit didn't feel right to Ace. The same clapping sound he heard from outside rang 3D in his ear. So he rushed to the back room of the house, grabbed his gat, stuffing it in his waistband and flew out of the door.

Ace ran so hard and so fast it almost looked like his feet barely touched the pavement. He prayed to God that BG's sudden silence and the double shots he heard had nothing to with his homie getting crossed up. But he didn't believe in coincidence, so he pushed up the two blocks even faster.

When he saw a group of people huddled in one section, Ace knew to go there as well. He slowed up to a jog, surveying the scene. The closer he got up on it was the wilder his heart raced. *Shit ain't right*, he thought when he saw the girl BG pushed up on traumatized as she looked down at the body he still wasn't close enough to recognize.

"Aye, man, don't go over there lil' brother." The OG stretched out his arm to block him, but Ace pushed it out of his way.

He walked up on the backs of people, blocking his view. He needed to get see what they saw. Ace speared his hands between two bodies. "Move! Move!"

They parted for the teenager and when they did and he caught his first glimpse. He spun around and lurched forward. *Bluh! Bluh!*

Ace heaved up the contents in his stomach when he saw BG's bloody body sprawled on the ground with half of his face blown off. He threw up so long he was barely able to breath.

On lookers knew the boys' relationship all too well. They never saw one without the other. The fellas were thick as thieves and virtually inseparable, so when Ace started bawling, everyone knew why.

"Aaaahhhhhh!" Ace groaned in agony. Never had he felt pain like this before. Even when his own brother was murdered it didn't devastate him like this was. Then again, he was fortunate not to have seen him slumped over the steering wheel of his car when he was shot up, either.

The crowd grew bigger and circled around BG, looking at him like some spectacle. That angered Ace, so he pulled out his gun and waved it from left to right, right to left.

"Back the fuck up. Ain't shit to see here." Tears still cascaded down his face but he was serious than a muthafucka.

They took heed to his lethal warning and spread the fuck out. Satisfied with the distance, he placed his gun on the ground as he kneeled down beside him. Removing the shirt off of his back, he covered BG's face. No one else was going to get the opportunity to see his homie that way.

Snot ran from his nose and over his lips as he blinked back unstoppable tears. "God, why mannnn? Why the fuck you didn't protect him, bruh?"

Ace looked at BG from top to bottom, noticing his finger curled around the trigger of his gun. He removed it from his hand, then he grabbed his off of the ground, placing them both in the small of his back.

He stood to his feet and hovered over BG in the same manner a watch dog would its property. He slid his arm across his face to remove some of the wetness as he mugged everyone.

Then the chime of a BG's phone ringing broke Ace's stare down at every person who stood at bay, waiting to gather enough *he say she say* to run tell that.

The phone lay not too far from BG. He swooped down and picked it up to see Munch's number across the screen.

"Fuck!" He didn't want to be the one to tell him his little brother was gunned down but he knew he had no choice. His body shook from bad nerves, causing his voice to quake as he answered. "Hello."

"B—Ace? Put BG on the phone, dawg." Munch was looking at the time. BG should have been there by now.

"Ah. Umm." Ace started to tell him but paused.

"Dawg, what the fuck wrong with you? Give him the phone."

"Ahh, Munch, mann," Ace began breaking down.

Ace was tripping over his words and Munch didn't have the patience to coax it out of him. He knew enough to know something was wrong.

He didn't know what the hell that something was but in about twenty minutes, he was sure to find out.

Uptown, New Orleans...

Turning down S. Claiborne Ave., Munch made a left on Louisiana Ave. where a mob of people and flashing lights on emergency vehicles congregated. His gut told him to pull over and when he saw Ace, he definitely parked and ran up on the scene.

Ace was standing off to the right with his hands on the top of his head and his eyes glued on BG when he noticed Munch run up on him from the side.

'What the fuck happened? And where BG?" Munch looked around the crowd for him but the sky was darkening its hue, making it hard to distinguish faces from afar.

"He gone, bruh." Ace started crying some more.

"Gone where?" His denial was ever-present. Munch noticed a body off to his side but he wasn't about to accept that the corpse under the sheet had any business to do with him. But he had to be sure.

Munch pushed Ace out of his way, knocking him off to the side as he bum rushed a path to face his fear.

He ducked under the crime scene tape and made a beeline for the person he prayed wasn't his brother.

"Get back behind the line." One officer directed but Munch wasn't hearing that.

He jogged over to the body, kneeled down by the head and snatched the sheet off of him.

"BG! Noooo, man. Fuck no!" he said in horrid disbelief. Tears dropped on command as a surge of pain clutched his heart so strongly he thought he was about to stroke out.

Then suddenly, he was yanked away by Officer Santemore. "You're contaminating the crime scene."

"Fuck off me!" Munch growled, elbowing the cop off of him, jerking his way out of his hold so he could go back to where his brother lay.

Santemore pulled out his nightstick and hemmed Munch by the neck, cutting off his air supply and dragging him backwards.

"You think you can do what you want just 'cause you mad? Huh?" Santemore spoke aggressively in his ear as he pulled the stick tighter against his throat. "You're in my will house. You do as I say!" He removed the billy club, shoving a gasping Munch off to the side.

Munch stumbled into a few nearby people who caught him. Once he regained his footing and his breath, he charged back toward bitch ass Santemore but a different cop intervened, stopping him.

"Calm down, man. You don't want to get arrested for whatever you're thinking about doing. Now let me help you. Do you know the victim?" He started off asking when Munch overheard Sante-more talking slick to one of his own.

"He's one less criminal we gotta worry about," Santemore said to his colleague, speaking of the deceased.

Munch looked past the policeman attempting to get information on BG and called out to Santemore as he sidestepped around the interrogating officer, pushing him out of his way. "Fuck you and that badge, you pussy bitch!" He pointed his finger dead at him, so there'd be no mistakes who he was gunning for.

His eyes were flooded with retaliation and he was going to make Santemore regret speaking so loosely about his brother. If he would have armed himself with his strap that was in the car, he would have given the coroners another body to examine.

He attempted to march into the lion's den of cops, a black man's last standing, but was taken down hostilely by three cops yelling expletives.

"Get down now!"

"Don't move!"

With his arms chicken winged behind his back, one cop kneeing him in the back, another on his legs and the last one smashing his head against the pavement, all he could was watch his brother lay cold from ground level.

That one was for you, Hakeem, G'Corey thought before he disappeared into the night.

Coffee

Chapter 30

A week later...

BG's funeral was about to start but Munch couldn't get out of the limo. He couldn't look upon the shell of his baby brother, a boy he raised as his own son for twelve years, and not spazz all the way out. It was best for everybody if he mourned him in solitude.

Reds opted to stay with him. She was unsure how to console him. But she wanted him to know if he was feeling alone, he wasn't.

The red rims circling Munch's puffy eyes was evidence of hours' worth of hardcore crying. He was so devastated. So angry. His fists were tightly balled into his lap. He looked crazed as he stared off into nothingness, looking like he was going to snap at any moment.

Reds was afraid, not of him but for him. His breaths were short, he was factually struggling to breathe. It seemed as if the loss of his BG was literally taking the life away from him.

There was no way the man responsible wasn't going to pay with his own life.

Reds feared the consequence that the slaying of his brother would bring because she knew there would be one since Munch planned to take vengeance from the Lord's hand and place them in his.

***

Hours later at the graduation...

The principal called the names of the graduating students one by one. "Shondrick Davenport."

Ace stood in place, feeling throwed off. He was supposed to be joked out, looking back at BG off in the distant line. But he wasn't. A day promised to the both of them was now only being given to one.

This shit ain't even right, God.

"Shondrick Davenport." He announced his name again when Ace didn't budge, waving him onto the stage.

Ace stood at the edge of the steps, mesmerized. He heard his name being called but he couldn't manage to lift his foot.

His classmate behind him understood his hesitation. Every student in the auditorium knew the reason for his pause.

"Come on. You got this." She encouraged as she slung his arm around her neck and grabbed him around the waist.

As he took guided strides, his knees almost gave out on him, causing him to buckle but she caught him.

A minute later, he stood in front of the principal, who handed him his diploma. The girl had stepped out of the way so the photographer could take his picture. But by this time, Ace had broken down fully. The photo was sure to capture the look of a young man who was suffering.

Several names were called after his but the one that brought everyone to their feet out of respect for a fellow Lion was the call of BG's.

"Nicholas McMillan?" The principal announced and Munch, with a heavy heart, walked across the stage in his place and in honor of his brother.

The principal extended his hand to Munch and pulled him into him. "Our condolences are with you, young brother."

He then placed the diploma in his hand and everyone cheered and began chanting: *BG! BG! BG!*

Tears welled in Munch's eyes for mixed reasons. He was both proud and filled with unbearable grief. He took his hand with the scrolled certificate in it, doubled tapped his chest and then looked up, pointing it up above. That was how the photographer commemorated the moment. Munch saluting his BG.

Later that night...

Yuriah, Kamal, Ace and Keyz all sat in the living of Munch's house. Everyone was processing their next moves as they kept an eye on Munch. There was no way to predict what he would do. He'd been too quiet for anyone's liking.

"I can't figure out for the life of me why that thuggah would come for BG. Mannn, Munch ain't hard to find. Why didn't he come at his neck?" Ace knew for a fact it would had been a different result had he confronted Munch.

Tonight they would have been partying, riding the highs of what spoils BG's rap career would bring him with Ace as his hype man. But instead, he trying to understand why life had to be so fucked up.

Munch sat silently as he listened to the evil inside of his head. He was consumed with hellacious fire that could only be extinguished with him knocking G'Corey's head off of his shoulders.

Yuriah sat back and admonished himself. He took blame for everything. The shooting at his wedding, Munch catching a gun charge, Minnie's paranoia and now BG's untimely death.

Yuriah thought on a quote from Machiavelli: *If an injury had to be done to a man, it should be so severe that his vengeance need not be feared.* "Why the fuck didn't I smash his bitch ass when I had the chance?"

"Fuck that! We ain't takin' no mo losses. I gotta a team of head bustas that are trained to go. If that boy is in the city, he will be found tonight! Give me the word." Keyz looked to Munch.

Munch's jaw was so tight it sealed his mouth shut. Kamal looked over to Keyz and answered for Munch. "That boy long gone but if he stupid enough to be here, bring him back alive."

Keyz' adrenaline spiked. "A'ight. I'm on that shit. I'm out."

"There will be no rest until that muthafucka is left with his dick in the dirt," Kamal spoke to everybody.

"He gotta know his day coming." Ace thought back two years ago when Magnolia Munch had to let it be known what time a day it was when it came to his BG.

The corner of Magnolia and Sixth was crunk as usual. Everybody was outside when Chuckie, 3rd ward's biggest and most feared D-Boy, pulled up on the scene.

His presence commanded the attention of everyone because he flaunted how well he was eating off of the streets by the flashy clothes, jewels and cars his money afforded him.

He was an arrogant S.O.B., quick tempered and over confident and the only reason he hadn't been faded was because of the gorillas he was associated with.

Chuckie parked his black on black Mercedes along the curbside. Then the three doors of his whip simultaneously opened once the engine shut down. One, his baby's moms. Two, his lieutenant. And lastly, the man himself.

He stepped on the block, dapping up a few cats that worshipped at his Jordans. His baby's moms and right hand man stood close in tow like two trained pits.

"What y'all thuggahs outchea doing?" Chuckie pulled out a joe, lit it, and puffed ringlets into the air.

"Bustin' some rhymes. These dummies think they lyrical beasts, but they ain't shit compared to me." The neighborhood spitter boasted.

Chuckie prided himself on his freestyle abilities and thought to take the opportunity to shine brighter than the thirty thousand dollar jewelry that draped around his neck.

"Let me get in on this, ya heard me." Chuckie inserted himself into the mix.

The two men went back and forth and the crowd that circled around them went wild. They went at it, spitting bars until Chuckie hit below the belt, making his opponent bow out. It wasn't because he couldn't come harder, he just knew it wasn't worth the drama if he did.

"Awww, man, he so phony, dawg. He went in on that man, stuntin' fa his bitch, no doubt." BG sucked through the tight space between his teeth.

"Oh, but that boy still cold, though." Ace gave Chuckie his props as he called out the next amateur to step up to the plate like he was on 8 Mile.

"Mannnn, get off his nuts. You actin' like homie be giving you free turkeys during Thanksgiving or something." BG clowned Ace as he elbowed him in the side. *"I'm much colda than he is."*

"A'ight, then. Go eat him up." Ace pointed in his direction.

"Like dog food," BG pounded Ace with the biggest Kool-Aid grin. *He hopped off of the porch and walked over to the inner circle, adjusting his nuts by lifting the crotch of his jeans. "Wuz'am? I got next."*

Chuckie looked BG down from head to toe and laughed. "Lil' BG? I don't wanna bring it to you, son. Let somebody else get this verbal lashing." He turned to his lieutenant to co-sign.

"Yea, whoa. Get back on tha porch where it's safe, lil' hoe-mie. It's piranhas outchea." He G-dapped a laughing Chuckie.

BG caught the emphasis he placed on hoe but he wasn't a sensitive dude, so he didn't give a fuck.

"Man, fuck all that, ya heard me. Just gimme my rounds." BG folded his arms across his chest as he waited.

"Should I give it to youngin', baby?" Chuckie asked of his baby's moms.

She nodded her head yes. "Give him the business, boo."

He smiled at her approval, began a light sway and started the battle.

Chuckie: *I got the "Blood of a Boss" in me/And when my "Thugs Cry" I let them slugs fly 'til my guns empty/You'sa bitch and ya "Loyalty is Blind"/BG, Big Girl, likes to get it from behind.*

"Ooooooo." The crowd chorused, inflating Chuckie's ego.
BG waited for the noises to die down and then he shot his verse.

BG: *I'm fifteen with "A Hustla'z Ambition"/And he's dumb as fuck on a suicide mission/I get love in these clubs and from the city blocks/And you get love from homo thugs in the jails, eatin' cock.*

"Ooohhhhh!" The people went crazier. Chuckie wasn't feeling the shift of the oohs and ahhs to a pup twelve years his minor, so he turned it personal.

Chuckie: *I'm allergic to the fake and "These N****s Ain't Loyal" too/I'm talkin' 'bout you, ya pussy brother, and ya road dawgs too/They gon' "Bury Me A G" when I go, neph/And my goons will get "Street Justice" when it goes left.*

"Y'all all can get it!" Chuckie crafted his fingers into the shape of a gun, aiming it at BG. Then he smiled and soaked up the roars of those bucking him up.
BG looked over to Ace who stood at his side. "Were shots just fired?" Ace booted up and nodded his head up and down. Getting up on Chuckie, BG swiped his thumb against his nose and went for the jugular. It wasn't over like Chuckie assumed. BG wasn't bowing down.

BG: *Dick sucka/ Forgot I know you silly fucka?/I got the scoop on you and ya crack head mother/And ya girl servin' ass 'cause she a "Silver Platter Hoe"/So when you kissing her, you kissing every thuggah I know/And that bastard ain't yours, he fa the thuggah down the street/She the hood freak/Ya bitch lettin' everybody skeet.*

"Ooohhhh!" The crowd egged.
"Talk that shit nah," BG started off a DJ Jubilee hit.
"Roll wit' it," the people automatically finished the rest of the bounce verse for him in a boisterous manner.
BG dapped and slapped up a few females and fellas who cheered him on, declaring him the winner as he was stepping off.
"We ain't done." Chuckie informed on a low growl. There was no way he would let a kid disrespect him in front of his hood and his lady.
"Dude, take yo fuckin' L and be easy," BG said, trying not to take it there but Chuckie was already on his level.

Chuckie reached for his piece and pointed it at BG. "I said we ain't done."

Munch was at the other end of the block, talking to his dip when she pointed down to the ruckus brewing at the other end.

"It's always some shit, I swear." She shook her head, disinterested in the reason it began to sound like a jungle.

Munch looked down there and waved it off as he continued to run it with her.

He was seconds away from leaving off with his girlfriend when Ace ran up on him.

"Munch! Chuckie pulled out on yo brother and I don't got my strap." He hurried his words, taking no breaths in between.

At the little homie's word, Munch took off running down the street, pulling his ratchet from out of his gym shorts. His plan was simple: Shoot first. Fuck asking questions later. When it came to his lil' BG, any and everybody could end up on the coroner's list.

The moment everyone saw Chuckie's pistol, they moved out of the way as to not be in the line of fire.

"Apologize for insulting my gangsta."

BG was itching to even the odds by reaching for his banger but he knew the first sign of him going for his waist would indefinitely have him chalked out and on the evening news.

BG didn't flex, though. His pops told him, "A man dies on his feet, never his knees." So if he had to go out, that's how it was going to happen because he wasn't giving him no apology.

"You'sa a thunder cat, huh, lil' thuggah?" He glanced at his mans and baby's mom to the left of him with his gun still trained at the center of BG's face. "If he was humble, he could have been on my team." He shrugged his shoulders. "Tell yo dead pops I said what up."

Chuckie cocked one into the chamber and BG involuntarily squeezed his eyes shut so he wouldn't see death coming.

275

Boc! Boc! Boc!

"Aahhhh! Aahhhh!" Most of the people began screaming. Everyone scattered. Some ran, taking different directions while others squatted behind cars to take cover.

When BG realized he wasn't hit at the first sound of fire, he pulled out his piece and started dumping on Chuckie, too. It only took seconds for Chuckie's right hand man to see that surrendering was his only way out of it alive, he was too fat to get far if he tried running, so he got down, raising his hands as he did.

With his arm extended, Munch continued running up, blasting on Chuckie from behind until he stood over him alongside his brother. Their spray of bullets caused his body to centipede.

Pow! Boc! Boc! Pow! Boc!

His baby moms muffled her screams with her hands as she watched on. She trembled with anger as she looked over to his mans do nothing to protect him, avenge him, so she reached for her .22. She came from behind a car she ran to when bullets started flying. And in an irrational manner, she yelled out in distress as she lifted her weapon to shoot.

BG turned her way and sparked her up.One shot to the chest crumpled her.

When the brothers looked over to where Chuckie's partner waited his fate, Munch made eye contact with BG, nodding his head to the side of them as if to say, "Go handle that business."

BG walked over to him and stood directly in front of him with his gun pointed at the center of his forehead. "How you want it? Like a man or a coward, thuggah?" BG gave him the option..

Remaining on his knees, he spoke angrily through the tight curl of his mouth. "I don't got beef with you, bruh."

BG lowered his weapon and then glanced at his brother before looking back down at the man in plea position. "A coward it is."

Raising his gun, he blasted once.

Pow!

One remorseless shot to the dome, executioner style caused him to fall over and onto his side. BG knew it was either going to be Fat

Boy now or him and his brother later because street life was never forgiving.

When the smoke cleared, three were left slain, swimming in red pools. It looked like a scene from the Wild Wild West but it was just another day in the Wild Magnolia.

From that day forward, the projects respected BG and Munch's mind more so than before.

Baby Goon was a G with his. He never started but he'd finish. And Munch, they knew that fucking with his BG was like signing their own death certificate and everyone including a Goliath like Chuckie could get it in blood with no questions asked.

Thinking back on that day alone reassured Ace that if a death wish was what he had, Munch would be granting that for him.

Munch stood to his feet and all eyes went on him. He looked them each in the face and then spoke his first words of the day.

"He want me? Well, mu'fucka got me." Munch walked out of the living room and into BG's bedroom, slamming the door behind him.

Coffee

Chapter 31

Late June...

"**A**hhhhhhh!" Samiyah yelled through gritted teeth. She was so exhausted from already having pushed out the first one but her intolerable contractions required her to continue pushing to get the second one out.

"You're doing great, Samiyah, just breathe and get ready to push on my go," the doctor said as she saw his head crowning.

She whined that she couldn't do no more and unrealistically begged the doctors to take the wheel but Cedric stepped in to coach her.

"You got this and in a little while it's gon' be all over." He wiped the sweat off of her forehead. Then he looked to Lil' Acacia, who was resting her head on his shoulder, "Mama got this, huh?"

Samiyah answered for her. "No, I don't. It's hurt so badddd. It hurts so..."

"Push!"

"Aaahhhhhhh!"

Three months earlier...

"Thank you for meeting me. I wasn't sure you would." Samiyah took a seat on the bench at Audubon Park where Cedric told her he'd meet her.

"You said it was important, so I'm here. What was so urgent it couldn't be said over the phone?"

To answer his question, Samiyah removed Lil' Acacia from out of her stroller. "Look at her?"

"What am I looking at?" He glanced at the baby and then did a double take, staring at her harder this time.

"What do you see?" Samiyah asked.

He looked to Samiyah and then back to Lil' Acacia, shaking his head. "How could that be? That's impossible. I had a vasectomy."

"Clearly it was a successful one because all I know is she's yours and just so there is no doubt I'm hoping you'll agree to a swab test to confirm it."

"Yea, but how in the—." He agreed to take it but he knew she was a Melancon. He knew she belonged to him.

Cedric reached for Lil' Acacia and stared into her eyes. She looked just like his son who passed away, just like him. He couldn't believe he was holding his flesh and blood. He never dreamed of being a daddy again but clearly she was meant to be.

Cedric hugged Lil' Acacia tightly as he smelled her baby scent. *"This is my lil' girl,"* he spoke emotionally. *"I have a little girl!"*

Samiyah watched Cedric gaze at their daughter like she was a relic and wished it would have dawned on her sooner, so he could have loved her from the start and she wouldn't have hurt Eli or Gerran, for that matter.

"Damn! I love her already. But why are you just now telling me?" Cedric was baffled as he continued looking at the seventh month old in his arms.

"Well, the story goes something like this..."

Samiyah rotated her head from one side of the pillow to the other. It didn't matter how many times she was told it would be over soon, it wasn't happening soon enough.

"The baby's head is out. I'm gonna need for you to push one more good time on the count of three. One. Two. Three. Push!"

"Aaaaarrgghhhh!" Samiyah's face trembled as she pushed with mighty vigor.

Moments later.

"Waaahhh! Waaahhhh!"

Samiyah cried tears of relief and joy as she heard the doctors confirming that both of her babies were healthy. Then two nurses walked on each side of her holding them up to her face so that she could see them.

Cedric directed their daughter's face so she could get a good view of her mommy and new family. "Do you have names picked out?" he asked as he looked at her cuties.

Samiyah looked at the first to be born. "Her name is Amiya." Then she looked at the second one. "And his name is Amir."

The next day...

Everywhere Minnie had to be, Yuriah was with her. One slip up could have cost him gravely had G'Corey been off of his rocker when he approached her some weeks ago, so Yuriah wasn't taking any chances moving forward.

So, it was a no brainer to go with Minnie to the hospital when she told him she wanted to visit her friend.

It was mid-morning when Minnie knocked on the door and entered into Samiyah's room with her husband behind her.

"Good morning, second time mommy," Minnie sung as she entered.

"What's up, Yah?" Yuriah addressed her with a kiss on the cheek.

"Hey, y'all," she spoke to them both before she looked to Minnie. "I'm so happy you were able to make it considering circumstances."

"I'm gonna step over here and make a call, a'ight?" Yuriah addressed Minnie before stepping away to leave them to their talk.

"I know it's been real hectic. I'm scared all of time and to know the guys say G'Corey is behind BG's killing only has me that more spooked. I don't feel safe leaving my house at all. But I wouldn't miss seeing you for the world."

"And that's what makes seeing you so special. I love you," Samiyah said tearfully.

"I love you, too."

Samiyah then reached out for Minnie's wrist, pulling her down toward her so they could have an intimate discussion.

"I spoke with Cedric and he is prepared to put together a security detail that will keep you safe and give you peace of mind until Yuriah is able to do what he do with G'Corey. Will that stop you from moving away?"

Minnie shook her head *no*. "That's the thing. I don't want to live like I need protecting. G'Corey has gone too far. His last few emails to me flat out said he will have me by any means necessary. I am scared out of my mind and since Yuri said he'd do anything to make me feel safe, getting as far away from New Orleans is what it's going to take for me to feel that. I mean, we'll still keep our house because I want to return to it one day but for now—"

She cut herself off and silently broke down. Samiyah pulled her into her arms. Yuriah dropped his phone to his waist and attempted to head over to them but Samiyah mouthed that Minnie was alright.

"I understand, friend. You have to do what you have to do. Me, Cedric and my children can always come to you when the twins are old enough to travel."

Minnie dried her face and sat up to look at her. "I just hope this nightmare ends soon."

"Me too, sweetie. Me too."

The ladies talked for a half an hour more but they ceased conversation when they heard the opening of her door.

"Oh, my God!" Samiyah sounded displeased when she saw Gerran coming in.

Minnie took his arrival as her que to depart. So she said her goodbyes, promising to talk with her later as she and her husband left to give the troubled spouses their privacy.

Samiyah rolled her eyes upward. "Who told you I was here?"

Gerran walked over to her with a beautiful bouquet in hand. "Your mama called me."

Dang, Mama!

He handed her the flowers to smell but she didn't reach for them, so he sat them on the table adjacent to her bed. Gerran then sat by her, taking her hand into his.

"You don't have to touch me to talk to me." Samiyah snatched her hand back and used it to wipe under her misty eye.

Gerran dropped his head. "I know this isn't the best time to talk to you but you've been ignoring me."

She glared at him. "You played me from day one and because you have a mind to start reaching out to me, I'm supposed to jump for joy? Well, I'm not your Johnny-On-The-Spot. It doesn't work like that."

"Look, I don't want to argue with you."

"So, don't!"

"Look, Yah, I called you a lot of untrue names and said many unforgivable things."

"Yes. You have!" She looked the opposite way. She didn't want to feel compassion for him finally apologizing.

"I was hurt so I hurt you."

"You damn sure did hurt me." His callous behavior was a sore spot for her.

"Look at me, Samiyah." She didn't listen to him, so he shifted her face in his direction. "Look at me. I'm sorry and to prove it to you I don't need a paternity test to tell me those children are mine. I knew it from the dump but I just wanted to slam you for what you did in the past and I was down bad for that, I know."

It felt good listening to him eat the filth he threw at her, but his words came too little too late. "That won't be necessary. I want you to get the test done so there's no throwing it in my face later."

"Fair enough. Well, let's work on us. Let me come home and we be a family again."

Samiyah frowned. She couldn't believe what she was hearing. "Why now? What's changed to make you think I even want to try?"

"Because you still love me just like I never stopped loving you. Yah, I know I did the fool but I was only…"

Gerran snapped his head in the direction of the door opening and when he saw Cedric entering holding Samiyah's baby, his jaw twitched. "What the hell is he doing here?"

Samiyah looked at Gerran disgustingly. "He's here because he can be. So, don't start nothing up in here." She looked to Cedric, who was unfazed at the anger in his eyes. "Do you mind coming back in a few minutes? I need to wrap things up here."

He answered her while looking at Gerran. "I can do that for you."

Cedric was over the beef from the brawl they had over Samiyah but the man in him had to let it be known that he'd take it there if he needed to.

When Cedric walked out and the door closed, Gerran's eyebrows drew inward. "So, he's your boyfriend now?"

"That's your problem. You're swift to assume things. No, we are not together. He's Lil' Acacia's father."

"Wait a minute. I thought Eli was—"

"Well, you thought wrong." She shook her head. "You fought that man without knowing why he even showed up at the hospital that day. You're so quick to stop me from making a fool of you that you're making a fool of your damn self."

"I can admit that I've jumped the gun on plenty and I can apologize for that too. Look, Yah, we not gon' iron our issues out on our own. Let's get marriage counseling and get back right."

"Just like that, huh?"

"No, but it will be a start. I've been miserable without you and I can't keep frontin'. I love you."

"Don't say that."

"I know I haven't shown you lately but it's true. If you won't try for me, do it for our children."

Ten minutes later...

Cedric reentered.

Gerran continued looking at Samiyah as if they were the only ones in the room. He kissed her on the forehead and then stood up to leave. "Think about it."

He walked past Cedric, glancing at the baby as he did. He missed her although he didn't show that either. Gerran looked over his shoulder and caught her eyes before he walked out.

Cedric eyed him as he did and once the door was closed, he walked over to Samiyah and took a seat next to her. "What was that all about?"

"He wants to make us work." She sounded exhausted by it.

"What do you want?"

"I thought for sure divorce but now I don't know. I have children with him and—"

"And a child by me since you want to bring up piecing families together. What about ours?" Cedric came out of left field with that, taking Samiyah by storm.

"Cedric, you never mentioned this before, so why are *you* doing this now?"

"I didn't think I had to mention it. Come on, nah. I've spent just about every day with you since you walked back into my life with our baby. You had to know nothing about the way I felt for you changed, ya heard me."

Samiyah covered her face. She couldn't believe she was at that point of choosing between them again. Hands down, she still loved Cedric and he was a better friend to her than Gerran had been a husband over the last few months, but Gerran was still her husband.

"I love you but if I don't see this all the way through with him, I'll never forgive myself." Samiyah decided marriage counseling was what they needed to be able to move forward.

***

Tracie was sitting in a small room, waiting to be called into trial. She was nervous about the outcome but she was willing to do what she had to do.

She ran her hands over the last letter she received from G'Corey two weeks ago. It gave her the strength to do what she needed to do today. And although she read the letter to the point where she memorized it line for line, she still decided to reread it.

Dear Trace,

Your auntie told me that your trial date is approaching and my heart is heavy. A thuggah tried to get his money up but wasn't nothing shakin', ya heard me. I wanted us to blaze out on those bitches, but it didn't work out the way we planned it. But have no fuckin' worries because yo man got you.

Coffee

You know I ain't never met a woman more down than you and I regret not seeing it until now. But I corrected that shit. You ask how? Well, read that muthafuckin' divorce decree I sent with this letter. I had to let her go 'cause she could never be you. You been tried to told me, ya heard me.

Anyway, baby, I love you. I rarely said it before because I was trippin' but I'm sayin' it now. Stay strong and know that me and baby boy gon' hold you down until we can figure out a way to get you from behind them walls.

Love,
Your G

"I love you, too." She kissed the letter.

Just then her state attorney walked in. "Good morning, Ms. Terry. Today determines your future. I have advised you numerously on what you should do but ultimately, I work for you. Have you made a decision?"

She looked at the letter in her hand. She refolded it, closed her eyes and held it to her heart. "I'm gonna do what I said I would. G'Corey needs me and he's all that matters."

Chapter 32

A few days later...

Elias was feeling pretty damn good. The women in his life had things a little crazy for a while, like his uncle warned, but everything was kosher now.

After having gone weeks without talking to Samiyah, they finally hashed things out with a heart to heart talk. It took him some time to accept that Peaches wasn't his but she assured him that his place in her daughter's life wouldn't be dimmed. He found peace with that.

School had been a slight challenge because he'd been out of the educational loop for years but he had been doing well with his business courses.

But it had been Blu's solid support throughout everything that was the cause of his upward mood and that's why he had special plans for her that evening.

***

Blu used her key to unlock the door of her parents' home. As she stepped inside she saw her sister sitting on the sofa curled up with a book. She didn't just want to walk past her although ignoring her was her first inclination, so she spoke. "Hey, sis. What are you reading?"

"The Ultimate Betrayal." She didn't bother looking up when she replied.

"Sounds like boo-coo drama." She shook her head at it. "Who's it by?"

She was on a really juicy part and simply not interested in Blu's attempt to make small talk. "Phoenix. Damn! You nosey." La'Tasha rolled her eyes.

"What's your problem, huh? You always wear such a stank attitude with me."

She closed her book shut, tossing it next to her. "The problem isn't with me. It's with you thinking we cool. But we're sisters, not friends."

Blu gave an astonished look. It wasn't surprising that La'Tasha didn't see them as such but it puzzled Blu because she never understood her heartless ways toward her.

But it was all good because Blu had a confession to tell her as well. She opened her mouth to speak but her phone rang. It was Eli. She took his call as a sign to keep quiet and leave La'Tasha to be evil-spirited by herself.

She walked away from her and answered, "Hey." Her tone was clipped.

"What's up, boo? What's the matter?" He caught her agitation.

"Nothing I want to talk about. What's up, baby?"

La'Tasha mocked her underneath her breath as she picked her book back up. *What's up, baby?* she gagged.

"What time you gon' be on your way?"

"Ahh, I can be there shortly. I just stopped by my mama and 'em for a second."

"A'ight. Well, I can wait on you to take my shower, then."

"Or you can go ahead and take it and just leave your door unlocked. That way if you are, I can just let myself in because I won't be long." She gave him another option.

"Cool, I'll do that. See you in a bit."

Blu smiled before she hung up but once she turned around and looked at the smug look on La'Tasha's face, a frown appeared on hers. She thought to bite her tongue but decided against it. La'Tasha needed to hear the truth.

"You know what? I don't even know why I try with you because the truth of the matter is I hate you. You are a petty, selfish and a manipulative person and you feel like the world should bow at your feet. So you're right. We ain't friends and when we see each other, we can pretend we don't."

"Awww, Little Miss Perfect doesn't have enough sprinkles in her fairy pouch to convince me to like her and she's mad." La'Tasha spoke like she was five years old but then switched to her condescending voice. "Well, if you hate me now, just wait 'til later."

"And what does that mean?" Blu spoke with her hands.

"Did you come here for Mama or me?" La'Tasha brushed her off.

Blu flung her hand in the air. "Whatever." She turned and left out of the living room and into the back of the house, where she knew her mother would be.

***

Twenty minutes later...

Elias didn't want to wait too much longer before he got ready, so he went ahead and unlocked his door.

After ten minutes of singing and showering, Elias turned off the water just in time to hear his front door closing.

He yelled out. "In the bathroom, Blu."

Nice! she thought as she removed her dress, dropping it on the floor. When she walked into the bedroom, he was still in there. So, she climbed into bed and waited to surprise him with a little opening act before the headliner later.

As Elias was drying his face with a hand towel, he stepped into the bedroom. With his face covered, he said, "Boo, I got some shit planned for you."

"As do I?"

The sound of her voice made him quickly remove the towel. His mouth flung open and then balled tightly when he saw La'Tasha sitting in the center of his bed with nothing but panties on.

"What the fuck is you doin' here?" Eli snarled as he rushed up on her to throw her out of his crib.

***

"I have no idea what he has up his sleeve. He just told me what to wear what he bought the other day and I did it," Blu talked to Kanari on her cell as she drove to Eli's.

"You think he's gonna pop the big question? I mean, he's taking you to a fancy smancy steakhouse and the selfie you sent of your outfit screams *special occasion*."

"I doubt that but if you're right, I'm ready to say *yes*. I'm lovin' on him." Blu felt the usual butterflies in the pit of her stomach but as she pulled up on Eli's house, that flutter suddenly turned into tight knots. "What the fuck?"

"What? What's wrong?" Kanari became alarmed at the sound of her voice.

"I'ma call you back!"

"Blu, wait—" Kanari tried to say before she was hung up on.

She instantly felt sick and her chest tightened seeing La'Tasha's car in front of her man's house.

Blu parked behind his truck and jumped out of her car. She kicked off her heels, leaving them in his front yard as she raced up his steps and burst through his door. She immediately spotted La'Tasha's dress in the middle of the floor and she was ignited with rage.

Blu dashed to his bedroom, stopping shy of crossing the seal. She was taken aback to find him on top of her sister.

"Eli!" she shrilled.

"Blu!" He turned in her direction, standing up and away from La'Tasha. She walked in on him wrestling to get her out of his bed. "Let me explain. This shit looks fucked up but nothing is going on."

Blu eyes narrowed below his waist, she walked up on him and then snatched the towel from around him, revealing his bare essentials. "Nothing, huh? Nothing but hard dick!"

His rise wasn't a result of his desire for La'Tasha but an instant reaction to seeing her nakedness, but he wasn't about to expound on that.

He grabbed the towel back from her and wrapped himself in it. "Baby, it ain't what it look like. I promise you that."

"Don't tell me what I'm lookin' at ain't what I'm seeing. It looks like I busted you about to fuck my sister!" Blu scrunched her face and looked about the room in confusion, elevating her voice. "And when did you find time to cozy up to this trick?"

"Aye, watch it. Don't get loose with your words." La'Tasha looked at her casually.

Elias snapped around to La'Tasha. "Mannn, shut the fuck up and get the fuck out!"

"Nah, she ain't gotta go nowhere. I wanna hear from the both of you what the fuck is goin' on."

"You can hear it from him. I'm pretending not to see you." La'Tasha sarcastically threw Blu words back at her.

"Blu, do you think I would invite her over here knowing you were on your way? I don't even fuck with her like that no more and on top of that, I left the door unlocked expecting you, not this bitch."

Blu threw her hand up. "Wait a minute. *No more?*" she asked incredulously.

Elias dropped his head and then lifted it back up. "Fuck!" He didn't mean to say that but he was out there now. "Boo, I been fucked and ducked this hoe. It was a long time ago, ya heard me. And I told you about her. I just never called this rat by her name." He nodded his head off to the side in a vexed manner. "This Cujo, man."

Damn! La'Tasha thought as she listened to his colorful recap of their dealings. "Ruff!" She waved. There was no limit to her bitchiness.

"Look, man, I didn't know this broad was your sister until I came by yo peoples' house and I wanted to tell you but so much shit starting happening afterwards and it just never seemed like a good time."

"*Tsss.* So, this is the woman you were in love with?" Blu felt deflated. Hurt. Betrayed—again. First it was Samiyah and now her. "After the Peaches' situation, I asked you if there was anything else I should know. Anything! And what did you tell me?" She mimicked his smooth voice, "*Nah, boo, nothing else.* Well, you lieeedddd!" She broke down crying. "And I am sooo done!"

Elias reached out for her but she stepped back two spaces, throwing her hands up.

"Boo, I didn't keep this shit from you because I wanted her on the slick. Things were already strained between us and when shit got good, I didn't want to jack it all up."

La'Tasha kept quiet and watched on as things fell apart because when it was all said and done, she'd be there to pick up the pieces. Eli's goods belonged to her anyway. *She licked it.* And there was never a man she had once that she couldn't have twice.

"Just when I thought my fool days were over, surprise." Blu turned around to leave but Eli grabbed her.

Blu started swinging on him wildly. "Don't fuckin' touch me! Don't fuckin' touch me!" she screamed.

Elias let her go. "Baby, let…"

In a mild hysteria, she blurted. "I hate you! I swear to God I do. You and that bitch deserve each other." She ran out of his house and jumped into her car. She was gone.

He was hurt. Not because of her punches, those licks didn't faze him. It was the wounding words she spewed that was a blow to his heart that rocked him. He could only pray she didn't mean them.

Elias then bit down on his lip and rushed back into the room by a giggling La'Tasha.

"Awww, come to mama and let me make you feel better." She pinched her chocolate nipple. She was thoroughly turned on and she knew deep down he was too.

She just popped Blu's bubble and now her old fling was about to pop her pussy, or so she thought.

"Bitch, you like playin' games? Well, tell me how you love dis?" He yanked her off of his bed roughly. There was no negotiating her up out of his house.

He snatched her by the arm. "Heyyyy! Eli, what the hell?"

Elias walked her through his house so fast, her feet barely had time to touch the floor. He spotted her keys on the sofa where she placed them, swooped them up and slapped it into her hand. Then he shoved her through his opened door. She stumbled forward trying to catch her balance. La'Tasha then spun around, covering her mounds with one arm and extending the other.

"Eli! My clothes!"

He drove his upper lip into a high arch. "Drive naked, bitch!" He slammed his door in her face.

Elias hurried into his room and threw on anything. He had to quickly catch up with Blu and make her understand what the hell happened as best as he could.

***
Two weeks later...

Eli hadn't seen or heard from Blu. He went to her bar every night but she wasn't there. And when he questioned Kanari about her whereabouts, she pled the fifth. She hadn't been home, either. He checked at different times every day to know that much. And her father was less than approachable when he tried talking with him once.

Eli then utilized his ace in the hole and pulled some major strings. It cost a grip to make it happen but he was sure to get her attention so it was worth it.

As he waited to walk inside, he thought back on the slick shit he told her. *"...Keep that shit up and one day you gon' walk away from me and I won't be bothered by that shit."*

But the joke was on him because one day wasn't yesterday, wasn't today and it sure wasn't going to be tomorrow. And if shit was going to be over between them, it wasn't going to be on behalf of her rudy-poo ass sister.

However, he wasn't trying to see an end date on them, she meant too much. Besides, he just came to terms with losing one baby, he wasn't about to lose his other.

Elias got out of his truck and stepped inside of the building. Front desk signed him in and then escorted him down some hallways where he was greeted by some unfamiliar faces. Finally, he reached his destination and walked into the room where a man sat waiting for him.

The gentleman stood to welcome Eli with a man hug. "It's show time. You're ready?"

"I stay ready." Eli bobbed his head as he took a seat.

A few minutes later, they were cued. "We go live in 3, 2…" The engineer informed them.

In a silky-smooth, baritone voice, Papa Smurf, the host of Quiet Storm radio, began his spiel. "Welcome back. If you're just tuning in, we have a guest with us tonight who'll be hosting the Lovers Only hour with me, Papa Smurf. Go ahead and introduce yourself, young brother."

He adjusted the drop of the microphone. "You got Elias in the building."

"And tell all the romantics out there why you're here tonight."

"I messed up and now my baby Blu ain't got no holla for me. And since she always listens to your show, I had to show her how sorry I am."

"Blu, if you're out there, crank the volume just a little bit louder and listen as Babyface sings *Never Keeping Secrets* from Eli to you."

I didn't want to lie to you but I didn't want to let you down/It never did occur to me sooner or later that you would find out/You know how much I care for you and I would never want to cause you pain/I know that there is no excuse how could I ever treat my baby that way

That's why I'm telling everybody that I (that I) know I was a fool/But I don't give a damn about it 'cause I wanna get back with you…

The next song to play was *Since I Lost My Baby* by Luther Vandross and a host of similar songs that had put Eli in his feelings.

After the last song played, Papa opened the lines to take callers. The switchboard was on fire. He took the first one. "Blu is that you, caller?"

"No, this isn't Blu. This is Yolanda. Listen, if she don't want you, Elias, I do…"

Papa chuckled and took another call.

"I'm just calling in to say Blu if you're out there, it sounds like he's really sorry. Give him another shot."

The lines lit up over the next ten minutes but none of them were his girl.

Elias was disappointed but he hoped it was only because she couldn't get through.

"Well, that wraps up our time with Mr. Elias. Anything else you want to say to Ms. Blu before you leave us?"

"Yea, Blu, I know you listening, so I want you to meet me at our spot. Don't leave me hanging, ya heard me. I love you, boo."

"We'll be right back after this commercial break," Papa announced before he stood up to walk Eli out of the door. "Good luck getting your girl back."

Elias dapped him. "The way I fucked up, ya dig, I'ma need it."

He left out of the room and back down the halls to get to his exit.

The moment Elias opened the doors of the building he stepped into a literal storm. The rain was blinding.

The twenty seconds it took to get inside of his truck had him drenched already. But he wasn't concerned about that, only the fact that he couldn't see even with his windshield wipers on.

"Awww, fuck! Ain't this a bitch?"

He had to wait an eternity for it to slack up but when it did, he was on his way to Romeo his Juliet.

***

A couple of hours later…

Elias walked inside of his house completely saturated from having waited outside for an hour and a half at The Lake and in the rain, all for Blu not to show up.

Feeling like his energy had been zapped, he plopped down on the sofa. Mustering the strength to use one foot to remove the soggy shoe of the other, he kicked them off.

He was in a state of disbelief. That was the most romantic shit he ever did, yet it yielded him nothing. Eli glanced over at the stereo's remote sitting atop the coffee table and decided to pick it up and turn FM98 on.

He was never an R&B type of thuggah but he and Blu listened to Papa Smurf's *Quiet Storm* every night and he was missing her.

He caught the tail end of one sad song going off as another was coming in.

That's when he heard the infamous whine of Keith Sweat crooning through the speakers. He had a mind to cut it off before R&B's legendary crybaby took him down that distraught road but he was already there.

You lied to me, baby/Why did you have to lie to me, baby...

Eli closed his eyes at the intro of *Come Back* and shook his head slowly as he felt where Sweat was coming from when he heard his phone chiming. Jacobi had been calling him periodically over the last two hours.

Deciding against letting his voicemail answer for him, he picked up. "What?" He sounded as flat as his deflated ego.

"'Bout time you answered yo phone. I heard yo ass on the fuckin' radio. Bruh, I know you love her but—wait, is you listenin' to Keith Sweat?" Jacobi heard the *down in the dumps* music playing in the background.

Eli rudely started singing.

Told me you'll never, never, never, never leave me/But tonight, I'm all by myself/I'm all alone, with nobody else/Hoping that you'd come back to me.

"Elias? Elias?" Jacobi had been trying to get his attention the moment he belted the first off key note.

"Dawg, I stood out there with the dick look when she didn't show up, looking like Oran *Juice* Jones from that wack ass 80s video."

Jacobi tried talking sense to his Day-1 but he could tell Eli wasn't feeling him. He wanted to be pissy. That was clear the second Eli interrupted him to sing the bridge.

'Cause I miss you so so bad/And if I could win your love back/I surely surely would, baby/I wouldn't give you reason to leave like you did, girl/Nooooo no no, I would not, baby...

Jacobi frowned and his eyes tightened. "Are you lookin' as ugly as you soundin'? Never mind that. I can't take this feminine shit from you. Quit soakin' like a lil' bitch, dawg. I'm on my way over there to get you the fuck up out your feelings." Jacobi ended the call.

Elias hung up, too, but he kept singing.
Come back/Come back—to me, baby…

Thirty minutes later…

The ongoing sound of the hard-hitting rain crashing against his window pane mixed in with the rush of knocks sounding at his door. Still listening to sappy love jams and in no mood for Jacobi's company, he ignored him.

The knocks didn't stop, though.

"Mann, go home. I'm good." Elias called out but it was obvious Jacobi wasn't going to leave.

Eli knew he didn't have a reason to be aggravated at his boy, but he was. He shut the stereo off and dropped the remote on the sofa as he stood to his feet.

Swinging the door open, he was prepared to blast him for being annoying during a time when his jokes weren't welcomed, but it wasn't him on the other side of his door, it was Blu.

"Baby, you came." Eli felt the weight of loss lift off of his shoulders.

She could tell he wasn't himself, she hadn't been either.

"You know I heard you on the radio and you touched my heart. I'm surprised I was able to see past the tears in my eyes on my drive over. But when I heard your plea for me, I knew what I had to say couldn't be done over the phone. I had to say this in person."

"I have something I want to say—I need to say. Let me start off by saying—"

Blu stopped him. "It's over."

Coffee

Chapter 33

A few days later...

G'Corey hopped the fence from Yuriah's neighbor side of the yard where he'd been camped out and into his backyard.

Today was the day of reckoning. There was no more waiting. No more hesitating because there was no perfect plan. He had to go King Kong and take his girl and kill anything that stood in the way of it because time was no longer an ally of his.

Standing at the top step, he lifted his gun to his shoulder and raised his Timberland boot to do a kick door. However, he hesitated when he heard the faint sound of a car door closing from up front. He ran along the side of the house to investigate if someone had come by or if they were leaving.

When he reached the wooden fence and peeked through the hole in the gate, he saw Yuriah sitting behind the wheel of his truck with his window down but he didn't see Minnie. He pressed up against it, scanning the tiny scope he was allotted but his view was limited. Then suddenly he heard her. It appeared she was standing on the porch from the projection of her voice.

"Baby, how long are you going to be again?" Minnie didn't want to see him leave but he had business to handle.

"No longer than three hours but of course you know it will be sooner than that if I can help it."

"Okay," she bobbed her head.

"Nah get inside and put the alarm on. I'ma pull off when I see you in, ya heard me."

G'Corey stuffed his gun in his waist and jetted to the back of the house. He removed one of his shirts while in motion, wrapping it around his fist.

He decided to punch through the glass window of the door. It would be quieter than the thud of the door crashing against the wall, allowing him to sneak in undetected since she was still outside.

Effortlessly, he was inside within seconds. He hurriedly closed the door back and he did so just in time because the security system's intercom said, *Alarm activated.*

***

Reds looked in the mirror and giggled softly at her reflection. She was on cloud nine and she was about to lift Munch up there with her.

Every day since BG was killed and G'Corey lived on untouched was hell for him. He barely ate, slept or talked. And there was nothing Reds was able to do to shake him out of his madness, until today.

Thinking back to one of their many controversial nights, she smiled even harder because she was sure she had the power to change his hellish mood.

It was 4 a.m. when Munch walked inside. Reds was up to hear him come in because she was having a difficult time sleeping without him.

She walked into the living room and cut on the light. She didn't want him to take her concerns out of context but she couldn't keep her fears bottled up.

"Baby, you've been coming inside like this every morning for weeks and I'm scared every time you leave out of the door because I wonder if you're gonna walk back through them."

Munch understood her worry. He heard her cries and he felt her pain but he was unable to cater to them. It wasn't that he didn't care because there was no denying she was his world but it was just that his brother was his life.

"What you want me to do? Sit on my hands and forgive those who trespass against me? Nah, I'll leave that shit up to some holy roller. I believe in street justice so I gotta do this."

"No, you don't! You not the only one who's out for blood. You keep lookin' for his troubles and you will find it. And I don't want you to die, Munch. Do you hear me? I don't want you to die!" Reds screamed at the top of her lungs.

She was shaking as she watched him stare straight ahead, seemingly unfazed. But then he turned to look at her. The pain he carried in his heart was engrained on his face.

He wanted to make her understand why he was adamant about his brother's business but there was no way he could. He tried and it didn't work..

Reds was having a difficult time trying to calm herself down, so he stood up from the sofa and walked over to her, holding her trembling body. She buried her head into his chest but cried even harder.

She didn't want to lose him but he wasn't trying to lose.

After minutes of being in his arms, Munch tore her away from him. What he was about to say wasn't going to put her at ease but she had to hear it.

"Bae, if death comes, ya heard me, I gotta be ready for it. It's not that I'm lookin' for it to happen but death is the consequence of the living."

That conversation hadn't left her since she heard it but she was hoping after today she could help him see things a little differently.

When Reds walked into the living room, she found Munch on the phone. She whispered, "I'm ready when you are."

He nodded his head and then returned his attention back to his call.

"If you not at the house, I can just pass through tomorrow and get them thangs, ya heard me." Munch wanted to relieve him of the choppers he had scored from an old connect of his.

"We pullin' out 'round four in the morning." Yuriah looked at the time. "So, I'ma lay up there and turn around. Minnie's at the house but I don't want her touchin' that. I can be there in twenty."

"Nah, don't change your plans for me. I'll just dip through before you kite out."

"It's all good, bruh. Shit ain't gon' start 'til I get there so you straight. Come through."

"A'ight then. I'm on my way." Munch hung up the phone and turned to Reds. "We gon' need to holla at Yuri before we do your thang, ya heard me."

Coffee

Reds smiled and agreed. A quick detour wasn't going to offset what she had planned.

***

Minnie turned the television on in the living room and had a seat. She channel surfed, looking for anything to occupy her time until Yuriah got back.

She looked around at her home and felt sad to leave it behind. Her and Yuriah made so many wonderful memories in it, but she couldn't enjoy being there comfortably. Not anymore.

G'Corey crept down the hall, stopping at the entrance where Minnie sat with her back facing him. He treaded softly so he wouldn't be heard.

He stood behind her for a moment inhaling her eye rolling perfume and his mouth watered. He then raised his hand and delicately brushed her hair from off of her shoulders.

"Ahh!" Minnie yelped as she jumped out of her skin and off from the sofa. She turned around and then every muscle in her body froze when she saw G'Corey standing there.

"Honey, I'm home," he smiled. "You look surprised. I'm guessing you wasn't expecting me but you should have known I would come for you."

Her mouth made several clipped *aah* and *oh* sounds as she tried to speak. She shook her head *no* then finally answered verbally. "What are you doing?"

"To take you far away from here." He walked around the sofa to stand on the same side as her but she inched away as he did. He saw fear spilling from her eyes. "Are you scared of me?"

Her voice shrilled as she spoke, betraying her. "No—ooo, I'm not." She continued moving away slowly, casting her eyes off to the side in search of anything blunt she could use to defend herself.

"You are scared. But of me? Imagine that."

"You just shouldn't—shouldn't be here." Her voice was shaky.

"You shouldn't be here, either." G'Corey looked around at the lavish yet cozy tri-level home and then back to her. "You should be with me. And I'm not waiting another day for that to happen." He balled his mouth and forced his next words. "I can't and I won't."

She followed his shifty eyes and saw they glanced at each of her packed boxes. She had to think on her feet. "As you can see, I am leaving him to be with you but if things are going to play out smoothly, I need you to leave and once I get my things out of here, we'll run away together. I promise." Her words were weakly spoken but she hoped he believed them.

G'Corey allowed his sudden laughter to die down to a weak smile. "I love you so fuckin' much, but when did you become a liar?"

"Wha—what am I lying about?"

"Everything! You lied about it all because if you meant half of the shit you was saying in those emails, you wouldn't be looking like you wanna piss your pants right nah. But you clearly was playing me, telling me all the shit I wanted to hear and for what? So you could get ghost on me? Oh, but you didn't know that *I* am Ghost? I was everywhere you were. Even the day you had your ole punk ass man show up in your place. I was there, too. And at the time, I spared his *ain't shit* life so you wouldn't be all fucked up but now it don't matter. I gotta drop him because he has some kind of hold on you that somehow made you forget our vows. 'Til death do us part. You remember that?"

Tears slipped from her eyes. "I do."

"Exactly! You said *I do*. So, I'm not the bad guy just because I want what you promised me, what is owed to me."

Minnie wished, in that moment, she had listened to Yuriah and not go behind his back by getting involved when he said he had things covered. But she feared ignoring his relentless emails and thought she could satisfy G'Corey with false hopes of their togetherness to keep him at bay long enough for her to slip out of the city.

G'Corey was smaller in size from how she remembered him but his unwelcomed presence was huge. His stare was icy yet his tone was warm. Everything about him, his energy, his movements, his reason for being there was frightening.

She clasped her prayer hands up to her lips. "G'Corey, you *are* scaring me."

He chuckled. "Finally, some honesty."

"Listen, G'Corey, Yuriah will be home any minute." She began choking through her tears. "You gotta go. Please just go and I promise we will leave off together."

He clenched his jaw. "Now you're lying again."

She whined her words. "I'm not. I swear I'm…"

"Shut up!" He raised his voice and it shook her up. "You think I give a fuck about that thuggah? He took my soul when he took you away from me. I want him to come back so I can return his ass to sender." G'Corey pulled out his gun and Minnie's body almost shut down at the sight of it.

"Please, please, please, don't hurt him. I'll do whatever you say. Just don't hurt him." Both cheeks were coated with her tears.

G'Corey looked at her sideways. "You really beggin' for this thuggah's life? You love him that much?" He snarled.

Minnie didn't know how to answer and that infuriated him. Now he had a mind to make her remember who she truly loved.

He motioned for her and she moved, stepping out of his reach. "Come here." She didn't listen as she circled the sofa. He leaped for her and missed. "I said come here!" She ran and he began chasing her.

She ran around the open floor plan with hopes that she could make it to one of the doors and get help but when G'Corey fired a shot into the air, she stopped almost instantly. She was paralyzed with terror. Minnie was so fearful of where the next shot would land that she couldn't even turn around to face him as he walked up behind her.

"Please don't hurt…" she managed to say.

"I won't hurt you, baby. I could never do that," he said as he placed his gun on the table in the foyer and yanked her pants down.

"No, no, no, no," she shook her head, pulling them back up.

"Don't fight me!" He jerked them back down, pushing her to the floor as he unzipped his jeans.

She scooted away from him and stood to her feet, trying to pull her pants from around her ankles so she could run but he grabbed her foot, yanking her toward him and causing her to smack the floor hard, face first.

"Aaahhh," she cried as blood began filling her mouth.

By this time, G'Corey had his jeans and boxers girdled at his feet. He turned her onto her back and climbed on top of her. "I don't want to hurt you. I just want to make love to you so you'll remember it's me you want."

She struggled to move from under him but it took no exertion for him to pin her and manipulate her body at his will. He had her panties and pants all the way down to her ankles again.

"Please don't do this. Please don't do this!" Minnie cried out but he wasn't listening. She still felt him maneuvering his penis toward her opening.

She settled on the fact that she had to fight, so Minnie went berserk. She began hitting him on both side of his face, screaming for help.

"Somebodyyyyyy! Hellpppppp!"

G'Corey covered her mouth with his kisses but she was still clawing at him, making it impossible for him to make love to her.

"Shut the fuck up!" He head butted her twice, quieting her screams. "Don't resist me!"

He grabbed ahold of his aching dick and pushed it inside of her. He groaned at their connection and she gasped from the pain of him penetrating her dry walls.

"Oooow! You're hurting meeeee!" She clawed at him to get off of her.

He stopped pumping. "Yell again. Hit me again and I will kill you!"

That deflated her fight. She turned her head off to the side and cried as she felt him resumed his savage attack on her body.

"Oh, shit, Minnie. Grrrr. Damn! You feel so good. Oh, I missed you. I missed you." He began kissing on her neck, breathing his breath in her ear as he moaned with every hump.

With Minnie now under his full submission, he was free to make love to her that way she liked. He tenderly ran his hand under her shirt and bra as he pulled out one of her big breasts and sucked on its nipple.

He then pulled out of her and removed her pants and panties all the way off and slid back inside, resting one of her legs on his shoulder as he drove in deep.

"That's still your spot? You gonna cum for me? Huh, baby? Ohhhh! Shit! I'm gonna cum for you. All inside you." He talked her through each stroke.

Minnie lay there motionless. No reaction. No sound. No tears.

"Oh, baby, I'm 'bout to cum in you. I don't want to but I'm 'bout to." He dropped her leg and began pumping fast and then faster. "Ahhhhhhh! Ooooohhhh!"

Minnie closed her eyes. She didn't want to see what was to come next.

He wanted to go again but he had time for that once he whisked her away to some state up North, where no one could interfere with them again.

"Get up, baby. Grab your keys and let's go." G'Corey stood to his feet, fixing his clothes before snatching his gun.

She couldn't move. She didn't try.

"Minnie, get up. I'm not playin' with you."

Still no movement.

G'Corey let out a gruff sound as he tucked his gun in his waist so he could use both hands to bring her to her feet. Playing possum wasn't going to stop destiny.

Meanwhile...

Yuriah pulled up to his house. He thought to sit outside and wait for Munch but decided to head inside and see what Minnie was up to.

Right as he was walking up his steps, he heard the blares of police sirens growing louder. They were coming down his street.

He found that odd, considering his neighborhood hardly ever had use for the N.O.P.D.

Nonetheless, he continued on to his porch and unlocked the door. He called out for his wife while stepping inside. "Oh, bae..."

Yuriah cut himself short when he saw G'Corey standing over his wife with half of her clothes off.

G'Corey looked over his shoulder and went to reach for his gun but couldn't pull it out in time.

Yuriah had already ran down the stretch of his hallway, grabbing G'Corey with him and ramming his back into the wall, knocking the wind from him instantly.

Yuriah was so crazed at what he walked into that it brought out the animal in him and he fought with random viciousness. He shaped his hand like he was reaching for a bowling ball and gouged into G'Corey's face, trying to puncture his eyeballs out of their sockets with one hand while punching him upside the head with the other.

Disarm alarm. Disarm alarm. The security system forewarned before it was set to shriek its alert signal.

G'Corey managed to remove his burner and banged his gun against Yuriah's head, cracking his skull.

That made Yuriah stumble but it didn't keep him at bay long because a second later he rushed him again, maneuvering the gun out of his hand and onto the floor.

"Aaahhhh!" Yuriah picked G'Corey up and body slammed him, straddling him immediately. He then looked over to Minnie who was now sitting up watching him in horrid disbelief.

The bloody look on her face fueled his inner demon and Yuriah roared anger. "Aaaaaahhhh!" He began squeezing G'Corey's throat with the determination to crush his windpipe.

"Aarrggh! Aarrgh!" G'Corey was gagging as he tried to reach for the gun that wasn't close enough for him to grab.

Then a flush of policeman who responded to his neighbor's report of a single gunshot came running through the house.

Yuriah didn't notice them coming. He could care less they were there. He was on a mission. "I'm gonna kill you!" Spit flew from

Yuriah's mouth and then his entire body spasm'd as his grip around G'Corey's neck grew weak and he fell over.

"Nooooo!" That's my husband." Minnie stood up to yell on the cop who tased him.

"That may be so but he's under arrest right now," the officer stated.

Minutes later...

What in the hell happened here?" Reds sat up on the dash as she looked at police cars lined up in front of Yuriah and Minnie's home.

Munch's adrenaline spiked as he brought his car to a halt. He placed it in park and looked to his left to see Yuriah being thrown to the ground and Minnie hysterically petitioning for them to let him up.

Munch gritted his teeth and hoped to God they didn't catch him down bad with those guns. He reached into his pocket and handed his phone to Reds. "Call Shenae. Tell her get here and bring Kamal."

He was about to get out of his car when he noticed bitch ass Officer Santemore bringing a handcuffed man to his feet and walking him to a police unit.

Munch couldn't recognize him by his side profile but when G'Corey turned his way for a brief moment, he identified him instantly and his heart started beating wildly.

"...just meet us here. Hurry!" Reds hung up with Shenae.

He kept his eyes glued on G'Corey but gave a stiff order to Reds. "Get out!" His lips barely moved.

"Munch, baby, why?" She was alarmed by his unnatural tone.

"Reds, I'm not saying it again. Get out the fuckin' car! Go!"

His last word came out so forcefully, she jumped. Tears came spattering from her eyes but Munch couldn't let that soften him. She looked at him fretfully and moved her mouth to call out his name but no sound came out.

Munch reached over her and opened the car door himself and then looked at her with disdain and somehow she knew what he was about to do. She wanted to beg him otherwise but he was an impenetrable brick wall.

"Oh, my God, baby," she cried as she scooted out slowly.

As she placed a foot onto the asphalt, he said, "Reds, I love you, ya heard me."

"Then don't do it, Munch. No, Munch. Listen to me. No…" was all she could say when she saw him pull his Dessert Eagle from underneath his seat.

He heard her cries but he was resolute in his decision regardless to the consequence. *No guts. No glory.* That's how he lived, plus he made a promise to BG that G'Corey would suffer the same fate as he even if the cost was his life. He put that on everything.

He stepped out of his car with his weapon at his side. Reds ran to the other side of the street and covered her mouth when she saw the scene flash in her mind before it happened. She didn't see it ending good for them.

G'Corey was griping and shaking his head side to side when he caught a glimpse of something moving out of the corner of his eye. And when G'Corey turned to face what the imagery was, he saw Munch wearing the look of man who was blood thirsty.

G'Corey opened his mouth to alert the policeman who had him hemmed up but he was silenced before he could make a sound.

With the skill of a marksman, Munch took aim at G'Corey's head. Squeezing one off, the bullet exploded his melon into red confetti.

The next shot he took hit Santemore in the neck, forcing him to grab at his skeeting wound before he dropped to his knees, expiring in seconds.

That was for disrespecting BG. God bless the dead. Munch took pleasure knocking Santemore off the map.

Minnie fainted.

Reds screamed. "Munnnncccchhhhhh!"

Yuriah yelled in a boisterous voice, "Noooooooooooooo!"

Every officer on the scene turned their weapons on Munch and without warning, they each opened fire.

Pow! Pow! Pow! Pow! Pow! Pow! Pow! Pow! Pow! Pow! Pow! Pow! Pow! Pow! Pow!

Munch got ate up by an assault of bullets. His body jerked and blood splattered from his mouth. With the last of his life, he saw Reds jumping and screaming hysteria, but there wasn't anything he could do about it. He was on his way to see if there was a heaven for a G.

Suddenly, his gun fell from his hand. Seconds later, he crumpled to the earth behind it. And that's when the police ceased fire.

Munch lay in the street with his eyes staring up into the skies.

No man knew the hour of their death but Magnolia Munch knew when that time came for him, he would die on his feet.

The five shooting officers rushed over to Munch with their guns trained on him, prepared to shoot again if they had to. But they lowered their weapons once one confirmed he was dead.

A week later...

A private ceremony was held for Munch. Only Yuriah, Minnie, Kamal, Shenae, Keyz, Shaunie, Reds and Ace were in attendance. They didn't want the traditional second line. Instead, they wanted to send a soldier home in the same manner he lived. Surrounded by family that would lay their life down for him or lay *it* down.

Reds stood off to the back. She wanted to pay her respects but she wasn't strong enough to do more than show up. The women stayed with her and fenced her in a sister circle, prepared to catch her if she was to faint again.

The men were visibly strong but on the inside they were broken pieces. Munch's death affected them for different reasons but his demise reached inside of their chests and squeezed at their hearts just the same.

The pastor spoke blessings over Kareem's time amongst the living and after the last of his eloquent words were articulated, each man individually walked up to his casket and placed significant pieces inside of his coffin.

Yuriah placed a picture of himself, Kamal and Munch from '88 underneath his hand. "We with you wherever you go. From the cradle to the grave. Love you, bruh."

Kamal didn't smoke but for his boy, he'd blaze one. He had two rolled blunts. One he slipped in the pocket of Munch's shirt and the other he sparked for himself. "Here's to those better days we talked about. I'ma get wit'cha again, one day."

Keyz pulled a Dessert Eagle from his waist and placed it at his. "You won't be needing this where you goin' but in case you run into a devil, send that bitch back to hell. I'ma miss you, big dawg."

Finally, it was Ace's turn to leave him with a memorabilia but his walk over to him turned into sludge. He couldn't do it. He broke down. "I ain't got no mo brothers, mannnn." He started crying.

When his own brother was murdered, Munch stepped in and took him under his wing. And he never discriminated between BG and Ace. What he gave his blood, he gave to him. "Who got me now? Huh, bruh? Who?" Ace cried out to him.

Yuriah stepped up and grabbed Ace by the shoulder. "You got me."

Kamal and Keyz stood alongside him. "And me," they both responded.

Ace turned around and hugged Yuriah. And the fellas double patted his back. He may had been forced to grow up early to survive the pitiless streets but he was still a kid in need of a father figure.

After a few more emotional seconds passed, Ace composed himself and headed over to Munch.

"Death is guaranteed to us all, so don't cry fa him and don't cry fa me when I go. Just make your life mean something while you here before your time is up, ya heard me."

Reflecting on the words Munch told him at his graduation somehow gave him strength. He cleared the croak in his throat, walked over to him and addressed him like the man he raised him to be.

"You asked me what I was gon' do with my life. I didn't have an answer then but I know now. I'ma go to Nicholl State just like you wanted to do. I'ma carry that torch, big brudda." He reached into the breast pocket of his jacket and pulled out BG's diploma. "I know you don't wanna get to heaven without this, so give this to our boy and save me spot at God's table, ya heard me. I love you, man."

When Ace stepped away, the quartet of young men from Minnie's church stood around the casket and began singing Boyz II Men, *It's So Hard To Say Goodbye,* as Munch was lowered into the earth alongside his brother and father. The McMillan men were reunited again.

Then, one by one, each man doubled tapped their chest, pointed to the sky and then to their brother, whom they buried a G as they grouped together and walked out of the cemetery.

And I'll take (take with me) with me the memories (take with me the memories) to be my sunshine after the rain/It's so hard to say goodbye to yesterday...

Epilogue
Two years later…

Minnie

Minnie looked out of the window from the passenger's seat as Yuriah chauffeured her, Reds and the baby to her friend's baby shower. The special occasion was a jubilant one but her mood wasn't. However, she promised Samiyah that her and the family wouldn't miss it when she spoke with her earlier that morning.

"Today just isn't my day," she mumbled under her breath.

"Baby, what was that?" Yuriah asked as he lifted her hand to his lips and kissed it.

She looked his way, smiled weakly and then she shook her head *no* as to tell him *never mind* her statement. She then turned her head back out toward the window and thought back on the aftermath of the rape.

Two years ago…

"Minnie, baby, what's the matter?" Yuriah gently called out to his wife as he approached her from behind, careful not to startle her. Ever since the incident, two and a half months ago, she'd become timid of her own shadow.

She turned her head slightly over her shoulder to verify it was him although she easily identified his voice. Not to mention they were home alone in their eight hundred square foot apartment, but she had to be sure. G'Corey violated her in such a way that she was mistrusting of even the things she was once sure of.

"Yes," she whimpered.

He placed his hands on each side of her arms and slowly tightened his grip around them. He learned to be extremely gentle since the rape because every touch surprised her. She was getting better but she was still plagued with remembrance.

"You've been standing at the sink, washing the same plate for the last twenty minutes. What's on your mind?"

Before she could answer, tears rolled down her face. "I'm pregnant."

He spun her around and hugged her securely, kissing the top of her head. Yuriah thought of this day and imagined how he'd respond when he heard those two words. Never did he imagine he would feel burdened.

"Did you take a test?"

"No, but I've missed two periods and I've been having all the symptoms from my first."

"How long have you known?"

"For some weeks." She looked up at him, trembling. "Baby, I'm scared. What if it's his?"

"But what if it's mine?"

Then suddenly, Minnie's body started to shake as if a cold chill came over her. She pushed away from Yuriah and covered her mouth to prevent herself from saying the blasphemous thoughts swirling her mind.

"Let it out, baby." He approached her but stopped when she stepped back.

"I keep seeing G'Corey's face while he was on top of me, taking me like he had the fucking right!" She screamed so loud it shattered a piece of Yuriah.

He went in and hugged her again. "I'm so sorry I wasn't there to protect you."

Minnie cried and inwardly, Yuriah cried too. Her pain was his but he couldn't fold because of it. He was her rock. Always had been and always will be.

After several minutes, Minnie simmered herself to a semi-calm and sloshed her tears away. She reached for her phone that was on the kitchen counter and made the call she dreaded making.

Yuriah watched on in silence.

The phone rang twice in Minnie's ear before the receptionist picked up. "Dr. Sonja Forrest's office. How may I help you?"

Minnie didn't say anything.

Love Knows No Boundaries III
Pandora's Box

"Hello? How may I help you?" The lady repeated.

Clearing her throat, she spoke. "This is Minyoka LeBlanc and I need the earliest doctor's appointment you have."

"We have a two o'clock today. Is that soon enough, ma'am?"

Minnie's heart raced. "That's fine."

She sighed heavily as she walked back into Yuriah's arms and sobbed some more.

Later that afternoon...

Minnie sat nervously on the table as she waited for her doctor to return with her results.

"It's gon' be a'ight, baby. I'm with you."

Minnie nodded her head but remained silent. It was hard to believe as he did because nothing since the day G'Corey broke into their home has been alright.

The push of the door caused both of their heads to sharply turn in its direction.

"Congratulations Mr. and Mrs. LeBlanc, you're pregnant."

Dr. Forrest smiled at both of them but neither returned her joyous expression. Feeling slightly uncomfortable from their lack luster reception, she continued. "Well then, if you can go ahead and lay back for me, I will do a vaginal exam before I perform an ultrasound and tell you how far along you are."

Minnie lay there tensed and unsure. Yuriah massaged her hand. "Breath, baby."

She exhaled slowly.

The doctor then retrieved the ultrasound machine, explaining that the measurements of the baby would allow her to determine how far along she is and the due date of expectancy.

"You are ten weeks." She headed over to her calendar so she could then tell her the arrival date for baby but Minnie stopped her.

"Doctor? What I need more than that is to know the paternity of my baby. Is there a way I can find that out now or do I have to deliver to know?"

"You can find out now. I will do a simple procedure called Cho-rionic Villus Sampling or CVS for short. I will insert a thin needle into the vagina and through the cervix, guided by an ultrasound. I will then obtain small pieces of the chorionic villi, which has the same genetic makeup as the fertilized egg. And as far as the potential father of your baby, a swab test collecting a saliva sample from the inside of his cheek will be all that's required of him. Both samples are then sent to a DNA center."

Minnie looked at Yuriah. *"We want to have that done. How long before we know the results?"*

"It ranges anywhere between three to five business days."

"Let's do it." Minnie didn't hesitate.

A week later...

"I can't open it." Minnie held out the letter of the prenatal paternity results for Yuriah to read.

He opened the envelope and pulled out the single sheet of paper. He read over it but Minnie wasn't able to read his reaction. *"Have a seat next to me,"* he said.

"Baby, just tell me. Baby!"

"Baby? Baby, we're here." Yuriah had to tap Minnie a few times to jolt her to the here and now.

She avoided eye contact as she unbuckled her seatbelt so he wouldn't see the gloss on them. "Oh, okay."

They both opened their doors. Minnie stepped out, but Yuriah turned to look over his shoulder.

"You comin'?"

"Yea, one sec. I need to change Kareem's pamper." Reds fanned her nose as she made stinky, scrunchy faces at her son.

"A'ight, we right outside."

"Okay," she acknowledged before focusing back on her big boy. "Who'sa stinky baby? Say, *Kareem Nicholas McMillan.*"

The toddler cooed at his mother's voice and playful touches.

Yuriah and Minnie began removing presents out of the trunk of the truck. Minnie wasn't enthusiastic about today and he couldn't pretend he didn't notice.

"I know what's bothering you and if this is gonna be too much, we can drop off these gifts and leave." Yuriah knew how hard it was for Minnie to be around pregnant women.

Minnie took the last two gift bags out before closing the hatch.

"I have to be here and I'm trying to get into a better mood, it's just hard, you know?"

Yuriah shook his head to show his understanding.

"It's been two years since the abortion and I do need to forgive myself for my decision but every time someone I know rejoices over being pregnant, it reminds me that I haven't conceived since I made that awful, murderous choice, which brings me back to why. But I couldn't carry my rapist's baby." Minnie shook her head because guilt told her it was her baby too. "And then the thought of not giving you any children makes me feel inadequate as a woman."

Yuriah placed the gift wrapped box down and walked up on his wife. Looking her squarely in the eyes, he spoke. "Well, you shouldn't. If you gave me nothing more than what you have already, you gotta know that's enough fa me. You're enough fa me."

Something about the conviction in his dark browns made her feel assured that she was indeed *enough*. "Thank you, baby. I needed to hear that."

"And I'll tell you every day of my life if that's what it'll take, ya heard me."

"I hear you," she nodded.

Reds got out of the truck. "Oh, my God. That's the last time I'm giving this boy beans." Kareem giggled. "I'm not playin' with you, stinka man."

"Let's get this show on the road." Yuriah picked up the gifts from the ground and nodded his head for both ladies to go before him and into the hall.

Samiyah

317

Samiyah spotted Minnie and the crew the moment they walked through the door. She put down her shrimp and sausage jambalaya and chicken drummettes, wiped her fingers and mouth with a wet one and then walked over to them.

"We come bearing gifts," Minnie smiled as she held up the two huge gift bags filled to capacity with unisex items since she didn't know what she was having.

Samiyah gave her a hug and kissed her cheek with hers. "Thanks, sis." She then looked over at Yuri. "What's up, brother-in-law?"

"I'm coolin'. You?"

"I'm getting some serious heartburn but I can't leave the spicy foods alone. I'm Creole down to my soul, I guess." She laughed. "Oh, silly me. I'm just a talking. The gift table is to your right and Kamal and Keyz are over there." She pointed in their direction.

"A'ight." Yuriah took the bags from Minnie, kissed her and then headed over to the table to drop them off.

"Give me my munchables." Samiyah wiggled her fingers in anticipation for Kareem.

"Hey to you too, Samiyah." Reds passed him to her. "I just don't get no love when he's around."

Samiyah nuzzled his neck with her nose, then she looked up at Reds. "You said something?"

Reds looked to Minnie. "See what I mean?"

"I'm only kidding, chick. How are you these days? Did you ever finish your book, *The Card I Was Dealt?*"

Samiyah asked one out of the two questions that were always difficult for her to answer. The other being, *How are you holding up today?*

"Yea, I did. It was so emotional for me to start. Hell, it was hard for me to finish but it's what Munch wanted." Reds fanned her eyes to prevent herself from crying but she couldn't stop them. They were already freefalling.

She hadn't learned how to deal with the weight of not telling him she was pregnant before they left the house that afternoon. In her mind, she believed it would have made the difference in his decision to retaliate against G'Corey and the cop he killed before his life was stole right before her eyes.

She spent every day wishing she would have because she was filled with depressive regret. It wouldn't have stopped him from going to Yuriah's but maybe it would have altered his mind frame.

The gory images of his demise haunted her ceaselessly. She saw the fatal scene flash her mind every night when she closed her eyes.

She was only thankful Munch gave her a reason to live on through their son because had she not been blessed with Kareem, she probably would have lost her mind.

Minnie rubbed her back in a circular motion. "Let it all out. Cry. You're amongst family."

"For real," Samiyah second it, absorbing her sadness.

Wiping her tears away, she looked at Kareem, who was a spitting image of his father and smiled. "I'm so glad I didn't move back to Jersey. You all are not just good for my son but for me as well. The support y'all have shown and still show gets me through."

"And that's what sisterhood is all about. Each of us have a story to tell that has damn near crippled us, breaking us down lower than low but here we are, standing," Minnie said triumphantly.

"And we're doing it together," Samiyah added.

"To sisterhood." Reds wrapped her arms around them to share a group hug.

They spent a few minutes more speaking on a brighter subject until Reds mood shifted back to a celebratory state when Samiyah saw Gerran walking up with the twins through the window, holding a baby bundle on each side.

Muah. Muah. Muah. Samiyah triple kissed Kareem's neck. "Here, take my big boy. Let me go help Gerran with my lil' crumb snatchers."

Reds reached for her toddler and they headed over to join Shaunie and Shenae.

Samiyah walked over to Gerran with her hand shielding the glare of the sun off of her eyes. "Why didn't you call me from the car? I could have helped you with them." She took Amir out of his arms and grabbed one of the diaper bags off of his shoulder.

He shifted Amiya to the front of him. "Daddy got this. Whatchu talkin' 'bout?"

"Ahh, you looked like the struggle, trying to carry these heavy duty booties."

"You see these guns?" Gerran flexed his muscle, bringing the curl of his bicep up toward his lips and kissed it. *Muah!*

Maaaa. Amiya repeated after him.

"You feel daddy, huh?"

Amiya bobbed her head up then down as she played with the diamond stud in his ear.

"Come on. Let's get them inside." Samiyah turned around and began walking away.

Umm umm ummm. Gerran admired the shapely bubble of her butt. He took all the credit for plumping her ass up because he insisted she didn't have nearly as much until he started hitting it from behind. "You know, speaking of booties, yours is getting fatter."

She turned around to respond but when she did, Cedric walked up on her and kissed her juicy glossed suckables. Wiping the watermelon flavored shine off of his lips, he said, "And I'm lovin' all of it, ya heard me." He responded cockily in a successful effort to smash to smithereens any inklings Gerran thought were possible about making a third time a charm. Cedric wasn't letting his family go like he had.

"Hey, hey. Not in front of our kids." Samiyah warned both her ex-husband and her fiancé.

Breaking the mild stare down between both men. Lil' Acacia started to shout. "Balloons, Daddy. Look." She jumped up and down, pointing at the pink and blue colors of the helium filled rubber bubbles.

Samiyah stooped down to give her daughter a kiss. "Aren't they pretty just like mommy's angel of mine?"

Lil' Acacia dropped her chin into her chest twice in a child-like manner while smiling her mother's smile to agree with her.

"How 'bout you go inside with daddy and get you one. Whadda ya say?"

"Yay!"

"Give me lil' man." Cedric extended one arm and reached for Amir. With his daughter's hand in his, he kissed Samiyah once again. "Don't be long."

"I won't be." She returned his smile then looked at her son. "Amir, say bye to daddy. Say, *see you later alligator.*"

He didn't wave or say a word. He was too invested in drinking his apple juice from his spill proof cup.

Gerran walked up on him and extended his hand. "Give me five, lil' man." Amir slapped his hand. "Love you, son."

Cedric then walked at Lil' Acacia's pace and into the hall.

"Hand me Amiya, please." She reached out for her sweet baby.

Adorning her with kisses all over her neck and tummy, forcing the cutest giggles to erupt from her belly, Gerran placed her in Samiyah's arms.

"You and brother had fun with daddy? Huh? What you say? That's a silly question, Mama? You're right. Every weekend is fun time with daddy. Well, I missed you. You know that?" Samiyah held a conversation with Amiya.

Gerran looked at his ex-wife adoringly. He couldn't help it. Despite the drama, he couldn't help but see all of his good days in her eyes. He missed being the reason behind the sparkle in them but being the man he was, he had to stand behind the *effed* up choices he made when he decided to let her go.

Samiyah spent a few more seconds cooing and talking with Amiya before she realized Gerran's entrancement.

"Ummm, why are you looking at me with that smirk on your face?" *Let mommy's hair go, Cupcakes,* she whispered to Amiya.

"Yah, didn't we almost have it all?"

"We did and we could have, but *almost doesn't count.* Those were your words, remember?"

He hung his head slightly. "You right."

"Look at this, though. Although we weren't perfect, we created two little people who are. And because of them, I will always respect you and show you mad love, but only as a friend."

"That's it, huh?"

"That's the bed we made."

Gerran bobbed his head then leaned down to kiss Amiya on the forehead. "Daddy loves you, Cee Cee. And Daddy loves your mama, too." He looked at both of his girls with the bluest eyes. "He always will."

A faint smile of sadness mixed with appreciation came to life on Samiyah's face. They'd been through so much turmoil in the past, it was nice to know that even when they swore their hatred for one another, love really did conquer all.

So, there was no denying Samiyah would have a tender spot for him. They had a teenaged love affair that was so magical it belonged in a fairy tale as well as a Shakespearean love that was both beautiful and tragic. But it was over and a love that once knew no boundaries ended.

Gerran placed the baby bag on Samiyah's shoulder and kissed her on the cheek. "Enjoy the shower."

"Thank you."

Gerran paused before he disappointingly turned away to go back to his car. He looked as if he wanted to say something else but decided against it.

Samiyah turned around to rejoin the celebration but her heart led her to turn back around. "Gerran." He looked over his shoulder before spinning completely around. "Don't forget, family dinner starts this Friday and every Friday after that for seven o'clock on the dot."

"I won't miss it for anything." He smiled and proceeded his trek to his car.

"Oh, and Gerran." Samiyah called once more.

"Yea." He spun to face her again.

"I'll always love you, too." On that note, she walked back into the party.

Gerran stood there motionless for a minute as a smile etched his face. He hoped that counseling would have brought them closer together but all it did was show them that they were best apart. So, he knew for certain she was gone forever but it felt good to know their love would never die.

Elias

"It's over."

"It's what? You can't mean that. You didn't even give me a chance to explain shit."

"Eli, neither or you. Let me finish."

Elias looked off to the side, unable to give her eye contact because he didn't want to remember the look on her face telling him they were done.

"When I say it's over, I mean the secrecy has to be over, not us."

"Huh?" He wasn't expecting to hear that. He knew he hurt her pretty bad when she walked in on him and her sister. So he was relieved to know he still had a chance with her. "So, we're not breaking up?"

She shook her head no.

"I don't want be without you, just the secrets. Damn, I hate that I love you so much but I do."

"Well, I ain't mad that I love you and no shit like this is happening again. That's on God."

"Right." She agreed whole-heartedly. Weeks without the one she loved most felt like an eternity spent in hell.

He then searched her eyes. "Do you really love me?"

She didn't need to think about it. Their time apart told her she loved him and it was nothing but love that had her leave her family's vacation home in Abita Springs, forty-five minutes outside of New Orleans in the pouring rain, just to let him know she did.

"I'll always love you."

"Well, in that case, La'Toria Salay Cormier, there's something I want to ask you…"

"You sure this the right spot, 'cause you gotta have mad connections to get hooked up with this joint. I tried to book this bitch twice and both times they hit me with that *try next year* shit." Jacobi disturbed Elias' thought.

He read the address on the building of the hall against the address in his text message. "Yea, this is it. You know Cedric do security for celebrities, so who knows whose elbows Samiyah was able to rub to lock this down."

"I've been here once, the inside is pure dope. I wanted us to book this venue for our thing, remember?" Blu asked Eli.

"You right. But it's hard as fuck to reserve. Illegals have an easier time crossing borders than securing a date for this place." Elias shook his head at the thought and then stepped out of Jacobi's ride.

Eli then opened Blu's back door, extending his hand to help her out. "You're such the gentleman," she admired.

He leaned into her ear. "That's 'cause you lettin' me hit it on the regular." He bit down on his bottom lip, steadied his hand waist high and began pumping his pelvis like he was sexing her from behind.

She looked at him with playful eyes but curled her lips as if she was about to chastise him. Shoving his shoulder backward with the sturdy push of her fingers, she said, "Boy, you play too damn much. Let's get inside so we don't be later that what we already are." She twirled him around and headed him in the direction they were to go.

"Yo, ain't your friend supposed to be meeting me up here?" Jacobi inquired as he looked at his reflection while approaching the glass door.

Blu shook her head, wearing a goofy grin. "You been trying for how many years and Kanari still hadn't come around? You might as well give up."

"That ain't my style, lil' mama." Jacobi then opened the door, waving her inside. "After you."

The second Blu's eight month belly made its appearance through the entrance, everyone yelled, "Surprise!"

Love Knows No Boundaries III
Pandora's Box

Blu covered her mouth and broke out crying tears of happiness when she saw seventy-five family and friends all congregated to celebrate the arrival of her bundle. She was standing in the middle of a gender reveal baby shower that she knew nothing about. *Eli is so slick*, she thought.

She looked over at a very proud Elias, smiling at the reaction she was giving. "You did all of this?"

"You shouldn't be shocked. I throw the best parties, period. Baby showers are no exception, although I did get a lot of help from Kanari and Samiyah on this," he admitted.

She went in to hug him around the neck. "Thank you."

As she walked around and greeted everyone, she couldn't help but feel outdone. The place was beautifully adorned, themed with royalty décor catering to the arrival of either their prince or princess. On one side, there were three separate gift tables that were unable to accommodate all of the presents that were all wrapped in solid silver and gold wrapping, thus extra chairs served as stands for them.

Off to another side were several food tables manned by Nola B's Catering Service, dishing out everything from an assortment of miniature po-boys to Cajun style red beans and rice.

There was a play area for the children in attendance in the back away from everything with three hired caretakers to ensure none of the women missed out on the fun and games Shenae was overseeing.

Lastly, there was an open bar serviced by one of the baddest mixologist to ever hold two shakers, Kanari.

"If I can have everyone's attention, please," Samiyah spoke into the microphone and called for everybody to turn their attention to the projector.

After the group of people faced the right direction. She pressed the play button and a three minute video cataloging Blu and Eli's time together as a couple played.

"Awwww," Blu became teary eyed. She was truly overwhelmed by the efforts everyone made to make this day memorable.

After two hours of eating, talking and playing classic Jack and Jill baby games, it was time to answer the big question: Baby Blue or Baby Pink?

Every woman wore either a blue or pink arm bracelet to signify which team they represented.

Shaunie, Minnie, Samiyah and Reds passed out fortune cookies and when everybody had theirs, Eli gave the green light for them to crack it open.

A lot of laughter and oohs filled the hall when they removed the slip of custom printed paper inside. It read: *We're fortunate to have a girl. We love you already, Devin Salay Dupree.*

The hand claps echoed throughout the building as everyone shared the excited that a queen in training would be born.

After congratulations were handed out in abundance, the pink cake with silver, white and pink sparkles on a white buttercream frosting was served.

Then DJ Poppa turned it out with kid friendly music at Elias' orders. And what started off at 2 p.m. turned into 7 o' clock easily.

Before it got much later and guest started to leave, Elias walked up to the microphone. He tapped it. "This thing on?" *Woooo*. The mic made a pitchy sound. "I always wanted to say that. But ummm, anyway, me and my wife have an announcement to make. *Come over here, boo.*"

"Eli, *my feet*," she whispered as she pointed at her wiggling toes to let him know she didn't have on her shoes.

He moved the mic from by his mouth. "*Girl, waddle yo sexy ass over here and quit playin'.*"

She began a slow rock to propel her to her feet but her beach ball belly made it nearly impossible to do on her own at times.

"We gotcha, mamas." Samiyah and Shenae both stood to assist her by taking a hand and pulling her to a stand position.

"This makes no sense." She laughed as she duck walked over to her husband.

Elias pecked her lips but then went back for a second kiss, this one a little bit longer.

"Alright nah!" Shenae blurted.

"*Alright nah.*" Lil' Acacia repeated after her, which made everyone erupt in laughter at her adorableness.

"My bad, y'all." Elias grinned as Blu tried to remove red lipstick from off of his lips. "I can't help myself sometimes."

"You're not supposed to." Samiyah responded to his statement.

"True dat. Well, we didn't plan on breaking news just yet but since everyone who's close to us is here, we might as well spill it. Once Devin is six weeks, we're moving to ATL to open our restaurant."

Everyone stood up to applaud them, whistling and hooting at his great news, except for Samiyah. Her mouth flung open as she sucked in a tiny amount of air. Although he told her their plans well over a year ago, it still shocked her to know the day was vastly approaching that she'd have to tell him goodbye.

"There's more," Blu stated as she felt him pulling her closer to him. "We already secured the two level, 2500 square space on Peachtree St. and after little thought we came up with the perfect name. Tell 'em, baby."

"I didn't even know that Chef Homeboy Dupree had a knack to cook some boss meals until one young little lady inspired me to do something more with my life. So, it is because of her that we're naming our family-style bistro *The Peach at Peachtree.*"

Samiyah excused herself from the table so she could step outside and get some fresh air. She was overwhelmed with his news and couldn't breathe.

Minnie grabbed some napkins off of the table and went after her. Elias looked to Blu and without him saying a word, she spoke his mind. "Go check on your friend. I'm good."

Elias walked outside and made it over to where Minnie stood holding Samiyah. He tapped Minnie's shoulder. "Let me get in there."

She stepped aside and Elias held her, rubbing her head in a consoling manner. Minnie looked on and felt her tear ducts brewing a batch.

Elias dried her face with the backs of his hand. "Yah, what you crying for, huh?"

"First of all, you're naming your restaurant after my baby. That touched me right here." She pointed at the center of her chest. "Then second, I can't believe you're really leaving me."

"For starters, she my baby too, ya heard me. I love that little girl and I owe so much to the both of y'all. I had no idea what unconditional love felt like until you made me a daddy. And secondly, don't you know we a short flight away? That means if you missin' a thuggah, you can come see me or when I'm homesick and I'm missing you, I can be on the next thing smokin'."

"I know but everything is changing, y'all. Eli *I'll Never Wife 'Em* Dupree is married with a baby on the way. Minnie is married to the man who's loved her from childhood and I'm shockingly not with Gerran. And of course the oddest change of this all is Acacia isn't here with us. I really miss that girl."

"I miss her, too," Minnie added.

Samiyah looked for Eli to say something but instead he looked at his watch.

"Eli?" Samiyah nudged him.

"A'ight, damn! I low-key miss her, too."

Out of respect, they partook in a brief moment of silence for the way things were.

Breaking that silence seconds later, Samiyah wagged her finger at Eli. "Back to you, don't you turn into no Dirty Bird jersey wearing ATLien when you go, no. This is still home."

"Never. I might be going to the land of 404 but I'm 504 wherever I be, beleed dat."

They shared a laugh and then Samiyah went solemn. "It really feels like these are the last days of us just kicking it as a clique."

"Well, Yuri and I aren't going anywhere so you'll always have me," Minnie assured her.

"Awwww," Samiyah pooched out her bottom lip and gave off sad eyes.

"Hold up. I got something I wanna do. Be right back," Elias skirted off inside of the building, returning minutes later with some beverages.

Love Knows No Boundaries III
Pandora's Box

"What's this for?" Minnie questioned as she took the long neck bottle from him.

"Shit felt worthy of a toast of sorts, so here it is." Elias raised his cup of Crown into the air. Minnie and Samiyah followed suit, lifting their wine coolers as well. "To an unbreakable friendship that knows no boundaries, you dig."

"Here, here." Both ladies chorused as they all touched each other's drinks to commemorate a bond that was too strong to ever be broken.

Many years later...

Elias and Blu earned the James Beard award for having the best New Orleans' cuisine dishes out of East Atlanta. And although there's no place like home, they are happily living in the city of Buckhead with their one and only child.

Minnie and Yuriah were unsuccessful with conceiving on their own despite their costly efforts with IVR treatment. However, they will be welcoming a baby boy once the adoption papers are finalized.

Samiyah and Cedric have expanded their family. After their wedding, they were surprised to welcome yet another daughter. They named her Amani. She has since tied her tubes to prevent anymore baby bombshells from happening.

Gerran is currently dating but hasn't remarried. And he has no plans to. Also, he hasn't missed a Friday dinner with his blended family, yet.

Tracie decided to make Baton Rouge her permanent home after she was released from jail. Her testimony against G'Corey Sr. set her free to raise G'Corey Jr. She vowed to never love another more than her son.

Coffee

Kawanna obtained her associates degree in counseling and is now a certified counselor at the Sweet Haven's Women's Center. She is currently dating herself until a single man comes along.

Reds became a permanent fixture on The New York's Best Seller's list and remains domiciled in The Big Easy, raising her son around his father's family.

Kanari is thriving as the new owner of The Bar at Aqua Blu. She, also, stopped denying her attraction to Jacobi. They're dating and her celibacy streak is over.

Kamal and Shenae opened a non-profit after school/summer camp in the 3rd ward named: *The MLJ Community Center* after three brothers. In an effort to atone for the sinful lives they've led in the past while creating a legacy worth leaving behind for Kareem McMillan, Yuriah LeBlanc and Kamal Jones.

~Fin~

Love truly Knows NO Boundaries

Love Knows No Boundaries III
Pandora's Box

Author's Note

Hi _____ (insert name here)

Life when lived is the greatest story ever told. Had it not been for all of my best and worst days along with the best and worst people I've met, I wouldn't have a story to tell.

Now on a more serious note, a man who has played an instrumental part in my life has ascended.

When writing was just a hobby, he believed I would do great things with it one day. And I just want to say *thank you* for everything, good and bad. Regardless to the storms we endured and even the ones that swallowed us up, I was blessed the day I met you and I'll always respect our rainy days, they made me.

R.I.P., **9th Ward Black**.
Earth was hell for you. So, I'm happy you were returned to The Most High. May your soul be at peace, black man.

And to my readers, those that really support me in sisterhood and in my art…

Merci Beaucoup,
Coffee

Coffee

Love Knows No Boundaries III
Pandora's Box

Available Now

LOVE KNOWS NO BOUNDARIES **I & II**
By **Coffee**
SILVER PLATTER HOE **I & II**
By **Reds Johnson**
A DANGEROUS LOVE **I, II, III, IV, V, VI**
By **J Peach**
CUM FOR ME
An **LDP Erotica Collaboration**
THE KING CARTEL **I & II**
By **Frank Gresham**
BLOOD OF A BOSS **I & II**
By **Askari**
BURY ME A G **I & II**
By **Tranay Adams**
THESE NIGGAS AIN'T LOYAL **I & II**
By **Nikki Tee**
THE STREETS BLEED MURDER
By **Jerry Jackson**
DIRTY LICKS
By **Peter Mack**
THE ULTIMATE BETRAYAL
By **Phoenix**
BROOKLYN ON LOCK
By **Sonovia Alexander**

Coffee

SLEEPING IN HEAVEN, WAKING IN HELL **I, II & III**
By **Forever Redd**
THE DEVIL WEARS TIMBS **I, II & III**
By **Tranay Adams**
DON'T FU#K WITH MY HEART **I & II**
By **Linnea**
BOSS'N UP **I & II**
By **Royal Nicole**
LOYALTY IS BLIND
By **Kenneth Chisholm**

<u>BOOKS BY LDP'S CEO, CA$H</u>

TRUST NO MAN
TRUST NO MAN 2
TRUST NO MAN 3
BONDED BY BLOOD
SHORTY GOT A THUG
A DIRTY SOUTH LOVE
THUGS CRY
THUGS CRY 2
TRUST NO BITCH
TRUST NO BITCH 2
TRUST NO BITCH 3
TIL MY CASKET DROPS

Coming Soon

TRUST NO BITCH (KIAM EYEZ' STORY)
THUGS CRY 3
BONDED BY BLOOD 2
RESTRAINING ORDER

CPSIA information can be obtained at www.ICGtesting.com
Printed in the USA
BVOW02s1823180516

448626BV00013B/75/P